Rose M. Long

The Fifth Season

by

Rose Mary Long

authorHOUSE®

AuthorHouse™
1663 Liberty Drive, Suite 200
Bloomington, IN 47403
www.authorhouse.com
Phone: 1-800-839-8640

First published by AuthorHouse 11/19/2008

ISBN: 978-1-4389-1159-5 (sc)
ISBN: 978-1-4389-1160-1 (hc)

Library of Congress Control Number: 2008909211

Printed in the United States of America
Bloomington, Indiana

This book is printed on acid-free paper.

The Fifth Season

Rose Mary Long

Foreword

My good friend Rose and I have worked together as volunteers for the Illinois Speech-Language-Hearing Association for over a decade. We've collaborated primarily on writing legislation regarding the practice of speech-language pathology in Illinois. It sometimes took creativity and persistence over several years for just one bill to be signed into law. Once we were on the phone during a severe thunder storm. I was searching for important details on the internet and passing the information on to Rose. We were so determined to be ready for the next day's meeting with lobbyists and legislators that we ignored the crackling of lightning in the phone. We survived and the bill became law.

At each victory we would celebrate, sometimes with a good meal. More typically we slammed down half a sandwich driving across the state, while we planned our strategy, debriefed, and shared family stories. In that process we became trusted allies and true friends, accepting each other and appreciating our different perspectives on life.

When I was elected president of the Illinois Speech-Language-Hearing Association Rose continued working on legislation. The bills that were passed made it possible for more qualified speech-language pathologists to be employed in schools and medical settings. That means more families are able to receive appropriate speech-language services. Rose became such a frequent visitor to the state capitol building in Springfield that the guards recognized her on sight. Countless speech-language-pathologists have benefited from her work, without knowing who she is. And now we get to read her fiction!

Very few stories are written by or about speech-language pathologists. Rose has written a gem, a story about a speech-language pathologist who is a lonely widow, a supportive friend, a passionate lover, a faithful Christian, an involved mother, and a determined individual repurposing her life after tragedy strikes. If you don't understand what a speech-language pathologist does before you read this book, you certainly will when you have finished it. If you are a speech-language pathologist, you'll delight in this story about one of us who helps others regain the ability to communicate at work while she regains her ability to love at home. I can't wait for the sequel! I have the highest respect for Rose and am excited that she's exercising this other creative side. She is a woman of many talents with a wise heart and keen sense of judgment. Enjoy!

Christy Strole, M.S.,CCC/SLP, past president
Illinois Speech Language Hearing Association

Author's notes

This book is a work of fiction, dedicated to the compassionate speech-language pathologists around the world who are devoted to healing the lives of others. The events, facilities, characters, and communities portrayed are fictional. The patients have been designed to represent the various types of personalities and kinds of disorders seen by a speech-language pathologist in a community hospital. The frailties of characters are intended to enhance the story. Any similarity to real-life counterparts, either living or dead, is purely coincidental.

I read the legend of Drops of a Spring Water years ago, but cannot find the source. For that I apologize. I did write the poem that frames this story.

In appreciation . . .

There are many individuals who have helped bring The Fifth Season to publication. Karen Young provided encouragement and inspiration at every stage from beginning to completion. My husband never doubted that it would be finished. He stayed at the wheel for far too many miles, so I could work on the manuscript. The constancy of his support gave me confidence to continue. Several individuals have read the various drafts and offered suggestions. My daughter-in-law Melanie proofread the manuscript the week before giving birth to twins. Sandy Mulligan found errors that were overlooked by all the others. The book would never have been completed without extensive guidance from my editor Arinne Dickson. She provided unbelievable attention to detail and gently gave me what she called her suggestions. For her faith in the characters and the story I will always be grateful.

Autumn: Season of Promise

East Wind plays with West Wind.
And like capricious youth,
they blow both warm and cool,
spraying seeds from pod and head,
promise of another year.
Together they repel the force of North and South,
a pattern known on earth since time began.

Chapter 1

Maren Kepple shoved the last box of Nick's belongings into the large trunk of her old blue Pontiac and slammed the lid as hard as she could, realizing she was closing another chapter of her life. The mid-August sun was already high in the sky. They were getting a later start than planned. Her youngest son didn't seem concerned about being late; he was just generally irritable. She knew that meant he was nervous. He had watched his brother, Matt, go off to college four years earlier, and only two weeks ago to law school. Now it was Nick's turn to leave home. Matt, already settled in on the West Coast, called to wish Nick good luck with his roommate. While they were finishing their conversation, Maren leaned against the warm metal of her car and took a moment to reflect.

Jack would be pleased, she decided. Since his death she had finished graduate school, Matt had completed college, and now their youngest was on his way to begin his studies. The last five years had been the most difficult of her life. Maren had survived primarily by concentrating on setting and achieving specific goals. She had completed her master's degree in medical speech-language pathology in the city. The commute both distanced her from the pain of her private life in Edgelawn and challenged her to focus on herself and others in a way she had never known. Working in the hospital had demanded all her concentration, so it had rested her mind from home duties. At the same time, her home life had given her a retreat from the grim realities of the large city hospital.

She had been excited by working in the medical setting; but being a practical person she had decided, after graduation, to stay closer to home until Nick was out of school. For the past two years, she had evaluated and treated children in Edgelawn's schools. Her contract for this year awaited her signature. If she hadn't been so busy with Nick's shopping and packing, it would already have been sent. She was planning to drop it off in person on Monday in order to meet the deadline.

Before her thoughts could turn to contemplating the empty-nest life ahead, Nick poked his head out the front door. "Mom, phone call for you."

It was Judy Harrison a speech-language pathologist she had met while working on an Illinois Speech-Language-Hearing Association committee. They had worked at the registration desk together during the ISHA convention and got to know each other pretty well during the quiet hours. Judy had been aghast that after all Maren's medical training she had taken a position in the schools.

"Maren, I hope I'm not holding you up," Judy apologized after they exchanged greetings. "I know Nick is leaving for college soon, and I was wondering… well…Is there any chance this might be a good time for you to make some changes in your life?"

Judy was employed by a contract company called Rehab International and through the company provided services at several medical facilities in the Chicago area. One of them, St. John's Hospital, a three-hundred-bed facility on the far west edge of the city, was not renewing their contract with Rehab International and wanted to hire Judy directly. The standard noncompetition clause in her contract prevented her from accepting the offer unless Rehab International released her. St. John's had negotiated with the company at length, and after some cash changed hands, RI had allowed Judy to take the position.

"So, I'll head the department I've been working in for two years," she explained now, "but to clinch the deal, I agreed to continue working for Rehab International three days a week for an additional year at other facilities." With that arrangement Judy wouldn't be able to cover the hospital by herself, even if she worked sixty hours a week.

"Basically, you want me to commit to a one-year full-time contract to hold the position for you," Maren stated for confirmation that she had understood correctly. She had to repress the surge of excitement she felt at the prospect of returning to a medical center—excitement that came in spite of the thought that it could turn out to be a temporary opportunity.

"Yes, but you know how large St. John's is. With you and me on staff full time I'm sure the hospital will have to open another position within a year."

One of Maren's externships had been at the Catholic hospital before Judy worked there, and she had fond memories of the experience. It was not quite as long a commute as Circle Campus had been.

Nick began honking the horn, interrupting Maren's thoughts. She let out a sigh of impatience. Now he was ready to go.

"When do you need to know?" Maren asked, deciding she would at least like to think it over for a few days.

"Today really," Judy pressed. "I only have twenty-four hours to sign the contract. If I can't find someone to help me cover the hours, I'll lose it."

The school contract looked up at Maren from the old oak kitchen desk. She wondered if the only reason she hadn't signed it was that she had been busy with Nick. As she studied the blank signature line the tinge of dread in the pit of her stomach made the decision for her. She knew there would be too many empty hours in her life once Nick was deposited in the university dormitory. It was time to set new goals.

During the first week at St. John's, Maren had a lot of relearning to do. She had worked carefully but slowly. Judy had taken a week of her vacation time retraining her. Now, Maren was on her own. She was starting the morning on third floor. She nearly dropped the medical chart for room 312-B. *Calm down,* she told herself as she opened the chart to the white tab marked History. Afraid she might not remember all she once knew, Maren forced herself to concentrate on the history section. A seventy-eight-year-old woman named Mary Kowalzic had suffered a dizzy spell and had been unable to eat dinner the previous evening. Her family had believed Mary was having a stroke, and when she continued having difficulty, they took her to the emergency room around 11:00 p.m. She had experienced some difficulty talking at that time, but had been conscious. Maren's body tensed as she imagined herself the daughter. *They must have been so frightened*, she empathized silently.

Maren flipped to the red tab, Radiology. A lacunar infarct was noted on the right side. Self-consciously, she reached for the medical dictionary to find that *lacunar* meant "small," not "moon-shaped." It could have been an old lesion. There was no previous CT scan to make comparisons. Next, she opened the chart at the blue tab, Doctor's Orders. It was crucial to make sure the doctor's order had actually been written. Sometimes mix-ups occurred. "Rehab consult to rule out CVA," it said. *Cerebrovascular accident,* she thought. *Another stroke. I've been working in the hospital only a week, and I'm beginning to think everyone in the world has had, or will soon have, a CVA.*

She went to the kitchenette and, on a small tray, collected apple juice, thickener, Lorna Doone cookies, applesauce, a spoon, and a cup of water, all things she would use to evaluate Mary Kowalzic's swallowing function. She forgot to check the chart to see if the woman had diabetes. Not wanting to take time to return to the nurses' station, she hoped the patient would be able to tell her.

In bed B by the window, she found a thin, white-haired woman, surrounded by a group of elderly folks, her friends and relatives. Maren introduced herself as the speech-language pathologist, pointing out the abbreviation "SLP" on her name tag. She pulled latex gloves from the box mounted on the wall, while trying to keep her voice calm and her movements as smooth and efficient as possible. Attempting to project an image of confidence, she poked her hands in the gloves and explained that her mission was to do a bedside swallow evaluation and speech screening.

The bright-eyed lady was sitting upright in bed, wearing the blue quilted bed jacket her husband had just delivered. She was beaming with pleasure at all the guests who had come to her hospital-room party and insisted upon introducing everyone. Her sister and husband were seated, and two neighbor women were standing at the end of the bed. Mary was a queen holding court. The introductions took care of the speech screening; her articulation was obviously normal. Every sound was clear; every word could be understood.

Maren began to relax and suggested the group visit the cafeteria for coffee. "It will be easier for Mary to focus on what we are doing without an audience," she coaxed. *Not to mention how much easier it will be for me to concentrate,* she admitted to herself.

Once the room was quiet Maren started the oral-motor exam. Mary puckered and everted her lips, saying "uuu-eeee-uuu-eee" as rapidly as she could. She puffed air in her cheeks, coughed, and cleared her throat, all without any apparent difficulty. At Maren's request, she protruded her tongue; Maren thought she noticed a slight tendency for it to deviate to the left. The stronger right side seemed to be pushing harder than the slightly weaker left side, but Mary corrected it automatically without realizing it had occurred. Maren asked her to repeat the task, but there was no evidence of the momentary deviation. She asked her to say "ah" and watched to see if her soft palate elevated evenly. It did. Her voice was initially a little raspy but improved after a sip of water. There were no real signs of muscle weakness or poor speech coordination that could be labeled dysarthria. Mary had no difficulty understanding or expressing herself which would indicate aphasia. She insisted she had no memory problems. *Pretty good for a woman of seventy-eight,* Maren concluded.

"I'm really embarrassed for taking up space in a hospital bed," Mary rattled on, conveniently forgetting that she had suffered some serious symptoms. She was a very lucky woman. Her scare was behind her, but Maren felt obligated to explain to her that sometimes symptoms are subtle or go unnoticed until you get home.

"It pays to check everything out," Maren cautioned, watching as Mary ate several spoonfuls of applesauce. A fat straw in the hospital drink mug caught Maren's eye. She handed the mug to her patient and watched and listened while Mary took a big drink. Not waiting for an invitation, Mary eagerly took bites of the shortbread cookie, assuring Maren she did not have diabetes. She chewed and swallowed, talking all the while. There was no cough, no signs of aspiration at all. Her swallow and her speech seemed to be within normal limits. Maren's impression was that Mary had experienced a TIA, a transient ischemic attack, a temporary condition often called a ministroke.

"Can I go home now?" the woman asked, the smile sliding from her pale face. The events of the past fifteen hours were catching up with her; she suddenly looked tired. "They said I just had to wait for the therapist to evaluate me."

Maren reminded her that a physical therapist and an occupational therapist would come to evaluate her sometime during the morning, since her doctor had ordered a rehab team evaluation. "You'll be ready to have a good nap when we are all through with you," Maren predicted.

"If I'm here for lunch, can I have a sandwich?" Mary asked. "I'm getting pretty hungry."

Maren admitted to herself she had forgotten to check the diet order. She promised Mary she would recommend a good lunch, and then she returned to the nurses' station to look for the order. "Full liquid diet," it read. That was the standard order from most of the older doctors. Many wrote the order from habit, not thinking that thin liquids moved so fast many stroke patients would lose control and choke or aspirate. Fortunately, Mary didn't have a problem. Maren wrote the request for an order to upgrade the patient to a general diet.

Maren sighed inwardly, grateful at how quickly the technical jargon was coming back. She wrote a brief report in Mary's chart and put it behind the lime-green tab, Rehab. She reread it to make sure she hadn't omitted anything important.

Looking at her watch, she realized she would have to learn to work faster. She avoided getting involved in the chit-chat with other staff members. There wasn't time. On Mondays, Judy had warned her, she would have to move quickly; there was always a long list of patients who had been admitted over the weekend. As she boarded the elevator for the first-floor radiology department, she wondered which radiologist would be on duty for the outpatient video swallow study.

On Maren's first day Judy had told her a group of older radiologists serviced the hospital. They were never present for the swallow studies, since they considered them to be the province of the SLP. The doctors were on site if there were questions, but didn't even review each tape. That was not the way Maren had been trained, but Judy had said just to call them in if she had any questions. On Friday Judy had informed Maren a new, larger group of radiologists had been signed to provide coverage. Now the SLPs couldn't be sure which radiologist would be on duty. Judy had warned Maren she had heard by the grapevine that several of the doctors could be difficult to work with. They insisted on being present for the video swallow studies and tended to direct them. Maren had difficulty communicating with Dr. Sudani from day one. She recalled the strained exchange.

"These swallow studies are rare, yes?"

"No, Dr. Sudani, these swallow studies are common."

"I have never done one, and I trained at Colonial General in Boston." A little research revealed that, much to the dismay of the SLPs in Boston, that major city hospital did not provide the service. Still, Dr. Sudani had insisted on being in charge. He gave loud orders to patients and technicians alike. Maren wasn't confident in the radiology suite and usually acquiesced to Dr. Sudani's demands. She sensed the same was true for the technicians.

Unlike larger hospitals, that would have a lead-lined booth where the doctor and SLP stood apart from the tech and patient, St. John's antiquated fluoroscopy suite was a single room. That meant the tech, SLP, and radiologist wore lead aprons to protect themselves from stray radiation and stood together in a confined space. Tension was palpable during a procedure that required close cooperation.

Maren hoped Dr. Churduri was working today. He had no experience reading video swallow studies either, but at least he had better social skills. "You just tell me what you want, and we'll do it," he had said when they met. His style was quite possibly the opposite of Dr. Sudani's, but it was certainly easier to function without professional competitiveness in the room.

Maren found the patient in the Radiology waiting area and introduced herself. John Steinkewicz had been brought to St. John's that morning by his twenty-nine-year-old son Jerry, who helped provide her with the history. John had suffered a mild stroke the previous week and had been released from the hospital without speech or swallowing evaluations. He lived alone in the home he had shared with his wife for over thirty years before her death. His sons and daughters-in-law were taking his meals in to him now and noticed that he often coughed during meals. John's new young doctor had ordered a video swallow study to rule out aspiration.

Maren liked John immediately; he was a Santa Claus of a man. It wasn't that he was heavy; he wasn't. And he had only a stubble of whiskers, no long beard. It was the twinkle in his eyes and his gentle manner that made her think Santa. They established an easy rapport. John was glad to have a conversation with whoever had time for him, and Maren was grateful for patients she could feel comfortable treating. She needed some positive experiences to build her confidence.

She assessed his speech and language skills during the interview. His wife had died two years earlier, he explained slowly. He had been retired these past ten years and had in fact been Santa at a local department store each year of his retirement. He loved doing it. "It's good," he drawled, "to be, you know, umm, useful."

Maren concentrated not only on what he told her but also on the way he worded it and how his muscles worked. He seemed to search for words frequently. Her intuition took over. She asked if he did any cooking for himself. His answer made it clear that he hated being a burden to his children.

"They tell me to let them help, they will bring in meals. I could cook, but there's not much food in the cupboard now." He hesitated slightly before pronouncing the word *cupboard*. His voice trailed off.

Maren noticed Jerry's eyes roll upward in obvious frustration as he interjected his side of the story. "Well, Dad, you keep forgetting to turn off the stove."

John looked down, ashamed. Maren prevented further argument by pressing on with the interview. John didn't believe he had any difficulty swallowing. It was true he coughed sometimes, but he thought that was because of his smoking. Jerry agreed they were uncertain about the cause of the coughing but noted it did happen while his dad was eating. John admitted he had trouble finding the right words to say and, as a result, was spending most of his time watching television. "I don't go to the Senior Center because I don't say the right things."

Maren's analytical mind shifted a gear. She wondered if he limited his activities because of difficulty understanding others and expressing himself. She would ask for an order for a complete speech-language evaluation.

Jerry decided to wait in the hall while Maren led John into the fluoroscopy room. There she put him through the basic oral-motor evaluation accomplished with nearly all patients. She noticed the tray of food had been delivered to Radiology for the outpatient video swallow study. There was always bread, cookies, a puree like applesauce or pudding, ground meat, and a drink. The radiology techs mixed barium with water in three Styrofoam cups and marked them appropriately, "thick," "medium," and "thin." Thanks to Judy's training, everything was ready. She watched John eat and drink before they positioned him in the small chair that the fluoroscopy arm accommodated. He ate a teaspoon of applesauce. There were no signs of aspiration, no cough, no gurgly voice.

Maren pulled on her lead apron and signaled with a nod to Janet the radiology technician to call the radiologist. She felt a slight dread; it was Dr. Sudani. They greeted one another coolly, and she briefly explained the reason for seeing Mr. Steinkewicz. Her voice sounded stiff and formal to her. *He probably thinks I have an attitude,* she imagined.

"Start with the puree," he directed, unaware that she was waiting for the identifying patient number to appear on the monitor. John's skeleton was sharply outlined on the TV screen in front of them, minus a number to document on the recording who this skeleton was. Janet sprang to action, leveled a teaspoon of applesauce, and inserted it into his mouth before Maren could object. "Swallow," commanded Dr. Sudani.

Maren would have preferred seeing if the patient could trap the bolus of food safely without letting any escape down his throat, but it was too late. John swallowed, and a very good swallow it was, too. With an edge to her voice, Maren managed to blurt, "We don't have a number on screen." Once the identifier was recorded, she continued, "I'd like to see a bigger spoonful, please."

She hated feeling intimidated and fought the feeling by being increasingly assertive. This irritated Dr. Sudani, who clamped his lips into a tight, thin line and said nothing. Some ingrained instinct let him know he would have to watch this one or she would undermine his authority.

Janet gave John a rounded spoonful of applesauce. This time Maren asked John to hold it in his mouth for a moment. He complied, and then swallowed efficiently. They all watched the black blob on the screen as it entered his mouth and was propelled to the back of his throat. Then, blip, it went through the opening to the esophagus and disappeared off the bottom of their screen. All the while, Maren used the remote control to record the procedure.

Now Dr. Sudani was getting restless. The patient obviously had no difficulty. He did not aspirate or have reflux. As far as the radiologist was concerned, the test was over. He sighed loudly, indicating his boredom. Maren was rapidly losing what little confidence she had. Before he could terminate the study, she managed to say that she needed to observe liquids. The doctor had to acknowledge that they had not watched the prepared drinks. Janet, well aware of the radiologist's preferences, grabbed the thin liquid and handed it to John before either professional asked for a specific quantity or consistency. John had gulped half a glass of barium before Maren could say, "That's enough." The thin barium seen as a black line on the screen was swallowed without a problem.

Dr. Sudani stepped back from the fluoroscope, now convinced it was time to end the study. In the barium studies he directed, if a patient drank a glass of thin barium safely, the test was over. But in Maren's interview with John and Jerry, they had reported that he choked when eating, not drinking. She had only one clue why that might be. Jerry had said his dad took big bites, and John had admitted to the charge.

"He does choke when he's eating, Dr. Sudani," she said brazenly, contradicting his unvoiced opinion. "I'd like to see him eat something more challenging." The statuesque doctor nodded wordlessly and stood by while she directed Janet to make a sandwich, dip it in the barium liquid to coat it, and hand it to John. Maren didn't want to hope John would aspirate, but neither did she want to miss something and have him admitted next week with pneumonia. She waited nervously.

John took the interlude to complain about the taste of the barium. Maren assured him the sandwich would take the taste out of his mouth and that after a few bites they would be finished. Dr. Sudani looked impatiently at his watch, an unnecessary gesture since there was a large wall clock hanging in full view.

Janet handed John the sandwich, Dr. Sudani turned on the fluoroscope, and they all stared again at the TV screen while John chewed the barium-laced ham-salad sandwich. He did take large bites, just as Jerry had reported.

"There," Maren nearly shouted, "did you see it?" A black teardrop-shaped blob the size of a pencil lead dropped from the back of John's tongue directly into his airway. The three professionals were incredulous that John didn't flinch. He didn't cough. He didn't choke. He clearly did not feel the food that fell directly into his lung—silent aspiration. His mouth was still full, and he swallowed again. Two more, smaller dots entered his airway. "Cough," Maren directed as she reached over to take the sandwich from him.

They never did see the material come back out of the airway, and the study ended abruptly. She asked Janet if she could use the room to review the video with John and Jerry. "No problem," Janet shrugged. Janet directed Jerry into the room while Maren returned the video to the beginning.

"Probably 30 or 40 percent of patients have silent aspiration," Maren counseled them. "They don't feel the material in their throat. Maybe that's why John takes such large bites."

"Oh, I think that's a long-standing habit," volunteered the son wearily.

She gave them instructions for preventing further aspiration, which included taking small bites and chewing thoroughly; then she suggested John might benefit from some speech therapy. "If your doctor writes an order, I can see you as an outpatient right here at St. John's to help with your word-finding problems as well as the swallowing problems."

They agreed, after seeing the video, that some therapy might be a good idea. Maren felt drained from the tension of the radiology department and gladly escaped to the deserted cafeteria to finish writing the report over a cup of coffee. She didn't realize until then that Dr. Sudani had not uttered a word after the aspiration. He hadn't asked the patient to cough. He hadn't terminated the study. He simply took off his lead apron, without the usual assistance from Janet, and walked silently from the room while Maren was explaining to John what had occurred. She naively hoped Dr. Sudani would be pleased to have learned more about the functional nature of video swallow studies. She never would fully understand that in her quest to provide the best service for the patient, she had threatened his ego and established her first enemy at St. John's.

Chapter 2

The commute was long, but Maren had time to spare. She alternated between the Metra and driving, and today she was driving. Both fascinated and repulsed by the city, Maren was excited to be working there but rarely stayed in town for dinner or social activities. This morning the sun shone blindingly through the windshield, making her wish she were on the train. Traffic always seemed worse on sunny days. It was stop-and-go, leaving empty minutes for her mind to replay old tapes. The car seemed to know the way without much attention from the driver.

During the past few weeks Maren had established a routine at the hospital. She was feeling more confident, more comfortable. She was grateful for that, because this morning was the ten o'clock staffing where she expected to see Paul McCloud, her one-time mentor. It was a special meeting on the med-surge floor to resolve some issues for a surgical patient. Speech Pathology had been invited to sit in to field any possible swallowing questions. Dr. McCloud was the surgeon.

The last time Maren had seen Paul he was in his last year of ENT residency at Circle Campus Hospital, where she had been a graduate student. They had officially met during the winter quarter when she had been assigned to shadow him. He was a good-looking surgeon with a very bright future whose ready humor made him as popular with the staff as he was with patients and students. Everyone had called him by his first name. Maren had gone to his office, followed him on hospital rounds, and observed him in the operating room. She had respected his skill and admired his integrity back then. He had seemed so young that it hadn't occurred to her to be intimidated.

Judy's note yesterday stated the staffing was for Dr. McCloud's patient. Maren had felt nervous immediately. *Maybe it just makes me feel like a student again*, she told herself. At eight-fifteen Maren parked, and a few minutes later met Judy for coffee and a briefing session in the cafeteria. She decided to talk it over with Judy.

"I know the surgeon for the staffing today," Maren volunteered. "I had him as an instructor at Circle. Is he still as easy-going?"

"I couldn't compare since I didn't know him then," Judy responded. "Paul McCloud is very well liked. He's in an old, well-established practice." She exaggerated the words to indicate the doctors in the practice were much older and probably anxious to maintain the status quo until retirement. "Gossip has it that he's not happy since he had hoped to specialize in pediatrics. The old docs have mostly senior citizen patients who have been with them for forty years. They have no interest in peds. Hey, I've got to get up to Rehab. Oh, by the way, you're in luck—Dr. Churduri's in Radiology today."

Maren finished her coffee, mentally drifting back to the day she met Paul, almost two years ago. It was January 22, his thirtieth birthday. Maren was already forty. The secretaries and staff had been chanting "Happy Birthday." Paul had taken full advantage. "Don't I get any birthday kisses?" he had encouraged in his soft, quiet voice. She had joined in the spirit of the occasion, glad for the informality. She had congratulated him and leaned forward to plant a kiss on the side of his neck, the way she frequently kissed her tall sons. Paul was a bit shorter than the boys though; her kiss landed on his jaw, and their cheeks brushed. He was definitely not one of the boys nor one of their peers. His face was more masculine than the boys' soft skin.

She jerked herself back to reality, dumped her mug on the conveyer belt, and headed toward the stairs. There were other patients to see before ten o'clock. The first, a forty-five-year-old female outpatient, was waiting in Radiology. Maren was pleased to see that Janet, the radiology technician on duty, had already seated her patient in the small waiting-room-style armchair in the fluoroscopy suite.

Frequently, Radiology ran late, but not today. Maren believed in signs to a certain extent and began to relax a bit. She reached into one of the pockets of her white lab coat and found a sterile-wrapped tongue depressor and small penlight. *Lab coats are mainly good for carrying various tools of the trade,* Maren thought. *The more pockets the better.* Judy had taken a short case history by phone yesterday, but Maren asked the woman to review her complaints to assure that nothing was forgotten.

"It feels like food sticks in my throat. I try to gag it up. Sometimes I vomit."

"Does it feel better then?"

"Usually, but sometimes I stick my finger down my throat and dig stuff out of my tonsils."

That rules out hiatal hernia—too high in the neck, Maren thought. She focused the light in the woman's mouth. Hard palate, teeth, and tongue looked normal, and predictably no sign whatever of tonsils. The tonsils had completely atrophied, as might be expected in an adult. Maren began to suspect gastroesophageal reflux, stomach acid that could creep up through the esophagus and swish around, irritating the back of the larynx and the throat. A classic symptom was a globus sensation.

"When you feel the food, does it feel like a lump in your throat?"

"Yes, until I dig it out of my tonsils."

"Let's take a look with fluoroscopy."

Janet went to get Dr. Churduri while Maren put on the small yellow lead apron and a blue thyroid collar. She stood by a corner cabinet and laid the paperwork on the countertop, where she would periodically take notes. She held the remote control in her left hand and waited until Dr. Churduri took his place behind the arm of the fluoroscope. He smiled his most charming smile and greeted her warmly. "Good morning, Mees Keeple," he pronounced, lengthening the vowel in her name. Maren returned his greeting cordially.

"Just hand her the pudding—she can feed herself," Maren directed Janet. She turned her attention to the monitor, pushed Record, and watched the black blob that was the barium-laced vanilla pudding being inserted into the woman's mouth. Dr. Churduri was good about not focusing in too closely. Maren could see part of the tongue, as well as the throat. It took less than a second for the pudding to be propelled to the throat and less than a second to enter the esophagus. Nothing stuck. The oral phase was normal.

"It usually happens with bulky food," the patient volunteered.

Maren asked Janet to make a quarter of a sandwich with the ground meat and bread. Again, everyone watched a perfectly normal swallow. Just to be thorough, they observed while the woman drank thick, medium, and thin liquid consistencies. All swallows were within normal limits.

"That's all I need, thank you," said Maren, allowing Dr. Churduri to excuse himself. She loved it when things went smoothly.

"You are very welcome. It was a pleasure," he said with a smile. There was obviously no aspiration, and there was no need for him to comment further. He smiled at Maren again as he turned his back for Janet to untie his apron. Without another word, he left the room.

"Thank you, Janet. Nice job," Maren commented. "Could we have this room for a few minutes to review the video?"

"No one's scheduled," Janet responded with a shrug as she dumped the barium remains in the hazardous waste container. She untied Maren's apron and left the suite.

Maren played the video back for the patient, pointing out the speed that the bolus, the lump of food, traveled. She showed her that there was neither hesitation nor residue. She kept forgetting the woman's name, so quickly glanced at the video swallow form she had begun to fill out on the counter.

"Mrs. Garvey, has your voice changed at all recently?"

"Why, it has, actually. I'm just getting older, I suppose. I used to sing in the church choir, but I just can't hit the higher notes anymore. In the morning it's awful until I cough for a while."

Maren had asked earlier if the woman took any medications, even an occasional antacid. Mrs. Garvey's response had been a simple, firm negative. Now Maren tried it another way.

"Do you ever have stomach discomfort, belching, or—"

"Oh yes," Mrs. Garvey interrupted, "I've had reflux."

"But you don't take any medication?"

"No. When the prescription ran out, I didn't get it refilled."

"And you don't take any over-the-counter antacids?"

"No. I don't like to take medicine."

But, she doesn't mind gagging herself, vomiting, and digging food residue out of her throat, Maren thought impatiently. She explained that the symptoms were consistent with a reflux problem and suggested that Mrs. Garvey discuss a new prescription with her physician. After walking the patient to the door, Maren returned to the counter to finish filling out the form. It was a short report. Under Recommendations she suggested reinstituting treatment for the patient's GERD. Hopefully, her doctor would write a new prescription and give her a pep talk about continuing to take it.

Paul was sitting at the table writing notes in the stack of charts in front of him while staff members drifted in and chatted among themselves. Maren was not the last to arrive. She was sure he didn't know she was on staff. She felt she had some kind of an advantage, knowing he would be there. It would be fun to see his reaction. She was right; Paul was surprised. When he looked up to see which staff member was joining the group, his jaw dropped, taking his normally glib tongue with it and rendering him momentarily speechless. She enjoyed watching the transitions. First was the surprise, then the recovery when his face relaxed, and finally the cheerful response.

"Fate has been keeping us apart. Where have you been hiding, Siberia? We didn't get a single postcard." He kept up a series of one-liners while collecting his thoughts. Paul didn't mind surprises. It taught him to think on his feet, but this morning he was glad to be sitting down. The last time he had seen Maren Kepple she was a new widow, struggling through multiple new roles. The difference was startling. Maybe, he considered, it was just that those dark circles and bloodshot eyes were gone. He studied the frame of auburn hair, which emphasized her green eyes. Her hair had been almost shorter than his. Now it was longer and some natural wave made its presence known. She actually looked younger—no doubt the healing of time. He left unsaid a one-liner that hung between them: *Fate has brought us together again.*

Paul was curious to know why Maren had returned to St. John's after more than two years, but there was no time for personal conversation. He had heard from an audiologist at Circle that after all her medical training she had taken a job in a school near her home, undoubtedly to be near her son. Kind of disappointing, he had empathized. Kind of like his own situation—disappointing. He pulled his thoughts back to the present and asked staff members to begin their reports.

"We would like to see that NG tube out as soon as possible," Maren began when it was her turn. "It restricts laryngeal movement and degrades the quality of the swallow." She was distracted, noticing that Paul hadn't used her name. She knew that a lot of staff members and students come and go every year. Maybe he didn't remember it.

"You're not recommending an upgrade to a PO diet?" Paul asked now for clarification.

Maren confirmed that the patient was not ready for oral feedings, and Paul wrote the order to continue the NG feedings at home. With the feeding tube that went through his nose and into his stomach, the man could be seen for swallowing therapy on an outpatient basis. If he couldn't meet his nutritional needs by mouth after three weeks, Paul would order a G tube placement directly into his stomach. There was every reason to believe he would eat by mouth again, as long as the cancer didn't return.

As the others filed out of the cramped space they called a staffing room, Paul returned his attention to Maren. "Hey, welcome back. What brings you all the way to the big city?"

"Judy offered me a job. It isn't as long a commute as Circle, and I said yes."

"Well, welcome. It's always good to have a staff member with some brains."

Without another word he dashed off to the elevator, leaving Maren basking in the glow of his compliment but also feeling a little let down, wondering if he remembered her name. She went to room 326 to look for the patient they had just discussed, but the man was not available.

The elevator was making lengthy stops at each floor, and Paul wished he had taken the stairs. The woman's auburn hair in front of him kept him reminiscing about Maren. There had been an aura of wisdom about her. Maybe it was because of the grief. She had known how to keep her mouth shut though. He had appreciated that. That trait was probably why she had been assigned to him. He didn't have time for giddy twenty-two-year-olds. He had agreed to have a student shadow him but had charged Gerry not to give him any of the gabby, slow-witted ones. "Give me someone with some brains," he had insisted. Gerry had known whom he preferred.

Paul used humor to create a friendly wall which he wore to maintain his privacy, but his wall had almost come down during those days. Maren's presence had caused him to be constantly on guard. She somehow reminded him of his family. He couldn't explain it exactly; he just felt some connection to her. He had been impressed with her quick wit and curious mind. He admired her determination and candor. "She's not intimidated," he had told one of the SLPs on staff. He liked that. He found no fault with her appearance either.

As the elevator doors opened, he heard his page. Back to three. He shouldered his way out of the elevator. This time he would take the steps. As was his custom, he sprang up the back steps in twos, quickly passing the gray blocks of the outside wall and the window at second floor. He swung the door to the third floor wide and stood face-to-face with Maren who was on her way down. After a nervous regreeting, they talked more easily. Maren briefly reported that she had sold the big house and she and Nick had moved to a three-bedroom townhouse on the east side of Edgelawn. It was in a new subdivision, adjacent to a winding creek. She told him about taking Nick to the University of Illinois the day of Judy's call. Oddly, no one came through to use the stairs, giving them a short interlude of quiet conversation. "What about you?" she asked. "What's been happening with you?"

Much to his surprise, he shared with her his personal frustrations with the senior partners in his practice. "Maybe that's why I started the mission trips," he said with a grin, while reaching for the door handle, "to get away from Lancaster and Granger."

"Mission trips," she repeated, inviting an explanation. Now that was a side of Paul she hadn't expected. He had always been so flippant, not the spiritual type. He briefly told her he had been to Guatemala and Haiti in previous years and was scheduled for Africa in a few weeks. Maren had always been interested in medical missions, but she couldn't see any way to participate at the present time.

"I'd really be interested in learning more about how that works."

"After I get back, we'll have coffee, and I'll bore you to tears."

"Oh sure," she quipped, "westbound promises on an eastbound flight." It was an old aviation saying she had learned from Jack and their friend Steve. She was startled that it had popped out after all this time. She was about to apologize when he laughed, opened the door, said he'd better answer his page before they sent the dogs out with a brandy flask to rescue him, and was gone.

File folder and forms in hand, Maren slipped in the back entrance of the kitchen. The order for the inpatient video swallow study had been written that morning, probably the result of the doctor's rounds. There had been no time for the kitchen to get the order and prepare the video tray, so Maren briefly enjoyed the aroma of fresh peanut butter cookies baking for lunch and picked up a container of applesauce and a package of Lorna Doones. Rae Jean, the kitchen supervisor, was generous today. She stopped her work and quickly produced a small ham salad sandwich for Maren's tray. Maren thanked her and hurried to Radiology.

She loved it when Janet or Larry worked, and today it was Janet. They always had the barium drinks properly mixed and clearly marked. Some of the other techs weren't as efficient and not as friendly either. Two lead 2s were already taped in place. That meant Janet had already checked the handwritten list kept in the cabinet. Mr. Gibbs would be the twenty-second patient recorded. Maren set the tray on the countertop, took the lined notebook sheet from the cabinet, and wrote, "22: George Gibbs Inpatient."

She pulled on the heavy, blue lead apron and a blue thyroid collar. *Where is the small yellow apron?* she wondered while Janet tied the over-long tabs on the apron. The tabs had Velcro, but the apron was obviously designed for a much larger person. Janet had to wrap them around Maren and tie them in back. Maren wished the hospital would budget an upgrade of the radiology department. *It would be nice to have a lead-lined booth and eliminate the aprons,* she thought for at least the tenth time since she had started working there. She hadn't yet been issued a radiation badge to wear, so there was no way of checking how much radiation she had already been exposed to. *It must be a small amount,* she reassured herself. *After all, the techs work here all day long, and they stay within the limits.*

George Gibbs was wheeled through the door in the black, reclining video chair. Judy had talked the hospital administrator into buying the secondhand chair from a major medical facility that was upgrading. Janet positioned Mr. Gibbs with assistance from Maren. Pushing the chair was like guiding a large, top-heavy stroller. Turning it and backing it into position so they could observe the standard lateral view was akin to backing a semi-truck to a loading dock. The patient was seventy-eight, had a possible diagnosis of Parkinson's disease, and had a definite diagnosis of bad temper. Yesterday, he had thrown his denture across the room, barely missing Libby, one of the occupational therapy assistants. Today he looked glum but seemed docile.

Maren hadn't seen him before, so began by engaging him in conversation. She loved getting to know the patients. A little small-talk also gave her the opportunity to listen to his voice and evaluate his respiration and cognitive function. He told her about his experiences in the war. He had been a pilot. Pilots never seemed to lose their passion for their flying adventures nor for the machines that allowed them freedom from the earth. The memories were as fresh today as they had been years ago. His speech was intelligible and the content focused.

"Now, let me hear you say 'Ah,' and hold it as long as you can."

"Ah-uh-ah-uh-ah-uh-ah-uh." His voice quavered, a definite vocal tremor. It was either early Parkinson's disease or essential tremor. She put her hand to his neck, feeling near the thyroid cartilage for rigidity.

"I just want to feel you swallow," she explained. Very little laryngeal movement occurred, making it more likely to be Parkinson's than essential tremor. She would probably see liquid pooling and possibly residue. That would create a risk of aspiration. They would see for sure in a few minutes. Briefly, Maren gave Mr. Gibbs a simplified explanation of the procedure, as she nodded to Janet to let Dr. Churduri know she was ready.

"No, it doesn't matter that you just ate a snack," she answered his concern. "Janet will only give you a few bites and some swallows of liquid barium to drink. The barium will make the food and liquid show up on the x-ray so we can see exactly what happens when you swallow. We'll just be looking at your throat though."

Dr. Churduri was, as usual, in a sunny mood. He focused on the lead numerals to make sure they were recorded, without being reminded. Because of the suspicion of Parkinson's disease, Maren initially asked him to focus on the oral cavity as well as the throat. She wanted to document any tongue pumping. Frequently, Parkinson's patients were referred for videos because they couldn't consume enough food to meet their nutritional needs, but that was usually in the later stages.

A video swallow study really wasn't needed to see the tongue pushing the food forward if the movement was pronounced, but the video might reveal more subtle movements. There were none though, judging by the first half teaspoonful of puree. Dr. Churduri kept the black bolus of applesauce on screen, as it passed over the back of the tongue, into the part of the throat called the pharynx, in and out of the grooves called valleculae at the base of the tongue, and into the pyriform sinuses. That was where 10 percent of it remained, stuck in the carved-out sinuses just above the entrance to the esophagus. Maren's suspicions were confirmed. She had the patient try a prolonged swallow. Most of the bolus moved through. The rest cleared with successive swallows.

If this was Parkinson's and was treatable, the prognosis would be good. His swallow would deteriorate over time though. Maren had seen patients whose family members spent as much as two hours trying to feed them each meal. Eventually, the patient would tire of eating or aspiration pneumonia and severe weight loss would occur. Then they were faced with the option of placing a G tube or allowing starvation. That was never an easy decision. While they waited for a transporter, Mr. Gibbs's grew tired and began to complain that he was uncomfortable. His previously friendly tone changed to one of annoyance and anger.

"Would you like to watch the video to see what happens with your swallow?"

"No, I don't want to look at the video. That's your job. I want to get back to my room. My daughter should be here, so you could show her. She said she'd be here, but she's too busy. She's always busy, never got time to spend with me."

"Your nurse told me she was planning to be here but was detained on other family business."

"Aw, she's always detained," he complained.

Although Maren had been told his daughter came early every morning on her way to work, she didn't argue. "We'll take you back to your room right now." She nodded to the tech. *I'll bet Mr. Gibbs could keep his daughter busy full time, if he was given the opportunity,* she thought sadly. She resolved to meet the daughter tomorrow to be sure family members understood the results of the study. Mr. Gibbs did not aspirate, but the residue placed him at risk. Under the recommendation section Maren wrote a suggestion to repeat videos at nine-month intervals, sooner if coughing or choking occurred during meals. She thanked Janet for a great job and, standing at the counter, hurried to finish writing the report.

Maren went from the first-floor radiology department to the rehab wing on four, hoping to fit in some routine speech therapy with a couple of stroke patients who were scheduled twice a day. Judy had seen them early in the morning. Maren would have to catch them between physical therapy and occupational therapy sessions. Unfortunately, lunch was already being served to Rehab patients. She should have remembered that they were on the early meal schedule.

Deciding to check for new orders and phone messages, she took the elevator to the basement and went back to what was referred to as the Physical Therapy Department. PT always seemed to get top billing, but occupational therapy and speech therapy were located in the same area, used the same main office, and shared the same secretary. PT did have the largest, most expensive equipment and undoubtedly carried the greatest number of patients. *There's always that bottom line. You can't argue with the revenue PT generates,* Maren thought.

Rita Wilden, the Rehab secretary, had been hired for the position when it was created. She scheduled outpatients for all the therapists, served as the central clearing desk for doctors' orders, and did whatever else it took to make the department run smoothly. She considered advice-giving part of her job description. She was a brick of the hospital. "Listen to her," Judy had advised. "She knows everything and everybody."

"Any orders I should take care of before I eat?" Maren asked.

"Go to lunch," directed Rita now, in spite of the new orders that had come down on the ticker tape. "You've got two outpatients first thing this afternoon. That cafeteria will be packed if you wait another minute."

"Anyone I've seen before?" Maren asked about the afternoon patients.

"Yes and no. One is an adult battling oral cancer. The other is little Jason Newson." Maren had worked with Jason since her first week at St. John's, but pediatric cases were few in number. Although Maren enjoyed working with adults, she missed the joy of seeing the rapid progress children could make. She answered Rita facetiously, "A child? In this hospital? Really?"

"Now you know we do have them from time to time," Rita returned patiently. "In fact, the nursery is full of 'em. Anyway, I thought you wanted to get away from the schools."

"The bureaucracy and constant groups of kids, yes, but it is nice to have some balance."

Taking Rita's advice, Maren turned and retraced her steps past the elevators and on down the hallway to the cafeteria in the east end. Paintings by local artists were displayed on the yellow, concrete block walls. Some were for sale; some were just for display. Ordinarily, Maren enjoyed looking at them, but she didn't take time for even a glance now.

Choosing from multiple vegetables and toppings, she created a large salad on a disposable plate. Her mind was already going over the afternoon schedule. She was first in line, weighed the plate at the cashier's stand, paid, and took it to the speech office at the west end of the hall. She began to eat and review the charts for the outpatients.

The adult was Jerry Taggert, referred by Dr. Leslie Randall, a prosthodontist in the area. According to the patient intake form, Mr. Taggert, only forty years old, had recently had an oral resection, a surgical restructuring of his mouth, due to cancer. Consequently, he was edentulous. He was to have impressions for dentures taken in Dr. Randall's office as soon as possible. A video swallow study done at another hospital had documented dysphagia. He had silently aspirated thin liquids. Maren had only a printed report, no videotape to review. She expected there would be poor speech intelligibility as well as the swallowing disorder, but there was no mention of a speech evaluation in the file. She wondered why he didn't continue his therapy at the medical center where he had the surgery. Possibly the distance involved to get there, she conjectured.

The second folder contained the history of four-year-old Jason Newson. Judy had seen him for therapy since the first week of August. These last few weeks Maren had been seeing him because, as Judy put it, "You're the child expert." When Jason was three years old, he had been diagnosed with childhood apraxia of speech. By the time most children are three years old, adults usually can understand 90 percent of what they are saying. Only 20 percent of Jason's spontaneous speech was intelligible even now. He had concerned parents, who had pursued private therapy, and he was making steady progress. Too bad the pediatrician assured the Newsons he'd outgrow it; he could have started therapy earlier. Typical though.

The diagnosis of apraxia meant the brain had trouble programming his muscles to do what he wanted them to do. Apraxia could be limb apraxia, where the person wanted to reach for one object, but the hand picked up the wrong thing. It could be visual apraxia, where the person couldn't focus or track appropriately. Or, as in Jason's case, it could be oral apraxia. Jason had difficulty moving his tongue, lips, jaw, and soft palate on command. The automatic functions of chewing and swallowing were, as Maren's neurology professor used to say, spared. Adults with neurological injury were more easily recognized as having apraxia than children, but with either population it could be a difficult diagnosis to make.

It was like Maren's inability to back a car with a trailer, she mused. Looking in the rearview mirror, she could see where she wanted to go; she just couldn't get there. Her performance was inconsistent, just like the patient's ability to pronounce a word. An adult might say "tumsub" for toothbrush one time and "toosbum" the next.

In children, the speech sounds hadn't yet developed, so therapy might be a matter of painstakingly teaching every single phoneme. Sometimes there was speech, but it was garbled and almost completely unintelligible. The more words the child tried to say, the worse the speech became. Individuals who had no language or cognitive impairment and suffered from apraxia were usually highly frustrated. That was Jason's case. He seemed to have oral as well as visual apraxia, but he was very intelligent. She thought again how Jason's big dark eyes reminded her of a Precious Moments figurine. His lashes were so long and curled he could easily have been a child model. Unfortunately, his frustration at not being able to communicate resulted in a short attention span as well as behavior problems, which Mrs. Newson referred to as a short fuse. He had a history of slugging anyone who didn't understand him.

Maren visualized Mrs. Newson, a thin, jittery woman with a very rapid, irregular rate of speech, a poor model really. She had tried to work with him at home, but her ability to be patient was quite limited. Now she mainly wanted to turn her child over to a professional twice a week to be cured, and the sooner the better.

She certainly needs a lot of encouragement, Maren reminded herself.

The road of habilitation was neither short nor easy for children with apraxia, but therapy would win out in the end. The very nature of the disorder did make it resistant to traditional therapy, so Maren used a combination of techniques and goals with Jason that addressed specific speech sounds, the length of his phrases, and his breath control.

Today she would start by having him blow through a straw to make soap bubbles in a jar. In September Jason had not been able to blow more than one bubble with his straw at any depth of water. That showed that his respiratory control was so poor he didn't have enough air to say even a three-word phrase. Now he could make a stream of bubbles for five or six seconds with the end of a soda straw in as much as eight centimeters of water. As a result of therapy, he was now putting two and three words together to make phrases. Maren was overjoyed with his progress.

The ringing phone interrupted Maren's chart reviews. It was Rita's crisp, professional voice announcing that Mr. Taggert was in the waiting area.

Mr. Taggert was a lithe man who, at first glance, appeared to be an active, healthy individual. *I'll bet he was heavier before his illness*, Maren guessed silently.

She introduced herself and led the way to the speech office. He was talkative, but as Maren predicted, she had difficulty understanding him. That made her a bit nervous. Everyone assumed that because she worked with individuals with communication disorders she would be able to understand people with foreign accents and poor speech patterns, but that wasn't always true. She wasn't sure if he said he worked for the post office or Fed Ex. She picked out enough intelligible words to know that he drove and delivered packages or something, and that he wanted her to call him Jerry.

With gloved hands, Maren did a very careful oral-motor evaluation. He reported very little feeling in the left lower lip, which allowed food and liquid to trickle past, unnoticed. The left side of his tongue was severely restricted. The right side of his tongue reached for the roof of his mouth but couldn't make contact. What made matters worse, his hard palate was extremely high. She wondered if his tongue had ever made good contact with his hard palate for speech or swallowing prior to his surgery. No point speculating; it wouldn't reach now. She noticed that his soft palate didn't move much, and what little gag response he had was triggered on the very back wall of his throat, directly in back of his uvula.

Maren watched him take a half-spoonful of instant pudding. He swallowed five times to clear it. Too slow. Eating a meal was out of the question. He had a bottle of iced tea with him. It didn't appear to be thickened, even though he had a history of silent aspiration on thin liquids.

He has no warning sensation or protective cough, yet he drinks whatever he wants. Still, she reminded herself, research suggested that if a patient was physically active, the lungs could tolerate some aspiration without causing pneumonia. Then she made out the word *cab*. He didn't deliver packages. He drove a taxi.

"When I'm thirsty, I just stop for a drink. I can't be mixing that thickener stuff in the cab," he said, confirming her suppositions.

She was getting used to his speech pattern now and understood more of what he was saying. He was good with gestures and facial expressions. That helped. He told her his weight was the problem; that was the main reason he had come. He needed to be able to gain weight.

"Do you use some kind of supplement to increase your calorie intake?"

"Yeah, I drink that Jevity."

"You mean Ensure, don't you? Jevity is poured through a tube, directly into the stomach. It would taste dreadful."

"I know. That's what we used when I was on the G tube, but the insurance will pay for that, not for Ensure. So I drink it."

Maren had heard patients did that but had never met one who did. She acknowledged the financial disaster of a battle with cancer. Then he coughed on the swig of tea.

"Actually," she said bluntly, "that could be a sign of progress. According to your last swallow study, you didn't feel the aspiration, so you didn't cough."

Drops of liquid he obviously didn't feel stood on the hairs of the mustache and beard he had probably grown to hide a now-lopsided face. He began to relay to her how food would stick in his throat, and she sensed the panic he experienced when that happened. He and his wife had met with a speech pathologist while they were at the other medical center. The SLP there had recommended Mrs. Taggert learn the Heimlich maneuver. Although it was good advice, Maren got the idea the Taggert's weren't happy with the service there. She didn't invite details, but she intuitively felt a need to be cautious. Some patients weren't happy with any service. She would be sure to explain the course of his therapy very clearly, so his expectations would be realistic. She knew she needed to protect herself as well, since she had never before done what the prosthodontist had requested.

"Today is just to establish a baseline," she began. "Next week Dr. Randall will give you a set of wax dentures. Then he wants me to evaluate you again and mark the upper denture wherever it might need to be built up. That will actually lower the roof of your mouth. Hopefully, it can be lowered enough so your tongue can create sufficient pressure against the hard palate for more efficient swallowing. A lower palate should also improve your articulation, so you can be understood better. Today I can understand about 25 percent of what you say. Hopefully, we can improve on that."

One thing concerned Maren. She had expected him to sound hypernasal, whiny; but he was actually denasal, plugged up as if he had a cold. He reported he did not have either a cold or allergies. If he sounded denasal now, how would he sound when a good part of the oral cavity was filled by a bulky prosthesis? Would he be trading one cause of poor intelligibility for another?

Jerry loved to talk, and continued a monologue all the way back to the rehab desk.

"Stay out of bars. There's nothing to do there but smoke and drink. The smoke and alcohol, they don't do you any good. I'm not letting my son ever smoke or drink. He's twelve. Do you have any sons? I wouldn't let them smoke if I was you. I'm sure that's why I got this. I don't smoke or drink no more."

It took some effort for Maren to transfer his attention to Rita, who would arrange his next appointment. Mrs. Newson and Jason were waiting. Maren hated getting behind, so she would write the note in Jerry's chart later.

She collected Jason and took him the long way to the speech room, through the PT area. They stopped at the utility sink for the bubble blowing. Jason got to choose the food coloring they put in the soapy water to turn the bubbles a pretty color. She encouraged him to blow the soap over the top of the container.

Following the blowing, which was not Jason's favorite activity, he got to choose a toy from the shelves in the speech office. He chose the play barn. He nearly always picked the barn. There was just room for a child-size table in the corner of the speech office, and he set the toy on it. As he opened the barn door and unloaded the figures, Maren elicited speech in a number of ways. She named each figure and asked him to repeat after her. Establishing the pattern of imitation was crucial to therapy. She tried to get him to complete phrases and to say spontaneous words.

"The dog says I want to . . ."

He completed her sentence with something that sounded like *ride*. She repeated her part, encouraging him to respond again. He did. She used judgment developed through years of experience to determine how often and how many times to have him repeat a response. While they worked, her thoughts turned to the parent education at the end of the session. Today she would give his mom some specific guidelines for use at home. Maren was sure Liz went overboard in demanding repetition of words. There was way too much tension at home over Jason's speech. Maren didn't want talking to become any more of a battleground than it already was.

Jason said many word approximations during the session. He tried to repeat nearly everything Maren said. She was excited about his progress and wished Mrs. Newson could see and hear his efforts. A renovation project was underway in the department, and an observation window for parents and students to use was promised in a few more weeks. Until then, Maren met with parents following each session to summarize their activities and to update an ongoing home program.

When Jason finally tired of the barn, Maren pulled out the picture cards and a board game she had placed under the play table. She wanted him to practice as many words as possible in a short time. As he used the spinner and moved Thomas the Tank around the board, he knew he must name the objects on the cards. At this session it was words starting with the phoneme /f/: fire, fan, fight, four, five, fairy. Sometimes he named the card using appropriate articulation. Sometimes he needed help.

Originally, Jason could not say the sounds for K, G, or F. By using hand-to-face touching, called motokinesthetic cues, he could now use his new sounds in words and sometimes in short phrases. Longer words were always more of a challenge.

"Tie-man. Fie-man." The missing /r/ did not concern Maren.

She focused Jason's attention on her face saying "Look" and laying her index finger horizontally under her lower lip. When he looked up, she tucked her lower lip under her upper teeth and exaggerated, "F-F-Fireman."

She started to reach for his face, but he pulled back, placed his own index finger under his lower lip, tucked it under his upper teeth, and pronounced, "F-fiaman."

"Good job," cheered Maren.

The best sign of progress was the change in Jason's attitude. Initially he was belligerent and uncooperative. Now he seemed to understand that Maren was helping him learn to talk. He could maintain attention for thirty to forty minutes now. She would soon increase his therapy session to an hour. Judy had said motherhood had trained Maren to be a better therapist. Maren did enjoy play therapy and wondered if the preschoolers took her back to simpler times, and happier days.

They finished the session by pulling a picture book from the shelf. Maren wished more parents would spend book time with their children. Stories were such good vehicles for teaching speech, language, auditory memory, and social skills. Besides, there were additional side benefits, such as providing parent-child closeness and demonstrating the importance of books. Maren originally had a hard time getting Jason to sit with her to look at a picture book. Now, he brushed the thick shock of coarse hair off his forehead and eagerly chose one of his favorites. Maren watched him. He had a well-to-do look about him, a Kennedy-ish quality, she decided; but his family wasn't wealthy. She knew they depended on insurance to pay for his therapy.

She knew Jason would do most of the storytelling today, because he chose a book they had looked at several times before. With new books he wanted her to read. "Reading" meant she would make up short sentences and say them slowly to explain the story line. Real reading would present too rapid a model for him to be able to repeat any of it. With the picture book today, he had the opportunity to try some phrases. Without the pictures for clues, she wouldn't have been able to understand him.

He laughed at the picture of the puppy tearing a hole in Baby Bop's bag. They found laughter in each activity. Today, Jason was sunshine itself, and the half hour passed quickly and pleasantly. On days when Jason was tired and uncooperative, Maren needed to switch to a variety of activities and games. He could be a challenge, but she knew what her goals were and could usually find some way to incorporate them with almost any activity.

Liz Newson came into the tiny room on the half hour for her assignment and to hear what Jason had accomplished. Maren reinforced that they were to work on only K and F and only at the beginning of words. Maren gently pointed out that trying to get perfect speech too quickly would only create more frustration for both Liz and her son.

Maren hoped she wasn't nagging, but couldn't help calling down the hall after them, "Remember, only ask him to repeat a word two or three times, no more."

She sat at the desk she currently shared with Judy to write notes for both Jerry Taggert and Jason. After filing them in the outpatient cabinet, she glanced at her watch. Midafternoon and she still had to see the rehab patients on fourth floor. *Don't reflect—move,* she commanded herself.

Chapter 3

Maren stopped outside the back door, stretched, and looked around. It was good to take time to breathe in the fall beauty, not just inhale but to really take in the colors and enjoy the warmth of the sun on her face. The brilliant reds and delicious yellows of the deciduous leaves were stunning next to the tall evergreens.

St. John's kept the grounds looking lovely, year-round. There were signs of a walking-jogging path that was under construction around the perimeter. The hospital was focusing more on preventive medicine, and the trickle-down effect meant encouraging staff members to take better care of themselves. Hopefully she would be able to make use of the path by spring.

She sighed and began walking across the parking lot toward her car. It had been an especially hectic few days, but thankfully it was midweek.

I should be making plans for the weekend, she counseled herself. Nick seemed content at school and wouldn't be coming home. It was still a challenge for her, filling the lonely hours. *Maybe Bonni will be in town*, she hoped, as she spotted her car in the first row, just after the doctors' reserved area.

Paul McCloud had his hand on the open door of his white Lexus when he saw her. He was parked directly in back of her blue Pontiac. He had been enjoying watching her and waited until she got close enough to greet her without shouting. She had the sun in her eyes, and he knew she hadn't seen him. Paul was finished for the day, his first full day back, and he was tired. *Maybe still culture shock or jet lag,* he theorized.

"It's a beautiful day, isn't it?"

"Yes, it is." She smiled broadly. They had talked several times in the halls after their reunion morning, but she hadn't seen him for a few weeks now. She noticed as she got closer that he needed a haircut. "It's a great day to be alive."

"I'll second that. It's also good to be back in the USA again."

"That's right. You've been in Africa, and you promised to tell me all about it." He was tan, but also looked more tired than she had ever seen him—and older. She thought he must be embarrassed about his hair because of the way he put his hand on the back of his neck. He seemed to be trying to make the long strands disappear.

The African trip was still on Paul's mind. It hung on him like an oversized, wet trench coat, weighing him down, making every step and every action more difficult. The trip had changed him in ways he couldn't yet define. They had returned to Western culture less than a week ago; and he had slept for the first twenty-four hours, not even calling his parents.

His hand went to the back of his neck again and touched a bead of perspiration that had gathered there. It sent him mentally back to Burundi. He had been sitting in the transport truck. The political balance had taken a turn for the worse even as their plane landed. The local military had closed off their destination village while the mission group was en route. Their truck was stopped at dusk and was held for twelve hours. It had been ninety degrees, even at midnight. Armed guards had interrogated them individually throughout the pitch-black night. He could still smell the sweat, caused by fear more than heat. The three doctors and five nurses had talked, sung, cried, and even prayed together.

Maren noticed the smile slide from his face and saw that his eyes were no longer focused on her. "A-hem," she cleared her throat, breaking his reverie.

He came back to the present and began to tell her about his week, how hard it had been to get back to his old routine. As they chatted, the sun sank lower, until Maren no longer needed to hold her hand up to shield her eyes. Many staff members passed them on the way to their cars. Few spoke. They were anxious to get to their homes. The air grew cooler and the sky darker, as wisps of stratus clouds passed between them and the sun, changing its color and blocking its light.

Just as Maren expressed her curiosity about his trip, his pager beeped. She expected they would be interrupted eventually, but they had been talking longer than she realized. She would be in the thick of rush-hour traffic going home now. Dinner would be very late, and she was already hungry.

He looked at the window of the pager, pressed a button, and looked back at her, an idea forming in his mind. "It's getting late to be standing out here. How about meeting me down the road at the Yellow Duck? We'll get a bite to eat, and I'll tell you more about the trip. I have to call the office. Then I'll be over."

She agreed and wrote the directions on a scrap of paper. It wasn't far.

He called the office and was told there had been a call regarding the laryngectomy patient at St. John's. He decided to go back inside to check Henry Wilson in person. As he walked, he mentally reviewed the events of the early morning surgery.

Paul had watched as the new resident Dave Lasota drew a blue line across the neck of the sixty-one-year-old man. Henry Wilson would never again speak with his own voice or breathe through his nose. After repeated recurrences of cancer, the decision had been made to perform a laryngectomy. They removed his larynx, a vital organ most people called a voice box. Henry probably drank a quart of whiskey a day. When he wasn't bending his elbow for a drink, it was to take a drag of the ever-present cigarette. Not everyone who got laryngeal cancer was a heavy smoker or drinker, but the majority of those patients were.

Now that he had no larynx, Henry would breathe through the stoma, a hole in his neck, for the rest of his life. It was aggressive surgery, not the kind Paul preferred. He would have been pleased to have handed off to the resident, except the resident today was Dave Lasota. Usually Paul got a resident started, then walked out for a break. That gave the new surgeon confidence. Paul had a knack for judging the skill level of residents and for returning at just the right time, to assure that all had gone well. Only rarely was it necessary for them to page him before he returned.

Dave Lasota was far from being a gifted surgeon. Paul hoped he would take up practice in some rural or far-suburban area, where difficult cases were referred to major medical centers in the city. Paul had talked him through the entire procedure. He had trusted Lasota to write orders in the medical chart for feeding, medications, and speech therapy. *That was probably more than he could handle,* Paul thought ruefully as he summoned energy to bound up the stairs.

He checked Mr. Wilson, adjusted the order for pain medication, and stopped to wash up in the physicians' locker room. Catching sight of himself in the mirror caused him to wish he had a fresh shirt. He did keep a razor in his locker. At least he could shave.

That's when he felt it again. He hadn't noticed for a while, but now that gnawing feeling returned to the pit of his stomach. He had felt it the first day back in the States. He had eaten crackers, chewed gum, and taken antacids. It still returned when he least expected it. Maybe it was anxiety, but he didn't rule out the possibility of some jungle virus. He hadn't mentioned it to his family when he had visited with them, but he knew his mother had sensed something was bothering him. She hadn't questioned him, though.

The discomfort in his stomach continued while he shaved and reminisced. Much of Sunday had been spent at his parents' condo near the lake. Gloria McCloud had hugged her only son a long time. Paul knew she was relieved to have him back in the States. "I'm so glad to get you home again," she had said on Sunday, "but I wish Penny was here." Paul's sister had been out of town with her husband Jim and daughter Erin.

Paul admired his mom. Now in her fifties, Gloria was still healthy and active both physically and mentally. Her quiet graciousness belied the toughness she had developed as a Navy wife during the first ten years of her marriage to Robert McCloud. She hadn't had the opportunity for formal training after high school, but certainly possessed the ability. When Bob took the job of financial advisor and fund-raiser at St. John's Hospital several years after his retirement from the Navy, Gloria had settled into a more traditional lifestyle.

Paul pictured his mom and smiled. She was blond, but not by birth. Much to her parents' dismay, she had improved on the mousy brown Mother Nature had given her with peroxide when she was a junior in high school. It had set off her hazel brown eyes and made her look older back then. Now the blond hair made her look more youthful. She had devoted herself almost totally to her two children and her husband, but somehow, over all the years, she had managed to keep a sense of her own identity. He particularly liked that about her.

Paul's thoughts shifted to his dad as he rinsed his face. It had been good to talk more with his dad, even though Bob didn't understand Paul's desire to go on the mission trips and had let him know it. Bob had seen enough of third-world countries during his Navy days. There was no place like the U. S. of A., in Bob's opinion. He was close to his son though; so, while puzzled, he had not been entirely surprised. Bob's own brother was a Maryknoll priest who traveled all over the world, and Frank and Paul had always been close. Bob assumed that's where the desire had been born, rather than from his own example.

Paul often looked at the photos in the family album and knew their stories well. Bob McCloud, a decade older than his wife, was a man of passionate beliefs. He had been quite the rebel in his youth, but he met his match in Gloria. He used to pick her up on his motorcycle, and they would ride like the wind. In later years his parents rode with the wind on Bob's modest sailboat. Bob still had the boat and on rare occasions Paul made time to join him for an afternoon.

Paul splashed some aftershave on his cheeks, ran a comb through his hair, and patted a stray into place. His dad's hair, now white, was still thick and wavy. At sixty-four Bob was still in perfect health. He played doubles tennis three times a week. Paul hoped he would fare as well in his later years. He hoped to emulate that level of activity and health as he aged, too.

He was sure his dad had never been unfaithful to his mom. The thought intruded like a stray wildflower in the bland lawn of his thoughts. He had heard Bob say he never wanted to be with another woman after he met Gloria. Father and son often disagreed on issues, but because of Bob's kindhearted nature he was mellowing into more of an armchair philosopher than an argumentative old man.

Paul took a deep breath and returned to the present. He felt better for having washed up. He checked in the mirror for stray bits of shaving cream. Finding none, he stood a little taller and took a last survey of his overall appearance. Clearly, his penetrating blue eyes were from his dad.

Not questioning how or why his thoughts had become so focused on his parents, he grabbed his black case and pushed through the locker room door.

He took the stairs down and walked quickly back to his car, recalling the comfort of his parents' home on Sunday. Paul, as usual, had declined his dad's offer for a drink. Gloria had poured herself a glass of wine and had reached for Paul's usual cola when he asked instead for 7-Up. They had sat by the sliding glass door, with a view of the lake, while Paul told them about his latest adventure. He had edited out the parts about facing his own mortality as well as theirs. Some things just weren't meant to be shared with parents. If they realized there were omissions, they hadn't let on. Maybe he would share more details after talking it over with Penny. It had been still too unsettling on Sunday.

Starting to feel more normal, Paul picked up his cell phone to call Chad, the owner of the Yellow Duck. He had the number programmed, memory-five for the restaurant. One was University Circle Hospital, two St. John's, three his office, four his parents, and six Penny and Jim. Chad answered immediately. Paul explained he would be there within minutes and that he was meeting a woman with auburn hair whose name was Maren. Before Paul could ask for favors, Chad's heavy accent interrupted. "Don't worry, Dr. Paul, we'll take good care of your lady friend. I already put her in the back booth and gave her a hot drink."

⸺

While Paul was shaving and reminiscing, Maren stepped through the door of the Yellow Duck and into a new world. The lights inside looked like lanterns and gave everything a soft glow. There were perhaps fifteen tables, each draped with a white cloth under a glass top. Mirrors on one wall made it look larger; so that the room felt cozy, not cramped, and the aroma of cooking wafted from the kitchen via the pass-through.

An Asian man with dark, thinning hair greeted her. He looked rather formal in his black, sleeveless vest over a long-sleeved, white dress shirt. He led her beyond the tiny reception area and past a tall divider that was a series of S curves extending the length of the room.

Attached on either side of the divider were curved padded bench seats, but they didn't stop at any of those. On her right, the wall side, were free-standing tables with self-contained booths in the corners. The Asian man gestured her into the corner booth, handed her a menu, and left. Although she requested nothing, he returned moments later with a cup and a large pot of hot jasmine tea. She surveyed the room as she sipped it, enjoying the soft mauves and muted greens. There was no Chinese red, gold, or black, as she had expected.

"Miss Maren?" He approached her again.

"Yes," she answered automatically, surprised to be addressed by name.

"I am Chad," he announced precisely but with a heavy accent. "Dr. Paul called to say he will be here soon. May I get you something else to drink while you wait?"

"Just more hot tea, please." She studied the rugs hanging on the wall next to her and the stack of pillows that stood like sentries, strategically placed between tables. She opened the menu but mainly enjoyed the tea and surroundings for nearly a half an hour until she saw Paul in the entryway. He chatted momentarily with a smiling Asian woman who pointed to Maren's table and then strode quickly to her.

"Sorry to keep you waiting; had to go back up to third floor. What do you think?" He gestured around the room, without waiting for a response to his first comment.

"It's charming, and I just opened the menu. I like Chinese."

"That's good to know." Paul smiled. "But this is Vietnamese. Do you know Vietnamese food?"

"Not really. Jack was in Vietnam but didn't bring back any recipes." Instantly she regretted mentioning Jack. Not because she didn't want to remind Paul of her marital history. He certainly had always been aware of that. It was because of the bad memories the mention of 'Nam brought—Jack tossing and turning, up in the middle of the night, finding him on the couch or in the easy chair, the giant-size bottle of sleeping pills that emptied without explanation, the appearance of a new bottle. It wasn't as if there were hard drugs. Jack, thank God, didn't come back like some of the others, hooked on heroin or having a crack habit. He just never slept well.

He had never talked about 'Nam, not to her anyway. Maybe he had talked to Steve. Jack's dad had died just before he left, and Jack had bonded with Steve Wagner in basic training. They had gone through flight training together and managed to be in the same unit for two years. They had served before antiwar sentiment got so bad, before the heaviest fighting really. But war was war, she supposed. Eventually, she had come to believe his insomnia might stem from his experiences in 'Nam. If it hadn't been for the war, he likely would have made a career in the service.

The thoughts flashed through her mind in an instant, but Paul caught the change of expression that crossed her face and felt her lack of focus. He couldn't access her history, but the last thing he wanted was to start the evening with morbid memories. He realized for the first time that her husband must have been some years older. "I'm sorry," he began, "I didn't think—"

"It's okay, really," she interrupted. "I didn't know him then, and I don't have any bad vibes about Vietnamese food. You're too young to remember the war," she mumbled, embarrassed and acutely aware of their age difference.

"No," His face brightened. He was determined to change the topic of conversation, "but this place has been a bachelor's home away from home for quite a while. Chad and Connie take very good care of me."

"Then you are a bachelor," she half teased, and the mood was light again.

"You didn't know that?" he asked, using the question to avoid volunteering any information about how he had found the Yellow Duck. It had been during his Oriental period, especially Oriental women. Susie, Chad's niece, had been in nurse's training when they dated. Paul had been fascinated by Vietnam stories and the boat people, maybe because of his Uncle Frank's stories. He had been seeing Susie almost a year when she decided to visit friends in California. She fell in love with the coast and made it her home. Paul had continued his friendship with Chad and Connie and made a home away from home at the Yellow Duck.

"Well, I like to get my information directly from the source, not rely on gossip. You never really said, you know. You talk about your parents and sister and brother-in-law, but not about . . ." She almost said, "Your love life," but stopped. Unfortunately, no other phrase leaped to mind.

"My social life?" He completed her thought with a wicked, teasing smile. He leveled his eyes directly to hers, paused for emphasis, and before she could respond, continued. "Maren, I'm not married. I've never been married, and I'm not going with anyone. In spite of what the male scrub nurse says, I'm not gay either."

She wished she could think of an appropriate reply, but instead just continued to look into his unblinking eyes. His blue eyes fascinated her. They weren't pale, washed-out blue; they were really blue. No family member or friend that she could recall had eyes like that.

Just when she realized she was staring, Chad returned from the kitchen to set another pot of jasmine tea between them. The moment passed.

Paul offered to order, and Maren was relieved to let him. They would have Number Five, something with shrimp and pineapple. She did opt for the steamed rice.

"Would you like a glass of wine before dinner?" Chad asked.

Paul looked questioningly at Maren. "Just water with lemon," she answered, shaking her head. She intended to stay very sober. She hadn't admitted it even to herself, but now had to acknowledge inwardly that she had always felt physically attracted to Paul. He held up a hand, indicating none for him, and Chad was waved off.

"How did the surgery go this morning?" she ventured, attempting to return to safer topics. A laryngectomy was rare at St. John's. They usually went to one of the university hospitals, and she had overheard the nurses talking about it.

"Oh, Dave Lasota is so slow. If he were in neuro, he'd be a half-brain surgeon." Paul's intellect was quick, and his wit could be sharp. He had little patience with mediocrity and none for ignorance. "But we're not going to talk about patients tonight."

"We're not?"

"No. No patient talk allowed." "I've turned off the faucet. I'm not even on call tonight," he finished with a smile.

"The faucet," she repeated. It was an odd metaphor, but she understood him to mean the door to the work world was closed.

Paul poured tea for them and changed the subject again. Maren had expected him to have an agenda, to be efficient, methodical, goal oriented; but he seemed content to just drift from topic to topic. She learned that he had played trumpet in high school and during his college years. He had even thought of majoring in music at one time. He learned that she loved to sing and had been in both a community and a church choir. She had been originally named Meran, M-E-R-A-N, after a British ancestor. She had changed the spelling when she married hoping to extinguish the family nickname Ann. It was still pronounced the same, to rhyme with Karen.

"How did you find this place?" she asked before he could pose another question.

"It was in the neighborhood." He intentionally dodged her question. He told her instead about wanting a home of his own, rather than an apartment. He had drawn circles on a map to define the area that would satisfy hospital requirements for his availability. He told her about how his sister had helped.

"It felt so good to have a house of my own, and having Penny handle the decorator was a real help. She would come up with two or three choices she thought I would like and bring them to me. It was that process that regenerated our relationship."

He talked so easily, opened up so readily, and seemed so comfortable. She was more reserved, but eventually stopped expecting his pager to go off and began to relax. She became more spontaneous as they shared stories of their growing-up years. They asked and answered all the usual questions and discovered each had a relative who was a missionary. Maren's was a great-aunt she hadn't known well. Paul's was Uncle Frank McCloud. From the way Paul talked about his uncle Maren could tell Father Frank had played an important role in Paul's life.

Paul wanted to know more about her family, and she wanted to know how he decided to become a doctor and specialize. As the food was served, he began telling her about Penny. His little sister had been born with torticollis. Her neck was twisted, pulling her head to one side, and it had been misdiagnosed, repeatedly. As a young boy, he had gone with his mother and sister to a long list of specialists. Doctors had thought it was scoliosis. His parents had tried chiropractic, physical therapy, and even acupuncture. As Penny grew, it got worse, and she became known as the girl with the twisted neck. Of course children thought she was an oddity. She had confided to Paul that she felt like a female hunchback. When he and his parents visited Notre Dame, he was the only one who knew that she had refused to go because of the connection in her mind. Her anomaly had held her back socially and scholastically, but that wasn't the worst. The worst had been the constant pain.

"When Penny was in high school, my parents took her to a major university where the ailment was diagnosed as spasmodic torticollis, when it was actually congenital torticollis. The recommended treatment was botulism toxin, Botox injections. She had a series of eight, at three-month intervals. There was no relief but plenty of side effects. She ate nothing but pudding-consistency food for months because of resulting swallowing problems. She was without a voice for weeks after each injection. Imagine, a teenage girl with no voice," he finished sadly.

He spoke so tenderly of his sister that Maren was touched. "What's happened to her since then?" she wanted to know.

"When I was in med school, I did a lot of research. I found Bill Schram, a pediatric head and neck surgeon in Iowa. He changed both of our lives. He diagnosed her with congenital, not spasmodic, torticollis and surgically disconnected her sternocleidomastoid muscle at the clavicle. Other muscles were affected in her back, too. It wouldn't have been so serious if it had been caught earlier. She was voiceless again for eight weeks because of damage to the vagus nerve. After the surgery, she could hold her head up for the first time in her life. I guess I wanted to be able to do that kind of thing for other kids." He gave a shrug of his shoulder. "She still has some pain but not continuous or unbearable."

"Didn't you say she's married to a great guy and they have a beautiful, normal three-year-old daughter?"

"Yes, and I'm Erin's godfather, and a very active uncle. What about your family, Maren? Parents? Siblings?"

"My mom died from the side affects of a drug used to treat her rheumatoid arthritis the year I was married. My dad died of a heart attack a couple of years later. I have an older sister Ruth. She's married, has three children, and lives in Maryland. She moved out to DC right after college to work for a congressman, so we haven't been as close as you and Penny."

"How did you meet Jack?"

She told him about her last year at Purdue. "I lived in an apartment with two friends on the first floor of a big, old house. There was a small apartment upstairs and an office attached to the back. Jack and his friend Steve were insurance agents in that office while they finished school. That was before they joined Dean Whittier," she explained. "We met in the lot where we all parked our cars. I thought he was so worldly. He'd already been to Nam."

"I thought he was a pilot," Paul interrupted.

"He and Steve flew choppers in Nam but wanted to change to fixed-wing aircraft. They were taking aviation courses at the university airport. Jack took me flying on our second date. I was very impressed. I was twenty-one when we were married, right after graduation. We had Matt a year later and Nick four years later."

Paul managed to get a bite of shrimp between questions. "How did he die, Maren?" He knew he shouldn't ask, but he had been curious for so long that he couldn't stop himself. He had thought it might have been a plane crash, so was surprised at her story.

Maren's stomach tightened. No matter how many times she went over it, no matter how many years passed, talking about Jack's death was always painful. Still, the words came more easily with the passage of time.

"Jack and Steve had gone to the cottage we owned together to go fishing. They were on the lake in a bass boat when a storm came up. It had been unseasonably hot, and what was forecast as severe thunderstorms turned into a sizeable tornado. They hadn't been able to start the motor for some reason, so they paddled to shore. Steve told me they relaxed when they hit the sand. Steve jumped out first and yelled at Jack to help haul the boat up on the beach. They had gone only a few steps when it hit. Steve was knocked unconscious by flying debris. He was drenched and bruised when he woke. He found Jack lying in a pool of water, face down, where the boat had been. It was gone. Steve tried CPR right there on the beach in the storm. Technically, Jack drowned." She spoke more quietly at the end.

"And in the fall you decided to start graduate school?" he asked, incredulous at the sequence of events.

"That was already planned. The boys were old enough, and I had been getting restless. Speaking of being restless," she said, ready to change the topic, "you were going to tell me about Africa. Did you sign up for that because you were restless?"

Now he was embarrassed. He had been so enjoying their easy companionship, he had neglected to share the story he had promised. Penny wouldn't approve. "Women like to be asked and need to be told," she had counseled repeatedly. Paul often had trouble figuring out which things needed asking and which should be told. This for sure needed telling.

"Over dessert," he promised.

"What is Vietnamese dessert?" she wanted to know, relieved that the conversation was changing.

"Chad," he called, "two special dessert drinks."

"Two coffee with Tia Maria coming right up," Chad called back. The two men laughed at what was clearly a private joke between them.

Suddenly, Paul looked serious.

"What?" she asked.

He waved off her concern. "It's just that it's the first time I've laughed out loud since I got back from Burundi. I . . ." he prolonged the pronoun and continued more slowly, ". . .find it very easy to talk with you, Maren. I thought that would be the case. I was so convinced, in fact, I made sure there wasn't much opportunity."

She was astonished to think that anything about their relationship was other than coincidence. That he had been purposely avoiding her was incredible.

He continued before she could speak. He told her, over several coffees, about the mission trip. He described their group, their living conditions, and the children he had treated there, some of whom he knew would live only a matter of days. He left nothing out, but he did save the story of the night before they entered the village for last. He shuffled his feet under the table as he tried to find the right words for that.

They had all been fatigued from trip preparations and the long flight before even beginning their mission. There had been no indication that there was political unrest, or the sponsors wouldn't have supported the venture.

"We still don't understand what's happening there, but mark my words, we'll be hearing more about that part of the world. Military of some sort stopped our trucks. They mainly wanted bribes but evidently were supposed to detain us while some action was going on in the village that was our destination. The guards harassed us all night, but one nurse more than the others. Carrie was thin. She must have looked the most vulnerable. They were still hoping for bribes, although most everything the group brought with us had already been given up. Carrie cried most of the night. I knew she missed her husband and children. No one knew the trip would be so dangerous. We were told by our translator that the guards were separating the men from the women in the village, while we waited in the truck. Between sobs Carrie said, 'It's not good for man to be alone. It's the first thing God declared was not good.' It was an odd thing to say.

I knew we might not live through the night. My own thoughts had started to focus on that possibility. Death doesn't frighten me. I've seen it too many times. I don't have a wife or children, and my parents would still have each other. Somehow the events and Carrie's statement triggered a realization that my parents would one day die, leaving me alone. They're so alive, so active. I never thought of the possibility of them dying, not yet. The idea of losing them caused a sense of isolation in me that I've never known."

The personal nature of what Paul was sharing took Maren by surprise. He searched her face, trying to determine her reaction. She was so engrossed in the intimate details of his story that she couldn't speak. She nodded her encouragement for him to continue.

He hesitated, remembering the crushing sensation in his chest. He had thought it was a heart attack and had waited to identify symptoms. He could almost feel now the terrible ache that had permeated his being. It had engulfed him until he recognized it as the emptiness he had never allowed himself to experience. He always had crammed his hours and minutes full of activities to avoid this very feeling, but it caught up with him in a transport truck in Burundi. He had felt absolutely paralyzed.

"I don't pray often," he finally continued, "but I did then. Carrie's scream broke my self-absorption. One of the guards was threatening to take her for interrogation." Paul had felt a surge of protective instinct flush the ache from his body. He had reached quickly into his medical bag and brought out a new Canon camera he had hidden there. He stretched out one arm with the offering toward the guard and put the other around Carrie's bony shoulder, pulling her further into the tenuous safety provided by their transport.

"At that instant my mind filled with a thought, or a directive. I'm not sure which. It filled my mind and then melted away. I felt calm again, but confused. I just held Carrie against my chest until she was quiet."

Maren pictured the intimacy of the moment. "But, what was the thought, the directive?"

Paul shuffled his feet again, determined to phrase this as honestly as he could. All the encounters he had ever experienced with Maren had crystallized while he kept his arms around Carrie. He resolved then to confront his relationship with her when he returned.

"I don't know if you believe in divine intervention," he continued, "but several times in my life I've had the sense that another power was transmitting a message directly into my mind, without words, although I try later to put the thought into words."

"Yes," Maren responded empathetically, "I've had similar experiences. I believe it is divine intervention. Is that what happened in Africa?"

He nodded.

"What was the thought?"

"You, Maren, the thought was you, that I should come back and talk to you and . . ." He stared down at his spoon and turned it over and over. He didn't want to scare her. *Get the words right, McCloud*, he charged himself silently. He looked up and met her eyes again. " . . . and get to know you and be with you, in friendship, in a relationship."

Their gazes were locked. Maren was only beginning to comprehend what he had already lived with for weeks. She wasn't prepared for it. She didn't have the right mindset. She focused on one word, *friendship*.

"Friendship. You're talking about expanding our relationship into a friendship. That's very flattering."

"It's not a compliment, Maren. It's an offer, an invitation. I want to explore a relationship with you. I thought about this the whole time I was in Africa. I even prayed about it." He waited for her to reply.

While Maren struggled to regain her composure, she reviewed a document her mind had secretly constructed without her awareness. It was a list of reasons why a romantic relationship with Paul was out of the question. First, of course, was the age difference. It would be different if he were older, but she was the old one. She knew he was Catholic. She could never accept that form of worship. He was a doctor, married to his work, and she had already spent too many days alone. He was too attractive; it sometimes made her feel nervous, out of control. He was city, she suburban. He was childless, and should have the opportunity, the joy, of fathering and raising his own children. She had raised her children. But most important of all, she had promised herself years ago, if she ever had another relationship, it would have to be three-way, including God from the beginning. *If only he hadn't said it just that way, my answer would be easy,* she thought. *But he said he prayed about it.*

Paul was openly anxious now. He began to scuff his feet again. She swallowed the last mouthful of coffee.

"Friendship," she said aloud. "I can't think of anything I'd like better than having a friendship with you."

Paul sensed that she did not totally understand all he had tried to convey. Maybe he hadn't explained enough about his parents or the emptiness that engulfed him that night. At least it was a start. He had opened the door.

He checked his watch. They had been sitting in their booth for nearly four hours. Although he didn't realize it until later, the gnawing feeling in his stomach had dissipated, and it never returned.

They were alone in the restaurant, which was normally closed by this hour. Chad and Connie had retreated to the kitchen to give them privacy.

"I need to stretch. How about a walk?" he suggested.

The walk was short, the drive to Edgelawn long, but the coffee kept Maren wide awake long after she tucked herself under the covers.

Chapter 4

Maren had first seen the thin, seventy-something Alice Benson the previous week, on third floor. The order had been for a bedside swallow evaluation. The original medical diagnosis was heart attack. Maren remembered her particularly because Alice had seemed so refined. Maren, sitting at the counter in the intensive care area on fifth floor now reviewed every detail in her mind, wondering if she could have done something more for the woman. The first time Maren had seen Alice, her nurse had said she hadn't been eating well.

Maren had sat at the counter in the nurses' station a long time that day, reviewing the chart extensively, looking for a clue as to why the possible swallowing disorder. Mrs. Benson had an NG tube. Maren had found the order to discontinue the tube feedings and begin PO with a general diet, but there was originally no swallowing evaluation order.

A sharp RN named Marsha had checked the I/O chart to see whether Mrs. Benson was getting sufficient nutritional intake by mouth. With budget cuts so many nurses were working part time that it was difficult to provide continuity of care, but Marsha was one nurse who was quick to identify patients who needed new orders. Marsha had told Maren the patient had trouble taking her meds, and since being on a PO diet had eaten almost nothing.

Maren had taken a stethoscope to room 308 and had noticed a voice barely louder than a whisper. Alice had been too weak to feed herself. She had taken the half teaspoon of ice cream Maren put in her mouth. The multiple swallows which resulted might not have been noticed without auditory cues heard through the stethoscope. The woman had coughed on thin and medium-consistency liquids and had difficulty swallowing the thick liquid.

It was odd that the feeding tube remained in her nose with no order to continue tube feedings. It would of course restrict movement of the larynx and degrade the quality of the swallow somewhat, but could have supplemented her oral intake. It should have been pulled when the discontinue order was written. No relatives or friends had been there to advocate for Alice.

God help those without loving relatives or friends to stand guard, Maren thought.

After the evaluation, Maren had found Dr. Landry sitting at the counter and had reported her findings to him. She recommended reinstituting tube feedings immediately while monitoring input for a pureed diet with thickened liquids. A video swallow study was always recommended when patients coughed during the bedside evaluation, but Maren had suggested that Mrs. Benson was too weak. Dr. Landry had seemed surprised his patient had not been receiving tube feedings all along, so Maren had pointed out the written order, which had been followed by many nurses before Marsha questioned it.

This morning the OT assistant had stopped Maren in the hall and asked if there was anything she could do to help Alice Benson communicate. The patient now had a trach and was on oxygen. She still had the NG tube as well as an IV drip. She was so weak her lips trembled. She couldn't lift her hands to her face.

Staring off into space at the ICA counter, Maren came back to the present. *Too little too late*, she reflected. *Still no relatives or friends. Why is she so alone?* Maren felt compassion for this woman. Although her nose was caked with blood and her hair disheveled, Alice maintained an air of refinement. That's what caused Maren to repeatedly speculate about what Alice's life had been before her illness and whether better treatment might have prevented her present state. *I don't know what I could have done differently. I don't even know how I can best help her now. She can't produce voice. She doesn't have enough strength to write messages.*

After talking briefly with the nurse, Maren went to get a communication board. *People believe a communication board is a magic talking device for the patient*, Maren thought ruefully. In fact, a simple board was only a series of pictures and letters for the patient to point to. Maren wondered how many patients actually used them; it was such a painstaking process. Maren felt the little communication board she offered was woefully inadequate. She left the intensive care area feeling depressed, wondering if Alice Benson would make it through the week. She was sorry that her prediction had not come true. "You'll feel better in a few hours," she had promised. If Alice did live, she was in for an extended convalescence.

A long week passed that Maren rarely saw Paul. She began to question whether she had understood him. Then, this morning, he had asked her to meet him in the cafeteria. She was holding the hot mug of coffee in both hands, waiting for him to get to the point. She wondered what was on his mind, but knew better than to interrupt his thought process with questions. He was rambling on about the hassle of the parking garage at Circle Hospital. She smiled and took in more warm liquid, half listening.

He must have seen a lot of life in a short time inside the walls of the city hospitals, she reflected. She was not easily impressed, but she did admire the sensitivity he had preserved in spite of a training process and work schedule that could be dehumanizing.

She had observed him in the clinic and the OR. His style was calm and noncritical, but he could be acidic at what he considered stupidity. He had always been the patient's advocate, as was Maren, but the mission trips had sobered him, matured him. She had seen a greater depth of character during their meal at the Yellow Duck.

Paul came to the end of his story, but didn't move on to another topic. She gave him a quizzical smile, and had no option but to make small talk by recounting her own traffic adventure the day before.

"That's why I took the train today," she finished her part of the conversation ritual and waited again.

"Maren, will you"—he paused—"stay in the city tonight?"

Startled at the abrupt change in topics, just when she had decided there was no agenda for their meeting, she tried to swallow and protest at the same time. The coffee caught in her throat, causing a sputter.

"I know it's the middle of the week, but I have family obligations on the weekend, and I'm getting frustrated trying to find some time for us to get better acquainted. If you stay for a late dinner, I'm five minutes from home, but you would still have a long drive."

"Paul, this could get too complicated. I'd have to pack for an overnight."

"I should have asked you ahead of time," he admitted, "but could you pick up a few things after work?"

She knew her list of reasons why the overnight wasn't a good idea had more to do with something other than the logistics, but it was all muddled in her mind. Being unable to verbalize clearly put her at a disadvantage; and consequently, in the end, she agreed. *After all*, she convinced herself, *how can we pursue a friendship if we never have time together?*

At noon she took a taxi downtown to buy a few necessities. She bought toiletries, night clothes, and a bag she called her Chicago bag, too large for a purse, too small for a suitcase. Perfect. While it could pass for a briefcase, it actually held the robe, gown, toiletries, and a change of clothes for the evening. There was no room to add an outfit for the next day, but she was out of time. *I'll have to wash things out;* she planned as she adjusted the strap to fit on her shoulder. She charged everything, tucked her small purse into the new bag, and hurried out to the street.

Grateful for the small umbrella that came with the bag, she knew neither she nor her purchases would get wet in the now-steady autumn rain. Hopefully, there wouldn't be ten conventions in town, and she would be able to get a hotel room. It would be an expensive overnight, but it would be a rare event, she rationalized. She would make a quick call to Sandy, her neighbor. Sandy kept an emergency house key for Maren's townhouse. She would feed Saturn, Nick's thirteen-year-old cat.

By five thirty the patients had all been seen and Rita was gone. *Good,* she thought, closing the door, *I'll change clothes here.* She wished she could get a shower, but a dusting of talc would have to do. She was glad she had added it to her purchases at the last minute. It did make her feel fresher.

Suddenly, her stomach began to churn with butterflies. *Relax,* she counseled herself. *It's just dinner.*

Her cab stopped in front of the restaurant at six thirty. She paid the driver and pulled the umbrella from her new bag. The building didn't look very promising in daylight; tonight, in the rain, it was positively gloomy. The two-story red brick was illuminated only by the long light over the painted wooden sign, "Yellow Duck." She reminded herself how cozy it was inside and stepped through the door. Predictably, Paul was held up at the office and didn't arrive until seven-thirty. By the time he paid the bill and Chad retrieved their coats, it was late.

They stepped out into the October night together, hoping for a walk. Feeling a light mist in the air, Maren immediately pulled her small umbrella from the Chicago bag. Paul surveyed the umbrella's size and commented drolly, "One of us is going to get wet."

"Won't hurt me a bit, just make my hair more wavy," she quipped.

Paul held her umbrella over them with his left hand and put his right arm around her shoulder to crowd under it. She, of necessity, put her arm around his waist. They had to stay in step, he pacing his strides to hers. As they walked, he was silently criticizing himself. He should have brought his umbrella to begin with, but was glad he had not. At the same time, she was hoping he didn't think she offered to share her umbrella with him in order to create this physical closeness. By the time they reached his car, the rain was heavy. There would be no more walking. The evening was over.

"I need to get a cab," Maren stated.

Paul was puzzled. He expected to take her to his house, to get her settled in the guest room.

"I have a reservation," she explained, seeing his blank look.

"I thought you would stay at my place. I never meant to leave you on your own. You'd like Penny's guest room," he added hastily so there would be no misunderstanding.

"I'm used to being on my own, Paul. I already reserved a room."

He felt disappointed and like a poor host. *Penny would say I didn't communicate my intentions, and she'd be right. Nothing to do about it now, except apologize.*

He had no choice but to relent. "I'll drop you at your hotel, but next time you stay in my guest room. You'll have to buy hotel stock otherwise." He wanted her to understand that he meant for them to spend many more evenings together. She didn't answer, and they drove to the hotel in silence. As she gathered her bag and umbrella to get out of the car, he stopped her arm with his hand. "It'll be better not to publicize our relationship at the hospital," he warned.

"If anyone finds out, I'll know you talked," she countered with a smile.

"Thanks," they both said together. She stepped out in the rain, alone.

There were more patients on five than usual. Five was ICU and ICA, the most seriously ill patients in the hospital. Maren's next patient was a seventy-six-year-old man with multiple subdural hematomas. Cindy, his nurse, glibly told Maren he had tripped and fallen while getting decorations from storage. Maren, as always, did a thorough chart review but found no documentation to support Cindy's story. That kind of incongruity always left her feeling unsettled. Did the nurse remember a different patient's history? Was the story true but not reported on admission?

Whatever the case, he was in front of her now, clear plastic tubing protruding from his skull. Bloody drops were visible as they were being evacuated from his brain to prevent further complications, and oxygen was administered via a nasal cannula. She felt drained just looking at him. His gaze did follow her as she walked around the small cubicle, but he made no effort to move or communicate. She was still wondering whether this was a multiple spontaneous bleed that should be considered a stroke, or if it had occurred due to a traumatic brain injury. She wasn't sure then whether to expect right hemisphere symptoms, traumatic brain injury symptoms, or none at all, since the bleed was not in the cortex.

She knew that not all SLPs bothered with such conjecture. They simply addressed whatever presented itself. Maren thought she probably wore herself out needlessly. After all, whatever symptoms he had would speak for themselves. He didn't answer her greeting and lay elevated at a sixty-degree incline, silently watching her. She quietly explained why she was there, then listened with her stethoscope at his neck to establish a baseline before feeding him. Resting respiration revealed no sounds of congestion. When she asked if he would like something to eat, he nodded.

She moved his bed to almost a ninety-degree angle, gave him a teaspoonful of applesauce, and listened to the swallow. *Swish*, it sounded as it moved in a timely fashion through his throat and into his esophagus. She gave him a bite of cracker. He seemed to handle the mechanical soft item, including the crumbs, without difficulty. She proceeded to the liquid and listened again. *Click*, it sounded appropriately as the sip of water zipped through his pharynx.

She straightened up and continued to observe him. She began to believe there was no problem, scolding herself for all her anxiety about his neurological status. Then he coughed. It was at least twenty seconds after the swallow. He coughed a second time, and she hadn't administered anymore liquid.

"I cough a lot," he finally spoke.

"Do you smoke? Do you have a cold?" she inquired, each time receiving a negative response. *He may have acquired a cold, it could be the beginning of aspiration pneumonia, or there could have been pooling I couldn't detect.* She knew that material could have remained in his pharynx and fallen into his airway many seconds after the swallow. The only way to tell for sure was a video swallow study. She would also recommend a cognitive evaluation. Maybe he was just the silent type and didn't want to communicate, or maybe he did fall and consequently had cognitive issues.

She called Radiology from the nurses' station before contacting the doctor. Might as well be able to tell him when it could be scheduled when she did speak to him.

Carolyn Ballentine, the head tech, answered. She had worked at the hospital since the construction of the present building. "Can't do it today," she stated matter-of-factly. "Only one radiologist here this afternoon."

It seemed odd to Maren that there would be only one radiologist on duty all afternoon. Emergencies had a nasty way of not happening on schedule. There was nothing to do but schedule it for morning. Only one problem—tomorrow was Saturday. There would be a radiologist, but no rehab services were provided. Originally, Judy had arranged to come in for videos on an as-needed basis. Then the new group of radiologists claimed Saturdays were minimum staff days and refused to schedule videos on weekends. Mr. Crandall would have to wait until Monday morning.

"Not early, though," Carolyn was saying. "We're already scheduled heavy from nine o'clock on."

"What about eight or eight-thirty?" prodded Maren.

"No, Dr. Jasmine is on, and she doesn't walk in until nine. Then she drinks her coffee and looks over the schedule for a half hour."

Incredible, thought Maren silently, frustrated and angry. She tentatively scheduled for eleven o'clock on Monday morning and called the doctor to get a telephone order for the study. She reached an automated answering service at his office. After being on hold for five full minutes, she hung up. She found the nurse, gave her the results of her evaluation, and finished by relaying her experience trying to reach the doctor.

"I know," Cindy sympathized, "I spent twenty minutes in that maze last Monday."

Nevertheless, Cindy agreed to reach him and get the order. If he declined to give the order, they could cancel with Radiology. Carolyn would be glad for the break. Feeling increasing tension gathering in the small of her back and rising to her shoulders, Maren stood, tried briefly to stretch the tension out, and headed for the elevator. Cindy called her back.

"Aren't you going to see Mr. Ladonski in 510?"

Maren hadn't gotten the order, but Cindy showed it to her in the chart—another swallow evaluation. It would be nice to see someone for speech or language, but that was not likely on fifth. Maren wished she could go back to the speech room and see an outpatient, get a chance to look out a window, and grab a cup of coffee. She was feeling irritable and beginning to detect abdominal cramps. Instead of giving in to her desires, she took the chart from Cindy and reviewed another puzzling history.

Mr. Ladonski had a trach tube that had been in place for fifteen years. He spoke around it. That meant he breathed through the hole in his neck, yet produced sufficient air pressure and flow to vibrate his own vocal folds, without even covering the opening of the trach tube. Some air was lost through the tube, which projected out of his neck, reducing his loudness, but he could be heard.

Oddly, no one, not even the patient, knew why the tube had been placed. Alvin Ladonski had had a slight stroke several days before but seemed to be progressing nicely. The swallow evaluation order was standard protocol following a stroke.

"I certainly hope he's swallowing well," Cindy stated. "He's been eating a general diet for two days now."

The diet order had been written on the recommendation of a nurse. Nurses weren't always trained to assess swallowing function, though some did an admirable job. Maren proceeded with the evaluation and concurred with the nurse's recommendation that Mr. Ladonski continue on his present diet.

Maren was anxious to get to the rehab unit on four to check on Jeff Fritche, but heeded her body's warnings that she needed food and something for cramps before continuing. As she walked the steps to the basement cafeteria, she reviewed his history mentally.

Mr. Fritche had been in-house for weeks. Judy had evaluated him when he was admitted to acute care with what appeared to be a massive stroke. They had thought he had global aphasia, a total inability to understand or use language. The lesion was in the thalamus, and Judy felt that was the reason he was so unresponsive. By the time Maren had seen him on the rehab wing, he was beginning to respond. Judy had specifically asked Maren's opinion because Maren's neurology class had been more recent than her own. It wasn't neurology notes that helped, though; it was an aphasia text by Brookshire.

The first day, Maren had watched as Judy worked with him. He had answered some yes/no questions by nodding or saying "no." The percent correct had improved when she presented him with the printed words and asked him to point to the answer. Jeff's right side had been paralyzed, so he had been learning to use his left hand. They couldn't be sure if his responses were slow because of that, or if he needed extra time to process each question. His ability to identify a correct object when given a choice of two had been only a little better than 50 percent. He might have been guessing and done as well. Jeff dozed off frequently during therapy, indicating he was low functioning, but Judy's notes stated that she had heard him speak in complete sentences once or twice. Family members also had reported spontaneous responses during their conversations with him.

Today there was a meeting with staff and family in Jeff's room to determine his placement at discharge. He was still lethargic and unable to tolerate the three hours of daily therapy required to qualify for a rehab center. The meeting was to be right after lunch. Maren decided to review his chart after lunch in case any changes had occurred and make copies of a graph to present at the staffing.

Maren paged Judy and arranged to meet her in the cafeteria. Maren was in need of some company. Working on the floor was lonely; she rarely stopped to socialize with other professionals. Judy was in her thirties, single, and fun-loving. She could always distract Maren from the grim realities of the fifth floor. Judy had moved to Chicago after graduate school in New York to live with a medical student, but their love didn't survive the demands of medical school. Judy's love of Lake Michigan and hospital life had more than survived; it had blossomed.

Maren thought Judy could have been a doctor, except for her belief that at least half of life should be devoted to recreation. Her easy-going, light-hearted nature made her a favorite wherever she worked, and she always did a good job. Since the two therapists had been working directly for the hospital, goodwill, confidence in, and understanding of speech services had improved dramatically. That meant more orders and more services provided. The quality of patient care had, in Maren's judgment, also improved considerably.

As they ate, Judy reported her latest personal trauma. "I noticed gray hairs last week. Can you believe it?" Maren said she hadn't noticed and Judy continued. "I made an emergency visit to my hairdresser to have my hair frosted. It hides the incoming gray, see?" There wasn't much to frost; it was extremely short. Judy was a lithe and very active woman with no time for primping. The short cut fit her size as well as her personality.

After Maren confided that she had been coloring her own hair for some time, Judy seemed more relaxed. "I never knew that. It looks great."

She began to fill Maren in on the latest news from the meeting she had attended that morning. "Metro Head and Neck Surgeons are coming to St. John's in a big way. That's bound to mean increased business for us. Dr. Weingarten wants a videostroboscopy unit in the spring," Judy continued in an excited voice. "He asked if I would accompany one or two doctors from their group to Wisconsin for a five-day training seminar the first week of March."

"And I can tell you said yes," encouraged Maren. "Better you than me."

"Of course I said yes. I tried to get them to send both of us, but could only get passage for one."

"That's okay. I don't think I would be very good at it. I don't know much about voice disorders, and I know I wouldn't like doing flexible endoscopy. I have no interest in inserting a scope in a patient's nose."

"Most of the time it's a rigid, oral scope, and once you learn it will be just like doing a video swallow study."

"If and when it comes, I'll be content to learn from you. I've been pleased that we don't get many voice cases here. It's not my area of expertise."

"Well, you'll be interested in this." Judy leaned closer and used a confidential voice. "There have been complaints about the radiology group."

"Really." Maren perked up.

"Quality-control issues. They take too many x-rays."

"I've noticed some of them take two or three stills during every video. I've never heard of that being done. Is it to generate revenue? Does the cost get passed on to the patient?"

"No, the hospital is eating it. Conjecture is that they take so many because they are unsure of themselves. Carolyn's keeping her mouth shut, though."

Judy's pager went off, ending their conversation abruptly. Maren didn't finish her lunch, but chugged two more Advil and headed back to fourth floor for a stop at the copy machine before the meeting.

—

Three therapists were waiting: occupational, physical, and activities. Jeff's nurse, the dietitian, and three family members followed Maren into the room. Darlene, the rehab nurse-supervisor, started the meeting by saying they were having the meeting in Jeff's room so that he could hear their discussion. She bent over the obviously sleeping patient and addressed him, "We want you to know what is being done to help you."

The others squirmed in discomfort but dutifully began to recite Jeff's goals, activities, and accomplishments to him, as if he were awake and attentive.

Physical therapy had it easy, thought Maren. They could manipulate his limbs and keep him awake by getting him out of bed. He couldn't walk by himself, but with support on each side he had taken a few steps. Occupational therapy spoke next. Their therapy focused on the smaller muscles and fine coordination for bathing, grooming, dressing, buttoning, and so on. Not much to report. He usually wasn't awake for therapy.

Diane represented Dietary and at her turn said he was getting pureed food, on the recommendation of speech therapy. Jeff was often lethargic or too fatigued to eat much, but he was getting enough calories. Diane had asked about his favorite foods and explained to the group that pureed food at St. John's was processed in a blender; no baby food was served. "If we have macaroni and cheese on the menu, that's exactly what is processed and brought to Jeff," she explained proudly.

When it was Maren's turn, she began by giving credit to Darlene for including Jeff in the meeting. Maren was sure Jeff was sleeping and did not even hear what was being said, but she wanted to reinforce the concept she was about to present.

"Understanding and expression are two different functions," she explained. "Just because a patient doesn't respond, you should not assume that he can't understand. In fact, Judy told me she heard Jeff speak several times in complete sentences."

Jeff's son interjected several examples of his dad's verbal participation. He had wanted the basketball game on and managed to speak enough words to say so. The revelation that Jeff spoke not only appropriate words but used sentences had been Maren's first indication that Jeff did not have global aphasia. She now began an explanation of Jeff's communication status and his prognosis.

"Jeff had a hemorrhagic, not an occlusive, stroke. There was bleeding in his brain, not a blockage of an artery. That means there is still blood in there that needs to be carried off. Until that is completed, he will have limited progress, so I don't want you to get discouraged." She pulled out the copies of the line drawing that displayed the six-month recovery pattern for mild, moderate, and severe deficits caused by occlusive versus hemorrhagic stroke. She handed them out.

"Recovery from an occlusive stroke is like this"—she demonstrated with her hand—"up quickly the first four to eight weeks, then leveling off. With a hemorrhagic stroke, the progress is minimal for four to eight weeks." Again, she drew her hand through the air to demonstrate the flat line. "Then there is often a rapid recovery and the person stabilizes at a level usually above that achieved by patients with an occlusive stroke."

As her hand stopped level with the top of her head, she sensed the effect her presentation was having on the family. They had hope again.

She looked at the sleeping patient. "I don't want you to be discouraged if Jeff isn't able to go to a rehab hospital when he's discharged from here. He may need a facility where he can rest and recover until he has the endurance for three hours of therapy a day. He'll benefit more when he does go through rehab."

Darlene listened intently and thanked Maren for her input. She obviously had been unaware of the basic recovery patterns. Maren felt proud of her profession and her training and was grateful she could provide important information to family as well as staff. It wasn't direct therapy, but it was certainly therapeutic.

Mrs. Fritche began to ask questions about skilled nursing facilities, and Maren excused herself. Her next patient was having a procedure in his room, preventing her from working with him. Part of the frustration of working in the hospital, Maren found, was that some time was inevitably lost just waiting or looking for patients. It was almost time for the video swallow study anyway. She checked in with Rita before going to Radiology. Little Jason's appointment had been canceled. He had a strep infection.

The video swallow study was for Emily Jackson, a white-haired octogenarian. She was a sweet lady, but fidgety. She had been admitted from her nursing home to see if it was safe to upgrade her diet from pureed food and thickened liquid to more challenging consistencies. In the past she had consistently and silently aspirated on mechanical soft items as well as thin liquids. She had recently suffered a right CVA, but it was not her first stroke. There had been at least two before that. She had no functional speech, due to both apraxia and aphasia, but she did comprehend simple directions. Her perpetual grin was from anxiety. She would relax once she got used to the therapist or nurse who was treating her, but was fearful of new people and circumstances.

Maren pulled on the lead apron and thyroid collar and began filling in the paperwork. Larry poked his head in the door to say the food tray had arrived. Emily was in a wheelchair. They had the option of trying to get her up into the video chair or transferring her to the armchair.

"Let's put her in a regular chair," Maren decided. "She doesn't weigh much. Even if we have to lift her, it'll be easier."

They easily placed her in the armchair, and Maren attempted to calm the woman while doing an oral-motor exam. The apraxia was so severe that the only way they would really obtain any usable information would be by watching her under x-ray, while keeping conditions as natural as possible. Patients with apraxia often did better at the table than during the artificial situation created by the video swallow study. Such patients could swallow automatically but not on command. The liquids were ready, and Larry called Dr. Sudani.

"Good afternoon, Miss Keeple." He pronounced her name with his heavy accent.

"Maren would be fine," she said, inviting him to call her by her first name. He didn't answer her, but did introduce himself to the disabled woman and looked at her expectantly.

"She can't communicate. There is severe apraxia and aphasia," Maren explained.

As if he didn't hear her, the radiologist continued speaking to the patient in stern tones. "You just sit quietly. Do as you are told, and we will be finished quickly."

Maren considered explaining that there wasn't much chance the woman could understand him let alone reply, but decided to let it go. Emily was not without feelings, however; she reacted to the stern tone with tensed body muscles and fearful eyes. Maren hoped to complete the test before anything else could upset the woman. She asked Larry to give her a teaspoonful of applesauce. Emily clenched her teeth and started to turn away. Larry smiled and coaxed. The applesauce went in. Emily continued to look around the room, moving her head to and fro. Consequently, Maren had to concentrate on an image that bounced back and forth on the screen, watching for any trace aspiration that might occur. Then Emily swallowed. *Great, no problem,* thought Maren.

"Let's do the bite of cookie next," Maren announced, saving the liquids for last. As she chewed, Emily became more agitated and moved her head again.

Before Maren could try to calm her, Dr. Sudani reached over the arm of the fluoroscope and grabbed the woman's head like a basketball player would palm a ball. "You must hold head still. You must hold head still," he repeated loudly, over and over. "Do not move. Do not move."

Emily began to cry. The more she cried, the louder he commanded her to be quiet. It was definitely bad-dream material. Somehow they finished the study. They did not see aspiration, and Maren recommended upgrading the diet. She was furious with the way the radiologist had treated the frightened woman, with seemingly no understanding of what apraxia or aphasia meant.

Maren thanked Larry and exited as quickly as she could. She retreated to the speech office to complete the paperwork and call the nursing home with results. *God only knows what Dr. Sudani wrote in his report,* she ranted inwardly. She was too angry to speak to him.

She paged Judy and was relieved to hear she had seen the patients Maren had missed. Judy was leaving early. It was Friday night. "Date night, remember?" she hinted.

Maren didn't take the bait. "Have a good weekend. See you Monday," she said, ending their conversation and managing to avoid giving an account of her own plans by not asking about Judy's. She would no doubt have to answer for that next week.

Chapter 5

Four weeks had elapsed since the first dinner at the Yellow Duck, but it seemed longer. So much had transpired. A week after their second meeting, Paul had asked Maren to dinner on a Friday night. He reminded her during the week that her hotel reservation was already made. She had to wait forty-five minutes for him in a busy restaurant that night. He was apologetic, but it was unavoidable. He convinced her then to take the key to his front door for their next meeting. She could go directly to his house, where she could shower, change, and wait in comfort. After that, they met more frequently. His key lay in a small compartment of her purse now.

It was drizzling again as it did the night of their second dinner at the Yellow Duck. November in Chicago wasn't pretty. Although it was only five-thirty, it had been dark for over an hour. Maren stretched her slender legs out of the taxi. She took the key from her purse, paid the driver, and followed the old brick walk to Paul's front door. She wondered if taking taxis and meeting Paul at his place would become routine. It was, as he had pointed out, more comfortable than sitting in a booth. Four weeks ago she couldn't have imagined she would consider this so logical and sensible a solution, but clearly it was.

She closed the door behind her, hung her coat in the guest closet next to the front door, wiped her feet on the braided rug that protected the honey-colored hardwood floor, and walked straight through to the kitchen. She placed the key in the middle of the small round kitchen table before going up to the guest room. She was adamant about leaving the key each time. It would avoid any awkward confrontation in the future, should he want it back. Paul had tried several times to get her to keep it but eventually realized she wouldn't change her mind on this issue, at least not for a while.

Maren did love the house. It was done in earth tones—lush browns and tans with muted greens and rich creams. Here and there was a touch of sky blue. *The house is like Paul,* she decided, *a solid exterior and a cozy interior.* The oak floor in the entryway gave rise to a curved, dark oak stairway leading to the second floor. The living room was to the left of the entry. She stopped on the steps to look in. It had a real wood-burning fireplace. *No gas log for Paul.*

The dining room was to the right of the entry. Paul had it enclosed. It was now hidden behind louvered double doors and served as an office or, more exactly, a library. Every wall was shelves full of books, tapes, CDs and DVDs. The stereo equipment hid behind smaller slatted doors where a built-in buffet had once been. Paul had built-in speakers installed in every room in the house, with the main controls neatly concealed behind the small louvered doors. There was a beautiful, old, hickory library table in the center that he could cover and set for dinner when his family came. He usually ate on a sturdy TV table next to his easy chair in the living room. Casual meals with a single guest could be taken at the little white kitchen table.

It was all surprisingly traditional. *Jack was as traditional as men get,* Maren reflected, *but insisted on contemporary furnishings. Paul, on the cutting edge of technology in his work setting, surrounds himself with traditional furniture like the overstuffed couch with large rolled arms.* She looked through the archway into the living room. True the couch was covered with leather, the softest, faun-colored suede; but the wing-backed lounge chair was done in a soft traditional plaid of green, tan, and blue, as was the oversized ottoman.

Her eyes fell on the fireplace. It was of the period of the house, a white wood front, marble hearth, and a wide, white, wooden mantle. Everything was neat and clean, she noticed again. Paul had a housekeeper, of course, but it was apparently some old family friend who came in once a week, someone named Jamie.

Maren let her hand slide around the graceful curve of the banister as she started upstairs. Suddenly, there was music. She turned and went back to the dining room door. After opening it to see if anyone was there, she realized that Paul must have programmed some CDs for her enjoyment. She was amazed at the thoughtful things he found time to plan. The music was something classical, probably Mozart or Haydn, she wasn't sure which. The night he had shown her his music center she had looked over some of the hundreds of tapes and CDs to see what kind of music he collected. She had found an abundance of classical and musicals, but mostly jazz. His medical school days in New Orleans had left a lasting imprint on the young doctor. His tastes had matured since then, but he still loved jazz.

Enjoying the warmth of the music, she turned back to the stairs. They hadn't decided where they would go tonight. Still, she wanted to change and freshen up.

She turned the white ceramic handle and pushed open the dark wood door of what Paul referred to as Penny's guest room. It was a beautiful room. Paul had told her Penny suggested painting the woodwork white, but on that he had disagreed. He had insisted on stripping and refinishing all the wood in the house. She turned the light on and walked into the dressing-room-sized closet. The guest room was under the peak of the roof, so the closet ceiling was sloped. Maren had purchased some city clothes and left them here in the odd-shaped closet. She had the hall bath to herself. Paul's bedroom, on the other side of the stairs, was a master suite with a huge private bath, obtained by sacrificing the third bedroom. The arrangement was ideal for house guests.

When she got out of the shower, she heard jazz wafting up the open stairway. She was beginning to like the music of David Benoit, and Paul knew she preferred the quieter numbers. Most of their dinner dates were followed by a walk, but she had stayed overnight the previous Friday to attend a concert. She had looked through his music CDs prior to returning to Edgelawn on Saturday and pointed out some of her favorites.

Matt and Nick knew she had been spending time in the city. She had told them openly she had become friends with a young doctor she had known during graduate school and that she used a guest room in his two-story house. In the midst of their consuming studies and college activities, it never occurred to them that she might be dating. Like most children, they couldn't imagine their mother being seen as desirable by a man other than their father. They asked no questions. She volunteered no details.

Maren assumed that the times she and Paul spent together were scheduled around his workload and family commitments. She occasionally wondered if he might also have other female companionship. She was so enjoying all the new experiences, she didn't question. Disarmed by his unexpected openness in conversation, she was also pleased that there had been no push for physical intimacy. She simply didn't want that. It would ruin everything by complicating a great friendship. *We've become companions,* she decided.

A collection of older musical numbers came over the speaker placed at the corner of her room above the door. He knew she had a fondness for music from movies and musicals.

She felt like she was coming down with a cold and momentarily considered writing a note and leaving for Edgelawn. She remembered how her dad used to make a hot toddy for her when she was suffering the effects of a bad cold. When she was living in her apartment during her college years, she would curl up on her sofa with a hot toddy and fall asleep under an afghan her mother had made. That's what she wanted to do as soon as her hair was dry. She turned on the new hair dryer and pushed the diffuser on its barrel.

Erruup. The power went out in the bathroom and dining room. *They must all be on the same fuse,* she reasoned. She put on the full-length green fleece robe she had purchased to leave at Paul's, zipped the front, and headed for the kitchen. She knew there was a flashlight in the drawer. She also knew Paul could be absentminded about simple household maintenance. She hoped there would be a spare fuse where she could find it in the basement.

—

Paul's surgical case at University Circle Hospital lasted longer than he had planned. It was considered a big case, an infant boy trached at birth because a tumor at the root of his tongue occluded his airway. It was benign but life-threatening. A tracheotomy had been performed in the delivery room and an NG tube placed for feedings. *Not much bonding with his mother that day,* Paul sympathized.

The pediatrician knew of Paul's surgical skill and adeptness with children and had spread the word about the case. Consequently, there was a room full of student and intern observers in the OR. The surgery was successful, but Paul, feeling drained by noon, had no time for lunch. He had grabbed two giant chocolate chip cookies from the physicians' lounge to eat on the way to his office. He smiled, remembering. Maren always said she never met a man who didn't like chocolate chip cookies. Paul would always respond boyishly, "I never met a chocolate chip cookie I didn't like."

The waiting room was full when Paul got to the office. *They can't all be my patients,* he thought. *It's Dr. Granger's day off, and Dr. Lancaster never has more than a few appointments a week.*

"You're late Dr. McCloud," Edith greeted him, stonily. She delighted in finding him lacking, in comparison to her long-time employers. She had been with them for twenty-two years.

"Dr. Granger started seeing his patients already."

"What's Dr. Granger doing here?"

"Dr. Lancaster went to visit his daughter in Oregon. Since Dr. Granger was here for Dr. Lancaster's patients, he just had me fit in some of his patients, too."

The seventeenth-floor office had limited space, and the three had worked out a careful schedule to avoid conflicts. Once when Paul had come up to see a child with acute laryngitis on his day off, Roy Granger had taken him to task, "Junior partner, know your place . . . could have seen him at the hospital . . . inconvenienced Dr. Lancaster as well."

Paul often wondered if buying this practice was worth the emotional toll it was taking. He was standing in line like a good little boy, waiting his turn. It was impossible to keep up in a high-tech field though, when the old boys wouldn't increase the thirty-five-dollar charge for office visits. Maren had visited the office when she was a student. That was when he had first started with the practice, thrilled to be in an office in the city. He didn't want to be banished to the boondocks, he had told her then. Now he was no longer impressed with anything about the practice, except his patients.

Paul walked to the closed venetian blinds behind his desk. When Maren had been here, she had asked him to open the miniblinds so she could see the view. He never looked out anymore. She had so enjoyed seeing the lake from seventeen floors up. He remembered the thrill in her eyes as she spotted Grant Park.

"It's all right outside your window, and you don't even look," she had accused.

He peered out now, and sure enough, it was all out there. *It has to be*, he thought bitterly. *It sure isn't in here.* He pulled on the freshly starched white coat and stepped into the narrow hall to review the first chart. Granger bumped into him outside the examining room.

"Oh, McCloud, been meaning to talk to you. Bob and I are heading out to Florida for some fishing December 10th to 18th. You'll cover."

The odd inflection meant it should have been a request, but it wasn't. It wasn't even a cordial order. Not, "We'd appreciate it if . . ."— just a statement. Maybe that's the way it was when they started out. And they were no more interested in changing relationship traditions than updating equipment or adding another room for outpatient surgical procedures. "If it was good enough then, it's good enough now" was their philosophy. They were just coasting to retirement. *I hope I'm not like that in twenty-five years*, Paul thought.

The two do-si-doed past one another without another word.

The heating system wasn't working properly again. The suite was usually too hot in the summer and too cold in the winter. Today the thermometer behind Edith's desk read eighty-two. Paul shed the starched white coat and took off his tie. He was rolling up his long sleeves when Granger made a derogatory comment about maintaining a proper appearance for the patients.

Paul could handle hospital politics in a rather offhanded, easy way. University Circle Hospital was a hotbed of political allies and adversaries through which he deftly maneuvered. St. John's, being private, wasn't nearly as bad. He managed to stay fairly neutral at both of those sites. But the politics of what was supposed to be his own office caused his stomach acids to pump.

He pushed out of the revolving door at five forty-five. He didn't care if the rain drenched him; maybe it would wash off the sweat, oil, and frustration of the day. He threw his brown, double-breasted suit coat over his shoulder and stepped off the curb just as a cab ran the light and drove its right front tire squarely into a pothole filled with rain and sludge. The muddy water splashed from Paul's shoes to his white shirt. Before he could move back, the cab's rear tire spun as the driver attempted to speed up. A filthy spray dotted the rest of his shirt and face. The jacket didn't escape the spray.

The only saving grace of the day was the successful surgery for the infant Brandon Koss. *Nice of Petersohn to refer the family,* Paul thought, trying to focus on something positive as he walked to the parking garage.

He began the process of turning off the faucet in his brain, though it would be more difficult tonight. He had gotten that phrase, along with fatherly advice, during med school, when he had been particularly stressed. "When you walk into your home, turn off the job like you turn off a faucet. Be open to your home, family, and friends, closed to the outside world. Otherwise you'll burn yourself out and destroy half your life-- your home life."

His dad had been right, as usual. Although there wasn't a wife and certainly no children waiting, Paul made it a point to read engrossing novels, watch intriguing plays and movies, and most of all listen to good music to refresh his spirit. Most times he enjoyed his solitude. He had practiced the skill of turning off the faucet until he could relax quickly and completely.

Solitude, he mused in anticipation. *All the years of living alone have been beneficial.*

Then he remembered. Maren would be waiting, expecting to go out. He groaned inwardly. Tonight he would rather just stay in. He had scheduled their times together so carefully, allowing each of them extended time to be alone. He had realized the potential of their relationship suddenly and dramatically in Africa. He knew Maren had no such experience to build on. He wanted to give her time to adjust and also make sure that each of them didn't neglect family and other friends. Now he had to admit to himself that he wasn't entirely ready to give up his solitude and privacy to allow another human being inside his wall on a constant basis, especially after a day like this.

He wasn't exactly sure how she felt about him, either. Their friendship was deeper, but since that first night walking under the umbrella, they had not so much as held hands. He kept reminding himself that she had another perspective. She had grown sons to think about, as well as learning a new job, which included figuring out the idiosyncrasies of several dozen doctors at St. John's, not just Paul.

He was as committed to their relationship as he had been the first day after his mission trip, but Maren still didn't seem to know their friendship was a relationship. In spite of his commitment, Paul was discouraged. This morning he had happily picked out the CDs and set the timer, wishing he could see the smile spread across her face, exposing the dimple in her cheek, and her green eyes light up. That was before the events of the day. Tonight he just wanted to be alone in his house, build a fire, make a stir fry, and eat alone. But she was already there, invading his space.

He parked in back and walked around to the front door. The house was curiously dark when he stepped in, and no music was playing. Before he could move, the lights came on, and the music started in the middle of a medley from Camelot. "Sssprring-time."

Maren suddenly appeared in front of him at the top of the basement steps, by the entrance to the kitchen. White lace peeked out above the hastily drawn zipper of her robe. She was so startled she jumped and squealed when she saw him.

"Paul, I didn't hear you come in."

"What are you doing in the basement?" he began.

"I blew a fuse," she started.

"They're circuit breakers . . ."

"I know," she corrected herself. "I found the right one." She flipped on the entryway light.

"What happened to you?" she asked, inspecting his dirty, wet, disheveled clothes.

He looked down and for the first time fully realized the extent of the damage the taxi had caused. For once no smart comeback escaped his lips, just a loud sigh and a look that spoke volumes to Maren. He hung his coat on a hook rather than a hanger.

"Let it drip. It's been a drippy day. I need a shower and some food and . . ." He almost added, "some time alone."

"And I'll bet going out would not be your first choice."

He didn't deny it. Now he was chilled. "I was looking forward to a fire," he said lamely, his eyes on his shoes, avoiding her face.

"I'll start a fire while you shower. Is there something I can fix here? Or," she added, "We can order something delivered."

"Let's just start with some crackers and cheese," he suggested. "Maybe after I warm up I'll be in a better mood and I'll fix you a stir-fry."

"You can cook?" she asked, her eyes wide, in mock horror.

He did smile then. "My mother told me no woman would put up with my hours, so I'd better learn to feed myself."

While Paul showered and changed, Maren found crackers in the kitchen pantry and several kinds of cheese in the refrigerator. Camembert unopened, moldy Swiss, and Co-Jack--salvageable. She fixed a platter and set it on the drop-leaf table, which abutted the back of the sofa. Paul kept a log holder next to the hearth, though where he got real logs in the city mystified her. She had traded for a gas log when she moved to the townhouse, but she still remembered how to set a real fire. Everything was there. Obviously, he used the fireplace regularly.

Paul came down in jeans, loafers, and a freshly pressed long-sleeved shirt, sleeves rolled up, or rather rolled under. She hadn't seen him so casually dressed before, in spite of their numerous dates. They spent virtually no time alone together in his house, except for changing and sleeping. He frequently left before she woke, or they went out for breakfast. He wore the look well, she acknowledged, trying not to notice the shape of his chest and upper arms, outlined by the cotton shirt. He seemed more muscular than she had realized. He actually was more muscular than when she had seen him in surgical garb years ago. Since his last mission trip he had been working out with weights regularly. He couldn't have explained why exactly; it was just another consequence of the trip.

A smile spread across his face at the sight of the fire. Was there anything this woman couldn't do, he wondered. The girls he had dated had been so helpless. Maren hadn't had time to return to the guest room to dress, but he noticed she had drawn the zipper to its full closed position to cover the white lace. The green robe was flattering. It fell straight from her shoulders to the floor. The sleeves were wide cut and long. The only decoration was the white lace panel that wrapped around the mandarin collar and extended to her chest. It was feminine without being frilly or provocative.

Music from *Phantom of the Opera* came from the CD player. Maren pointed to the tray of crackers and cheese. "I didn't know what you would want to drink with it."

"Maren," Paul began firmly, "I know you don't approve, but I'm going to have a drink."

"Why do you say I don't approve?"

"Well, you've never had anything alcoholic in all the times we've been together."

"Oh, I . . ." she stammered. The truth was she consistently refused anything alcoholic to make sure she kept her head and didn't say or do anything Paul might misconstrue, anything that might reveal the extent of her attraction to him.

She was blushing; she could feel the warmth in her cheeks. "Look, if we're staying in, I'll have a glass of Chablis with you." She was too embarrassed to reveal her thoughts, and Paul couldn't guess what they were.

He didn't keep Chablis, but found a bottle of unopened blackberry wine. "Uncle Frank gave this to me for my birthday last year. Hopefully it wasn't sacramental wine."

The sweet wine didn't appeal to Maren, and once more she remembered her desire for a hot toddy. They decided to save Uncle Frank's wine for another time. Maren fixed each of them a hot toddy, and they sat on separate ends of the couch, reaching over the back of it to the table for snacks. They cleaned the platter, sipped their drinks, listened to music, and watched the fireplace.

Maren waited silently, without asking questions. She enjoyed Paul's talkative nature, but if he needed an evening of quiet, she wasn't about to complain.

After a half hour the fire warmed the room. Maren had fluffed her hair occasionally, until it was dry. The ceiling light in the entry hall spilled into the living room, but otherwise there was only firelight. Light and shadows from the flames danced on the walls and ceiling. Maren got up to add another log, a slightly larger one now that the coals were hot. He watched her intently, wondering whether she ever had time to think about him, whether she thought of him as more than another friend from the hospital.

"Maren, I'm glad you're here," he began. She didn't know, of course, that a little over an hour ago he had wished she would vanish before he got home. She took his meaning to be about tending the fire.

"I'm a little out of practice," she apologized as she poked the log into a better position. "Do you want to talk about what happened today?" she asked, returning to the couch.

"I'll tell you tomorrow. Tonight I just want to forget it."

The fire sputtered and spit a hot coal onto the marble hearth. "I'll get it," they said in unison and jumped up together. As he pulled the screen closed and they turned back to the couch, he noticed the mild fragrance of her talc. It was fresh and helped wash away the strong, unpleasant odors and emotions of the day.

Before she could retreat against the rolled arm of the couch, Paul caught her wrist. "Don't sit way over there. I could use some company over here."

The day, the brandy, the warmth of the fire, and the soft robe were wearing down his resolve to let their relationship progress slowly. He was getting impatient, and the firelight gave her such an appealing glow.

"I just want to touch your hair." He drawled out the words as he inched his hand slowly across the back of the couch. His sensitive fingers lightly tested the curl, and then slipped under her hair to her neck. An ache engulfed him. He wanted to pull her to his chest, as he had her surrogate in the transport truck. Still, he resisted moving too quickly. He didn't want to frighten her or risk their future.

She froze, unable to blink or breathe while his fingers slowly traced the curve of her neck and carefully retraced their path, up to her jaw and to her cheek. She felt the breath rush from her lips as a shiver coursed through her body. She turned to look at him directly, giving him the opportunity to trace each lip with his thumb. She closed her mouth over the softness of his hand, unable to speak. Realizing she was kissing his hand, she covered it with her own and held it to her lips and cheek. Her eyes were closed, her mind whirling. It happened so suddenly; her usually analytical mind was reduced to only sensation.

He began to caress her face and neck, sliding his fingers to the back of her head to explore the curls again. She shivered and let out another small sigh. He saw her closed eyes and that she was leaning her head against the back of the couch. He held her head and face in his hands, preventing her retreat. Pulling her closer, he touched his cheek against hers. She tried to speak, but again only a small sound escaped her. "Oh." Before she could regain her voice, he covered her mouth with his own in a long, soft, gentle kiss. For a moment she quietly savored the sweetness of his lips on hers, but as his kiss lingered, the passion she thought had been extinguished stirred. Feeling her response caused his body to surge with desire. His hands explored the softness of the robe and her shape beneath it. He knew she was surprised and was now vulnerable.

Don't, his inner voice whispered. *Don't. You know what you need to know.*

His arms encircled her, pulling her gently to his chest. His cheek was against hers again, his face in her hair, inhaling her fragrance. He kissed her neck where only a moment before his fingers had experienced her skin for the first time. His heart was pounding as fast as hers. He held her tighter against his chest, protecting her, protecting them both. Her arms were around him, giving him feelings of relief and passion at the same time.

He leaned back against the cushioned arm of the couch and held her motionless against him, as he listened to her rapid breathing. He allowed himself to enjoy the passion she returned with her kiss once more, then held her quietly until their passion subsided.

She began to realize what he had done. She put her forehead down on his shoulder and was embarrassed and ashamed, not of her feelings but that she had allowed him to discover them.

"I'm sorry, Maren, but I had to know . . ." he whispered.

She also knew. She had deluded herself, but now she knew the truth.

"I had to know," he repeated softly, "and you didn't give me a clue."

"I didn't think it could be returned. I was afraid if you knew how I felt, it would be the end."

"Maren, why?'

"Paul, do I have to say it? I'm a decade older than you, just to start the list."

"That's not the kind of thing that matters at all. My dad's ten years older than my mother."

She sat up and curled her feet under her. "That's different."

"Why is it any different?"

"Are we arguing?" she asked, passion now behind them.

"No, we're discussing."

"Paul, I prayed it would be just platonic."

"You want it to go away!" he accused, amazed and hurt.

She had been trying to prevent a relationship she knew would be a painful dead end for both of them, while he had been trying to nurture their friendship into something deeper. She couldn't let herself believe that he could be physically attracted to her, or that their relationship had a future. She saw too many obstacles. He saw none.

"We need to talk," she began.

"Maren, this isn't going to go away if we talk for a month," he said with certainty. "Let's get some dinner."

They moved to Paul's cozy kitchen. She sat on one of the spindle-backed chairs at the table for two in the corner, watching him chop chicken and vegetables on the square butcher-block island in the center of the room. There was a cooktop built into the island, with a huge exhaust fan canopy hood overhead. It was one of Penny's ideas, so he wouldn't have to face the wall to prepare food or cook. While he worked they watched each other warily, like respectful competitors who have called a truce. She was reminded of when she had watched him in surgery. Those boyish hands were so quick, so sure.

The first time she observed surgery it was a tonsillectomy, and Paul was the surgeon. The six-year-old boy was Maren's patient. She had recommended he be evaluated for a possible tonsil and adenoidectomy numerous times, but the pediatrician always had the same reply, "There's nothing life-threatening here. No surgery needed."

Peter had a serious speech problem and snored nightly with frequent sleep apnea episodes. He had chronic tonsillitis, too. That Friday morning Janis Garliner had brought her son to the emergency room. He had a fever, and his tonsils were so swollen he couldn't swallow. The ER physician had taken one look and paged ENT. Paul had answered the page. Maren had seen Janis walking beside Peter's cart, while Paul himself pushed the cart. He told Maren later that he had grabbed a scalpel in ER in case he had to trach the boy in the hall. The tonsils and adenoids had become so enlarged they were about to totally obstruct the airway.

Maren had asked to observe the surgery, and of course Paul wouldn't forbid it. It was a teaching hospital. He had been concerned about her watching a boy she knew, especially since this would be her first time in the OR, and because she had sons. A mother might identify too much. The scrub nurse had shown her where to change. She had pulled the booties over her shoes, changed into the scrubs provided, covered her hair, and fit the mask over her nose. She had put her contacts in her purse and had worn her glasses. A glimpse of her image as she hurried into the surgical suite confirmed that she was not even remotely attractive.

Paul's eyes had locked on hers as soon as she walked into the OR. He had a way of looking into people. If the eyes were really windows to the soul, Paul McCloud had the ability to look in. Of course, if you had the courage to meet that look of his, you could, in those moments, also see into Paul's soul. It had been a moment like that. He had looked into her. She had met his gaze. She had begun to understand then that it didn't matter what she looked like on the outside; he could look past the glasses, past the mask, into who she was. It had been a silent conversation, the width of the room between them.

They were having a silent conversation now, with only the width of Paul's kitchen between them. She had never looked away from his gaze after that day in surgery, not until tonight on the couch when she closed her eyes, overwhelmed with emotion and hoping to prevent him from seeing the extent of her feelings. Nothing about Paul was accidental, she was learning. He was decisive and direct. He had touched her intentionally, to see if she would respond. Then why had he stopped?

Paul watched her peripherally while he chopped, diced, and mixed. He had assembled many a stir-fry; he didn't need to think about it.

He had learned a little more about her tonight. *She's been so controlled these past weeks. Maybe it's her British heritage,* he rationalized. *I was beginning to doubt myself.* He had actually considered the possibility that the whole relationship idea was just an intellectual exercise that grew from his imagination after the experience in Africa. Now he knew. It was no intellectual exercise; it was not his imagination; it was a viable relationship. It was mutual.

"Why did you stop?" She interrupted his thoughts.

"It's done. It's time for dinner."

"No, on the couch why?"

He knew what she was asking. As he scooped rice and vegetables onto the plates, he interrupted, "Maren, we have time. Expressing love with your body is a gift. It should be a great joy. I want to make sure it's the right time for both of us—no doubts, no regrets, not an accident, but a decision, a commitment." He put plates on placemats designed to fit the round table and sat down opposite her.

"Do you pray?" she asked quietly, now waiting to see if he would meet her gaze.

He sat down and took her hand. "Creator God," he began, looking into her eyes, "we are grateful for this food and for our friendship and for this night. Help those with no food, no home, and no hand to hold." There was no "Amen," so Maren added it.

She was ready to continue their discussion, but Paul stopped her. "Let's enjoy our meal, Maren. We can talk tomorrow."

Chapter 6

Thanksgiving had come and gone. Thanks to Steve giving Matt a complimentary ticket, he had been at the table with them. They had planned for Christmas, of course, but assumed once the whole continent lay between them, Matt would miss turkey dinner with Maren and Nick. Steve and Pam had invited them all for a meal on Friday, and it had been wonderful to see them, again. All through the growing up years, Maren's boys and Megan had been like cousins.

Matt had been content just to be home, but Nick spent most of the weekend trying to convince Maren he had to have a car on campus. She had been inclined to agree after driving Matt to O'Hare and Nick to Champaign on the same day.

She had enjoyed retreating into the role of mother, housekeeper, and cook, but now she was ready to return to life at St. John's. It was a good thing Judy would be there all day; the list of outpatients and stack of new orders was impressive.

The local suburban school district routinely gave St. John's name to parents for medically based speech-language evaluations. Schools were required to provide for children when they turned three. Maren wondered how it would be possible to serve increasing numbers of students in schools when SLPs were always in short supply. She knew districts had only a few options. One was to have an agreement with a local medical facility such as St. John's, and Judy was hoping they would get a contract to provide services routinely. For now there were lots of evaluations for children above the age of five, but not much therapy.

Insurance policies often paid for evaluations, but some companies expected schools to provide the therapy "for free."

Usually only one pediatric evaluation was scheduled on any one day, but today, thanks to Rita's creative scheduling, Maren had three multiply handicapped preschoolers to evaluate. Judy was working to cover the inpatients, so Maren decided not to reschedule anyone. *Besides*, she reasoned, *usually there's a cancellation.*

Evan Jennings arrived promptly at nine o'clock. His father brought him; the mom was working. He was just two years old. The Jennings family had moved from a rural area to the suburbs in order to have more services available for their only son. Evan had cerebral palsy, and his sister had recently died of a brain tumor. The parents had learned a lot during the girl's illness and applied it for Evan's benefit. During the intake interview, Maren learned that both children had been adopted. Will and Debbie Jennings were special parents. They had requested handicapped children.

Evan was a handsome boy, thin, with shiny brown hair and pretty, delicate facial features. He couldn't walk. He rolled, but didn't truly crawl. He had a G tube; Maren could see the protuberance above his naval, through his shirt. She expected to be doing a detailed feeding-swallowing evaluation, but Will assured her that he and his wife were experienced with infant-toddler swallowing issues from having worked with Evan's sister. Their answers to Maren's questions confirmed their competence. Debbie did most of the feeding, since she had the most success. They poured his formula into his stomach via the tube, so he was guaranteed sufficient nutritional intake. They fed him by mouth as much as possible to help him develop eating and speech skills.

He couldn't respond well enough for the use of a standardized test, so Maren used a parent interview form with Mr. Jennings to assess Evan's development. She did bring out some toys to observe his reactions. Evan needed physical therapy desperately. Maren made a mental note to check with Judy about the possibility of co-treating with PT. It made so much more sense than each discipline scheduling him separately.

Immediately following Evan was Tony Scanlon. He had been diagnosed with a seizure disorder shortly after birth. He was given several medications to control the seizures and several more to protect his liver from the side effects of the first drugs. They had moved to the area from Kentucky when Billy Scanlon lost his job. They lived in their ten-year-old station wagon until recently when Billy got a job and a government-subsidized apartment became available. Tony, at three years old, was the baby, the youngest of four children.

Terri Scanlon put her son on the floor, and he melted in a puddle of flesh. The referral said "low muscle tone." *That's an understatement. He's like a wet noodle,* Maren assessed. Maren had never seen a case as severe. Evaluating speech didn't take long. Tony didn't have sufficient muscle control to provide the respiratory support necessary to even coo. Developmental scales placed him at the level of a newborn, but a newborn with deficits.

Mrs. Scanlon was not a good historian. She was not even focused. Tony had a history of pneumonia, so a video swallow study had been done at University Circle Hospital. Mrs. Scanlon said it "confirmed the CP." Maren was not sure what she meant. Was she referring to cerebral palsy or insufficiency of the cricopharyngeal sphincter, the muscle that opens the esophagus? She wrote one note to get the results of the study and another to see if PT, OT, and Speech could work out a schedule to co-treat Tony on some kind of rotating basis. She didn't need to see him every week. Mostly she would provide consultative services until he was ready for direct intervention.

It was obvious Mrs. Scanlon was stretched to her limits with three school-age children and this multiply handicapped boy to cope with day and night. *I can't expect much from the parents in addition to the physical care they are already providing. There is hope, but it will be a long and difficult road.*

𝓴𝓴𝓴

Maren's third pediatric patient was scheduled for right after lunch. She paged Judy, met her in the cafeteria, and told her about Evan and Tony. Judy was all for the co-treat plan. "It's one way a smaller hospital can provide something extra," she agreed.

Then she filled Maren in on the latest problem in Radiology. Carolyn had called her to say the techs no longer wanted to feed patients for the video swallow studies. "She said they didn't want to be responsible for patients aspirating barium. I think it's probably just considered below their dignity to—and I quote—'spoon-feed adults.'"

"Where did this come from? Janet and Larry do a great job, and they haven't complained to me. You have the system laid out beautifully. The purpose of a video swallow study is to document aspiration, in a controlled way, of course. Naturally, patients will aspirate barium. Something must have caused this glitch."

"Well, a new tech named Nora Gates came over from Halstead Hospital. She told Carolyn the SLPs feed there. The techs position the patient and handle the remote control. That's it."

"But that's only one facility," objected Maren.

"Doesn't matter. Nora is some relative of Dr. Granger. Carolyn doesn't want to do battle, so we will all have to adjust until we can collect some data to present to the board. I know you're not looking forward to the change, but you'll have the opportunity to try it out at two thirty, right after the last pediatric eval."

Jake Samuels was twenty-four months old but was the size of a five-month-old. He had been born with Prader-Willi syndrome. Maren didn't know much about the syndrome, but she had looked it up. Failure to thrive and inability to suck were the characteristics that stuck in her mind. Obviously, Jake failed to thrive in every way possible. His eyes looked glazed and moved in an uncontrolled pattern.

"Yes," his mother confirmed, "doctors suspect severe visual deficits." That made Maren wonder about his hearing, but Mrs. Samuels said they had the auditory evoked response study—she called it the BEAR test, for brain stem evoked auditory response. "He does hear," she stated.

Maren laid the child on a mat on the floor to examine him. He was surprisingly active, kicking so hard he bounced himself around in a circle. She pulled off his shoes in self-defense. Down on her knees next to him, she used a penlight and tongue depressor to get a look inside his mouth. His tongue barely protruded to his lower lip. She looked more closely and noticed the right side of his tongue protruded more than the left. And the tongue was heart shaped, constrained by a short lingual frenum. She peered inside hoping to see a low, flat hard palate. She was disappointed. The hard palate was extremely high and very narrow. *Physically impossible that this tongue could contact that hard palate,* Maren observed. That didn't bode well for speaking or swallowing.

She looked further, pressing on the back of his tongue to check for soft palate elevation. Nothing. She was disappointed again. She pressed harder; still no response. She lifted the tongue depressor to the soft palate and gently pressed; still nothing. She watched, without palpating further, while he vocalized loudly. Finally, with determined pressure directly above the uvula, the muscles contracted and he gagged, but only slightly. There was no evidence that the soft palate elevated without such pressure. That meant he would lose air through his nose during speech. It confirmed what she thought she had heard earlier during his cries, nasal air emission.

Jake did produce some vowel-like sounds, in addition to snorting sounds. Mrs. Samuels' biggest concern, however, was that he had been taking a bottle for the past ten months and suddenly refused, unless he was very hungry. He still had a G tube in place, which had been his only source of feeding for the first fourteen months of his life. Tina Samuels had been thrilled when he began to suck; now she was distressed that they might have to resort to tube feedings again.

Patiently, and trying not to be judgmental, Maren asked Tina to demonstrate how she fed Jake. The mother took out a spouted cup that looked like a cream pitcher. She poured the liquid into his throat, and Jake gulped it down. She told Maren that they fed him table food, too, just shoveled it in the back of his throat and washed it down with liquid. It frightened Maren to think what might be happening. He had not developed aspiration pneumonia, at least not yet.

Jake was also scheduled for PT and OT evaluations during the afternoon, so they ended their session right on time. Maren knew she had a lot of counseling to do with these parents. She made notes with a list of recommendations. Hopefully she could convince Tina to return for a few sessions of feeding therapy.

No time to write the reports; she had to get to Radiology for the outpatient video swallow study. The patient's name was Carl Kinsington. He was a nursing home patient and reportedly had a supportive family, although they weren't present today. Maren checked his saliva swallow, often called a dry swallow, while he was in the waiting area. It was weak but present. He followed directions. He was terribly thin and had a pasty color; obviously a sick man. Was it aspiration pneumonia, a new stroke, or the latest virus? She wanted to rule out at least one of the possibilities.

She went into the fluoroscopy suite. Although Radiology was busy this afternoon, Janet walked past wearing her parka. Her daughter had fallen at school, probably a broken arm. She would not return to work today, and it was Larry's day off. Carolyn was busy with a CT scan. Nora, the new tech and relative of Paul's senior partner Dr. Granger, would do the video with Maren.

Nora was not a newcomer to her profession. Maren judged her to be in her fifties. She used heavy makeup, had no facial expression, and wore long, thick, bangs which covered her eyebrows. Maren introduced herself in the hall and asked who the radiologist was. She started to add that she hadn't yet met Dr. Jasmin, when a wide woman an inch or so shorter than Maren motioned for her to come into the hall. Nora nodded her head to indicate this was the radiologist.

"Good afternoon, I'm Dr. Jasmin. I trained at Boston Colonial with Dr. Sudani."

Oh no, that's where they don't do videos.

When Maren verbalized her thoughts, the radiologist waved away her concerns. "I was downstate for two months at Collinsville Medical Center. We used to sit in the office and push the button for the fluoroscopy when the tech would call for it, so I know all about the procedure. And we only give these patients liquids and puree," added Dr. Jasmin loudly and confidently.

Maren was stunned. Not thinking about being tactful, she began to protest. Dr. Jasmin quickly let her know that she was a guest in the radiology suite and the doctor would make the decisions. Nora passed them, pushing Mr. Kinsington in a wheelchair toward the fluoroscopy suite. She helped him transfer to the armchair by the fluoroscope and left him, momentarily, to report to Maren that she didn't know how to set up the recorder. Maren turned her attention to the equipment while Dr. Jasmin retreated to her office until all was ready for her presence. Nora hadn't mixed the liquids either. She was willing, if Maren would give her the formula. Since the techs had always provided the setup,

Maren couldn't give her specific measures. Maren did it by look and feel.

"Thick should be like honey, medium like fruit syrup from a can, thin as close to water as you can get it," called Maren while she reconnected the TV monitor cable to the fluoroscope monitor. Reluctantly, Maren handed Nora the remote and told her they were ready for Dr. Jasmin.

Nora, a concerned look on her face, returned with the heavy-set physician. As Dr. Jasmin got the patient's image on the screen, Nora thrust the remote at Maren.

"I'll feed," she stated adamantly. Maren couldn't have been more surprised. It was Nora who had instigated the big brouhaha and caused the change in protocol. It was Nora who didn't want to be responsible for feeding patients. Now suddenly she wanted it the other way.

"Are we ready, are we ready?" prompted the radiologist impatiently. "Let's go. I have another CT scan to do."

"Yes, ready," answered Maren. But before she could ask Nora for a half teaspoon of applesauce, Dr. Jasmin took control.

"Good. Give him the cup of liquid."

Maren was stunned. No one ever started with liquid by cup. It would be the most likely to be aspirated by a weak patient. Before she could object, the tech flew to comply with the doctor's order. She watched, horrified, as Nora snatched the cup of thin liquid off the tray and directed Mr. Kinsington to drink. A mouthful of liquid barium flowed into the patient's mouth, spilled into his pharynx and airway, and fell toward his lungs.

"Aspiration! Aspiration!" called Dr. Jasmin loudly. "I end the test right now."

"Cough!" directed Maren loudly, "cough hard." Very little of the black blob reappeared on the screen.

In retrospect, Maren thought she would have been wiser to have run from the department as fast as she could at that moment, but her concern for the patient kept her there. What could she recommend given this "study"? A G tube, based on one inappropriate trial? She approached the doctor and conferred briefly about the size of the bolus. By now Mr. Kinsington had been away from his quiet nursing home schedule for over two hours. Aides there, knowing he would be getting a radiology procedure for swallowing, had assumed fasting would be in order. No meal had been served to Carl Kinsington since yesterday. He was frail on good days. Today he had a fever and had been sitting in a cold waiting area for over an hour because the ambulance had arrived early. Now he had at least a tablespoonful of barium in his lung.

"It was a fiasco," Maren stormed at Judy afterward. "He must have an ounce or two of barium in his lungs."

"I already heard. It's all over the hospital. Everybody has already heard. They called Larry in from his day off because Nora ran out. He said the fluoroscopy suite looked like a war zone when he got there." She giggled, in spite of Maren's obvious distress.

"If it was my family member, I would sue the hospital, the radiologist, and everyone who touched the patient all day."

"You need to fill out an incident report," Judy counseled.

"Will it have any effect?"

"It will be read by the medical board. It'll be one more piece of evidence."

"Why don't they just dismiss this group and get different radiologists?"

"The group will cry racism," stated Judy bluntly. "The hospital discharged a Hispanic nurse a month ago. He's suing. It's going to take a lot of evidence to avoid another nasty lawsuit."

"And what will the repercussions be for the rehab department and for me if I file a report?" questioned Maren.

"You do what you have to do," answered Judy simply.

Paul had a late nasal surgery at St. John's, a simple deviated septum and polyps. He finished packing the nasal cavity, wrote orders, and headed for the locker room.

Thanksgiving had been good. Penny, Jim, and Erin had come. Aunt Elizabeth had been there, indomitable as ever, even after the laryngectomy. It had taken her a long time to learn to use the electrolarynx, and she still wasn't really proficient with it. At least she was back at her travel bureau, teaching Penny all she would ever need to know about the business.

Uncle Frank had even come, a rare treat in recent years, since he traveled more and more for Maryknoll. "Don't they let you old priests retire at sixty?" Paul had joked, knowing Frank didn't have the time or the inclination to retire. Managing money ran in the McCloud blood, his dad for St. John's and Frank for the Maryknoll Order. They always made money for other people, though there wasn't that much of their own. What they did have, they worked hard to get and spent sparingly in order to save for bigger things, like Paul's education, Bob's sailboat, and the family house in Pine Bluff.

Eighteen years ago the four McCloud's—Bob and Elizabeth in Chicago, Cloris in California, and Frank—went together to buy the house in Pine Bluff, Colorado. They had decided on Colorado as a kind of midpoint. Bob had to have a lake, Cloris needed mountains, Elizabeth asked for trees, and Frank wanted peace and quiet. The teenagers, including Paul at that time, needed activities. Pine Bluff was the perfect choice. Lake Dillon and the ski slopes were close. None of them lived there, but there was plenty of coming and going. Thanksgiving was usually spent in Chicago though, and Cloris, Mike, and the boys ordinarily didn't come. Their boys were in various graduate schools and professions now, but not married. They always said they were waiting for Paul to take the plunge first.

Paul had actually gotten all day Thursday off. The family had met at his parents' condo and spent the day cooking, eating, and catching up. They had asked to hear more about Paul's mission trip, and he had given everyone an abbreviated version. Somehow, in all the weeks since he returned, he had never gotten around to telling his folks about Maren. It hadn't seemed appropriate to bring it up in the group on Thanksgiving Day, either. He had begun planning an introduction though, and Maren was always present in some corner of his mind.

Without realizing what he was doing, he now took a detour from the surgical suite through the basement. The detour caused him to pass the rehab department on his way out. There was still light spilling under the partially open door of the speech office. He poked his head in.

"Maren, what are you doing here? It's after six."

Startled, she jumped up from her desk. "Hi. I had some paperwork to finish."

There was no light in her eyes, no smile, no dimple.

"Are you okay?"

"Just a really hectic day."

Immediately he thought of her sons.

"Are your boys okay?"

"Oh yes. We had a wonderful Thanksgiving. How about you?"

He told her briefly about his family gathering, and she did smile a little when she referred to his family as the clan.

"A meeting of the clan. Only the clan and select friends were present," she teased, mimicking a news broadcaster. "How's little Erin?"

He didn't answer, because of his concern for her travel back to Edgelawn. "Maren, do you know there's a blizzard outdoors? It's mostly lake effect, but driving was already getting bad when I came in."

She looked stricken. She didn't like bad-weather driving. It had been one of her concerns when she took the job. Her expression was all it took. He insisted she ride home with him. No use even taking two vehicles.

They settled for spaghetti and garlic toast; it was all Paul had in the house. He sensed that she was preoccupied or stressed about something. She had stared silently out of the window all the way home. She didn't laugh or even smile at his humorous cracks. She didn't contribute to the conversation, leaving him feeling shut out. If it wasn't on the home front, he assumed something had happened at the hospital. Even though he took care of other people's needs all day, he still wanted to take care of her. Tonight, for once, she let him.

"A little food and drink will fix you right up," he promised her. But when he questioned her, she resisted.

"You always say to turn the faucet off at the end of the day."

"Well, you're obviously not doing that on the inside. Let's make a deal: you download at night and then shut off the faucet. I'll turn off the faucet at night but open it and download in the morning."

She ignored the mixed metaphor; she was touched by his sensitivity and concern. After they ate, she did tell him about the day, ending with her quandary over whether or not to file the incident report.

Paul put on his professional persona and asked a few questions. "Was the study completed? Did you recommend a diet or feeding techniques based on the study?"

She had to answer yes. Because Maren had been persistent, they had tried smaller presentations of puree and thickened liquid. The study was mostly completed, but they didn't try anything chewable and tried thickened liquids only by teaspoonful. She had recommended a diet. Now she wondered again if it would have been better to have terminated the study while it was obvious that the doctor had ordered an inappropriate trial.

"Technically," Paul said, "it was a minor incident. If the patient doesn't develop pneumonia, there won't be any long-lasting consequences." He knew the tech was Granger's niece and that Granger had voted yes to bringing in the group of radiologists. Granger also sat on the review board. Older doctors often believed speech pathologists shouldn't be involved with swallowing, and Granger made no secret that he subscribed to the philosophy that if an older patient choked or aspirated and contracted pneumonia it was time for the patient to die. "Pneumonia is the old man's friend" was the mantra.

Paul was aware how complaints such as Maren's were processed, but he didn't offer advice. *She will have to make her own decisions*, he reminded himself, wondering how much to say. He gave her examples of incident reports and how they had been resolved. Eventually she asked pointedly who was on the review board, and he confirmed that Roy Granger was one of five.

Later, while Paul read by the fire, Maren showered. One thing he had in common with Jack, Maren thought was tremendous physical stamina. The shower sapped what little energy remained in her body. She came down in the green robe and white scuff slippers to thank him and tell him goodnight. He stood and took her hands. He wished they could sit on the couch by the fire again, but knew she needed sleep.

"I'll walk you to your door," he said gallantly, but when they reached the foot of the stairs, he stopped and took hold of her shoulders. "I think I'd better say goodnight right here." He pulled her closer, leaned down, and gently kissed her.

In the morning she felt better about the incident report. A doctor's perspective was certainly different from her own. As long as no one died, it seemed to be no big deal, she reflected cynically. *It's a big deal to me, and I'm going to file the report.* Paul only nodded when she told him.

In the car he asked her to meet his parents the following Saturday. He knew Nick would be home for a long Christmas holiday soon and suspected she would be too busy with holiday preparations if they put it off any longer. She agreed to meet them for dinner at the Rose Garden Cafe and have dessert at their condo.

—

When Judy called to check in, Maren told her of her decision to file the incident report. Judy advised Maren to go to Leonard Slaker, their supervisor. Lenny wore several hats at the hospital but had no official title that Maren knew. She was aware that his wife was a nurse on third floor. He was a large, white-haired, easy-going fellow, and believed that in a hospital doctors were always right. Maren told his secretary she needed to speak with him briefly and was allowed to go in without a wait. She walked the few steps through the hall to the open door. Lenny, seated behind his unassuming metal desk, motioned for her to sit down.

Maren began to explain why she was there and produced a copy of the incident report she had completed. For a while he just listened, a blank expression on his face. *Obviously I'll get no sympathy here*, thought Maren.

"We never did these tests," as he referred to the video-fluoroscopic swallow studies, "before Judy worked here. Maybe we just shouldn't be doing them."

Maren wondered if that was a challenge, ignorance, or a real option he was proposing.

"That's something the hospital can certainly decide, if it wants to limit the scope of services in that way," she responded evenly.

"I'm just saying, our techs haven't been trained to do this procedure."

"Well, if they go to work elsewhere, 90 percent of the hospitals would require them to know how to function for swallow studies."

"It doesn't seem to be a very safe procedure if a tablespoonful of barium can drop into a patient's lung."

Maren felt anger rising in her throat at his challenge. She had never seen or heard of such a large amount being aspirated and realized she hadn't mentioned the size of the bolus. Judy had been correct when she said the whole hospital was talking about it. Someone had gotten to Lenny before Maren.

"The food amounts and consistencies are supposed to be directed by the speech pathologist. It's a functional test. The radiologists here have had no experience with it, but some of them insist on directing the study anyway. Dr. Jasmin herself told me she had never been in the room during a swallow study. She sat in another room and pushed a button to activate the fluoroscopy when a tech called to her. She has never examined patients prior to the study or reviewed the video recording after a study, yet she insisted on issuing orders. Nora jumped so fast to comply, I didn't have time to object. Even if I had, I doubt it would have made a difference."

Thinking she had been too emotional and too detailed, Maren stopped abruptly. When Lenny didn't answer, she finished in a quieter, more controlled tone. "I have no desire to watch a patient choke to death in front of me or contract pneumonia because of gross aspiration. If I was part of that man's family, I'd sue this hospital, the radiologist, and everyone connected with the study."

Silence hung heavily between them. She had thrown the dreaded "s" word on the table.

"Okay, file your report," he said lightly. "I'll talk to Carolyn."

That was all he said. She felt dismissed. Not much response from him, she mused. She really couldn't tell whether Lenny even had an opinion. She walked out, feeling let down.

The snow didn't let up. It got worse. Maren had arrived at work at six o'clock in the morning because of riding with Paul, so she left early. The day had been quiet, thankfully. Judy was at a Rehab International facility, and Maren kept a slower pace, thanks to the low inpatient census. There were mainly outpatients. She co-treated the three babies with Amber, the physical therapist. Progress would be terribly slow, but Maren enjoyed the interaction with Amber and Libby, the OT assistant.

Maren continued to reflect on patients as she drove west to Edgelawn. The high point of her day had been a phone call from Jerry Taggert's wife. She had called to clarify what food textures Jerry could eat so he could go on a fishing trip. The way she talked about his swallowing and therapy was so poignant. Maren wished she could have recorded it.

"Everything social revolves around food. You can't go anywhere without having food and drink, and Jerry can't eat or drink anything from a restaurant. He's cut off from his friends because they can't understand his speech. We thought he could at least have breakfast with them. He went with the group last time, thinking he could get eggs down, but they were scrambled so dry he choked. The guys tease him and make fun of him. They have never seen what cancer can do."

Thoughts of Jerry and his wife moved in and out of Maren's thoughts like the snowflakes wafting past her window. It was three o'clock; she was halfway home. The plows were keeping up with the flurries. The flurries turned to rain as she got farther from the lake air. She was anxious to be home.

Chapter 7

At precisely three o'clock Pam Wagner retrieved the mail from the box outside the front door. She returned to her dining room table, poured another glass of Merlot, and sat studying the dramatic picture on a postcard as she sipped her third glass of wine from the crystal goblet. She had started having an "afternoon drink" shortly after Megan went to college. At first it had been just one. Now it was three or four, more if Steve was on a trip. The picture was so beautiful, she thought dreamily. Little sail boats drifted along under the orange, layered clouds. The silhouette of a bird, she supposed it was a seagull or pelican, looked free. It was rising up from a single dark cloud to a larger cloud bank that was lined with the yellow-orange reflection of the rising sun.

The card was from Mandy, her younger sister. "Wish you were here. Come see for yourself how wonderful life can be," Mandy had written. Mandy was the free spirit of the family. She had never put down roots. This year it was Key West. She was earning a little money as an artist's model. At least she wasn't living with this one; she had gotten a small efficiency apartment on her own. If Pam wanted to come down, Mandy had said over the phone on Saturday, they could get a bigger place. Now this card had come, to further tempt her.

Why not, Pam thought, realizing she had drained the bottle. *There's nothing to hold me here. Once Megan leaves for school each fall there's nothing for me but laundry, cleaning and cooking. That's my whole life. Steve's always leaving or recuperating from a trip, constant jet lag. Three days out, two to recuperate. Two days out, one to recuperate. Only there are never enough days between trips for recuperation.* He loved it as much as Pam hated it.

When they met, Steve was a financial planner. They had long-distance, romantic, aviation dates before they were married. She had been a flight attendant. Steve would rent a private plane and come see her at her layover cities. Sometimes he would hop the flight she was working, and they would spend her time off together. When her carrier folded, Pam had planned to get on with United or American, but Steve had proposed first. She had believed back then if Steve could get on with an airline, the travel and romance would never end.

It had surprised her that she had enjoyed their lifestyle better when he was in business than when he was a commercial pilot. They originally had entertained and gone to parties with business acquaintances. *Then Alan Daley had to ruin it all,* she reviewed mentally. *He had to tell Steve that Eastern Airlines was hiring anyone with over three hundred flight hours.* Of course Steve had jumped at it. With his military flight time it had been a sure thing. Steve had gotten on with Eastern and had tried to take Jack Kepple along. Pam had always wondered if Maren had stopped him, or if Jack really preferred spending his time at home and in boats on the lake.

Pam got up to open another bottle and continued mulling over the past. When Eastern folded, Steve had gone back to Dean Whittier. Pam had hoped the pilot bug was out of his system, because she had discovered she hated being alone all the time when he was away. *I liked traveling, but Steve loved flying.* Her thinking was getting confused from the alcohol, but she thought she and Steve had been happier when they were on the go, traveling or partying, not when he was traveling and she was home alone.

Being a pilot's wife had not turned out to be as glamorous as she had expected. *Steve loved airplanes, not people,* she decided ruefully. *Maybe that's why he was attracted to me at first. I was associated with aviation.*

She started another glass of wine. Her musings become increasingly muddled as the bottle was drained. Jack and Maren were already married and had Matt when Steve had proposed. Maybe Steve was left with too much time on his hands. *Maybe,* Pam thought, *we were just two people with no other goals, more in love with traveling and airplanes than with each other.*

She had assumed their relationship would improve after he returned to the brokerage firm, or at least that each would be happier. Before they could settle into the new routine though, a group of the pilots he had worked with at Eastern had called to say everyone was getting on at Continental. She had begged, but Steve had applied anyway. *Some men fly for a living. Steve lives to fly. He's addicted. He saves no time or energy for family or friends.* He had gotten on with Continental just before the strike had come. Pam had been reprieved again.

Life has been a roller coaster, she decided. They had been fortunate though, because Steve had always been able to go right back to Dean Whittier. They were always looking for brokers, and Steve had been trained. He wouldn't give up flying though. *Oh no. He had to apply to United.* Pam had thought he'd be too old, but his experience got him on ahead of many other men, and at a time when women with only a hundred flight hours were being hired to meet gender quotas. United had always been a solid company. It didn't look like he would ever be going back to Dean Whittier, at least not until he turned sixty, the mandatory retirement age for airline pilots. He stayed on Boeing 737s now, the short-haul trips.

Steve considered his present schedule to be exceptionally good, but his idea of a decent schedule and hers did not match. Pam was really brooding now.

A wife is entitled to have her husband's shoes under the bed. Even when he is home, we don't spend much time together. He has so many interests: the cabin, his own plane, his wood-working shop . . . She admired that about him, though—his interests and friends. *We just don't have much in common with each other.*

She shrugged, drew deeply from the wine goblet, and reminisced bitterly. *It was all Jack's fault. Jack died, and that took all the life out of Steve.*

He had never talked to her about it. As far as she knew, he hadn't talked to anyone about it. She would never forget the way he looked when she and Maren met him at the airport. He had put his arms around both of them, and his whole body shook with emotion, but he never really cried. He had flown the single-engine Comanche home that day while Jack's body had arrived by ambulance. People had told her Steve shouldn't have been flying, but Pam knew him well enough to trust that flying would calm him more than anything.

It had come slowly afterwards, the change in him. It was like a part of Steve had died, too. He rarely made love to her and then only when she broadly hinted that it was time. He had helped Maren with the house and financial issues, and Pam hadn't objected. *Jack and Maren would have done the same for me,* she reasoned, but somehow it seemed to Pam that Maren had survived better than she and Steve.

Jack's death killed what was left of our marriage. Maren made a new life for herself. She looks better than she has in fifteen years, no kids or husband, just herself to look after. She's free, like the bird on the postcard. Pam's thoughts had come full circle. *Maybe that's why Steve flies. It makes him feel free. What makes me feel free,* she wondered. She stared at the now-empty bottle, looking for an answer.

She rudely pushed aside a stack of *Aviation Week*, *Airline Pilot*, and AOPA magazines. They made her realize again that she had no such consuming interests.

I may be almost fifty, but I'm still attractive, she reassured herself. At five foot six inches and one hundred fifteen pounds, she was lithe and her long, blond hair gave her a youthful look. She didn't color it either. She was proud of that. She didn't need to. *I'm sure there are men who would appreciate me more than Steve does.*

It would be easy to pack up and disappear. I'll let Megan know, of course. Steve will take care of getting her back and forth to school. Maybe Megan would spend the holidays in Key West. That would be perfect. That's it then, she decided. She would send a letter to Megan and be gone before Steve's parents arrived for their annual Christmas visit. She could be gone before Steve returned. No one would miss her once he hired a housekeeper.

Pam knew the stories about pilots who came home to find the house and bank accounts cleaned out. The men always commiserated with each other with the disclaimer, "He didn't have any warning."

Pam really didn't wonder if Steve had read the warning signals. She didn't think about how long she'd be gone, or exactly what she would do when she got there. She hung onto the thought that she would be free and there would be interesting things to do. There would be new people who might think she was attractive and interesting. She packed two bags, wrote to Megan, called Mandy, and stopped at the bank on her way out of town. It didn't occur to her to leave a note for Steve.

———

Steve sat in the semi dark cockpit of the Boeing 737. He had been out for three days, as usual, and there were two legs left to fly. The jet engines were idling while they waited in the area pilots referred to as the penalty box at O'Hare International airport. It was an appropriate name—it penalized everyone. But they still had to complete ID 229 to Newark and back. Steve was scheduled back at midnight, but thanks to another thunderstorm rolling through, it would be much later. What they said about Chicago weather was true, "If you don't like the weather, just wait around. It will change." The public wouldn't have expected thunderstorms though, after the snow earlier in the day.

Steve's copilot was a quiet, uncommunicative sort named Hank Kolerov. Steve liked to talk—it helped pass the time—but for the past twenty minutes the two had stared silently at the radar scope, the best equipment in the industry.

Steve's thoughts drifted. *It was worth all the aggravation at Eastern and Continental to finally get on with UAL. The UAL labor disputes are past history, and my job is more secure than it's ever been.* He wished Pam appreciated the benefits more. She didn't seem to be pleased about the increased income, the job security, or their travel opportunities. Well, she did like the travel, but it was never often enough for her. It was true his seniority was not great, but it was good enough to keep him from being on reserve.

I do work some weekends and some four-day trips, but it will all be worth it. She'll see. Meanwhile, I'm flying some of the best equipment in the world. Fat Albert, as the 737 was affectionately called, was the smallest of the fleet, but it sure beat a single-engine Comanche anyday.

"One thing about thunderstorms, Hank," he reminded his copilot, "they come and they go." The two watched on the scope as this one did just that, and the tower finally began to move the planes out.

No use calling Pam when I get in. She'll be sound asleep by then. She's probably finished another bottle from the case of Merlot I gave her for her birthday. She sure has developed a taste for Merlot. The thought clouded his mind momentarily, but he pushed the worry aside as he shoved the throttle forward.

"Tell the passengers we're sixth in line for takeoff," he directed.

"There are going to be a lot of missed connections," Hank replied dolefully.

"We'll try to make up for the lost time," answered Steve, thinking of Pam going to bed alone, again.

Winter: North Wind's Season

Winter belongs to North Wind.
A time of frozen water.
A time of howling, painful gusts
that make the earth lie pale and still,
controlled. Sleeping life
and dormant seeds await a rescue from the South.

Chapter 8

Matt left on Saturday, Nick on Sunday. The brilliant afternoon sunlight streamed across the deck, through the sliding glass door, and fell on the round dinette table. Maren and Bonni sat in the upholstered swivel chairs looking out across the snow-covered deck at the frozen creek. They were finally getting their Christmas visit, although it was already the first week of January. Maren made tea in the hand-painted pot Bonni had brought from Japan. The two women had little in common, yet a close friendship had developed over the years since Jack's death.

They had originally met at an office party almost ten years ago, when Bonni's dad, Alan, had been one of Jack's clients. Alan was a retired airline pilot then, but had taught Bonni to fly light planes when she was ten. She had been one of the first females to be hired by United. There was a height requirement for pilots, and at five feet nine inches Bonni easily qualified. Her long legs and thin frame made her appear to be even taller.

Her short, jet-black hair accented her dark eyes and sharp jaw. She had a no-nonsense look that served her well on the flight deck. What she lacked in physical strength, she more than made up for in decisiveness and know-how. She knew how to fly 747s and loved it, no matter what kind of schedule she had to put up with. She had advanced quickly, not so much because of her outstanding ability, which was considerable, but because of the seniority system and quotas. Women were in demand in the cockpit.

In spite of working in a man's world, Bonni managed to maintain her femininity. She learned to be a good pilot from her dad, but her mother ingrained in her that a woman can do whatever she sets her mind to—". . . and she doesn't have to become a man to do it," she often said. When Alan Daley retired from the airlines, he had bought a Bonanza that he and Bonni flew frequently. Some of her happiest times with her parents involved aviation. She knew her dad had tried to talk Jack into applying with the airlines and that, as Maren had told her later, that Jack preferred the single engine plane, the boat, and the cabin.

Maren's relationship with Bonni had been casual until Jack's death. Shortly afterward they had bumped into each other at the brokerage office, and Bonni had asked Maren to join her for lunch. Since then they had supported each other in a variety of ways. When Bonni was looking for a church, Maren offered hers. When Maren needed a real estate agent, Bonni knew someone. They admired one another's abilities and were fascinated by their differences. Bonni was eight years younger, single, and traveled widely for work and pleasure. Bonni's career had long been her focus, while Maren's had been home and family.

Bonni fit in with Maren's family partly because they had friends in common, and those friends had common interests. But there was more. Bonni was fascinated with Maren's family lifestyle, one that had eluded her; and Maren was equally fascinated with Bonni's liberated lifestyle, one that had never occurred to her as an option.

This afternoon Maren and Bonni were just two women catching up on each other's lives after the holidays. Bonni so enjoyed having Maren share her motherhood side and always prodded her for more and more information about her boys.

"It was really hard this year," Maren was answering. "I knew it would be different with me working at the hospital. As much as I complained about working in the schools, it was wonderful to have extended time at the holidays with the boys." *And summers*, she thought wistfully. "We had some great times during the holidays, though. The boys are so good to help cook, clean, shop, whatever needs to be done. Still, I'm exhausted from the pace."

"It was so wise of you to have asked for Christmas week off, up front," affirmed Bonni, her eyes shining as Maren talked about her sons. "I was so disappointed when my trip didn't get out of New York in time to go to the Mannheim Steamroller concert with you. Did one of the boys have a friend use the tickets?"

Bonni and a friend had been scheduled to accompany them. When the friend cancelled Maren had invited Paul to go. She had examined her motive later, wondering if she had thought Bonni and Paul might have a mutual attraction. That would have solved what she considered her dilemma. But, Bonni was snowed in on the East Coast, and Steve had been like a lost puppy without Pam and Megan.

"I didn't get a chance to tell you, Steve Wagner went with us. I felt sorry for him being on his own, and the boys are so comfortable with him. It was really a special time."

Bonni bit her lower lip, trying for about two seconds not to pry. She couldn't stop herself from asking, "They're not the only ones comfortable with him, are they? Any sparks there?"

Maren didn't really even consider the question. "Oh, Bonni, Steve is an old and treasured friend. I've known him as long as I knew Jack. I guess that means I've known Steve longer, now." Her voice trailed off. "I do feel sorry for Steve, but truthfully, I've known for years that Pam was unhappy. An empty nest brings freedom, but also loneliness. Maybe having Megan leave for college tipped the scale for her. I haven't seen much of her since I started working at the hospital, but I talk with her occasionally. Either Steve or Pam calls me every few weeks, just to check up. You can't replace that kind of friendship." She sighed, sipping her tea.

"Do you think she'll come back?" queried Bonni, sorry to have the subject turned to the Wagners.

"Maybe, in time, but right now Steve is devastated. He called everyone they knew in the area, looking for her. When he filed the police report, they had him call every friend and relative in the country. Pam's sister Mandy told him she was there in Key West with her, but Pam wouldn't talk to him."

"Well," replied Bonni coldly, "she'll have to communicate with him for the settlement."

"Bonni," Maren remonstrated, "we don't know that they'll divorce."

"Wake up and smell the coffee, Maren. This has divorce written all over it."

Then Bonni got the conversation back on track. She wanted to know if either of the boys had a new love.

"Matt has mentioned someone named Ellie. I never know whether it's romantic or not, he has so many friends. He's still the stable one, a typical firstborn. He's there on a scholarship this year, did I tell you?" She had, but Bonni didn't mind hearing it again.

"How does he like law school?"

"Well, that could be a problem." Maren's answer surprised Bonni. "He complained about the content of the coursework, said he's not so sure he made a good decision."

"In other words, the social life in California is great, but the academic track isn't what he expected?"

"Exactly, and I must tell you I'm not surprised. Matt has a great analytical mind, but I think he was more excited about the climate and the prestigious scholarship than about the study of law. I encouraged him to finish the year to give it a fair trial, pun intended."

Bonni smiled. "You're a wise mother. What about Nick?"

"His freshman year is normal—hates his roommate, has a new girlfriend already, named Lois Maxwell. They spend a lot of time together, mostly at church activities. I think she's real involved in Campus Crusade ministries. I haven't met her yet, but he didn't mind going back to school. She must lighten the study burden, but now he really wants a car. That's all I heard about while he was home. I'm wondering if that has to do with Lois."

Bonni said she had a friend who worked for Campus Crusade for Christ in Champaign. She promised to ask him about Lois Maxwell.

The sun moved lower in the sky, and Bonni, finally satisfied with the home-front news, was curious to know what a speech pathologist did in a hospital setting. She began to interrogate her friend on that topic, first asking, "Who do you work with?" Instead of describing patients, Maren began to talk about co-workers. Paul's name came up immediately. Something in Maren's tone, or lack of eye contact, told Bonni there was more to the story.

The phone rang, interrupting Bonni's next barrage of questions. It was Nick. He was checking in, but he only had a few minutes to talk. He and Lois would be going to a discussion group at a friend's apartment. A mutual friend with a car would pick him up.

"It would sure help to have my own car," he cajoled again. "Then I wouldn't have to rely on you and my friends to haul me. There's no university rule against it, and I could park it at a friend's apartment complex for free." Maren was pulled into his persuasive arguments and began to listen to the details as to where a car on campus could be parked.

Bonni made herself at home, poking around in the refrigerator while Maren was preoccupied. As she expected, there were some leftovers. Leftovers at Maren's house were better than first servings in most kitchens. Bonni got out two chunks of lasagna and a bottle of wine from the back of the refrigerator.

When Maren hung up, the warmth of the day was past, and the kitchen was cool. "How about eating by the fire?" Maren suggested. "Let's make a salad, too."

While they worked, Bonni deftly returned the conversation to Dr. McCloud. "So you knew him before?"

Eventually she heard it all, the invitation to the Yellow Duck, the key to the house, and the other outings, even his inclusion for the family holiday outing with Steve and the boys. "Then you're dating! Why so secretive? I haven't heard any of this," she sputtered. Abruptly she stopped her expression serious. "He's married, isn't he?"

"No, no," Maren answered hastily. Feeling a little trapped, but relieved to have someone to discuss it with, Maren looked at Bonni across the island where they were preparing the salad. "Bonni, I am attracted to him, but . . ."

"What?" Bonni was a little alarmed.

"He's much younger."

"Younger than me?" Bonni was flippant.

"Um-hm," Maren nodded.

"Oh! How much younger?"

"He's almost eleven years younger."

"Than me?" Bonni was aghast.

"No, than me."

"But he's attracted to you?"

"Well, he seems to think so."

Catching her drift immediately, Bonni retorted with her usual rapid-fire rate. "Seems to think so? Maren, he's a grown man, not a college boy. You've told me he's a competent doctor, a specialist, a surgeon. Don't you think he knows his own mind?"

It was hard for Maren to argue with Bonni's logic. Still, thoughts of the joys of child rearing, joys Paul would never know if their relationship became permanent, troubled her.

"That's true," agreed Bonni. "But I married Gary at twenty-one, expecting to have children immediately. No children came, and our relationship was empty." Bonni had never talked about Gary. Maren knew the marriage had been short-lived, but didn't know why.

"Does that prove my point then?" asked Maren, uncertain of Bonni's meaning.

"No," Bonni spoke slower now. "When I married Gary, we thought we were ready for a family. When no babies came along, we realized we had nothing to hold us together. We were in love with the idea of being part of a family, creating a family, but not really prepared to be life partners without children. It was strange—if there had been children, I don't think we would have questioned our marriage. The point is that no one knows the future, regardless of age. Paul could marry someone his own age"—*someone like me*, she thought miserably to herself—"and still not have children. Have you met his family?"

Surprised that Bonni would think to ask, Maren dutifully reported about the dinner at the Rose Garden Cafe. "I think only a few people get to meet the clan, but they were very nice. I really liked them."

"How did they react to you?"

"Oh, Bonni, they don't have any idea that we've been dating. I insisted Paul keep it very casual."

"You mean he lied?" Bonni challenged, thinking Maren was being naïve.

"No, he just said I was a friend from the hospital, and that's true. After dinner with Bob and Gloria we went back to their condo. Paul's sister Penny joined us for dessert, and I love her. She is sweetness itself. She reminded me of that Bible quote, 'In her there is no guile.' Her daughter Erin and husband Jim weren't there, so it really was just the immediate family and me. They made me feel very comfortable and"—she hesitated—"special."

Chapter 9

Paul couldn't sleep. When he finished the surgery, it had been after three in the morning. A gang member had taken a bullet in the neck that pierced his larynx.

What a way to start the new year, Paul lamented.

"They should give us a whole course in gunshot wounds," Paul used to say. Now he could teach one.

What a waste, he thought again, as he changed positions for the hundredth time. *No wonder drugs and alcohol are so tempting to the medical profession.*

Come morning, Maren or Judy would see this fifteen-year-old and work with him on swallowing. Paul had done all he could with the boy, who had displayed no emotion. He was so young to be lost. *Maybe psychiatry should have a talk with him,* Paul thought, as he dozed on and off, having crazy dreams.

At dawn he showered and dressed. He stopped at St. John's first to check on the young gang member. The boy still didn't say a word, just stared straight ahead. Paul dialed the pager number for Charles Ziffarelli, Ziff to everyone who knew him. Anyone who called him Chuck had to be a salesman. Paul's call was returned immediately.

While he waited in the physician's lounge for Ziff, he remembered the dream. Hard to believe he had slept long enough to dream. It had been so clear, like he was awake. He was walking out the front door of his house and saw one lone flower blooming beside the sidewalk. He stopped, and was so attracted to it he decided to take it indoors. He quickly snapped the stem, but as he did so, all the petals fell off. He was left holding a broken stem. He didn't know why he felt so sad about it; it was just a flower, just a dream. Still, he felt depressed.

"Looks like the weight of the world is on your shoulders," said Ziff as he approached, coffee in hand.

"Oh, just not much sleep," Paul said, dodging the real issue. The two doctors had been residents together at Circle Hospital. They still played tennis, when they found time, and enjoyed sharing an occasional patient. They quietly discussed Johnny Opaka in 356, a private room with a twenty-four-hour-a-day police guard.

Ziff then returned the conversation to Paul. Although Ziff was officially paid to care for patients, he was also expected to be available to staff, and he took the responsibility seriously. "Long night, huh?"

"I couldn't really sleep once the adrenaline was floweri . . . uh, flowing. Just bad dreams when I did doze off, no rest."

Paul seemed to have something on his mind. "Bad dreams, huh?" Ziff probed. "Anything specific? Are those bags under your eyes from just one night without sleep?"

"Do I look that bad, or do psychiatrists just see things other people don't?" Paul asked irritably. Then he told his friend briefly about the dream and how sad he felt.

Not into dream interpretation, Ziff tried a direct approach. "Is something in particular bothering you?"

"Well, I am concerned about a friend."

"A male friend?" asked Ziff, thinking this might really be about Paul.

"No, a woman. She's been a widow for almost six years and really hasn't, uh, dated much."

"A widow, huh?" Now Ziff assumed Paul was concerned about a family member or patient. "And you think she should date?"

"Well, actually she started seeing someone who's a little younger. The guy has never been married and there's some concern about, uh, their differences, in physical needs and, uh, expectations."

"Who's concerned?"

"I am," Paul emphasized. "I wouldn't want the woman to be hurt or disappointed in any way." Thinking he may have revealed too much, he hastily added, "Of course, there's nothing I can do about it."

Relieved that the problem did not involve Paul directly, Ziff asked a few more questions. "Was she married a long time?"

"Eighteen years."

"Oh."

"Is that bad?" Paul asked, nervously.

"Not necessarily. Were they happy? Any children?" Each time Paul answered, Ziff just said, "Oh."

"For crying out loud, can't you say something other than 'oh'?" Paul snapped.

"Well, I can understand your concern for her, but I'd be more concerned for the guy. He's the one who may suffer feelings of inadequacy."

"Yeah," agreed Paul, feeling even more miserable. "So any advice?"

"Well, if they spend enough time together, it'll probably all work out."

"That's it? That's your best psychiatric advice?" Paul was incredulous.

Just then Paul was paged on the overhead speaker, bringing their conversation to an end. Ziff stood, stretching his tall frame, and ran his fingers through his thick, curly, dark hair. He ambled off, whistling a quiet tune, satisfied that his friend was not in personal distress. Paul started down the hall, but realized in his preoccupation he had turned the wrong direction. It was a dead end. "How appropriate," he muttered under his breath.

⁓

Maren wished Judy didn't have so many administrative tasks. Once again Judy was in a meeting, and Maren would have to do the bedside swallow evaluation for Johnny Opaka herself. Wishing she could hand it off to someone else, she stopped in the cafeteria to pick up a cup of coffee. The usually busy café at the end of the large room had only one couple huddled in the corner, their backs to her. Maren was startled to realize it was Lenny Slaker and Carolyn Ballentine. She didn't want to think in a gossipy way, but they looked like they were on very friendly terms. She wondered how a friendship of any nature between the two of them, one of the hospital administrators and the head tech in Radiology, might affect her and the incident report she had filed.

Maren started for the elevator, turning her thoughts to the gang member who awaited her. She had seen the deadly tentacles of gangs reach even into the elementary school where she worked the last few years. The public thought gangs and drugs were in high schools, with some recruiting in middle schools. She knew for a fact there were whole families involved in gangs, and that gang members corrupted, maimed, and killed others, emotionally as well as physically. When they maimed and killed rival gang members, Maren could be hard-hearted, but she knew innocent people frequently got in the way of their bullets. She hated guns, even for hunting. Hunting had been one of the ongoing conflicts she used to have with Jack.

This morning gang member Opaka was sitting up watching TV. Maren moved slowly through the door, so the armed guard could read the photo ID badge clipped to the left lapel of her white lab coat. As reported by the other staff members, Johnny said nothing, made no sound. Maren had heard it was considered an honor in a gang to have been wounded.

For a fifteen-year-old he certainly looks hardened, she judged. She was not particularly gentle during the oral-motor exam; but he didn't flinch, and he silently complied with most of her requests. She had read the surgery note and knew swallowing would be painful. There had been no indication in the chart about the etiology of his dysphonia. He didn't answer her questions, did not say "ah," and did not cough or yawn with voicing.

She struggled to put her prejudices behind her. Her job was to evaluate this patient. Still, she knew she felt judgmental. She was angry at the street violence affecting cities all over the country, and this fifteen-year-old boy was a tangible symbol of it.

Why no voice, she wondered, trying to regain her professional perspective. *Not a sound. His volitional swallow seems intact, even if laryngeal elevation is slightly reduced.* Before giving him food or liquid, she tried once more to hear at least *ah* "Say ah, please. I need you to say ah."

No response. A flashlight in her left hand and a tongue depressor in her right, she made a calculated decision. She advanced the wooden blade and pressed the back of his tongue firmly. Still no sound. She lifted and advanced the stick, projecting it suddenly into his velum, the soft tissue behind the hard bony palate.

"Agh," he gagged with voicing.

"Oh, sorry," Maren apologized, feigning innocence. "Did that hurt?"

"Na," he responded automatically to the challenge.

Without giving him a moment to retreat, she challenged again, "Does it hurt to speak?"

"No, no."

"How about swallowing, any pain when you swallow?"

"No, it don't hurt," he insisted loudly.

Not likely, thought Maren.

Continuing to build the verbal responses, she asked which he would like to eat of the things on her tray. She looked away, fiddling with her gloves, so he couldn't get by with pointing. He hadn't had any food by mouth for many hours. Unwisely, he chose the cookies. They would undoubtedly cause the most discomfort, unless he chewed very thoroughly. Predictably, he did not. The pain would be worn like a badge, Maren knew, and in no time he would again be out on the streets with his buddies.

Back at the nurses' station, she started to write her report when her pager sounded. Judy was sending a speech pathology graduate student named Kim up to join Maren for the morning. She returned to the report. "Patient denied pain during phonation," she finished.

Dr. Ziffarelli stood behind her, reading over her shoulder while he waited to review the chart. "Dr. McCloud said the boy didn't speak. Did you get him to talk to you?"

"Yes, a few phrases. He'll be fine. No therapy needed."

"How did you get him to speak?"

"Oh, just my motherly manner, I guess." Maren shrugged and handed him the chart.

Just then Kim arrived. After introductions they went to fifth floor.

"Maggie Wright is a seventy-nine-year-old female, status post CVA," Maren explained to Kim. "The outstanding thing about her is that this is her fourth stroke. Several were on the left side of her brain; this one occurred on the right. She has some residual aphasia and dysphagia. This CVA left her severely impaired. She was admitted yesterday and was NPO, nothing by mouth, until the swallow evaluation. There's an IV in place for liquid nutrition." Kim seemed to follow all that Maren said and asked no questions.

Maren introduced herself and Kim to Mrs. Wright, who was weak but cooperative. Initially no swallow response was elicited. Her velum drooped at rest and moved only slightly with stimulation.

"Not good signs," Maren pointed out to Kim under her breath, so Maggie wouldn't hear. "Alternate feeding method for sure, but since this is her fourth CVA, her doc might be thinking permanent G tube or J tube, as opposed to temporary NG tube." Kim nodded, indicating she was following the explanation.

Maren worked with the woman, moistening her mouth with drops of water dispensed through a straw. She began manually moving the woman's larynx, while Kim watched. Finally, Maren provided some stimulation in the patient's throat with an ice-cold, long-handled mirror. Suddenly, Maggie Wright swallowed. Maren repeated her trial therapy and asked her patient to swallow again and again.

Success three out of ten tries. I'll recommend direct intensive therapy and a temporary non-oral feeding, an NG tube.

Kim followed her into the hall where Maren spoke to the family, a husband of fifty years, a son, and a daughter-in-law. She told them she was hopeful that in a week they could start Maggie on a PO diet, food by mouth, even though she might require supplements to help meet her nutritional needs. The family seemed relieved and went into the room while Maren and Kim returned to the nurses' station.

Maren didn't notice Paul sit down at the counter behind her. She was focused on what Kim was saying. She told Maren Judy had agreed to take her on for the internship and had been supervising her at her other sites until now. Kim was only allowed to observe at this point, and Maren remembered how tedious observing could be. She tried to draw Kim into the decision- making process. Paul's pen remained poised above the chart while he eavesdropped.

"Try to look first at the patient," she suggested. "Ask yourself, 'What's wrong here? What does this person need? What can I do or recommend that will help?' Then figure out how to fit that information in your report. When you start out, you may have to just fill in the blanks on a form, but if you remain at that level, you'll be a technician, not a speech-language pathologist."

Kim nodded and together they reviewed their findings. The patient was conscious but groggy. Maren explained that the initial lack of response and drooping palate were negative prognostic indicators.

Mrs. Wright's nurse interrupted them to ask if there was a possibility of recommending an NG tube. "Yes," Maren answered, "we'll recommend a temporary non-oral feeding method." When the nurse had gone, Maren explained her reasons for suggesting the temporary NG tube as opposed to the more permanent G tube.

Paul smiled. Maren was so careful to recommend rather than prescribe. He heard Kim offer her suggestion, to delay initiating therapy until after a reevaluation later in the week. Maren gently overruled her. "I can see how you would suggest that, since this is the first day after the CVA. We'll want to get an order for therapy, though. That way we can treat and reassess with one order. We did get a response today, and we want to build on that as quickly as possible."

Now Maren helped Kim form modest goals for the woman. "Response to three exercises: open and close mouth, protrude and elevate tongue, and vocalize on command. Swallow six out of ten trials. Increase velum elevation from no movement to elevation six out of ten trials." Maren numbered the goals on the page.

Paul finished writing but continued to listen. Kim was asking about Maren's techniques. "I didn't think she would swallow. How did you do that?" There was a discussion about pharyngeal stimulation versus thermal stimulation. Paul didn't really know if there was a difference, but he couldn't delay any longer. He stood just as they turned to leave. Maren was startled.

"Dr. McCloud, good morning. Any new patients for us?"

"Sorry, just a ruptured tympanic membrane."

They pulled another chart while Paul started toward the elevators. He had always known Maren was good. More recently he thought of her as gifted. Each time he heard of her work, he was more impressed. She would have made a great surgeon, he decided, stepping into the elevator.

As the elevator went down, he remembered a conversation with Dr. Wang soon after he had met Maren. The family practitioner had been talking about Maren in the lounge. His patient had suffered a massive CVA, and he had told the family the woman would probably never be able to communicate again. However, the next time Dr. Wang saw the family, they told him excitedly that the speech therapist walked in and had the woman talking in minutes. She counted, sang, and said words in conversation. Within a week she could repeat short phrases and was reading out loud. Dr. Wang had been astonished.

Paul had mentioned the story to Judy, who confirmed that Maren was more than a good diagnostician. Judy said Maren had a way of divining what a patient's potential was. More important, she knew how to get them started on the road to their maximum potential. Judy also had told Paul that Maren took her abilities for granted, assuming every speech pathologist could do the same.

When Paul told Maren about Dr. Wang's story she had shrugged it off. "It was apraxia, not aphasia," she had said simply. "With apraxia you can usually get some automatic response immediately. It's volitional speech that takes time and effort."

Maren heals patients, Paul decided, *while others merely provide therapy.* As the elevator doors opened, he vowed never do anything to interfere with her use of her gifts.

Maren's next patient was having a procedure, so she paged Judy and told her she and Kim would cover the video. She knew Judy was anxious to finish her administrative duties and be off to her rehab site. She would need the rest of the morning free from patients.

The video hadn't been on the schedule earlier—another surprise. Maren had asked Judy how to find out what caused the glitch in communications between scheduling and Rehab. Judy seemed to just go with the flow, while Maren was always more upset by scheduling surprises. In the old days Maren had complained that Jack was too programmed; he had to plan everything in advance. Maren was the one to go with the flow in those days. She understood him better after being on her own all these years.

Kim's short, heavy legs hurried to keep up with Maren's longer strides. Maren still hadn't heard anything about her incident report, so she was increasingly nervous every time she approached Radiology. Dr. Churduri today; hopefully no conflicts. The tension gathering in her back muscles relaxed slightly.

Sylvia Florence was already positioned in the black, contoured video chair. No family members were in the waiting area. Sylvia was only sixty years old, but was referred from a local nursing home where she had been on the same swallowing precautions for over two years. Nurses were looking for a diet upgrade, since they had never noticed a problem with the pureed diet. Maren wondered if perhaps the woman was cognitively impaired. Such adults frequently became wards of the state when caretakers themselves died or were incapacitated.

A trach tube protruded from Ms. Florence's neck. She greeted them with a voice that was quiet and mildly hypernasal. They progressed through the oral-motor exam. Kim held the evaluation form and tried to monitor what was happening.

"I just start on the outside and work my way in," explained Maren. "Face, eyes, nose, chin. Then lips, cheeks, tongue, teeth, hard palate, and soft palate."

Maren directed the patient, "Say 'uuu-eee-uuu-eee-uuu-eee.' Puff some air in your cheeks. Stick out your tongue. Try to touch your nose with your tongue. Circle your lips with your tongue."

When she got to the soft palate, Maren's voice stopped. Finally, she continued. "Say *ah*." She let Ms. Florence close her mouth and then asked her to open and say *ah* again. She stepped aside so Kim could look in. The student looked at her questioningly. At first Maren thought she was looking at a fistula, an extra opening between the oral cavity and nasal cavity. A dime-sized, hole was positioned just above and to the right of a structure resembling a uvula. Maren looked below the uvula-like structure for the opening to the nasal cavity, which should be accessible behind the velum. There was no opening there; it was smooth, closed. The hole was the only opening to her naso-pharynx.

"Must be the result of cleft palate surgery decades ago," she said to Kim.

Sylvia Florence didn't know why she had the trach tube or if she had been born with a cleft palate. Collecting her thoughts, Maren looked once more. It was incomprehensible. The oropharynx wasn't supposed to look like this. The woman couldn't move her soft palate, and she couldn't close the gap, which was the only opening to the cavity behind her nose. Air breathed in her nose would have to progress through the tiny hole and be routed tortuously around the tongue, to the pharynx, and then into the lungs. If she had food in her mouth, the chance of plugging her airway would be great. With the hole plugged and food in her mouth, no air could enter her trachea via nose or mouth. During speech, air would always escape through the little opening, causing permanent hypernasality and reduced loudness.

While all this was evolving in Maren's mind, Kim stood beside her looking confused. They proceeded to do a standard video swallow study. Dr. Churduri only commented that it looked normal on x-ray. Maren had never once seen a radiologist actually look in a patient's mouth. This would have been one to look at in three dimensions. It showed how deceptive a two-dimensional image could be, and how medical practitioners become so trusting of the particular instruments they use.

They found Ms. Florence's sister in the waiting room after the study.

"No," she said, "no cleft palate. Sylvia was born normal." This anatomical anomaly was the result of a tonsillectomy when she was five years old. The trach had been in place ever since. One glob of mashed potatoes could have plugged her airway, so she needed the trach to assure her of a patent airway. She would have to continue on her present swallow precautions and diet. Maren assured Kim things like this didn't happen in surgery anymore. She wondered if revision surgery was a possibility after all these years. As happened more and more frequently, she wished she could ask Paul. It was, of course, up to the woman's physician to determine her treatment.

On the way out of Radiology they heard Dr. Jasmin talking loudly with Carolyn Ballentine. Maren dutifully kept Kim moving out of the department and hoped Judy would find out in a day or so what the problem was between the usually placid Carolyn and the self-assured radiologist.

News traveled fast and Judy had already gotten the word by lunchtime. She hurriedly ate a chicken salad on wheat and filled them in, before leaving for her rehab site. "They were arguing about the procedure for a CT scan. Carolyn doesn't raise her voice often and tries to avoid conflict. She went straight to the top with this, though. I'd bet money that we've seen the last of Dr. Jasmin," stated Judy confidently.

Maren wondered who "the top" might be and remembered seeing Carolyn and Lenny huddling in the café. How Judy knew everything going on in the hospital was a mystery to Maren, but for a workplace that emphasized confidentiality, word certainly spread quickly. Still, Judy seemed to have no idea Carolyn and Lenny were friends; or maybe she assumed everyone knew that. Maren began to realize the importance of understanding the culture of the workplace and wished she had made a greater effort to relate to the quiet, but evidently powerful Carolyn.

Judy was proved right only a few days later, when she had lots of news for Maren. The radiology group agreed Dr. Jasmin would not return to St. John's, and Maren found herself wishing the same fate for Dr. Sudani. Judy also told her that her incident report had been addressed. Not much would be different, except Nora was never to be assigned to a swallow study again. Judy was to help orient new hires in the department, but that didn't include Nora. A new female radiologist named Idriss was to work from time to time, and the word in the halls was that she was an okay doc. Maren relaxed a bit, but preferred to have students with her in Radiology. The atmosphere seemed more congenial when there were outside observers.

Chapter 10

Mr. Wells came to St. John's for a video swallow study in mid-January. He was about seventy and had undergone surgery right after Christmas to dilate his upper esophagus because of what he described as a spasm. He told Maren he had suffered one problem after another, and she quickly realized he had lost the ability to relate his history consistently.

Maren wished she could phone the family and take a thorough history before the study. She wished she could call the gastroenterologist who had referred the patient to clarify some points. Unfortunately, Radiology had called her at two ten. "Your outpatient video scheduled for two o'clock is waiting." To complicate matters, an undergraduate student, not Kim, was observing for the day. Maren tried to direct the student to be helpful while she scrambled to gather materials.

The video clearly showed severe pooling and residue in the pyriform sinuses. Mr. Wells swallowed seven to ten times trying to clear it, but only a part of the bolus cleared the upper esophageal sphincter with each swallow. The dilatation was obviously a success, however some reflux was observed from the esophagus into the pharynx. There was no reflux as high as the nasal cavity, though, and no indication of poor velopharyngeal function.

Maren didn't know there was a Mrs. Wells until she walked the patient back to the waiting area. At first Maren wondered if the woman was his wife or his daughter. After introductions Maren asked her to go over the history. With Mrs. Wells's help the sequence of events became more clear. Swallowing function had improved briefly following the dilatation. Then he was treated for a fungal infection in his esophagus. Today he was in a state of weakness, dizziness, and discouragement. He had recently been prescribed a new medication for severe gastroesophageal reflux. About that time his swallow had deteriorated.

His voice was soft and minimally breathy. Mrs. Wells repeated that her husband had been suffering from fatigue and dizziness. Everyone in the county had been hit by influenza that week. Maren wondered if his resistance had been low and he was simply another flu victim. Or possibly there was some interaction with medications, or side effects. No CVA symptoms were present. None of the possibilities she came up with satisfactorily explained the severe pooling, significant residue, and reflux she had observed.

The explanation had finally come from Dr. Eichelberry, and Maren was left feeling even more inadequate. She brought it up with Paul after dinner, perhaps hoping for some sort of absolution. First, though, she hit him with the couple's age difference. "I wasn't sure whether she was his wife or his daughter," Maren reported. Paul got the message but ignored it, not giving her the satisfaction of commenting on their age difference.

"Maybe I wouldn't have missed the diagnosis," Maren complained, "if I had been given a chance to get a case history in advance."

Paul empathized with scheduling screwups. As a physician he knew you just did the best you could to work around the unexpected. He had noticed that Maren seemed to think all glitches could be eliminated.

"The student kept asking to see some compensatory techniques while I was trying to concentrate," Maren continued. "I was so puzzled I couldn't even think of possible treatment. If there was a neuropathy, I thought I should have heard hypernasality. I totally ignored the quiet breathy voice symptoms."

"So what did you document?" Paul asked.

"Besides what we saw, that pharmaceutical side effects should be considered and the speech pathologist would consult with the MD."

"Which you did?"

"Yes, I talked with Dr. Eichelberry myself the same day. After I overwhelmed his nurse with details, he came to the phone himself."

"What did he say?"

"That it was odd that the complaints started about the same time as the new meds. He asked me for the documentation of possible side effects of the drug."

"And you got back to him with that?"

"Yes, I sent a fax. The documentation turned out to be rather weak—low incidence reports of pharyngeal pain, weakness and dizziness, among a variety of other possible side effects."

"What's the problem then? It sounds like you did everything you could have done."

"Today I saw Dr. Eichelberry in the hall. He said he had just dictated a letter to me to give me the results of Mr. Wells's neuro exam." She stopped. Paul waited, eyebrows raised in anticipation. "Mr. Wells has myasthenia gravis. He responded quickly to Mestinon, confirming the diagnosis."

"That's great, Maren. What's the problem?"

"I totally missed it."

"The diagnosis?"

"Yes."

"You're not a neurologist. No one expects you to be."

"I should have seen the increased weakness, Paul. My neuro prof used to say you could tease out that diagnosis just by having the patient count to two or three hundred. Speech will deteriorate in front of you if the patient has no chance to rest. Every muscle is weak and has virtually no endurance."

"Maren, that may be true, but a community hospital is not a classroom or Grand Rounds at Mayo Clinic. You have to work within the limitations of your environment."

Maren stared at him, feeling a definite lack of sympathy for her chagrin. Paul started to speak again, but remembered Penny patiently explaining to him that it wasn't wise to try to talk a woman out of her feelings. Cheering her up was fine, just getting her to momentarily forget, but actually pulling her out of the pit wasn't considered helpful. She had to climb out herself. He really could only understand the concept if he reminded himself that self-help was the best help.

"Well, Maren, you did miss the diagnosis, but your job was to identify and document dysphagia. You did that appropriately.

Contacting the physician by phone and fax was above and beyond as far as I'm concerned. If he took the time to dictate a personal memo to you, he must have appreciated your effort."

"I think he sent the letter to let me know what a dope I was, focusing on the meds and totally ignoring the signs and complaints of weakness."

"Maren," Paul said evenly, "I don't think he would have taken the time for that reason. In medicine we try to help each other. Maybe he wouldn't have made the neuro referral without your input."

When Paul said, "You missed the diagnosis," she felt momentarily worthless; but when he went on to say that she had acted appropriately and that her efforts were probably appreciated, her self-worth began to return. It was like when the doctor pressed on the cause of your pain. He didn't inflict the wound; he just confirmed its existence. She felt affirmed and accepted, but not quite exonerated. She would have to do that for herself.

The letter arrived a few days later and indicated, just as Paul had suggested, that based on the documentation of dysphagia the patient had been referred to a neurologist. No one had all the right answers at exactly the right time, she realized. Still, she wished she had figured it out. *I guess I'm still learning,* she conceded.

—————

It was a few weeks later that Maggie Wright died, or committed suicide, only God knew which. Her swallowing had improved and Maren had begun more direct therapy when another TIA or CVA occurred. It had set everything back, but Maren still had hoped to regain what had been lost. Progress had definitely taken place.

Maren walked into Maggie's room Friday morning to find a new patient in Maggie's bed. Startled, she thought Maggie must have been sent to rehab. *I don't think she would have enough endurance for a rehab placement. Maybe she was transferred to a nursing facility to give her time to gain strength. A medical complication might have occurred, and she's back in intensive care.*

She asked the clerk, but it was a new employee who didn't know Mrs. Wright. The clerk looked at the computer screen. She didn't find the patient listed and didn't know what to suggest to Maren. Maren finally found the nurse for Maggie's room in the hall.

"You didn't hear?" Joanne asked in a hushed tone.

"Hear what?" Maren asked cautiously.

"She died." Before Maren could respond Joanne continued. "She kept pulling on that NG tube, so we had to tether her hands. Sometime in the night she got one hand free. She pulled on the feeding tube, maybe trying to take it out. She didn't get it all the way out though, and it was set on constant drip." Joanne paused dramatically. "Technically, she drowned. She couldn't swallow well enough to keep the fluids clear, she couldn't pull the tube out, and she couldn't push it back in. She drowned. The liquid just kept dripping until it filled up her lungs, and she just drowned."

Maren tried to block out the words, but Joanne kept repeating them, 'Drowned.' 'Couldn't swallow.' She was stunned. She had occasionally looked for a patient's chart only to find the person had died in the night. Patients died; that was a fact of life in a hospital, but she had never imagined being responsible in such a direct way for a patient's death. Her recommendation for an NG tube had a domino effect that resulted in her patient's death.

Maren felt sick. An unusual drowning. The words carried significant emotional baggage. Jack had died an unusual drowning death, but she hadn't felt responsible. She didn't answer Joanne. In fact she walked off the floor without speaking a word. In the cramped speech therapy office she sat and stared at a stack of paperwork on her desk, without making any attempt to address it.

Judy found her there when she came in. It didn't take long to get the whole story. She assured Maren that not only was it not her fault, it wasn't anyone's fault. Accidents happen in hospitals as well as other places. She wondered if Maren was emotionally sent back to thoughts of Jack's drowning. There was no logical connection, though. The incidents were totally different. She decided not to dredge it up.

They had some lunch and Maren seemed better, but was obviously still preoccupied. Judy began expressing concern about Maren driving home alone.

"I took the train. Paul wanted to see Edgelawn, so he was going to take me home."

"Paul." Judy stated blankly and then repeated quizzically, "Paul? Do you mean Paul McCloud?"

Instantly, Maren realized what she had done and was jolted back to reality. She watched the realization spread across Judy's face and waited for the questions. It wasn't a question that came forth, but reassurance and a warning. "You had better be very discreet. I won't say anything, but anyone who sees you getting in or out of his car could start tongues wagging." Judy recalled the year she had lived with the resident. Their every move had been common knowledge. It had caused quite a stir until he moved out of state.

Then with a sly smile Judy added, "And all this time I thought you had something going at the other end of the tracks."

Maren did cancel their date. She took the train home, saying she didn't feel up to a social evening. Paul was disappointed, but he honored her need to be alone. It would be better to experience his first visit to Edgelawn as a happy event.

When she walked in the back door, the phone was ringing. She thought it was Paul, checking on her. "I'm just in the door," she answered, instead of "Hello." Steve's voice responded. "Oh good, I thought I'd be leaving a message again."

Maren wasn't really surprised to hear from him. He had been calling much more frequently since Pam left, from home and a variety of cities where he had layovers. At first it was, "How do you cook corn?" Then it was, "Megan's got a new boyfriend." Sometimes he called just to chat. They always picked up right where they left off. There was no pretense between them, no posturing or game playing. Occasionally he wanted to talk about Pam; usually anything but Pam.

Pam finally had contacted a lawyer and had asked for divorce papers to be drawn up. Steve wouldn't object. He wanted her to be happy. He had hoped he would be able to make her happy, but obviously that was not the case. Steve bid for and got crazy schedules now—no need to be home. It didn't matter anymore what kind of hours he kept. In fact, he had put in a bid for 747s and was waiting a class date assignment.

Whenever he called, Maren took time to chat. It was the least she could do. Today he was home and just checking in. He knew by the sound of her voice she was feeling low. As always, he was full of good advice. "What you need," he said cheerfully, "is a change of pace, something to think about besides sick people." She couldn't argue with that. "I'll pick you up in twenty minutes. We'll go out for a burger."

Normally, Maren would have picked up on that phrase, but in her state of mind she missed it. "Go out for a burger" was pilot talk for "fly to a small airport for a bite to eat." That's exactly what they did.

Steve arrived within a half hour in his new BMW. "Probably lose it in the settlement." He shrugged, rapping his knuckles on the roof. He had been poor before; it didn't distress him that he might be poor again. He loved traveling and loved his job. Pam couldn't take that away. He drove straight to the Edgelawn airport, where they hangared the red and white single-engine Comanche.

"Where are you taking me?" Maren asked, totally forgetting the events of the day.

"I hear they make a very good burger at the new coffee shop in Rockford."

"I should have known we weren't going to be eating at Wendy's," she returned dryly, as she stretched to step onto the wing.

The cold wind caught her face and hair and seemed to blow the world of health care away. She stood enjoying the sensation for a moment, in spite of shivering, then slid into the left front seat next to Steve and fastened her shoulder harness and lap belt. She put on her headset and watched him go methodically through the items on the checklist, assuring that all was well with the engine. Before she could mentally drift back to her other life, they were racing down the runway into the wind. The needle on the instrument went quickly past the line for sixty-five knots.

Steve pulled the nose gear clear of the pavement at eighty-five. She felt the main gear retracting before her body was committed to flight, and the little plane climbed confidently into the sky. The cold air was predictably smooth, a perfect night for a flight. Twenty minutes later they were parking the Comanche in Rockford. The casual coffee shop was full of aviation enthusiasts who were drinking hot coffee, eating mediocre food, and telling exaggerated tales of their recent or not-so-recent adventures.

She could always identify the pilots—they flew with their hands during conversations, demonstrating climbs, turns, stalls, descents, and chandelles. Unexpectedly, she felt the pain of the empty place inside her that Jack had filled. This was the world he had loved, general aviation and the friendliness of people at small airports. That atmosphere just didn't exist at large airports.

When she pulled her thoughts back to the present, Steve was describing the grandeur of the Emerald Isle Hotel, where the crew laid over in San Diego, and the size of the filet he had eaten at the pub next door to it. They didn't talk about Jack or Pam. Each needed only to relax in the company of a good friend.

It was late when they returned, but Maren felt more refreshed for the getaway than if she had slept the extra hours.

"Flying always makes me feel as though I have escaped," she said, thanking Steve.

"Yeah, it was good for me, too," he joked, wiggling his eyebrows with sexual innuendo. He was an irreverent fellow, but good-hearted.

Tomorrow was Saturday, and she was thinking of inviting him for a home-cooked breakfast when he said he was taking an organ run early in the morning. He would fly to Kentucky, pick up a patient waiting for some kind of organ transplant, and fly to the designated hospital, quickly and without charging a fee. Usually he didn't get much advance notice about those flights. She was impressed with his willingness to donate his services, but was disappointed. She would cook dinner for him some other time.

Chapter 11

Pain! She woke with it. Maren didn't think of it as cramps anymore, just pain. It started in her abdomen, spread to her back, and grew to monstrous proportions until it was all she could think about. In the old days it had been held at bay with over-the-counter medication. Now she had a prescription. Usually the pills seemed to dull the pain; other times she wondered why she bothered to swallow them.

She went to the hospital only by train on days like these. Occasionally she made it until five; most times she left after lunch. She couldn't think, couldn't work, and could barely stand upright. Once home she would curl up in the fetal position in her bed and close her eyes.

It sounded trite to tell people she was leaving work early because of cramps. She was too embarrassed to say how much blood loss there was on those days. Maybe the worst consequence was it made her feel very old and dirty. She didn't consider it a subject for social conversation, so only her close friends knew how debilitating the symptoms of the fibroid tumors were.

Originally Dr. Logan thought it might be endometriosis, but eventually he told her it was the tumors. At the word "tumor" Maren had recoiled in horror, although they were totally benign. "Take them out," she had said naively, but there were too many and some were now quite large. He warned her a year ago that a hysterectomy was the only solution. It was a just a matter of time.

Fear had become part of her monthly cycle. She counted days and planned activities around those dreaded days. Sometimes she was afraid to sleep for fear of waking in pain or a pool of blood. What used to be five to seven days had grown to ten. She thought the main thing that kept her from scheduling surgery, besides the inconvenience and expense, was the unpredictable nature of her disability. Some months were mild or skipped entirely. Hormone therapy was tried, of course. She couldn't tolerate the side effects. Fortunately, today was Saturday, and fortunately Steve wasn't coming for breakfast. She could stay in bed late and pamper herself all day. She thought Paul might call to check on her, but he did not.

Maren didn't know that Paul had to cover at the office, or that he finished with Granger's patients early and decided to use the unexpected free block of time to tell his parents about his feelings for Maren.

Gloria made no response and waited quietly while Paul gave more details. She had decided before Paul was born that she would accept her children's choices graciously, as long as they were happy. Her own parents had caused deep and lasting resentment when they had disapproved continually of Bob McCloud. She wanted Paul to have a life partner, someone to encourage him in work and play, someone to show him another side of life. She wanted the marriage to be happy and lasting. Beyond that she had no requirements.

Bob was not critical by nature, but he was outspoken. He asked the questions. He liked Maren, he said, but then he liked almost everyone he met. He wanted to know about her boys, her background, and her religion. Paul did not hesitate to share what he knew. His parents would support whatever decision he made, of that he was certain.

"Well," said Bob slowly, "I always wanted grandsons. Naturally, I expected to bounce them on my knee before I attended their college graduations. This will take a little getting used to."

"That's why I'm telling you now, so you have a chance to get used to it as I get to know them."

Realizing now that Paul didn't know the boys well, Gloria also suspected that no wedding was planned. "How do the boys feel about you marrying their mother?" she pressed.

He confessed then about Maren's preoccupation with their age difference and her fear that Paul would one day regret not having children of his own. Gloria began to feel she knew Maren on a mother-to-mother basis. She could understand Maren's concerns and was pleased that she was being protective of her only son. Bob, who was adept at dealing with young people, wanted to meet the boys immediately. They both advised Paul to establish a good relationship with her sons without delay. "If you don't learn to love them, they'll always come between you," Gloria advised. Paul was grateful for his parents' input. That meant they were in his corner. Now maybe some progress could occur.

When the phone rang at noon, Maren was hoping to hear a friendly voice. It was. Bonni Daley wanted to stop by. Maren thawed some homemade soup, took another capsule, and headed for the shower. Lunch was her breakfast.

Bonni made aviation small talk while they ate. That wasn't like her. Not until they finished the soup and sourdough bread Bonni had brought from San Francisco did she get to the reason for her visit. She looked at Maren across the table and began, "I've been in touch with my friend Jeff, the one with Campus Crusade for Christ."

Maren had forgotten that Bonni had promised to find out more about Nick's new girlfriend and her church.

"Maren," she continued slowly, "Jeff says he doesn't know any Lois Maxwell in the Champaign group." Maren didn't offer a response, so Bonni continued. "There is a Grace Campus Crusade Group, but it isn't part of Campus Crusade for Christ at all."

Again Maren didn't know what to say. "Maybe I got the name wrong," she suggested.

"No," Bonni went on, "you had the name right, but it's believed to be a cult."

If Bonni had dropped a loaded gun in the middle of the small kitchen table, it couldn't have shocked Maren more. If there was a word that could jolt her emotions more than *gang*, it was *cult*.

"Cult"—she finally spit it out—"you mean like that Branch Davidian thing in Texas years ago?"

Bonni tried to calm her friend. She had talked to Jeff extensively about cults before bringing the news to Maren. Not all cults were bent on suicide, but they did hinge on control of each member, body and mind. Nick was being slowly sucked in by his new friend. Bonni began to share some of what Jeff had told her.

The group had started with only a few students. The leaders were from Tulsa. Since August it had grown to two or three dozen students. They had presented themselves as new spiritualists who interpreted Scripture together. Each student was encouraged to keep a journal of activities, thoughts, and dreams. The students would share these personal thoughts and events together in a leader's apartment. The leader would interpret their thoughts and dreams for them. Sexual liaisons were encouraged as a bonding technique, although there was no evidence of group sex during meetings.

Maren's stomach turned and tightened. She pushed back from the table and stood. That old nemesis, Fear, began to reach its fingers around her waist. As if to escape, she walked around the table to the sliding glass door and looked out at the wetlands behind her townhouse.

"So Lois is being drawn into this, too?"

"Maren," said Bonni gently, "Lois is one of the leaders."

The fingers of fear became a rope that tightened around her stomach. Despair began to wrap its tentacles around her throat. She rested her forehead against the cool glass door and closed her eyes, in a posture of helplessness and surrender.

In that instant she saw clearly in her mind's eye a scene that had occurred when Nick was only six. Jack had constructed a rope swing from a huge old willow tree trunk that hung over the edge of the lake. The boys would hold onto the large knots in the rope railing and walk along the thick, horizontal trunk until they were over the water. At the spot Jack had marked, they would jump, holding another rope until they had swung farther out where it was safe to let go.

Matt had gone first and had splashed safely into the water. On his first try Nick had inched his way along the rough trunk, but the bark had hurt his feet, causing him to lose his balance before he reached the place marked for jumping. As Maren had stood helplessly below, watching, he fell, not over water but directly over the rocky shoreline.

A prayer had formed automatically. It hadn't been a pleading so much as relinquishing, "In your hands, Lord."

Nick's small body had bounced against large branches, which he would have cleared had he maintained his balance to the marked spot. As he had rolled through them the branches raked his body, but also altered his fall, causing him to land in shallow water. The impact had been with the sandy lake bottom not the nearby rocks. Nick had been scratched, but not seriously or permanently injured.

Maren blinked, realizing she had been in a kind of daze. She stood up straighter and looked at Bonni, feeling revived, comforted, even assured. The fingers of fear and tentacles of despair had dissolved in that instant, replaced by a protective presence around her. "I need to make some phone calls," she said calmly.

Assuring Bonni she would be able to manage alone, Maren walked her friend to the door, gave her a hug, and thanked her. Neither Nick nor Steve answered her call. She did reach Matt, who offered to come home. Maren assured him it would be better if he would just stay in closer contact with his brother. Steve returned her call at eleven thirty. His familiar voice and their long-time friendship soothed her as she huddled under the covers and told him the bad news. Predictably, he promised to do whatever he could to help.

When she finally heard from Nick on Sunday afternoon, he sounded fine but would tolerate no criticism of his friend or her church. Unwisely, Maren had started the conversation by asking if he was making any new friends. That put Nick immediately on the defensive.

"What do you mean 'new friends'? What's wrong with the friends I have?"

"Oh nothing, I just hear you talk about Lois quite a bit, and I hope you won't be so exclusive with any one person that you'll miss other opportunities."

"We both have lots of friends," he answered curtly, ending the discussion.

"Are you still attending your Bible study?" she asked, knowing the study groups didn't really study the Bible.

"Yeah, we have our study group. Why all the questions? You were never very interested before."

More shrewdly, she steered the conversation to the possibility of buying a used car for Nick. She now saw the car as an opportunity to encourage him to come home more frequently.

"You know, I think we should spend some time looking for something for you soon. Why don't you let me know when you can get home for a couple of long weekends?"

At least they ended on a positive note.

Two weeks passed, and there had been no opportunity for Paul to visit Edgelawn or for Nick to come home. Maren had stayed in the city twice, but was constantly wondering if Nick might be trying to reach her. She phoned him at least every other day.

Paul was concerned and supportive. He arranged for Ziff to talk with Maren. Once he knew of the situation, Ziff checked with Maren regularly and counseled her patiently. Maren shared her concerns with her friends in Edgelawn, too, since they had known Nick since birth. Still, she had an overpowering desire to drive to Champaign and bring her youngest son home, by force if necessary.

The barometric pressure had dropped. Maren was sure that's what caused all the CVAs to occur en masse. Fortunately, Kim could now work independently with some patients. Maren was grateful, because the demand for speech pathology services had already doubled since she and Judy had been hired by the hospital directly. Maren was so busy at the hospital she had no choice but to focus totally on the patients in front of her, parking thoughts of Nick with her car in the lot.

Fred Winslow captured her attention and her heart. He was a nattily dressed seventy-five-year-old, traditional gentleman. Even in his hospital bed he looked like a man who had led a good life, in every sense of the word—good family, good income, good hearted. Now his eyes were usually closed. He had serious visual deficits. In the left eye, his daughter Gail said, he had worn a contact lens since his cataract surgery three years earlier. His stroke a few days ago, left him with homonymous hemionopsia, the left field of vision in both eyes was gone, destroyed.

Today he sat in the armchair next to his bed, glasses and dentures in place. A smart plaid sweater vest covered his long-sleeved dress shirt.

His freckled face wrinkled with a big smile as he greeted Maren. He had good social skills. That frequently made patients look better cognitively than they were. Fred's daughter June was on watch duty. The family was large, two boys and three girls. They took turns or came in twos and threes.

The first time Maren had seen him he had been in bed. The chart had documented a right CVA. Judy had evaluated him earlier for swallowing as well as speech and language. She had left goals for treatment in his chart and had noted that his prognosis was good. He appeared to be in pain that first session. He had squeezed his eyes shut, rolled his head back and forth on the pillows, and kept one hand across his forehead. He had answered "Yeah" a few times. He had opened his mouth on command, but did not protrude his tongue or say *ah*. Maren had talked to both June and Gail and had provided family education. That meant she had said the obvious in as kind a way as possible. She had hoped they understood at least part of her message. The message that morning had been, "It looks like your dad has had another stroke." They had agreed.

The next time Maren saw Fred, Fred Junior, Gail, and June had been present. She had reevaluated Fred's status. She had asked questions, required him to count to ten, asked him to follow directions, and chatted intermittently with him. What she did always looked like passing the time of day to the untrained. Then came the harder part—translating the results of the five-minute conversation for his children. What Maren had determined was that he didn't have apraxia, and he didn't have the recovery pattern of someone who had a hemorrhagic or ischemic CVA. His performance fluctuated too much, not only day by day, but from hour to hour. One time he would be lucid and conversational, the next time completely nonverbal. Fred Junior had stated, "We think he's having multiple TIAs."

Maren had been startled at his apt diagnosis. She had just reached the part where she would tell them that they could not rule out seizures, but had been interrupted. "I don't know how knowledgeable you are," she had begun. Fred Junior had interjected the children's theory that their dad was having a continuous series of transient ischemic attacks. Usually a single TIA would impair the patient momentarily or for up to twenty-four hours. Then function would return to normal or near normal. In Fred's case they seemed to just keep occurring. "We're pretty experienced," Fred Junior had assured Maren.

"I think that's a possible diagnosis," Maren had agreed, putting off the discussion of seizures for another day. Of course they hadn't totally understood the implications of their diagnosis. Maren had known immediately that therapy would not be beneficial. The attacks, whether TIAs or seizures or both, would come, leaving him temporarily unable to respond. Then he would return to his previous state or close to it. After many, many such attacks the near return to the previous function level would be lower and lower. Maren had felt the love in the room. Love and fear were tangible entities in the confines of a hospital room if you were open to experience them.

"We want aggressive therapy," Fred Junior had proclaimed, unaware of the incongruity of his diagnosis and recommendation. Maren had promised him she and Judy would continue to see his dad twice a day. She hadn't told him that was primarily to document lack of progress before discharging him. In the meantime, the family had been in need of support and further educational counseling. She had informed the social worker.

Now Fred looked up from his breakfast tray and began a conversation. Some of his sentences were clear. Paraphasias, words pronounced with mixed-up sounds, laced his speech. This was new, and it was significant. Fred's CVA was on the right side of his brain. The language center was almost always on the left. Patients with a left CVA often had aphasia, difficulty retrieving the right words. Often the words would come out with sounds mixed up. If the lesion was more anterior, or forward, in the brain, the patient would be frustrated, aware of the difficulty. If the lesion was on the left side but posterior, toward the back, speech was fluent but meaningless. In that case there was no frustration. Such patients weren't aware of their meaningless speech and usually didn't understand what was being said to them. Fred seemed unaware of his paraphasias now. It was a sign of a new incident, posterior and on the left side. Sadness akin to despair seeped through Maren's spirit as she worked with him.

When Maren's therapy made him uncomfortable for any reason, he closed his almost unseeing eyes and rolled his head back and forth. Now he rubbed his back against the back of the chair, like a cat trying to scratch an itchy spot. It didn't necessarily mean anything. Fred didn't follow directions now. He attempted verbalizations only about the old days, a common trait as the mind deteriorates. Its earliest treasures seemed to be locked deep inside and were the last to be given up. Fred had gone to Oxford years ago, he told her. It had been a magical time in his life; he was still proud of his accomplishment.

Maren knew even as she enjoyed his stories that she would discharge him today for lack of progress. June stopped her in the hall and reviewed his successes and failures. Maren reflected back to her his strong and weak points. Even June, the most stoic of the family, was red-eyed this morning. It was beginning to register with them that their dad, their dear, kind, good-humored father, was leaving them, bit by bit. As surely as drops of rain in a puddle eventually evaporate, this kindly, loving patriarch was evaporating as they watched.

Maren explained gently to June that her dad really had made no progress that could be attributed to therapy. She didn't need to say that he had actually lost ground.

She encouraged June to engage her dad in conversations about the good old days. "That's frequently a way to elicit some amount of language," Maren said. Maybe it would be comforting as well. She hoped so. The family had been afraid that allowing him to reminisce would be in some way detrimental. She assured June it would cause no harm and promised to check in later in the day to see how they were doing.

Following the conversation, she walked straight to the nurses' station and wrote the discharge summary. She planned to look in for a social visit only and to advise them that therapy would be discontinued.

The next day, however, Maren was called to room 460 again. The patriarch of the Winslow family was now having difficulty eating. The family had requested a swallow evaluation, and Fred's doctor had written the order. They didn't want to place a G tube, but weren't sure what the consequences would be if they did not.

After a bedside swallowing evaluation, Maren followed standard protocol and recommended a video swallow evaluation. Then she patiently went over their options. They needed to be advised that he was clearly at risk for aspiration. If the video swallow study documented aspiration on all consistencies, and she suspected it would, he would be at risk for pneumonia if they fed him. Their options would be tube feeding or oral feeding as tolerated.

It was within their right to accept the responsibility of possible pneumonia rather than to place a tube. Fred could be kept alive with a G tube for a longer time, if that's what they wanted. She showed them some techniques for giving him liquids. He already refused solid food. He just pushed it out or held it in his mouth without swallowing. When they began to ask technical questions about the effects of not placing a feeding tube, Maren referred them to their doctor.

She said good-bye as she left the anguished family and hoped fervently she wouldn't be called back to see Fred Winslow again. She was fairly certain they would not agree to a video swallow study, since he was already refusing to eat. She was positive they would not allow a tube to be placed.

All day Maren had looked forward to an early dinner date with Paul and planned on taking the train home afterward. She met him at the Yellow Duck. By now she felt Chad and Connie were her friends, and greeted them warmly. Surprisingly, Paul was already there. He had only an hour before leaving for a meeting downstate. Maren knew he went to Springfield from time to time, though they never discussed it in detail.

He told her about his conversation with his parents, but as with the downstate trips he didn't give her many details. His emphasis, he said, had been that they were dating and that he wanted his family to get to know her and her family better. She accepted that.

He was so much closer to his family than she had ever been with hers. She admired and envied their relationship. She couldn't help but be pleased at their acceptance of her. In the back of her mind she could imagine the boys calling Bob "Grandpa." What a great role model he would be. But calling Paul *Dad*? That she could not imagine.

She hated admitting to Paul that she was depressed, because she knew he especially liked her cheerfulness. She also knew he could take the bad with the good, so she did tell him briefly about her talk with Fred Winslow's family.

Paul admired her for her sensitivity, and empathized. "I don't think my dad would like going on for years with a tube in his stomach and no light on upstairs." He spoke so softly she could barely hear the words.

Maren tried to use the conversation to hammer on the age theme again. "What if this man had a sixty-three-year-old wife?"

"What if he did? What's important is what kind of life they had together." Paul felt renewed in his ability to win Maren over since talking with his parents. It might take the whole McCloud family to convince her, but they would get past this issue one way or another.

Maren opened her eyes and realized her head was resting on a soft pillow. There was hardly any light coming in a stained glass window. It was so quiet. She strained through the darkness to see who was standing beside her bed. It was Paul, but he looked so sad. He had tears on his cheeks. His shoulders were sagging. He reached one hand up and touched something just above her.

Why didn't he say something? She couldn't get awake enough to move or speak.

There were flowers behind Paul. There were flowers on top of her. Someone else was pulling Paul back and starting to put something on her. She was in a casket!

Maren woke with a jerk as the train lurched to a stop. She had fallen asleep in the upper-deck seat with her coat on top of her. Too hot! She roughly pushed the coat aside and tried to neutralize her feeling of panic by pressing her head against the cold window and then looking at fellow passengers down below. Some were chatting, some reading, a few were dozing. She hoped their dreams were more satisfying.

"Edgelawn, next stop," called the conductor. Maren quickly gathered her things. She needed to feel the cold air on her face. She hurried down the steps at the back of the car and stood waiting for the door to open. It wasn't hard to figure out the meaning of that dream. She needed to find a way to convince Paul about the seriousness of their age difference once and for all.

She drove home with her window partially open and didn't bother turning up the heat once she was in the house.

Steve had called and left messages on the recorder at half hour intervals. "I figure you'll come home eventually," his voice began in response to her outgoing message. "Why don't you start applying for jobs at hospitals closer to home? That commute of yours is a killer."

Good old Steve, she thought affectionately, always looking out for her, always giving her advice. Never mind that his commute was just as bad.

She turned in without returning his call. She simply didn't have the energy for conversation. They could talk about commitments, obligations, and schedules tomorrow.

Chapter 12

Why does everything go wrong all at once? Maren asked herself on the eastbound train the following week. Her whole body ached, but her eyes were the worst. She was suffering from sleep deprivation as well as lack of exercise, and she knew it.

Life seemed to be in a downward spiral. Her efforts with patients seemed to be one failure after another. The missed diagnosis of Mr. Wells seemed insignificant now. There was Mrs. Wright's drowning and Fred Winslow's demise. Her monthly problems continued. Nick was still involved with the cult. And now the Newson incident was both a professional and personal loss. Mrs. Newson had told Rita she was taking Jason elsewhere for therapy.

How could I have been so insensitive? Maren continued to beat herself emotionally as she went in the side door and down the steps to the speech office. She reviewed over and over how Jason had been doing so well. It had been the one continually bright spot in her life. Now that too had been extinguished. *It was my own fault,* she told herself.

She had been so pleased when the observation room was finally finished. She had set up the room monitor, instructed Liz on its use, and begun working with Jason. She had been concerned that he still wasn't using sentences at home, although he did so in therapy. She had used an adaptation of an old facial-cueing technique known as motokinesthetics. Jason had responded with repetitions of her sentences and formed some of his own using the carrier phrases Maren modeled.

"I want a truck. I want a car. I want a—" As he drew photo cards from the stack in front of them, he finished each sentence with the name of the object on the card.

Maren had seated him at the table so Liz could see the cues clearly through the observation window. Then abruptly she had decided to bring Liz into the room. She had found Mrs. Newson, not behind the window, but sitting at a desk in the room reading a novel. The joy of Jason's progress had dissolved in an instant. Maren had been hurt and angry, not so much for herself but for Jason.

"Couldn't you watch for just twenty minutes? I've been demonstrating techniques for you to use at home, and you've missed it all." Her tone had a definite edge. All the frustration of the last few weeks boiled over.

Mrs. Newson had replied that she watched Jason twenty-four hours a day at home, and that once in a while a mother is entitled to a break. Maren hadn't argued, but it was only with the greatest effort. The following day, Liz had called Rita and canceled. They had found a facility closer to home. Monday, the puppet Maren had loaned them was returned by express mail.

The joy of being a speech-language pathologist seemed to be strangled a bit more every day. Maren couldn't seem to get things turned around. She wished she could take a vacation. Two weeks was not even imaginable. Ten days might restore her, but in reality she couldn't get away for more than a three-day weekend.

Today was only Wednesday. After depositing her coat in the speech office, she picked up orders from Rita for three new inpatients that had to be seen by the end of the day, in addition to the regular case load and a number of videos.

Trying to forget the Newsons, she hurried to get ready for an outpatient appointment in the speech room. Jose Valesquez, it turned out, was the high point of the day. The first time she saw him he had spoken a constant stream of paraphasias and jargon, total nonsense that sounded a bit like a foreign language. His adult daughter had assured Maren his babbling meant nothing in Spanish either. His brain lesion from the stroke had to be posterior, because he neither comprehended what anyone else said nor monitored his own speech. From time to time he expressed frustration, but not at his inability to speak, at his listeners' inability to understand him. His was the kind of case Maren would rather not treat. *Without awareness what could you build on?* she asked herself.

Research showed that verbal expression improved in direct relation to auditory comprehension, so Maren's therapy for Jose had focused on listening skills. He had been a handful, and his daughter Martha had been at the end of her patience. Several entire sessions had been spent just getting him to pick up the appropriate household item as Maren spoke its name.

A pencil, tissue, cup, screwdriver, and shaver now lay on the table in front of them.

"Jose, give me the pencil," she said slowly and clearly. He still required two repetitions and frequently needed shushing to keep him from confusing himself with his own chatter. "Jose, put the tissue in the cup."

"Cupper under," he began while placing the screwdriver on top of the cup.

"Wait. Listen," Maren insisted. "I'll say it again."

This time he kept quiet, picked up the appropriate objects and looked to Maren for encouragement. She nodded her head as he completed the task. The first day he had been 20 percent. This morning he was an astonishing 60 percent, with one or two repetitions of the directions. Relatives would never be able to control him sufficiently to practice the task at home. The prognosis was still guarded, but Maren consoled herself that at least he was progressing.

At the end of the morning's appointments Maren tried to encourage herself, *I'm either getting used to the frustrations of working in a hospital, or I'm so tired I don't care anymore.*

She shuffled down the hall to the cafeteria to meet Judy. It was way past the lunch hour. They would be lucky to find any hot food. She asked for a cold sandwich and started toward the coffee cart.

She saw them there again, Lenny Slaker and Carolyn Ballentine, at a time when the café was usually empty. *What an unlikely couple.* Maren had seen them together regularly since the day she filed her incident report with Lenny. She would never have made the connection otherwise.

Judy was across the room, apparently unaware. Maren, determined not to gossip, sat with her back to the couple.

"What you need is a little diversity," said Judy, after Maren reported the events of the morning. Judy had plenty of diversity in her life. Last night's phone call from her mom had added to it. The date of her dad's bypass surgery was March 3rd.

"You're going, of course," Maren stated.

"Oh yes." Judy paused and stared at Maren. "And you know what this means?"

Maren stared blankly across the table for a moment, trying to figure out how the new complexity in Judy's life would impact Maren. Then it hit her—the five-day training with Dr. Weingarten and the Metro ENT docs. Judy had allowed Maren to opt out, saying someone had to stay to mind the store, but the new circumstances changed everything.

"The laryngeal videostroboscopy course . . ."

"That's right."

"How will you—" began Maren and stopped. "Oh no, you can't expect me to—"

"There's no other way, Maren. It's too late to cancel, and even if we did, it would be a tremendous setback for the program. You could do it, Maren. I know you don't want to be responsible for developing the strobe protocols, but you could represent us and bring back the information. I'll catch the next conference available, even if I have to pay for it myself."

Maren hesitated, which gave Judy a chance to continue. "I know you've been under some stress. Don't go if this will put you over the edge. But if you need a break, it might be a good thing." She had such a way of getting others to do things while seeming to be concerned only for the other. It didn't feel like she was being pushy, but she clearly was exerting pressure.

"What about coverage here?" Maren asked warily. "I thought someone had to mind the store." She was really more concerned about being even further away from Nick and less available. "I have some friends who could provide coverage," Judy answered, unaware of Maren's real concern, "or we could get the hospital to contract for short-term help from Rehab International." Maren promised to let Judy know by the end of the week, but she already knew that she would go.

Paul was supportive and enthusiastic about the idea. He offered to spend an afternoon with Nick midweek on his way to or from Springfield. He wanted to reassure Maren that someone would be in available to him. Surprisingly, Nick agreed to it. He had been curious about his mother's friend and was eager to get to know him better. When Maren asked what the two of them would do, Paul just said he thought two single guys would figure out something.

Steve was also supportive. He would spend his days off, which were on Friday and Saturday, taking Nick to get a used car. That would relieve Maren of the car responsibility as well as keep her from worrying. He said he wanted to repay Maren for taking Megan back to campus after the holidays—not just the driving, the talks, too. The trip to Northern Michigan had been a harrowing one, with an ice storm causing them to stop for almost twenty-four hours at a motel before it was safe to continue. He knew from his conversations with Megan it had been a special time for them. Megan had needed someone to talk with about Pam's behavior, and Maren was more than a good listener, she was an old family friend. She had guided Megan safely through a time that could have had serious repercussions for the young woman. Steve was grateful that the two were staying in touch.

Maren gave the car-shopping plan her blessing. Knowing Steve and Paul would be close to him made it easier for her to be away.

Chapter 13

Paul insisted she take his car. Hers was perilously close to needing new tires, and the heater had not worked well for several weeks. It would be a long drive, and his new blue BMW would be more comfortable and safer than her own.

The next day, one of the Metro group, Dr. Nolan, invited her to ride with him. Maren probably would have accepted, but she had already agreed to Paul's offer and had arranged to leave her car in the garage for the repairs while she was away. Paul would use one of his parent's cars and arrange to pick hers up when it was ready.

As she drove out of town Sunday morning, Maren couldn't help thinking about the message Judy had left on her answering machine. Maren retrieved it by phone from Paul's house, just before leaving. Sparky had died. The well-known professional clown had been a patient at St. John's and was loved by the whole staff—in fact, by the whole city. He and his wife had decided to become clowns late in life, and characteristically they had done it together. They had entertained thousands of people over the previous decade at parades, parties, openings, and even political celebrations. Now Sparky was gone, and Gram would have to continue alone.

Maren was glad she wouldn't be in town for the clown's funeral. It would be on all the radio and TV stations. *More sadness I don't need.* Although she tried, she couldn't prevent herself from thinking about the couple during most of her drive.

Maren had evaluated Sparky within two hours of his arrival at the emergency room. He had been only mildly impaired as far as speech, language, and swallowing. It might even have been a TIA. The doctor had agreed, and Sparky had been sent home. Two days later he was back.

"Same thing only a little worse, I think," Gram had told Maren. This time he was admitted. When Maren checked him the following day, she noted his condition had deteriorated. His voice had been weaker, not stronger.

"He choked trying to drink his coffee this morning," Gram had reported.

His speech had been slurred, too, and he had not scored as high on an aphasia performance scale. Before Maren could leave the room that day, Gram had insisted on showing her their promo pictures. It had been hard to imagine this elderly, frightened, quiet couple was really the famous duo Sparky and Gram. There in the picture Maren had seen the white daisy painted on Gram's cheek and Sparky in his black felt bowler hat and big, red, oval mouth. In costume it looked like a small hula hoop was holding up his britches. Gram stood only shoulder high to him.

Gram had tears in her eyes as she related the story to Maren. When their children were grown and gone, the two had looked for something to do together, something that would replace the laughter and fun their children had provided. They had limited resources, but Gram had known someone who belonged to a clown troupe. She hadn't thought her reserved Harold would ever do such an outgoing thing, but he had agreed, out of curiosity, to go through the training with her.

Gram had explained to Maren that each clown's face is unique. Once they created their faces and costumes, Harold had been transformed on the inside as well as on the outside. Under the cover of his new identity, he lost his inhibitions. Someone had commented during an early performance, "He's obviously the spark of the act." That's how he adopted the name Sparky. Gram explained that she had always wanted to be a zany grandma, and being a clown afforded her that opportunity.

The clown troupe had visited Sparky in the hospital several times, sometimes in costume. It hadn't escaped Gram's attention how their visits brightened so many faces there. They had never visited hospitals, Gram admitted, and she regretted that omission.

Maren continued to reminisce about the couple's personalities and the medical details of the case as she drove. She had watched the chart for test results. There had been no evidence of a bleed, yet the CVA appeared to be ongoing. Sparky had been discharged several times, but came back within a few days each time. It had been Maren who evaluated his speech, language, and swallowing function at each admission; and each time function had deteriorated. It had depressed her that she could do nothing for him, nothing for them.

Judy had insisted, "You are providing an essential service. The CT and MRI scans aren't showing anything. PT and OT can't document a difference. The small nuances of speech and language are documenting that something is going on."

"But what?" Maren had asked. "And what can they do about it?"

"That's up to the doctors to figure out," Judy had replied.

Maybe before the end they had figured it out. It didn't matter now. Judy's message said the clowns had been to the hospital in costume on Saturday to say good-bye before the body was removed. Judy's voice had sounded uncharacteristically emotional on the answering machine. "Maren, there is nothing sadder than a whole group of mourning clowns. I'll never forget it." Maren was grateful the conference would keep her away from the publicity. She didn't need to see newscasts or read accounts; the couple was forever etched in her heart.

The first few days of the conference were wonderful, just what Maren needed. She had to concentrate so completely on the lectures she really had little time for worry or anxiety over Nick or patients. She learned more about evaluating and treating voice disorders in the first three days than she could have anticipated. There were groups to chat with and an indoor swimming pool at the hotel where they relaxed in the late afternoon. She was overwhelmed with the intensity, but Judy had warned her not to let that discourage her.

Maren slept soundly for the first time in weeks, feeling virtually free of responsibility, since Judy had promised not to quiz her. "Just bring home the handouts and your notes," she had said. "I'll be able to learn as much as if I'd gone myself."

While Maren still didn't especially like the idea of nasal endoscopy, she found the rigid oral scope something with which she could feel reasonably comfortable. The speech pathologists practiced on each other and with student volunteers to learn the technique.

Judy called on the third night to report that her dad's surgery had gone well. She was ready to talk shop. Maren was happy to comply. "I'm beginning to appreciate the difference between endoscopy and stroboscopy. I always thought it was a miracle to be able to look through the flexible endoscope and see the vocal folds so much more clearly than with just a mirror exam, but I see now why they say stroboscopy is the gold standard. You can watch the mucosal wave move across the top of each vocal fold. I could see the tiny blood vessels of the vocal folds, and during one exam I identified a varix."

Judy had to cut the conversation short, so Maren didn't have the chance to explain how the equipment worked, but she was getting a better understanding than she had predicted. The instrumentation included a miniature camera and xenon light on the end of the rigid scope, which was held in the patient's mouth. The camera took photos based on the pitch of the patient's voice. The photos and voice were instantly recorded, documenting voice and vocal fold movement. Stroboscopy had become the most effective way to diagnose laryngeal abnormalities of anatomy and function. That was the reason ENT physicians and SLPs were working together to incorporate the procedure in their practices. The doctors diagnosed; the SLPs assessed function. The prospects were exciting, although Maren still thought it was too technical for her. She was happy to provide therapy for the patients in a community hospital, but she was sure Judy would love the challenge.

Rick Nolan, Alan Weingarten, and Jim Ferraro were all there from Metropolitan ENT, the group that wanted the strobe at St. John's. By midweek she was thankful Paul had given her his car, enabling her to decline Dr. Nolan's offer to ride with him. The conference appeared to be mainly an opportunity for him to "prowl and howl," as he called it. She heard from three SLPs during the week that he had tried to hit on them. He was amazingly arrogant, claiming to have more expertise than any doctor at the conference. The SLPs weren't sure whether he was claiming professional or sexual expertise. At least he didn't try to compete with Dr. Hiroshu, a world-renowned pioneer in the use of laryngeal surgery and stroboscopy.

The doctors were mainly interested in the lectures on surgical techniques, while the SLPs were fascinated with the presentations giving implications for voice evaluation and therapy. Maren did attend some of the physicians' sessions. All three of the doctors from Metro ENT were attentive and helpful to Maren, answering any technical questions she had. They were anxious to have the strobe venture get off to a good start. Communication and referrals would have to go both ways.

The conference ended Friday, giving participants the opportunity to relax before returning to work. Leaving the last session, Rick Nolan walked next to Maren. He invited her to join the Metro group for dinner at a nearby Mongolian restaurant. She agreed reluctantly, wishing for again for Judy's presence. No wives had come along, and unless other SLPs had been invited, Maren would be the only female. She was under the impression they would all four ride in one car, but in the lobby only Rick Nolan was waiting. He said the other two were placing phone calls home. He would take Maren ahead to assure a place in line, since the restaurant did not take reservations.

Maren reminded herself she was not the swinging single type, and chances were that fact had become obvious to Dr. Nolan during the week.

The others arrived within minutes, and it was just the four of them. The conversation at dinner was congenial, with Weingarten and Ferraro sharing openly about their families, as well as their plans for the strobe. Rick Nolan was a perfect gentleman, even though he out-drank them all. The others seemed not to notice, but Maren became concerned about riding back to the hotel with him.

Dr. Ferraro must have sensed that. He complemented Nolan on his new sports car and pointed out that it would be a shame if Rick dented it after the evening's drinks. Ferraro, Maren noticed, had not had a single drink, and she wondered if they had played out this scene before. Dr. Ferraro begged to sit behind the wheel for the short ride back to the hotel. Meanwhile, Alan Weingarten put his hand on

Maren's elbow, guided her to his car, and delivered her safely to the front door of the hotel.

She was grateful to get in early. She would be able to get another good night's rest before starting home. It was after ten o'clock, when the bellboy knocked at her door to deliver a tray of fresh fruit, cheese, and a bottle of champagne. She started to protest the mistake, but there was her name on the card. It was from Metro ENT. She couldn't refuse. She could have the fruit for breakfast. As the bellboy turned to leave, Rick Nolan brushed past him into Maren's room.

"We have to celebrate our new working arrangement," he said, without a greeting. "We'll have to cooperate to make this strobe investment worthwhile, you know." He picked up the bottle and began opening it. "We could even draw up some guidelines tonight."

She didn't want to be rude or cause a scene. "Dr. Nolan," she began.

"Rick," he instructed her.

"Rick," she began again, "this is very nice"—she gestured at the fruit and wine—"but it's been a long day. I don't think I could concentrate on writing guidelines tonight."

"Of course," he responded apologetically. "What a bore I am. Not very considerate of me. Well, let's just toast the new venture then, and I'll go."

She wasn't allowed to refuse. He had already popped the cork, filled the glasses, and was handing her a drink. Two glasses had been delivered, she now realized. Fortunately, her room was spacious. A small couch, armchair, and low table were arranged in front of a picture window that framed the lights of the city.

Maren resolved to keep the conversation on business. She began by admitting she was a bit hesitant about using scopes, but hurried to assure him that Judy was enthusiastic.

He didn't respond to her comment but began talking about his lonely life. His wife was an advertising model. "You can never touch her, you know, she's always got to be camera-ready. I'll bet you've had an interesting life. What field is your husband in?"

She was surprised that anyone at St. John's didn't know her story but reasoned that his group was just coming into the hospital. Before she could censor her own statements, she revealed that she was a widow. Rick stood up abruptly, extending his hand, as if to say good-bye.

"I'm so sorry," he offered, holding and patting her hand. "Life can knock you down sometimes." While he was talking, he pulled her to her feet, thanked her, and said he must let her get some sleep.

Surprised at his willingness to leave so quickly, she stood and took a step toward the door, attempting to free her hand from his grasp. He didn't move and didn't release her hand. Instead, he pulled her closer. Before she could sidestep, he bent and kissed her. She was still holding the glass of champagne and didn't have a free hand to put between them. As she struggled to pull free, the glass of champagne splashed down his shirt to the floor. Still he wouldn't relinquish his hold on her.

"Dr. Nolan, this won't help our new work relationship." She wasn't frightened at first; she had rebuffed unwanted advances before. Usually, the man would feel awkward and foolish, apologize, and be anxious to leave. Not Rick Nolan.

"I can't resist your red hair… your flaming hair." Obviously he had continued drinking after dinner and now misjudged her character as well as the color of her hair. She dropped the wine glass and pushed harder against his embrace. That seemed to excite him more. "I love a woman with faar." He slurred the word *fire,* and she realized, too late, she had misread the seriousness of the situation.

"Come down here . . ." He pushed her to the couch and pinned her there with his body.

In the movies the woman always threw a full glass of liquid in the man's face, but the wine and the glass were on the floor. *No chance of that now*, she thought in a millisecond.

He was heavy and reeked of alcohol. She felt his hardness and forced herself to think calmly. If struggling turned him on, she would fake unconsciousness. She went limp, and it caught him off guard. She used the instant's advantage she had bought for herself to bring her hands with full force against his chest, pushing him away.

His body thudded heavily to the floor, but Maren was moving before he stopped rolling. She went over the back of the couch and ran for the door. She didn't stop until she got to the check-in desk, where she claimed irately that she had been ringing the desk for a half hour to get someone to remove the tray. She demanded that a bellboy return with her, saying she couldn't sleep with the odor of the cheese and champagne in the room.

The bellboy, an older man with thin, gray hair, surveyed Maren's appearance as he unlocked her door. Odd that she hadn't taken her key. Dr. Nolan had gone, leaving the goblet on the floor where it had fallen. His glass was upright on the small table.

The bellboy took in the appearance of the room as he collected the glasses and tray without comment. He not only did not ask to check her phone, he apologized for the delay in retrieving the cart. To avoid making eye contact with him, she focused her gaze on the generous tip in her hand. He reminded her to use the chain lock. "Remember," he told her, "there is no room service available after ten o'clock."

Chapter 14

The day dawned crystal clear and piercingly cold as Maren opened her eyes. She got up immediately, anxious to be going home but realizing the memories of the previous night were going with her. *There seem to be more and more complexities to deal with at the hospital*, she lamented.

How can we pretend to work amicably together, she wondered, as she placed her bags on the backseat.

The drive home seemed longer than the drive north had been. After an hour she became aware of the beginning of cramps in her back. At first she thought it was from five days of sitting, followed by another long drive, but when the tension crept around her waist and spread throughout her pelvis, she knew she was in for what she called "cruel cramps."

She stopped for coffee and took three pills instead of two. If she hadn't been driving Paul's car, she would have driven straight to Edgelawn. The roads were dry, but traffic was heavy for a Saturday morning, increasing her tension. She knew she should have eaten some breakfast, but she couldn't force herself to risk facing any of the participants from the conference in the coffee shop. Being home was her priority.

She finally arrived at Paul's door at eleven. He wasn't home and had not left a note. She searched the bathroom cabinet and found a heating pad. Fear joined pain and they increased together. It had never before been this severe when she was away from home.

Just get into bed and plug in the heating pad, she told herself. She kicked off her shoes and slipped under the covers in the guest bed she had come to think of as hers. The pain continued to intensify until she was sick to her stomach. She forced herself out of bed and lurched into the bathroom, where she passed out on the green and white tile floor.

⸺

Jamie Bonet was late, not by minutes or hours, but by days. She usually finished Paul's house on Thursday, but she had taken on too many projects this week. Her hands ached from the arthritis, but she liked working hard and loved the McCloud family.

She had first met Bob and Gloria in New Orleans long before Dr. Paul went to medical school there. Jamie's mixed ancestry included one-quarter French, one-quarter African, and half Native American. She was not a large woman, but was solid with powerful arms. If she had an accent, it was Chicago. She could have passed for Italian. She was simply an American with a dark complexion.

Her father had been an alcoholic who left the family when Jamie was a toddler. Her mother had worked in a hotel days and waited tables at night to support them. She had tried to keep Jamie with her, but eventually had agreed to give her to foster parents until she could get a better job.

About that time the McClouds stayed in the small hotel where Jamie's mother worked. The McClouds met Jamie's mom again when they happened into the little bistro where she waited tables in the evenings. There they heard her story and decided they needed some household help for Gloria, who had two small children to care for. Bob and Gloria insisted Jamie be included, so she grew up in Chicago and married a kind, hard-working midwesterner.

Jamie and her husband now had several children of their own, and she cared for her aging mother as well as the McCloud family. She really didn't have to clean houses for the income anymore, but she liked the idea of taking care of the McClouds. She did Elizabeth's and Penny's as well as Bob and Gloria's and Paul's homes. They all trusted her implicitly. She was practically one of the family.

This week Jamie's mother had required more attention than usual. Jamie hoped Paul wouldn't mind her being at his place on the weekend.

Seeing his car in the back, she rang the bell instead of using her key. When he didn't answer, she let herself in. Not wanting to startle him, she called out. There was no answer. Maybe he was out with friends. So much the better, she thought; she would finish quickly and be gone before he returned.

She started upstairs to check the guest bathroom and bedroom. It was being used more frequently, she had noticed. She smiled, wondering who the lucky woman was. She flipped the switch at the top of the stairs to light the hall, turned into the bathroom, and let out a scream before she could stop herself. On the floor in front of her lay Maren Kepple.

Jamie dropped to her knees beside Maren, afraid the woman was dead. Maren felt warm though and moaned when Jamie moved her. She was breathing and didn't appear injured. Jamie wondered again why Dr. Paul wasn't there. Before she could decide what to do, Maren opened her eyes. Her knees pulled up automatically as she moaned with the next wave of cramping.

"Take it easy, take it easy," Jamie said "I'll help you to bed. Do you know where Dr. Paul is?"

"Maybe at his parents," whispered Maren. Her fear of the pain outdistanced her fear of the stranger.

"You're not pregnant, are you?" asked Jamie bluntly.

"Not a chance," replied Maren, summoning her strength. She told Jamie she had some medication for cramps in her purse.

Jamie snorted under her breath. "When you pass out on the floor, it can hardly be called cramps."

She gave the jar to Maren, got a glass of water from the bathroom, and retreated to the kitchen to brew some tea her mother's people used to make. The ingredients were leaves and roots of prairie plants and forbs. She kept Paul's kitchen stocked and considered these to be necessities, although he never used them.

She returned with the hot drink and asked Maren how long it had been since she had eaten. They introduced themselves then, and Jamie phoned the older McCloud's home. No answer. She left a message and tried Paul's pager, but it wasn't turned on.

Paul was, at that moment, leaving Penny's home, where the family had enjoyed a midmorning brunch followed by Paul, Jim, Bob, and

Gloria playing tennis. The others were going to spend the afternoon together and attend evening mass. They weren't surprised that Paul had other plans. He was looking forward to a long visit with Maren and a late dinner.

While Maren sipped the tea, Jamie fixed eggs and toast and brought the plate upstairs. Jamie wondered if Paul knew this woman was in his house. She must be an expected guest, maybe the regular guest. After all, Jamie reasoned, she got in.

As the food and hot drink soaked in, Maren began to recover. Now she felt more embarrassed than frightened. She began to make polite conversation, but Jamie was again blunt.

"Are you dating Dr. Paul?"

Taken aback, Maren stammered, "Yes...no..., uh yes, I, I suppose so."

"You don't sound too sure," prodded Jamie. "Most women would be proud to date Dr. Paul."

"Oh, Jamie, it's just not that simple. I really like Paul, but there are things . . . things which will always keep us apart." Maren would look back later and wonder how they had managed to have such a personal conversation in such a short time. That was just Jamie; she didn't make small talk or put up with pretense. Or maybe the tea had some effect.

"What things can keep people apart who love each other? Even when I was in a foster home, my mother found ways to see me and let me know she loved me."

Jamie's bluntness brought out bluntness in Maren. "Death, Jamie, death can separate people even though they love each other. My mother and father, and my husband are all gone, and I'm much older than Paul. I see no point in leaving him alone and childless when he could be making a good life and watching his children grow, with a companion his own age."

It was the first time Maren had expressed her pain and fear in such stark words. It was a passionate outburst, leaving Jamie silent for a moment, her lips clamped shut in a tight line. Then sadly she shook her head and said ominously, "Cautantowwit alone decides how many days and nights we each may have. Dr. Paul knows the legend. To some another season is given. You have no right to interfere with your fate, no right."

Maren felt for a moment that Jamie was about to cast a spell on her, but before she could respond, they heard the front door open. Jamie went to meet Paul. From the stricken look on his face when she told him what had happened, she immediately understood the depth of his feeling for Maren. This one was not a casual acquaintance. Jamie watched from the entryway while he bolted up the stairs, two and three at a time, to assess Maren's condition for himself.

Paul checked her pulse and observed her color automatically. The crisis was obviously past. He was alarmed that menstrual cramps had rendered her unconscious—another piece of the puzzle that Maren was to him. She had never mentioned having such a problem.

Jamie, like an old chief with authority, asked Paul to come speak with her in his study. She would return later in the week to clean, she told him. Then, "If you love this one, you should remember the legend of Drops of a Spring Water."

Before Paul could answer, she was out the door. He shook his head. Sometimes Jamie was as American as apple pie. Other times there was an eerie quality about her she must have gotten from all the summers on the reservation with her mother's people.

Paul made a fire and Maren came down for some of the Chinese food Paul had brought with him for their dinner. He wasn't hungry, but now that the pain had subsided Maren was famished, even after the eggs and toast. In between bites of egg drop soup she told him about the week, the good and the part about Rick Nolan. Paul's chest tightened and his fingers curled around the arm of the couch and dug into the fabric as he listened.

"Why didn't you tell the desk clerk what happened?"

"I don't know. Maybe I was afraid I might have been partly to blame."

He thought she might have some guilt about her manner or dress or some deep-seated problem with her sexual identity. "How?"

"I didn't want to drink on the job, so when Nolan kept pouring more into my glass at dinner, I poured mine into his when he wasn't looking. I did that several times at the restaurant when they went back to the serving tables."

Paul laughed out loud. "I'll bet he'll have a whopping hangover."

He started to tell her about the avenues for reporting the unethical behavior, but she held up a hand and stopped him.

"I'm not going there Paul," she stated adamantly. "In the first place I have enough on my plate right now. In the second place I've seen what women have to go through when they report such incidents. I'll just laugh this off and hope he won't remember it ever happened. Unfortunately, I think this is standard operating procedure for him."

She didn't know then that her words were not only accurate but prophetic.

—

Maren stayed overnight, after confirming that Nick was with Steve. She drove home after breakfast on Sunday, leaving Paul to feel that the house was oddly empty. It had never seemed empty when he had been alone there before.

He paced around trying to decide what to do next and found himself facing the bookshelves in his dining room study. There in front of him was the old leather-bound gift Jamie had given him when he graduated from med school: <u>American Indian Poems, Legends, and Medicine.</u> He wiped dust from the top of the old collection and took it to his wing-backed recliner by the fire.

He read for an hour, refreshing his memory about the old religious beliefs of the Navajo. He had actually read all of the volume at one time. The Navajo believed the winds were gods. To each was attributed certain characteristics. When you thought about it, the concept of a spirit-god with multiple personalities wasn't so different from the Christian belief in the Trinity. The wind-gods had children, some of whom were messengers to men, not unlike the concept of angels recorded in Christian scripture.

North Wind made the world pale in winter. South Wind joined East Wind and West Wind to defeat North Wind. Kind of like the battle with the fallen angel, Paul rationalized. The three winds extracted a promise from North Wind that the earth would be green for six months. The four agreed and made laws that governed the earth. South Wind would sometimes blow during winter to bring rain. In spring, South, West, and East winds could play together to melt the frozen land. In summer, West Wind would blow softly to comfort the land.

That part reminded Paul of the story of the great flood and the rainbow of promise.

"'The Legend of Drops of a Spring Water'—ah, here it is," Paul said out loud and began to read.

South Wind's offspring were four boys and a girl. The boys were Proud Rain Wind, Excrement Face, Rain Under the Knee, and Going Behind the Mountain. The girl was named Drops of a Spring Water. She was given in marriage to Frozen, a powerful force. She became frozen in his land and sent a message to her father to rescue her. South Wind dispatched one warrior after another to bring her back safely. The first three were driven away by impenetrable cold rain. Going Behind the Mountain succeeded because he approached slowly and enlisted his brothers to bring fierce rains to melt the frozen land. He brought Drops of a Spring Water home safely.

Paul stopped. He felt someone was in the room with him. He looked up, just as the fire sparkled from a gust of wind blowing down the chimney. He tried to shake off the eerie feeling, but the parallel didn't escape him. He had come to believe that Maren was frozen somehow. Something was keeping her from permitting an intimate relationship to develop, and his instincts did tell him to go slowly. He did want to bring her home to the warmth and safety of his love.

Undoubtedly, others have tried to rescue her, he realized in the back of his mind.

He went to the kitchen and made a cup of strong tea, mostly so the activity would bring him back to reality. Setting his mug on the lamp table beside his chair, he went to poke at the fire.

When he picked up the old book again, he found the poem he was looking for. Maren had asked him who Cautantowwit was, and Paul wondered what Jamie had been telling her. He remembered the name was from an old Indian poem. There was no author's name, no credit for translation. He read it aloud, as he had been taught poetry should be read.

Cautantowwit's Time

Winter belongs to North Wind.
A time of frozen water,
a time of howling, painful gusts
that makes the earth lie pale and still,
controlled. Sleeping life
and dormant seeds await a rescue from the South.

South Wind calls East and West
to play and dance and sing.
Warm rain melts the rigid land,
awakes the dormant ones,
and thaws the frozen lives.
Guileless play
defeats the great North Wind.

West Wind brings a time of comfort on the land.
Every living thing now has a chance
to grow, to rest, produce new seed,
and be the best that each can be,
before the cycle can repeat.
Gentle breezes blow.

East Wind plays with West wind.
And like capricious youth,
they blow both warm and cool,
spraying seeds from pod and head,
the promise of another year.
Together they repel the force of North and South,
a pattern known on earth since time began.

Cautantowwit rules the earth
and all that is upon it.
He completes the work or joy
left undone by other gods.
Days of windless warmth with clear blue skies
and long cool nights, lighted by the yellow-orange moon,
are numbered by Creator God alone.

Spring: Playtime of the Winds

South Wind calls East and West
to play and dance and sing.
Warm rain melts the rigid land,
awakes the dormant ones,
and thaws the frozen lives.
Guileless play
defeats the great North Wind.

Chapter 15

Maren grabbed the handhold on the outside of the cabin, pulled herself onto the wing of the red and white Comanche, and slid deftly into the right seat. Steve had picked her up at 7:30 this morning for the trip to Wisconsin. He had completed the walk-around and supervised while the line boy added fuel. Now they were ready for the preflight checklist. While he ran up the engine and checked gauges, Maren reviewed the sequence of events and emotions once more.—

Steve had asked her earlier in the week if she would donate the last Saturday of March to a worthy cause. He needed her to help him open their cottage on Lake Mazon for the season. He said he didn't want to face Pam's belongings alone, as if she had died. Maren realized that she was dead as far as Steve was concerned, and going through her things was not going to be pleasant for him. In his hurt and anger he would probably throw everything in a bag and trash it, if left on his own.

Maren continued to feel some allegiance to Pam. The women and their husbands and children had spent many days together at the lake house, especially in the early years. Maren hadn't been there much in recent times, but Megan and Pam had lived in the cottage the past four summers while Megan worked at one of the resorts in the area. Pam would undoubtedly have left clothing and other items in the house.

"Ready?" Steve asked through the headset microphone.

"Ready," she responded through her mic. They could talk comfortably to each other using the headsets, in spite of the noise of the one hundred eighty horsepower engine just outside the window.

That is, they could talk as long as air traffic control wasn't on. Steve pushed the throttle to the panel, and the plane accelerated down the runway into the wind. At eighty-five knots he pulled back on the wheel, starting a smooth, steady climb through four thousand feet. Maren watched a wispy puff of cloud brush past the wing. Through her headset she could hear Steve talking with ATC.

While Steve was occupied with the climb and talking to the tower, Maren returned to her private thoughts. Besides her loyalty to Pam and Megan, she felt she still owed Steve an immense debt for his help after Jack's death. She realized she would have had a much more difficult time without his assistance. It had been financial affairs, not personal belongings, that Steve had helped her clean up. Jack had always been so busy taking care of his clients' finances that he neglected his own. He had always said when he turned fifty he would set his financial house in order.

How could he even think that way, she wondered again, *when his father had died of a sudden heart attack before Jack's fifteenth birthday? Maybe it was some sort of defense mechanism, a denial of his mortality.*

All the old memories mingled with more recent memories and played through Maren's mind again. It had to be humiliating for Steve to lose his wife and need to ask for help. He was always helping other folks solve their problems, but seemed unable to solve his own. Maren wondered for the thousandth time what had gone wrong for them. She had known immediately that she couldn't refuse to help Steve, even though it meant breaking a date with Paul. Much to her relief, Paul had said he understood. He had no choice but to understand.

Flying was a freeing experience, and Maren began to relax and enjoy the panorama. She always got a new perspective up here above the earth. Each person and building looked so small. She always felt a little closer to God when she went up in their Comanche. Airliners didn't give her the same effect. She felt like a passenger in a big bus there, shades drawn, a movie playing. But here, sitting up front like this with windows almost surrounding her, she felt she got God's view of life. There were no lines to separate states, counties, or people, yet she was close enough to identify individual homes, cars, and even children shooting baskets in their driveways. *How small each of us is*, she thought, again.

Steve interrupted her reverie, asking if she wanted to fly. She smiled and shook her head. "No, but I'll hold the course for you until you get the sectional."

She took the yoke and kept the wings parallel to the horizon while he turned to his flight bag, selected the appropriate chart, and folded it to display their current position. She had never been interested in pursuing her own pilot's license, but Jack had insisted she learn enough about flying to safely hold a course for him and land in an emergency.

There wasn't much talk after that. They both watched for traffic that FAA controllers called out, and she reset the altimeter when a change in barometric pressure was reported. They were in a high-pressure area, so not much change was required.

It was just before noon when they circled the Lakeland County field. They had enjoyed the benefits of tailwinds all the way up, which had given them ground speeds of one hundred sixty-five knots and a smooth ride. She knew that could mean a long trip with headwinds going home, unless the wind diminished.

There was not even a Unicom base on the field, just a windsock to help pilots decide whether to choose the paved north-south runway or the east-west grass strip. Today the prevailing south wind called for use of the paved runway.

She reflected on all the lessons for life she had learned from aviation while Steve brought the plane skillfully to the runway. *Head into the wind for take-off and landing.* That meant face your problems head on—less chance of being unexpectedly and unnecessarily upset.

The left then right wheels met the pavement. *Errt, errt.*

Plan your trip carefully.

The nose gear touched noiselessly to the runway.

Always have an alternate destination in mind, just in case the flight doesn't go as expected.

This flight had been textbook perfect, and Steve's landing was gentle.

Know your options. She continued the mental list while he taxied to a tie-down spot. *Have a plan B.*

That was always a good idea.

Maren opened the door, stepped out onto the wing, grabbed the handhold, and jumped to the grass. Steve followed her. The air was bracing. Upper Wisconsin was considerably colder than Illinois, even with today's south wind.

She took the chocks from Steve and put the wooden wedges in front and back of each wheel. He quickly and expertly took the ropes that were attached to heavy metal rings imbedded in the ground, slid each through a metal ring on the underside of each wing, and tied the plane securely. They weren't expecting bad weather; it was just routine.

They zipped jackets and bent their heads into the wind for the short walk toward the shack that served as a planning area for pilots. Nearby was their nearly antique Ford station wagon parked and waiting. They had one of the year-round residents run it every couple of weeks, but Maren was always relieved to hear the engine start.

Although it was cold, the sky was clear and the sun bright, an ideal day for a flight or a drive. It would be a good day to be working in the cottage, she reflected, enjoying the warmth of the sun through the window of the old car while Steve loaded their things in the back.

Maren had set the wonderful lunch and homemade French apple pie she had baked on the backseat. There were no restaurants for miles, so they always took food. In the summer there were places along the lake to eat, but you had to go by boat. Steve wouldn't put the boat in for another eight weeks. The lake would likely be ice-covered until then.

It was a forty-minute drive to the cottage. As they rode, Maren remembered again how disappointed Paul had looked when she had told him. He had said only, "I understand," but she could tell. She was disappointed, too. They had planned to take a walk or ride bikes along the lake and have brunch today. Steve noticed her serious expression.

"Is this still hard on you, coming here?"

"Oh, no," she lied. "I was just wondering if I put everything in the lunch basket. I haven't done this for a while." She couldn't tell him she had made a sacrifice for him. She couldn't imagine how much he had sacrificed for her.

They pulled up to the cottage, which was a two-story house with a stone front facing the lake. The large jutting stones and green shutters made it look warm and friendly, even on such a cold day. According to

Jack, it had been built by two brothers. When one died unexpectedly, Jack and Steve had bought it for a song.

Over fifteen years ago Steve and Jack had installed a small oil furnace. Before that there was only a wood-burning stove, quite an experience for the boys and Megan. Pam and Maren visited more frequently as more amenities were added, although there had been indoor plumbing from the beginning.

Maren looked out at the icy lake and remembered how Jack had loved the water, whether it was river, lake, or ocean; he hadn't been able to get enough. He had died in the water, just a few miles from this house. Maren had been back only a few times since then, once to collect their belongings, once at Steve and Pam's insistence for a family picnic weekend. The boys had enjoyed a few more visits with Steve, but neither of them had Jack's passion for outdoor life.

Today was different. This was for Steve. He had lost his friend and now his wife. His life was torn, even as Maren's had been. He pushed the door open and walked through ahead of her, just in case some critters had gained entry during the winter. "One thing about life, it doesn't stay the same," Steve pronounced philosophically, looking around.

Maren wanted to console him. She quoted words she had heard him use many times. "Troubles are like thunderstorms, Steve. They come and they go."

He set to work making the plumbing operational, while she cleaned the red and white checked vinyl tablecloth that was always on the round oak table and laid out their lunch.

Paul felt empty but had no desire for food. He stepped outside his back door and watched a small plane overhead. He understood Maren's need to help Steve. He just hoped she wouldn't confuse that need with any other emotion.

Paul didn't fly. He didn't fish. He sailed a bit with his dad, but didn't venture far. He was a doctor, a surgeon. He had spent his whole life becoming a respected specialist, but on this sunny spring morning he felt distinctly deficient.

Penny found him standing there in his backyard, staring at the sky. "Hey, I looked all over for you. What are you doing, planning a garden?"

Paul turned around to see his sister walking toward him. The sun illuminated her face, giving her an especially radiant look. The handful of freckles sprinkled across her nose spilled out onto her cheeks, making her look younger than she was. He felt brighter just seeing her. She was always full of life, full of energy.

"Hey, Pen. What are you doing in this part of town? Is the shop closed?"

"Jennifer's working today. I'm grocery shopping while Jim's home with Erin. How about a cup of tea?"

"Did you bring some of your herb brew?" he teased.

"I knew you wouldn't have any decaffeinated, unless it was some of Jamie's potions. Have you had breakfast?"

He shook his head, remembering Jamie's potions and predictions.

"Well, why don't you make us an omelet? I'll get some fruit from the car."

"What makes you so sure I don't have fruit?"

"I know your lifestyle."

"Well, it so happens I have a quart of strawberries," he gloated. He didn't mention that they were to have been part of brunch after a bike ride that wasn't going to happen.

Penny was four years younger than Paul and had idolized him all her life. She felt she knew him better than anyone else. He wasn't home enough to have a quart of berries unless he planned on guests.

"Maren or someone new?" she asked.

Color crept into his face and he retorted more sharply than he intended. "What makes you think I only get food for women?"

"Plural?" she teased.

"No."

"Oh, just one then." Penny was the only one who could get away with such teasing or get him to divulge details of his private life before he volunteered. Usually he didn't mind. They had always been close, maybe more so because of her torticollis.

They walked through the back door into Paul's kitchen.

"Pretty sure you'd find me home, weren't you?"

"Well, you do usually sleep a little later on Saturday."

They went inside, and Paul cooked while Penny cleaned the berries.

"You going to tell me about her?" Penny asked.

He gave her a quick look and returned to chopping onions, making no attempt to answer. She became concerned. It wasn't like Paul to be so quiet.

"I'll tell you my secrets if you tell me yours," she coaxed sweetly.

"What secrets?"

Now she had hooked him. "You first," she urged.

"No, you first," he insisted. "You can't keep secrets from your doctor-brother."

"Do you promise to tell all if I do?"

"Penny, it is Maren, or rather, was," he admitted, without actually promising to reveal everything. "She broke our date this morning for another guy, an old friend. He's flying them to Wisconsin to open a cabin that they own jointly. That's it."

"Is she mad at you?" Penny probed.

"Penny," he warned, in an exasperated tone.

"Okay," she interrupted, "I'll tell you my secret, then you finish your story. Deal?"

"Sure," he half-heartedly promised. "What's the secret?" He was intrigued. Penny usually blabbed everything without preamble. She had never been able to keep a secret, at least not from Paul.

"I'm pregnant!" Her face lit up.

Paul was surprised and extremely pleased. No wonder she looked so radiant. He knew Penny and Jim had been seeing a fertility specialist. She had asked him for a recommendation to a clinic. Jim's diabetes had been diagnosed when they began investigating why they were unable to provide Erin with a little sister or brother. They had begun planning for in vitro fertilization. He had wished they wouldn't, because of the high risk of multiple births, but he had told her he'd be there with them whatever they decided.

"So, how many?" he asked cautiously.

"We didn't do it, Paul. We spent some time relaxing at Pine Bluff instead."

Pine Bluff had always been a great gathering place for the family and now obviously had become a perfect "honeymoon" spot.

"That's great, Pen."

"Due December 15th." She paused only a moment. "Now, it's your turn."

"Huh?" He tried to dodge but knew he was caught. He tried to lead her off the track by confiding about his increasing frustration with Granger and Lancaster. He had put out some feelers for other office space. In fact, he had found a medical suite that would be available midsummer.

"You'd go out on your own, no partner?" Penny probed.

"That's the idea."

"It would be like starting over, wouldn't it?" she asked naively.

"It would be starting over," he replied glumly.

"That sounds hard after all you've been through already."

"Umm," was his only comment as he concentrated intently on turning the hash browns. She tenaciously returned to the subject.

"But how are things between you and Maren, other than the pilot friend?"

"Well, she's still adjusting to life at the hospital." He dodged her question, not very skillfully.

"I was asking about your relationship, or is that too personal? You just look like there are some things on your mind."

"You are one very perceptive sister." He smiled for the first time.

They finished preparing the food Paul had bought for Maren and himself, and he shared with his sister things he would share with no one else.

"After dinner last night, we were eating Eli's cheesecake right here." He tapped the table. "Maren started telling me what it was like after Jack died. I didn't realize at first that she was preparing me for something.

"She was quite naturally grief stricken. She said she was numb and had very little energy. She spent what energy she could muster on the boys and getting started in grad school. She really didn't have the time, the energy, or the experience to deal with all the financial decisions she had to make."

Paul tried to read Penny's expression to see if she was following the story. His sister only nodded encouraging him to continue.

"Through it all Steve was always there for her. She said she couldn't have survived without his support. She would have had to drop out of grad school and that experience was what gave her hope for the future."

"It must have given her a break from grieving, to focus on something so demanding." Penny nodded, still not understanding the problem.

"Exactly," Paul confirmed. "This fall Steve's wife left him, out of the blue, so to speak. She took off without leaving so much as a note. It took days for him to locate her. She's definitely not interested in reconciliation. Their daughter is in college in Michigan. I think Maren's been trying to be a source of emotional support for Steve and his daughter. I know Maren took some time off work to drive the girl back to school for him after the holidays."

Penny, beginning to comprehend how interwoven the lives of the two families had been, recognized immediately the possibility that her brother would have his heart broken. She tensed, but did not interrupt.

"Last week," Paul continued, unaware of Penny's insights, "Steve asked Maren to help him open their lake house and clean out the wife's belongings. Even though we already had plans for today, Maren said there was no way she could refuse him."

Penny flinched. That didn't bode well for Paul's relationship with her. "Are you serious about her?"

He answered with a look and a sigh that told her everything. "I was feeling pretty inadequate when you showed up. I didn't think I wanted to talk about it, but I'm really glad you came."

Instead of answering, Penny asked for more information. "Mom and Dad said you've been keeping in touch with her boys."

"I e-mail Matt regularly, and I have made a couple side trips to see Nick when I had meetings downstate." The truth was, Paul had outright manufactured several excuses to travel through Champaign, just to spend a couple of hours with Nick.

"Is she doing any better about the age thing?"

"Not really." His answers were short now, a sign she was getting too close for his comfort.

"Sorry, Paul. I didn't mean to grill you. I just wanted to help."

"You just want to see me married." He smiled wearily.

"That too," she responded in a lighter tone.

They began filling their plates, and for a few minutes neither spoke. Then, attempting to say something positive to close the conversation, Penny tried to convey that Paul and Maren made a nice-looking couple. "Well, you two look well-matched physically."

Paul was startled, misunderstanding the comment. "What would make you say that? You don't know that's true at all. She had one lover for eighteen years. That's physical compatibility—not wondering, but knowing when and where and how to touch, how the other will respond. . . ."

It all came out in a rush. Some of the intensity diminished as he ran out of words to express his concerns, and he noticed that Penny had dropped a paring knife on the counter and was staring open-mouthed at him.

"So that's it," she said quietly. "Paul McCloud, voted most desirable doctor in three hospitals . . ."

"Don't rub it in Penny," he stopped her.

"No electricity?" she asked cautiously.

"On both sides." He half smiled and cocked one eyebrow, acknowledging their mutual attraction.

"Then, I don't understand."

"I just have this sense that she'll close down if we get too close physically."

Penny hesitated a moment, measuring her words carefully. "Paul, a woman can open her body to a man in the way you want, only if she has opened her mind and emotions and soul first. Is she opening up to you on those levels?"

There was the nagging missing piece. He hadn't been able to put his finger on it, but Penny identified it immediately. Maren did open up to him intellectually, without hesitation. With encouragement she was beginning to share her emotions with him. But her heart and soul were locked deep inside. He believed the evidence was that he had yet to visit her home in Edgelawn. She kept him separate from her home life, at the other end of the tracks.

"I'm not sure what all you mean by her soul, but she keeps her home life separate. How do I get past that?" he asked aloud.

As they ate, Penny studied Paul. She loved her brother so much. She had hoped Maren would truly appreciate him and be capable of giving him the love he needed and deserved. Now, she imagined Maren and Steve flying off to a secluded cottage on a beautiful spring day, a couple whose lives had intertwined for years. How easy it would be for them to slip into physical intimacy. Penny felt a surge of urgency. Something would have to change quickly, before the inevitable occurred.

"Why don't you take a couple of days off and take Maren to Pine Bluff," she suggested.

"Sure," Paul nodded, "that's a great idea, but how does that get me into her house?"

"The house isn't as important as you think, Paul. It's what it represents. And Paul," she warned ominously, "don't wait. Do it right away."

After lunch Steve left to arrange for the bass boat and his inboard-outboard boat to be moved from storage after the thaw. He returned to the house to find Maren had bagged nearly all of Pam's property, keeping a few things out that she felt Pam might like to have returned to her.

The sun would be getting low soon. It was time to start back.

"Steve, are you sure this isn't premature? Maybe she'll come back."

"I don't want her to." His answer was quiet, but hard. "It hasn't been good between us for years, but I didn't want to admit it. I wouldn't have made the break, and frankly I'm surprised she had the guts to do it."

"Oh, Steve." She tried to stop him from making statements that he might regret later.

He held up a hand to silence her. "Maren, I really appreciate your coming along today. Even if you hadn't sorted through these things for me, I just didn't want to come alone."

"I understand," she said quietly. "It's the least I could do."

They were standing together beside the heavy oak table, watching through tall, dirt-streaked windows as the bold orange sun started its descent toward the far shore of the lake. They had both lost so much and shared so much. It was tempting to stay and watch the sun set together, like seeing the final scene of an emotion-packed movie; but it was time to go.

Steve turned, put his hands on her shoulders, and looked down at her.

"Thanks, Maren. You're a good friend."

Instinctively, she put her arms around him and hugged him. "You've done more for me than I can ever repay, Steve."

Their cheeks were so close. He brushed hers with his lips. Instinctively, she returned his gesture, touching his cheek lightly with her lips. In that instant she knew he was going to really kiss her. Before she could decide if she wanted him to or not, he tipped his head until their lips met. When she didn't resist, he pulled her closer and held her with his kiss.

She felt suspended, the way a trapeze artist supports his lady by a cord held in his teeth. She was spinning below him now, like the partner at the end of the cord.

Steve controlled her thoughts through the power of his lips and embrace. His arms enclosed her, a storm of passion sweeping over him. She felt something in herself begin to stir, while he continued to control her with the thread of their kiss.

As he pulled her tighter against his body, she stiffened.

"Oh, Steve . . ." Her voice was hoarse with emotion. Her hands came around from his back to push against his chest, separating them. He allowed his hands to fall limply to his sides, offering no resistance to their separation, but his deep-set, dark brown eyes stared hungrily into hers, pleading. "We'd better go," she managed, lowering her gaze. He only nodded as he picked up the last of the bags.

The flight home was picture perfect and smooth as glass, thanks to the wind tapering off. Brilliant stars began to appear, suspended in a dark blue, then black sky. Steve glanced at her from time to time and smiled, as if they shared a new secret. Twice he reached over and patted her hand. Maren pretended to sleep.

Chapter 16

"You'll need an interpreter," Judy called as Maren headed for third floor. "We think he only speaks Spanish."

How could they know, Maren wondered, *if he hasn't spoken?* Obediently, she paged Flora, one of the hospital interpreters. As soon as Flora arrived at the nurses' station, they went to the patient's bedside. "Buenas días, Señor Perez," Flora repeated over and over. "Abierta la boca." Each time there was no verbal response. He did turn his head to look at them and smiled broadly while nodding his head. Whether that meant he understood remained unclear.

Señor Perez had been transferred to a local nursing home from out of state a week ago. He had developed several medical complications, including a bladder infection, dehydration, and impacted bowels, thus his hospital admit. The nursing staff was concerned because he never spoke. No one knew if he had suffered a CVA or if he had some other pathology that affected his speech. Swallowing was within normal limits; and he followed some directions, whether given in Spanish or in English, as long as ample gestures were used.

"It was the same yesterday when I came up here with Judy," reported Flora.

"Well, I'm sorry to call you for nothing. I could have said, 'Buenas días, Señor Perez.'"

"Ah," replied Flora with a knowing look, "but what if he answered you?"

Maren returned to the nurses' station and began to report her findings to Señor Perez's nurse, Carol. They were in the process of reviewing the patient's entire history when a young doctor bustled up to the counter talking loudly. It was obvious he was talking about Señor Perez.

"Oh, we were just talking about him. Maybe you can help."

"Anything to help such lovely ladies." His arrogance was apparent. Carol looked at Maren, encouraging her to continue.

"We've been trying to figure out why he doesn't speak," Maren explained.

"It's because the king is down . . ."—he nearly shouted—". . . the leveler of all humanity. That's why they sent for me. I'm the butt doctor."

"And you're going to help him speak?" Maren asked the gastroenterologist incredulously.

"When the king is down, everything is down," he continued, projecting his voice across the stage of the nurses' station.

Abruptly, he turned and began a verbal repartee with the clerk. Maren took the opportunity to move outside of the counter that enclosed the nurses' station. Carol followed her into the kitchenette.

"Who is that?" Maren asked with raised eyebrows.

"Just Dr. Branson, the gastroenterologist. He's quite a character."

"He's obnoxious. Why do patients put up with him?"

Carol giggled. "I guess because he's a really good butt doctor, and most people appreciate the comic relief."

Maren watched as Dr. Brad, as he was called, laughed with a physician at the elevator. It seemed safe, so she returned to finish her note in Señor Perez's chart. As she reached for a pen and pulled a chair over, she realized someone was staring down at her. A tall woman with large glasses was stretched over the counter to get closer to Maren.

"Is it you?" the woman asked dramatically. "Is it really you?"

"I think it's me," Maren said as if uncertain. She held her ID badge up for the woman to inspect.

"Patricia," gasped the woman, "I haven't seen you in years."

"You're not seeing me now either," replied Maren with a smile.

"Oh?" The woman, now looked at the name tag Maren held out. "Oh. Don't worry, I won't tell." She ambled down the hall, without looking back.

I'll bet she thought Patricia was a spy, Maren imagined. First the butt doctor, now this odd exchange. *Must be a full moon,* she decided, picking up the phone to page Judy. "I'm going back to the office. If there are any more patients on three today, you get them," she stated without explanation.

That was how they happened to switch schedules and Maren, not Judy, saw Allison.

She wanted to call her Peanut or Pip-squeak, she was so small. Allison weighed eighteen or twenty pounds, about the size of a ten-month-old, but she was already two. Maren was the first of the rehab team to evaluate her.

Allison went with Maren eagerly. She had such a big smile it made her eyes crinkle into half moons. Her tiny hand took hold of Maren's finger for the short walk down the hall from Rita's desk to the therapy room.

Maren had a copy of the Preschool Language Scale but wasn't sure Allison's attention span would be long enough to administer it formally. She brought a small box of cold cereal to use for positive reinforcement during testing, just in case. She frequently could coax children to continue performing far beyond the level where they wished to stop by using rewards, such as pieces of cereal.

Allison's only word through the whole session was "uh-oh," in a small, squeaky voice. Other sounds were just grunts, accompanied by gestures. She was tired of looking at Maren's picture book within fifteen minutes.

When Allison saw the food, all activity ceased until she obtained it. She seemed extremely hungry. Her tiny hands shook as she grabbed for the box. When a piece fell on the floor, Maren scooped it up and tossed it into the waste can. Allison bolted for the waste can, dug through the refuse until she found the crumb, and popped it into her mouth before Maren could stop her. Maren allowed her to finish the small box of cereal. The child's hands were more steady after the snack.

The presenting diagnosis was microcephaly, small brain. Maren wondered what else was going on with the child—low blood sugar, a muscle tone problem, some other neurological or endocrine disorder, or just excitement in a new environment.

Allison responded with alertness, unlike anyone Maren had ever seen with microcephaly. True, her speech was severely delayed. True, her head was small, but her body was also diminutive. And she was cute as the proverbial button with her long brown hair, straight-cut bangs, and big brown eyes.

She was, unfortunately, a ward of the state, the center of a bitter custody battle. She had been removed from her mother's care because of medical neglect. She could be simply suffering from malnutrition, or she could have a rare syndrome.

One thing about the medical field, Maren thought once more, there was always another mystery to solve, something else to learn. She was eager to solve the mystery that was Allison.

When PT, OT, and speech worked with a child as a team, a team leader was designated, depending on the child's most serious deficits. Maren would be Allison's rehab team leader for many weeks to come, as together they would try to solve the puzzle that came in this eighteen-pound package.

Maren returned Allison to the caseworker in the waiting room and picked up a new order for speech therapy for Howard Schumann. Rita had highlighted "Wm. Schumann, M.D." at the bottom of the sheet, not in the spot for the name of the physician who wrote the order, but where a note was made if the patient was a relative of a hospital employee.

Bill Schumann was a respected pediatrician. Maren had worked with him on several cases. She had heard he was taking over Allison's care after the next court hearing. He spent most of his time at the larger David Stone Medical Center for Children, but Maren had seen him coming into St. John's at five or six in the evening to check or recheck one of his infrequent patients. It made Maren a little nervous to think of making recommendations for Dr. Schumann's father.

The elder Schumann was eighty-nine years old, and as might be expected, his list of ailments added up to what Judy called WOB, worn-out body syndrome. Maren found him in a private room in the acute care unit. He had an IV for nutrition, and a nasal cannula was dispensing oxygen. He was sitting in a lounge chair next to his bed, holding hands with his granddaughter, a pretty young woman about twenty-five or so. He was thin, bone thin.

Maren spent a few minutes talking to the pair. The granddaughter had red-rimmed eyes.

"He won't stay in bed," she explained, "so they got him this lounge chair." She indicated the hospital chair, usually provided for relatives who wanted to spend the night.

He insisted on being dressed during the day. Today he wore dark gray slacks and a patterned sport shirt with a blue long-sleeved sweater. His voice was extremely weak.

"I'd really like some food, like oatmeal – or custard," he answered when Maren asked what she could do to help him. "I'm sure you would," Maren commented, not promising anything.

The granddaughter interrupted, pointing to the bedside table. "There's the list of exercises the other therapist left. We've done them at least once a day."

Maren looked down at the paper, a list of swallowing exercises, appropriate for rehabilitation patients, was printed in Judy's hand. Sometimes, Maren was finding, her perspective was quite different from her colleague's. This was obviously a dying man. There was no potential for rehabilitation. Judy had documented big-time aspiration when she administered his video swallow study the day after his admittance for worsening heart problems. Maren wondered what Judy had been thinking. Probably, to buy some time, she had suggested the NPO status be maintained for a few days while they tried to strengthen the swallow.

Maren had no intention of putting him through a series of exercises. She said she would check on them later and turned to go out, wondering what kind of note she could possibly write.

"I could use some inspiration here," she prayed as she sat down at the counter. Her inspiration appeared immediately in the form of nurse Helen Reese.

"Aren't you the speech therapist?" asked the nurse sharply, returning to the station from another patient's room. When Maren acknowledged that she was, Helen accosted her verbally. "Well, what are you going to do with him?"

She was obviously referring to Mr. Schumann, since Maren had his chart open in front of her. "You'd better do something about his swallow. They can't keep him NPO forever. Either recommend an NG tube or let him eat something. All he wants is a little bite of oatmeal or custard. Frankly, I don't think the family will place any kind of tube." Maren looked up at the nurse, sighed, promised to do her best, and thanked her for her input.

She studied the information in the chart for another few minutes. The picture was clearer. The family was opposed to tube feeding that would artificially prolong life. Perhaps that's why Judy had not recommended an NG tube. Maren stood to leave. "Let me review the tape of his video swallow study, and I'll see what I can come up with," she promised Nurse Helen.

Maren went to the storage closet, retrieved the tape, watched it repeatedly, and took notes. She was thankful for Judy's thorough and fastidious video swallow routine. It was easy to see why she hadn't recommended a diet. He had aspirated on all liquids and on mechanical soft. He didn't aspirate on the puree and extra thick liquid, but took twelve to sixteen seconds to clear it. The guideline for recommending a consistency was ten seconds. If a patient couldn't clear a bolus in ten seconds, he would tire before sufficient amounts could be eaten to maintain body weight.

Maren started thinking through her solution. *Mr. Schumann only wants some pleasure. I could recommend therapeutic feedings for pleasure. A speech pathologist would then give him ten teaspoons or less, once or twice a day. Seriously ill patients are often given six small meals a day. An RN could feed him ten teaspoons of puree three or four times a day. If we combine those two protocols he would get six very small, therapeutic feedings for pleasure each day.*

"Can we get an order for six small meals a day of puree and extra thick liquid, to be administered by the RN or speech pathologist only?" Maren asked Helen Reese when she was back in the ICU.

The nurse nodded and smiled. "We can."

"Each swallow will require ten to sixteen seconds to clear," Maren warned. "And you know his intake at that rate will not be sufficient to meet nutritional needs."

"And Dr. Schumann will know that, too," Helen assured Maren in a quieter voice than she had used earlier. "But we can leave the IV while we get this started, and go from there. At least he'll get some oatmeal."

"And custard," insisted Maren.

Tuesday Maren and Paul met at the Yellow Duck. He assumed he would have a hard time convincing her to spend a weekend in Colorado, so he came prepared with photos and anecdotes of family times at the Pine Bluff house. They sat in their usual corner booth. He didn't ask about the trip to the cottage; she didn't volunteer. She could be so closed, Paul decided. Now he appreciated what others meant when they complained that he was closed.

"I brought pictures to show you," Paul began after they placed their order. He felt a bit guilty as he handed her one of the house with him and his cousins standing in the driveway. The photo was taken twenty years earlier, right after the house had been built; but he wanted to present it as a family gathering place. "My dad and mom and all the McClouds decided to build a vacation home when I was a teenager."

When he said "all the McClouds," it made Maren think again of a clan, but she didn't interrupt to tease. He looked so serious.

"Aunt Cloris and her family were in California, Aunt Elizabeth and Dad were in Chicago, so the location had to be halfway. Dad wanted a lake, Cloris and Mike wanted to ski, Aunt Elizabeth preferred trees, and Frank need peace and quiet. The Rockies fit the bill. It's not too far from Denver's airport, so weekends are doable." He tried to read Maren's face to see what she was thinking, but her eyes were on the photo.

He handed her a more recent picture of a deer next to the house and another of the Denver skyline taken from the back deck at twilight. She stared at the pictures but did not comment. The last snapshot was of his parents standing at the back, looking up at the second-story deck, which ran the length of the house.

"I took these a little over a year ago to show how the evergreens have grown." They dwarfed the house in the photo. He had always enjoyed seeing the shorter aspens against the evergreens, and in the last photo he had captured the morning sun lighting up the newly turned yellow leaves. Looking at the photos with her, Paul was struck by the remoteness of the setting for the first time. His family had always considered it privacy, not isolation.

He worried about her reaction. He turned his fork over and then turned it over again. "I'd like you to see it in person sometime," he said weakly. She was focused on the people and how attractive and inviting the house looked. She had never been close to extended family, neither her own or Jack's, so she had been intrigued by Paul's clan from the beginning.

Now she mused about how the McClouds managed to schedule time, both together and separately at the mountain house, evidently without significant conflict. No wonder Paul kept such a distance from co-workers; he was always happily surrounded by family, a fact that left Maren feeling slightly envious. It didn't occur to her how secluded the house in the mountains appeared. What she saw was a family gathering place, where family or friends might drop in, a place where stress was left behind. She ached for such a retreat.

"Maren," he started again, with more determination, "I can't tell what you're thinking, but I'd like to take you to Pine Bluff this weekend." She looked up, surprised by the immediacy of the invitation. "I'd love to go to Pine Bluff," she answered without hesitation. "My only concern is about Nick. Ziff said to keep him away from the cult as much as possible, so I've asked him to come home repeatedly. He's always too busy. He didn't come home for spring break at all, but at least he went to spend time with Matt. I wanted to see him this weekend, to offer to go to Champaign."

"Why don't you think about it and check with Nick. You can let me know." Paul didn't want to pressure her into doing something that would make her uncomfortable or cause her to have regrets.

"I'll call Nick tonight, but would we be able to get tickets so quickly?"

"Ah, I have connections." Paul smiled broadly, reminding her of Penny and Aunt Elizabeth's travel bureau.

Oddly enough, it was Steve who solved the problem of keeping tabs on Nick, but Maren's first conversation was with her son at eleven thirty.

"How would you like to play host and tour guide for me this weekend? I need a getaway," she proposed after their initial greetings.

"Gosh, Mom, I was planning to come home for the weekend."

"Oh," was Maren's only response, not knowing how to proceed.

"I just finished talking with Steve. He's going to help me work on the car. It needs a lot more bodywork than I thought. Steve says we should change spark plugs and rotate tires, too. We were planning to work in his heated garage all weekend. I figured I'd be spending at least one night there. If you need a getaway, why don't you and Bonni take off for a day?"

"Actually," she confessed, "Paul invited me to visit the McCloud family cottage in Colorado, but I told him I hadn't seen you for a while."

"Colorado, that's cool, Mom. You should go."

"But you would be here alone. I couldn't go and leave you here alone."

"I'll bet Steve wouldn't mind if I spent both nights at his place. He'd probably appreciate the company."

Maren knew that was true enough, and Ziff had told her to encourage stronger relationships outside the cult.

"I'll call him. If it's okay with him, I'll go."

She couldn't resist one last opportunity to get Nick to question the cult leadership. It was another technique Ziff had told her to use. "Are you sure Lois and the group will let you go?" she asked carefully.

He took the bait. "Mom, they don't tell me what to do. If I want to work on the car for the weekend, I don't have to ask permission. You guys have it all wrong. Matt asked the same thing when I talked to him earlier."

Maren smiled, pleased with his response and that Matt had been able to use some of the techniques, too.

Not wanting to get into an argument, she ended the conversation on a positive note. "I'd better call Steve before it gets any later. Goodnight Nick, I love you."

"Night, Mom. I love you, too."

She phoned Steve immediately. "I hear you and Nick have a lot of work to do on the car this weekend."

"After you told me your doctor friend said to keep him busy, I made sure we bought a car that would need a lot of attention. I figure if he and I are working on the car, he can't be with them." Steve didn't refer to the cult by name, and Maren knew that he meant to spare her feelings.

"I'm so grateful, but I was hoping to get away for the weekend, and I don't want him here by himself."

"You need a getaway, after all the pressure you've been under lately," he emphasized. "I'll keep him here at my place. We'll change spark plugs, wipe out body rust, patch, and paint. If we run out of things to do, I'll have him help me with a couple of Comanche projects. I could use an extra pair of hands, and it would be fun to do some flying, too." Amazingly, Steve volunteered the arrangement without Maren being required to reveal her plans.

"Are you sure this is okay with you? You don't have to cancel a trip or anything?"

"I actually have the weekend off. I'll make sure Nick leaves here Sunday night too late to attend any meetings on campus."

Chapter 17

Wednesday was packed with activity both at work and home. Maren arrived at St. John's Thursday morning hoping for an easier day and an early escape to Paul's house. She had outpatients most of the morning, including little Allison, who now had a vocabulary of about a dozen words. During the session Maren heard *up, down, more, drink, no, uh-oh, home, juice, hello,* and the names of the girl's foster brothers. Maren wrote a list of the words and posted it for OT and PT. She had asked the foster parents to keep a notebook of words and phrases they thought they heard at home.

She had also requested more complete records on the little girl, and thanks to Dr. Schumann, the records had arrived. Rita handed her the envelope as Allison left the outpatient area.

Unable to take time to stop at her desk, Maren stood next to Rita's desk and browsed through the psychologist's report. Allison's father was currently in prison for sexually abusing two children. Authorities couldn't confirm that Allison had been abused, but the psychological report certainly left that as a possibility. Maren felt sick at the likelihood. Still, she believed that possibility and the girl's rapid progress helped rule out a diagnosis of microcephaly. She hoped Dr. Schumann would agree.

At noon Maren met with Stephanie, an undergraduate student who was to observe with her for the rest of the day. Usually, Maren enjoyed the students, but the patients she was to evaluate during the afternoon were almost all in the intensive care unit. It could make for a depressing afternoon.

Maren opened the medical chart for Brian Jeffers. The History section stated he had come to the hospital for an endarterectomy. "That's a procedure to open the carotid arteries to allow blood to flow more freely," Maren explained to Stephanie.

Only a junior in college, Stephanie had completed her general education requirements and was in the second semester of theory classes. Theory would prepare her for classes on disorders. Only then would she be allowed to work with actual patients and students. She didn't have a chance of really comprehending the complexities of Mr. Jeffers' history.

"What do all those letters mean?" Stephanie asked quietly.

"MI, COPD, CABG times three," Maren read aloud. "All those letters to say the man's heart and lungs are in terrible condition, and he has had triple bypass heart surgery. He is a CVA, a stroke, waiting to happen. Otherwise they wouldn't have scheduled the endarterectomy. Our job is to assess his swallow."

After evaluating him at bedside, Maren scheduled a video swallow study, which they would accomplish during the afternoon, if Radiology was on time.

"His hoarse, breathy voice concerns me. I'm fairly certain we'll document aspiration. I'm also going to recommend an ENT evaluation and a diet change to thickened liquids," she informed Stephanie. "I suspect he has a paralyzed vocal fold. That's always a possibility after chest surgery.

"The left recurrent laryngeal nerve lies lower than the right in the chest, then goes back up and into the larynx. That's the nerve that innervates the vocal fold. It's vulnerable to bruising or being nicked or cut during any chest surgery. Usually the paralysis is temporary, but it could last six months. It could also be permanent." Maren stopped, convinced she was talking over the young woman's head.

She reviewed the history for Jose O'Campo while Stephanie read over her shoulder. He was emerging from a coma. They walked across the hall and greeted the patient. He opened his eyes briefly for them but did not vocalize.

Maren saw several family photos on the shelf in back of his bed. She held them in front of the patient to provide stimulation. Jose seemed to look at Maren. Next he appeared to focus on the picture she held in front of him. She moved it to his left. His eyes followed, but he didn't turn his head. She slowly moved it to his right. Again, his eyes tracked the object.

She used a glass, a pack of tissues, and a comb, all objects from his bedside table, attempting to elicit the same visual response. The photos got the best result each time. She turned his TV to the Spanish station, and they left to find his nurse. Maren wanted his nurse to ask for Spanish music to be brought by family and played during the day.

"If they have time to tape record messages, have them leave personal tapes here, too." She wrote a note for Judy's benefit, primarily asking her to keep reminding nurses to use the audiotapes. Stephanie didn't ask questions or comment, just watched with a sad face. While Maren wrote, she asked the student to find the medical chart for Leanne Merriweather.

Mrs. Merriweather had a tracheotomy and was ventilator-dependent, following a serious heart attack. She needed a communication board. Maren would get her a simple board for expressing basic needs when she could get back to the speech office. The woman was too weak for direct therapy. She had barely opened her eyes.

Maren told the patient another speech pathologist would check on her on Friday. Other than Maren's voice the only other sounds in the room were made by the ventilator. Stephanie's face was blank.

The next two patients they saw were even less responsive, so Maren and Stephanie moved on down the list. George Crockmeyer was edentulous and had a nasal cannula in place to deliver oxygen. His mouth hung open constantly.

During the oral exam Maren noted a bulky residue in his throat. She retrieved a pink spongy toothette from the pocket of her white lab coat, un-wrapped it, and used a twirling motion to try to roll the residue out of his throat. It was so sticky that she resorted to a washcloth. With latex-gloved hand she reached in, gripped a chunk of the residue with the dry cloth, and pulled until she removed a rope of thickened mucus. Stephanie turned away. Maren didn't blame her, but felt more compassion for the patient than for the squeamish girl.

"I'm sorry you were uncomfortable in there," Maren said gently when they were in the hall, "but Mr. Crockmeyer was in real discomfort. I don't know why nursing staff or respiratory therapy didn't deal with that before it got so bad. I doubt he could even swallow." Stephanie only nodded. As they left the room a nurse and doctor waited to enter. The nurse introduced Maren as the speech pathologist.

"I understand there is an oral anomaly," the doctor began.

"Well, there were a lot of dried secretions. I just finished cleaning it out. It was quite a rope," explained Maren. The nurse, who had considerable hospital experience, jumped into the conversation.

"We couldn't get that mass to move. We thought it was a tumor or something."

"It was just very tenacious mucus. Humidified oxygen would help."

"Yes, I'll order that. Then it's cleared up? That was it?" he repeated impatiently, glancing at the embarrassed nurse. "Thank you very much."

Maren, openly watching the clock now, was hurrying to complete her note when her pager beeped. The message was from Radiology. She knew she would have to work Mr. Jeffers' video swallow study into her schedule. It was already four thirty, and Stephanie had fulfilled the required number of observation hours for her class. Maren signed the form and released the young woman. Stephanie said only, "Thank you," nothing about her experience. *She'll probably switch majors to marketing or recreation management, something fun,* predicted Maren silently, watching the girl walk toward the elevator.

As Maren prepared to leave for the day, Rita dropped in to the speech office on her way out to tell Maren that Dr. Schumann's father had died during the afternoon. Already drained from an afternoon of critically ill patients, Maren felt her mood drop even lower. Her eyes misted. "I hope he enjoyed the custard and oatmeal." Her throat constricted, preventing further conversation. She picked up her purse and followed Rita out the back door.

Her packed bag waited in her car's trunk. She and Paul had both managed to get Friday off, and Penny had arranged an 8:00 A.M. flight for them.

Paul's day was worse than Maren's, and much longer. Lancaster and Granger had milked his request to have Friday off for all it was worth. Granger left the office early to enjoy the spring weather, saying Paul could easily fit his few patients in between Paul's scheduled appointments. That was true, but it meant every patient was late. It was past dinnertime when he finished dictating notes and left the office.

As he drove toward home, Circle Hospital paged him. An eight-year-old boy riding his bike had been hit by a car. The boy was one of Paul's regular patients, and the parents had requested Paul's services to treat the facial injuries.

When he finally walked through his back door, he found that Maren was already sound asleep. He showered, made toast, added peanut butter, and poured a glass of milk. That's when the phone rang. It was just after eleven. Lancaster and Granger had also stipulated that in order to have Friday off Paul would stand call Thursday night.

It was St. John's ER on the phone. An intoxicated passenger survived an auto accident, but his face and head had smashed into the windshield. Immediate reconstruction was Paul's responsibility. The driver was dead on arrival. Neither had been wearing a seat belt. There were no air bags.

When he finally got home again, it was long after three in the morning. He stretched out on his bed with his clothes on, but couldn't blot out the consequences of the accident. He wasn't supposed to feel anything anymore, but he always did. He forced himself to focus on the escape that dawn would provide and hoped he would be able to sleep with the aid of the high altitude, the beauty of Pine Bluff, and Maren's company.

They didn't talk much on the plane. Paul read for a while. He wore his glasses rather than his contacts, and Maren liked the look. He appeared to be more scholarly, yet more like a regular guy. This morning he also looked exhausted.

She knew he had been called out for an emergency; she had heard him go out. This morning he only said he had spent several hours trying to put a young man's face back together. She knew alcohol probably caused the accident, and that the patient had no insurance. Paul would probably never get paid.

At least he slept on the flight; Maren did not. She prayed that they could both forget the pain and ugliness they were leaving long enough to have at least one decent conversation. She underestimated Pine Bluff.

They endured the long wait at the car rental desk and then drove in silence for forty-five-minutes. They wound around curves, up the mountain, and down several gravel roads. Seeing the roads Paul had to negotiate made Maren glad he had rested on the flight and that they had arrived in daytime.

She recognized the tall frame house built into the hill before he turned into the drive. It matched the photographs she had seen; but it seemed larger in reality, more like a resort. The aspens flanking the house were dwarfed by its size. Maren asked if the siding was cedar or pine, and Paul told her it was fir.

He drove up to the garage but left the car out. He wanted to take her in the front door. Immediately inside were steps. "These lead up to the living room, kitchen, and some of the bedrooms, and those go down to a recreation area and more bedrooms. Let's start up here," Paul said, carrying their luggage ahead of her into the living area. It was carpeted with plush, off-white, wall-to-wall carpeting, and the walls were wood trimmed. The walls themselves were a kind of plaster she had never seen before. It was creamy white with flecks of walnut brown and had a rough texture. Maren admired the stone fireplace that was built into the corner, so it didn't block the view. Picture windows, which extended from the edge of the fireplace chimney across the entire east living room wall, were covered only with sheer curtains. "Whether they're open or closed you can see the valley," Paul pointed out, proudly.

Paul took Maren's hand. "Come out here," he said, almost pulling her across the room and out the back door to an enclosed gazebo. From there they walked out onto the open deck, which extended across the entire back of the house. She commented that the elevated deck reminded her of the one outside her kitchen at home. "It's higher and much longer, though; and the view is certainly more spectacular than anything in Edgelawn," she observed, admiringly.

They stood without speaking, looking out at the valley below, the clear, blue sky above, and the evergreens, pines, and spruce in between. They breathed in the clean air and enjoyed the panorama before them. It was as if some kind of osmosis was occurring, which, if given enough time, could eventually transform them completely.

Reluctantly, they returned to the living room where they had left their luggage. Maren noticed again that the colors of the contemporary furnishings were typical of the Southwest—soft aqua, creams, clay, and wood tones. It was totally soothing.

Paul gave her a tour of the house and invited her to choose whatever bedroom she wanted. She decided on a room on the south side of the house that had access to the long deck on the east. Paul's usual room was downstairs, but he elected to stay in the north wing, where he had a spectacular view of the valley, but no access to the deck.

After unpacking and changing clothes, they both wanted to walk. "Don't ever wonder off alone," Paul warned her, as they started on a worn path behind the house. "Usually a mountain lion or bear wouldn't attack an adult, but they have been known to maul small children to death."

Maren took the warning to heart, but her attention was already on the variety of trees and early spring wildflowers. Delighted, she pointed out blue spruce, white pine, ponderosa pine, and Norwegian spruce intermixed with the budding deciduous aspens. She was thrilled when they saw the delicate, lavender and white Colorado columbine blooming in a patch of sun next to their walkway. It was really too early in the season to expect them, Paul told her.

He realized that in all the times he'd walked that same path he had never noticed the nuances of color or details of the landscape he was seeing today. The trees had been collectively just evergreens. He knew he had a new perspective because he was sharing it with Maren.

Within an hour hunger made its presence known, and the couple went back for the car. It was a short drive to an unpretentious bar and grill on the main highway for lunch—a sandwich and soft drink that Maren rated as one of the best meals she had ever eaten. Paul explained that the altitude would affect appetite as well as thirst.

"What about this incredible fatigue that's taking over my body?" she asked while stifling a yawn. Paul was relieved that he wasn't the only one craving sleep. They agreed to put grocery shopping on hold, and returned to the house to stretch out on their pillow-topped beds.

When Maren woke, she put on a jacket, pulled a chair to the deck, and opened a book she had found in the bookcase in her room. It was a history of the county. She managed to read only a few paragraphs because appreciating the view in front of her suddenly seemed more important than learning about the past.

The sun set quickly behind the mountain. She was pulling the chair back into her bedroom when Paul found her.

"Gets cool quickly, doesn't it?"

"It gets dark quickly, too," she answered, shivering in spite of her jacket.

"I'll get a fire started. You'd better get a sweater on. If you need one, I'm sure you can find something in one of the dresser drawers. Help yourself." He had obviously noticed that under the jacket she was wearing only a cotton T-shirt.

When she joined him in the living room, he was poking at the logs in the fireplace. He was hoping its warmth would help Maren relax. A few people now knew they were dating, and those who knew said Maren would help Paul unwind. The truth was, Paul did let go, through the discipline he had developed over the years. It was Maren who got so wound up she could get no release from her tensions. Yet, she had told him she relaxed more with him than almost anyone else. He looked up at her and thought she did look more tranquil this evening than she ever had during their evenings in Chicago.

He had brought a pitcher of water from the kitchen and went to the dry bar where he had set it to pour each of them a drink.

"You need to really push water up here at altitude," he reminded her again.

"It is dry up here," she agreed, realizing she felt strangely nervous now that she was alone with him here in the mountains.

Paul sat on the floor, leaning against the couch. The lighted Denver skyline was beautiful through the window, and she continued to stand, staring out, admiring the view.

He decided to plunge in, no preamble. "What was it like to be in one relationship for eighteen years?"

The bold question caught her off guard. Just when she would begin to think of Paul as a superficial kind of male companion, he always surprised her with something that took their relationship a step deeper. She began to speak without thinking through her answer. She could talk about it now, but not entirely without emotion -- nearly five years after Jack's death. She spoke slowly at first and quietly. Soon words poured out, as if they had been waiting for an opportunity to escape some walled prison.

"Jack was from a rather rural area south of Lafayette, along the river. He was a man's man, quiet, didn't show his emotions. I think the intensity of his emotions was just too much for words," she explained a bit defensively.

"He was a good father, although he never really had a strong desire for children before the boys were born. I think . . . I know the boys were the best part of his life. He loved it when he could take them someplace with him.

"He was always there for me. We'd argue about money or the boys or where to go for the holidays, but we both knew we couldn't function until we got over it. We never made up really -- we just kind of started again. We weren't good at talking things out. We communicated without words after a while."

She stopped talking and stared into the fire. She smiled. She felt she had succeeded in reporting everything in a good light, with an optimism she hadn't always felt.

Paul waited; he wanted to hear it all. She had spent eighteen years of her life with a man named Jack, loving him, hating him, sharing his food, his house, his bed, and his children. If Jack's children were to be part of Paul's life, he needed to understand.

He couldn't imagine living with anyone other than his sister and parents for a lifetime. He couldn't imagine what is was like for a man and woman to sleep together for eighteen years and suddenly not have that closeness. Paul was rarely nervous, but the thought of hurting Maren or letting her down, physically or any other way, was causing him more and more anxiety. He kept thinking he needed to know what had been.

"We went to church as a family," she resumed, without prompting. "We prayed at mealtime, but that was it. Somehow it was too emotional, or too personal, to pray, just the two of us." She was intentionally avoiding their intimate life. Two things you shouldn't discuss had been ingrained—sex and money.

Paul was persistent. "Maren, I've known a couple of women that I cared for deeply, one for as long as two years. Even though the relationships came to an end, I still missed their presence in my life. I can't imagine what it's been like for you."

He was as subtle as possible, but she understood what he was asking and she was embarrassed. She had never discussed her sex life with anyone, not even a woman friend.

She didn't answer. He tried again.

"Maren, you're still a young woman. How have you managed . . ." He stopped and started again. "Maybe I just assumed too much, but you implied you haven't really had a close relationship with anyone since Jack died. That's a long time now."

She swallowed hard and began again, with more effort. "Jack was shy with women, shy with me. We were clumsy lovers at first. We grew up together. It's a good way to begin, knowing one of you is just as innocent and naive as the other. I know times have changed, but I still have that perspective. Only, I can't go back. I can't erase what I've experienced and who I am, or what others have experienced."

Paul felt a stab of reality. It was true they could never experience such innocence together, but he accepted that. Why, he wondered, couldn't she? Now he lost his courage. He wasn't sure he wanted to hear more. "Come down here with me," he invited, patting the plush carpet.

Her feet and legs ached from hiking through the hills. She would rest tonight, she decided, and bring up their differences in the morning, over breakfast. She pushed off her shoes and sat next to Paul, leaning against the couch.

"Stretch out, and I'll give you a foot rub."

"How did you know?"

"The uninitiated always suffer from the first day on the trails. You got a workout today."

She lay on her stomach, facing the fire, resting her chin on her hands, and held her feet up for him.

"Oooh, nice," she moaned appreciably, more grateful that the uncomfortable conversation had come to an end than for the foot massage.

He finished her feet and continued massaging her legs, then her back.

"I may fall asleep right here," she threatened, trying to maintain consciousness.

"Do you feel safe to fall asleep here with me, maybe wake up together, knowing how we respond to each other?"

She turned over and propped her head in her hand, elbow on the floor. She was startled at the suggestion of his question, but was more calm now that the past had receded into its walled chamber. They had been alone together in Paul's house many times, and she had never felt threatened in any way. She rolled over on her back, resting her head on a pillow he tossed her, and looked up at him. "I do feel safe with you, Paul." Her answer surprised her. Haltingly she continued. "But I . . . I just can't start over. I . . ."

"No one can start over, Maren, you just keep moving ahead."

"I just don't know how to do that," she finished, feeling helpless.

He had been sitting next to her, massaging her back, and hadn't moved when she turned over to look at him. Now he slid onto his side, and she came back to her side, mirroring his posture. She was looking straight into his eyes.

"Does it feel comfortable when I put my arms around you?" he asked, holding her attention with his steady, clear blue eyes.

The house was so quiet and peaceful. The hospital, Edgelawn, Matt, Nick, and Jack were all so far away. She felt free from all her responsibilities, alone in a way she had never experienced in her adult life—alone but not lonely. Her heart pounded faster. "Yes," she replied honestly. "I like being in your arms."

He moved closer, slipped his arms around her, and pulled her against him. With their bodies pressed together, she felt his warmth spread through her, awakening her. It was like having coffee after a sleepless night. She wanted him to kiss her, but he didn't. She stared unblinking into his eyes, inviting him, knowing she was giving him mixed signals, but unable to be consistent.

"Maren, I'm going to kiss you, but that's all." When the fire burned hotter, he moved from her lips and face to her neck and shoulders. In the intimacy of the night he whispered once more that he would only kiss her. It was a promise he kept, although they stayed in the warmth of the fire's glow until it consumed all the logs and finally flickered out.

The morning light filtered through the slats of mini blinds and tiptoed across Maren's face. She woke with a smile, hugging herself, knowing she had dreamed some very pleasant dreams. She pulled on a flannel shirt and jeans, and then her nylon jacket.

The house was cold, and Paul was not inside. She found the thermostat and turned it up, but the furnace did not respond. On the kitchen table she found his note, saying he had gone to town for some groceries and had already called the oil company to have the tank filled right away.

She was still holding the note when she heard a vehicle in the drive. Thinking it was the oil truck, she ran down the steps and threw open the front door. An attractive man with thick, white hair almost fell in. Dressed in jeans, hiking boots, and a blue and black plaid flannel shirt, he had been bending to put a key in the lock when she pulled the door wide. They were both startled.

"Hullo," came a deep velvety voice that reminded her of someone. "Are you a friend of the family?"

"Yes, I am . . ." she stammered, still blocking the doorway ". . . of Paul's." Then she connected the face and voice. He was taller than Paul and heavier than Bob, but definitely part of the clan.

"You certainly look like a McCloud."

"I'm Frank," the priest announced.

Maren stepped back and offered to help him bring in his bags and parcels. He told her he had driven from Colorado Springs where his flight from San Francisco had diverted from its Denver destination the previous night. He had planned to go straight to Pine Bluff, but after the long flight from Manila through Hawaii and San Francisco, decided to spend the night near the airport. Maren explained that Paul had gone for groceries and that she was about to make some tea.

"You won't find tea here," Frank said, chuckling at the thought of tea in the McCloud's mountain house. "But I'll make you an exceptional cup of mountain-brewed coffee."

So it happened that she was face to face with Frank McCloud in the kitchen, instead of talking with Paul about their differences, as she had planned.

"Father Frank, I didn't know you would be here. Paul speaks fondly of you, and I'm so pleased to meet you." she said.

"Just Frank when we're with family," he instructed. He told her he came to Pine Bluff as often as he could. "Originally I came for sheer escape. In more recent years, I bring my laptop and work."

"Which is it this time?" Maren asked. She admired the warmth of his manner and the smile in his voice. His soft voice was similar to Bob's, but it was more than velvet soft; there was definitely hoarseness.

"Both," he confessed, unaware of her diagnosis. "I've about worn out my voice, and I need to work on a graduation address I've been asked to give in May. It's for St. Veronica's College in Minnesota, a Catholic women's school near the University of Minnesota."

While he found the parts of an old percolator-style coffee pot, filled it, and set it on the electric stove, they got further acquainted. Maren tried to explain herself as a friend from the hospital. Surely he would see that she was too old to be in a romantic relationship with Paul. The events of the previous evening would certainly cloud that issue, but Frank didn't know about last night. She underestimated the perception of the priest, as well as the closeness of the two men. Frank knew Paul wouldn't bring a woman here unless he was serious about the relationship. Casual friends were not introduced to the family, nor invited to the family retreat.

Paul had brought only one other woman here that Frank knew about, because he had the misfortune to have met her. She had been extremely intelligent, but had no spirit of warmth such as he detected in Maren. He was pleased; he had hoped Paul would find a life companion. He knew his nephew kept busy, but was sure he experienced terrible loneliness. Frank and loneliness were frequent companions. But his nephew had taken no vow such as he had.

Frank was impressed with Maren immediately. Besides warmth, she had maturity and intelligence. From her attempts to explain away her presence, he surmised that there were difficulties. He busied himself, setting mugs, sugar, juice, and canned milk on the table. When he made no comment, she returned to a safer subject. "What's the sermon about?"

"Graduation address," he corrected. "The woman at the well is the text, but I'm afraid I'll never get to tell the story. I keep resting my voice, but it gives out on me more and more."

Maren sensed his distress. "I'm a speech pathologist. Maybe I can help."

He broke out the cinnamon rolls he had brought to go with the coffee and juice. "Well, I need to do something."

He poured the coffee, his cup to the top, hers with room for cream. "Shall we give thanks?" he made an open, inquiring gesture with his hands. Automatically, she put her hand in his hand and bowed her head.

Frank, unaccustomed to praying while holding hands with an attractive woman, was momentarily taken off guard. Like his nephew, though, he had the ability to recover quickly. He gently curled his fingertips around hers, as if her hand was a sacred object. He did in fact believe that all parts of the human body were sacred. He asked a simple blessing on their meal and their new friendship. Maren was surprised that just as when Paul prayed, Frank's prayer was spontaneous, not memorized.

She began to question him about his voice. It was worse in the morning. He coughed a lot, but had given up smoking ten years earlier. He was extremely concerned about the possibility of cancer, since Elizabeth, the oldest McCloud, had already had a laryngectomy. He had become so concerned on this trip that he had seen an ENT physician in Manila. A direct laryngoscopy had been done. Maren's eyes opened wider. That meant a general anesthetic in a hospital with an oral scope inserted to give a magnified view, instead of a flexible scope exam in the doctor's office. It seemed unnecessarily aggressive to Maren, but perhaps it had been the best way to get a good exam in that city.

He withdrew a typed folded report from his shirt pocket, and handed it to her to read.

"From the doctor's description of the posterior commissure and your symptoms, I would suspect gastroesophageal reflux."

"The posterior what?"

"The back part of the larynx, where your vocal folds are attached," Maren explained, eliminating the medical terminology. She told him how acid could reflux up the esophagus from the stomach and seep into the larynx, causing irritation. "It's often stress related, Frank. Are you under a lot of stress?" she asked with concern.

He was not used to having someone tend his pain. She was so quick and perceptive, so personal. She was respectful, but not overawed by his priesthood. Blushing, he related to her some details of his life. He told her about traveling from place to place by himself to review finances at the various facilities, making decisions for cutting budgets that sometimes had far-reaching effects in the lives of others. He had no office staff, in fact no office to call his own.

"Yes, my lifestyle and my job are stressful," he summarized.

"Do you have someone to talk to about some of these things, someone interested in your well-being?" she asked, thinking of a counselor.

"I have a confessor," he answered shyly, "but I really haven't shared this with anyone else, not until now . . . with you."

The way he hesitated and then said "with you" sounded so intimate; she was afraid to invade his privacy further. She liked him immensely and felt drawn to him, but pulled back because of who he was. If circumstances had been different, she knew she would have wanted to pursue a relationship with him. She couldn't guess his age exactly, but it felt like she was with a younger Bob, or, she suddenly realized, an older Paul. She wondered if her attraction to him was because he reminded her of Paul, or if she was drawn to Paul because there was something greater that she sensed in each. Some part of their character, she decided, something . . . She searched for a way to describe it, something she could only describe as spiritual.

Just then Paul burst through the front door and bounded up the steps, whistling "Happy Days Are Here Again." He felt the warmth of the atmosphere in spite of the cold house, when he entered the kitchen.

Although Frank hadn't seen Paul on the road, Paul had seen Frank. He bought extra food and was delighted that Frank and Maren would have the opportunity to meet. He could tell they had already achieved a degree of closeness; and he was pleased, though not surprised. He had expected they would get along.

After an affectionate bear hug between the two men, Paul talked nonstop while he fixed a *real* breakfast. He polished off the remaining cinnamon roll while he worked. None of them noticed that the house was still cold. Since Frank planned to stay indoors to work and sleep all day, he volunteered to watch for the oil truck and call the company again if it didn't arrive by noon.

That left Paul and Maren free to sightsee. Paul wanted to show her some of his favorite spots. The first was an old wooden walking bridge over a stream. From it they could look up to see the stream's source, or rather, sources. The morning sun sparkled on the waterfall above their heads. Perhaps a mile from the waterfall a spring bubbled out of the ground. The spring water made its way along a tortuous route down the mountain, until it also spilled into the waterfall. Looking higher they could see the melting snowcaps that undoubtedly fed both.

The sun filtered through the trees, creating the light and shadows local artists were challenged to replicate. Maren felt like they were standing in a chapel.

"Paul, what do you want in life?"

He smiled a little, leaned on the age-darkened handrail of the old bridge, and tossed in the leaf he had picked up. "Just to have meaningful work to do, enjoy beauty, love someone, and have someone love me."

"That's almost exactly what Frank said this morning."

"You two really hit it off, didn't you? You didn't waste time on small talk."

"He said he wanted to know that the work he is doing is important in God's plan, to appreciate creation, continue to learn how to love, and know that he is loved."

"Don't compare me with Uncle Frank, Maren," Paul warned sternly. "He's living on a higher plane."

"Oh, Paul, he's just a man," she argued, remembering the pain in Frank's eyes as they discussed his voice problem.

Only a few rays of sunlight reached as far as the little bridge, but it felt warm on their shoulders, while the early spring air chilled their feet.

Reluctantly, they left the beauty and peace of the chapel-bridge, hiked the two miles back to the car, and drove to Lake Dillon. After walking around the town for a bit, they lunched in the upstairs of an old two-story house that had been converted to a restaurant. Their white wooden table was by a window directly across from the lake.

While Maren enjoyed the postcard-picture view of the lake and the snow-covered mountain peaks beyond, she wondered how many other women had enjoyed this view with Paul. She admitted to herself that the question's presence in her mind could only have sprung from jealousy.

After lunch they drove farther into the mountains to visit some of the McClouds' favorite skiing sites. Maren decided, without having seen it in winter, that the landscape was the most beautiful in the off-season.

Hiking at altitude left them thirsty and in need of rest. They took soft drinks with them to the car and drove back to the house.

Hunger surfaced again by the time they parked in the gravel driveway. Paul had bought steaks to grill for dinner. He was hoping his uncle might have started a salad, but Frank had slept and worked at his computer all day, just as he had planned. At least the house was warm.

As she walked down the hall to her room, the two McClouds began talking and preparing dinner, freeing Maren to shower and change clothes. She was impressed that they were so open and comfortable with one another. Neither was timid or hesitant in relationships, like the other men in her life had been. She heard Paul filling Frank in on his hopes for a new office,

During dinner Frank asked Maren about her family and interests, while Paul enjoyed watching their friendship expand. He enjoyed watching Maren anytime, although there was something different about her tonight. The dry climate had relaxed her wavy hair, giving it a softer, smoother look, and she had applied no makeup. He didn't think she needed any. Her cheeks were rosy from hiking in the brisk, dry air. She wore an olive-green, ribbed sweatshirt with three buttons that were open at the neck, exposing the soft flesh of her throat. She looked so contented. He wanted to reach out and touch her. He wanted to make love to her, he admitted to himself.

He forced himself back to the moment. She was asking Frank how the graduation address was coming.

"It just needs a little polish, but I'm feeling better about it."

The story of the woman at the well Maren knew fairly well. Jesus went alone to the city well. He had no way to draw water up, and all the women but one had already come and gone with their buckets. This woman had always been portrayed as a sinner, a loose woman that Jesus befriended. He asked her for a drink and told her he would give her living water. Then he told her all about herself.

Frank told the story with a different emphasis. "Jesus had sent the disciples on errands. He was tired and thirsty from the dusty journey and from speaking to crowds along the way. She was the only woman who approached him, and did so even though they were of different religious groups. She drew water for him, ministered to him in that way. He did tell her about herself in order to gain her trust, and he taught her some important truths. She was then empowered and went on to minister to others. He was refreshed from her ministering to him, and was able to return to his work." Frank finished his story, smiling at Maren and Paul.

"A very powerful message for a women's college," commented Paul, "that a woman can provide a crucial ministry."

"What did Jesus tell her that made such a difference in her life?" Maren wanted to know.

"I think just to accept the gifts that God wanted to give her," replied Frank, looking directly into her eyes.

As Paul and Maren finished the dishes, she wondered if Frank knew more about her life than she thought she had revealed to him.

Paul brought out the CD Maren had given him for his birthday. It was called *Great Trumpet Solos*, and featured music from Haydn to Wynton Marsalis. Paul obviously enjoyed it and made a point of telling Frank that Maren had given it to him. She put it on, and set it to play first, while Paul built a fire. Three lounge chairs opened out of the sectional couch, and Paul and Maren claimed two of those. Frank parked in the one free-standing lounge chair by the fireplace with his feet propped up.

The CD ended with the Canadian Brass playing "Amazing Grace," but Frank missed it; he was dozing in his recliner. About the time his body would catch up with Mountain Standard Time, he would be off to another time zone, thought Maren.

When the music stopped, he opened his eyes, excused himself, and went to his room on the lower level. Maren and Paul sat in silence, enjoying the quiet sounds of the fire. It was Paul who finally broke the silence.

"What about you?" he asked, continuing the morning's conversation as if nothing had transpired between their talk at the bridge and now. "What do you want?"

"What do you mean?"

"Out of life. What would make you happy?"

"I guess I've had it all. I don't know what could be left."

"Your life with Jack was that special, so good that the rest of life can't . . ." He uncrossed his ankles, rubbed the soles of his stocking feet on the footrest, and recrossed his ankles while looking for the right word. He didn't want to make direct comparisons. "Nothing else is even appealing?" he finished lamely.

Yesterday she would have lied, for his own good, of course. She would have told him it was so nearly perfect with Jack that she just couldn't ever be with anyone else again. But that was yesterday, a long time ago.

"I meant all of it, Paul—family, friends, work, health, a home. People ask for so much nowadays. I'm just grateful for what I've had, and it seems greedy to expect more."

Even as her words spilled out she remembered Frank looking into her eyes and saying Jesus wanted the woman at the well to accept his gifts. She ignored the nagging memory. "And, I'm afraid I misled you last night."

His heart seemed to stop beating, while he waited to hear what she would say next.

"I wanted to tell you just the good part. My marriage was good, but there were always . . . difficulties, right up to the end... serious difficulties."

"Maren, you missed the best part," he interrupted passionately. "It was ripped away from you by a storm. You were robbed of so much."

"Paul, sometimes we yelled at each other, screamed at each other," she countered. "You think I'm quiet and logical, but I yelled, I screamed. It scared the boys. I hope and pray it didn't scar them."

"You would have resolved your differences. Ask my mom and dad."

"But we didn't. I wish we would have, but we didn't. I didn't. And I bring that with me into any long-term relationship."

"You mean you believe if you marry again, you would relive the same pattern."

"Yes."

There it was. She was frozen in time. Well, he wouldn't try to talk her out of her belief. She would only find out if she worked it out for herself. There was no way to convince her it could be otherwise, unless she was willing to take a chance.

"Maren, I won't try to tell you it would be different for us. I'm just a man, like any other man. I want what every man wants, someone to be my companion, my friend, my lover, someone who will never leave me. I want someone to share my ideas and stories and time with. I want to know, without question, that my someone will be there for me when I walk through the door, when I sit down to eat, when I go to bed, and when I wake up. I want that someone to have stories and ideas that she wants to share with me. I want my someone to value my company and to trust that even if we disagree I'd still be there for her, and she would still be there for me. The truth is we haven't lived life together long enough yet to know that."

A few clouds obscured the sun and prevented it from dancing on Maren's face. Before her eyes opened, she realized it was Sunday, and she and Paul and Frank would be leaving Pine Bluff by noon.

When she went to the kitchen, Frank was preparing bread and wine to say Mass. Paul joined them, and Frank, the priest, began to say an informal Mass. He blessed and broke a new loaf of sourdough bread for communion. It wasn't like the Mass Maren remembered from her youth. She recognized some of the responses but not the form. She was spiritually moved by the experience and, surprisingly, felt closer to God than she had for a long time.

Frank had a morning flight and left after breakfast. Paul asked how Maren would like to spend their last few hours at Pine Bluff. She wanted to go back to the chapel-bridge to see the waterfall once more.

"We'll have to pack then and leave from there," Paul answered, pleased with her choice.

It was cooler outdoors and threatened snow. They stood at the bridge, protected from the wind. The sun moved high enough in the sky to be clear of clouds, casting its warm rays on the couple, as if choreographed for a movie. Maren's thoughts moved ahead to going home, back to the problems with Nick and Matt and the hospital. As if reading her mind, Paul asked if she had talked to Nick since they had been at Pine Bluff.

"I called Steve when we got here. I gave him the house number, since I don't carry my car phone. He remembered meeting you at the Christmas concert and was envious that I knew a family with a house in Colorado. Nick hadn't gotten there yet. I gave Steve strict orders to call if there was any kind of problem at all. He promised. So, I guess no news is good news."

She smiled when she remembered Steve's response. He had assumed the McCloud family was in Pine Bluff for the weekend. She hadn't intentionally misled him, but neither had she bothered to correct the misimpression. After all, she thought smugly, she and Paul were chaperoned by a priest.

Paul interrupted her thoughts. "I'm glad you came here with me, Maren. I want you to know it was a special time for me, the most special time I've ever had here. I think I know you better, and I'll never walk here again without treasuring the memories of this weekend. I see everything differently when I see it with you."

His poignant expressions always took her by surprise. He sometimes struggled with putting his emotions into words, but he persevered until he communicated exactly what he felt. She was so moved that it was she who couldn't express her emotions.

His hand rested on the old wood railing. She put her hand on his and said only, "Thank you, Paul. Thank you for a wonderful weekend."

———

The plan was for Paul to drive Maren home from the airport, but fate and airline schedules intervened. As they deplaned, the crew of the 747 at the adjoining gate was leaving the flight deck. Maren turned to look at the tall female pilot. It was Bonni Daley, pulling her wheeled flight bag behind her, looking as perky and cheerful as always after her long day.

Introductions were made, and they stopped for soft drinks to allow Paul and Bonni to get acquainted. Maren accepted Bonni's offer of a ride home, and once again Paul's visit to Maren's home was postponed. It didn't bother him as much this time. After all, he thought, some real progress had been made. He didn't yet appreciate the depth of her fear of repeating past patterns, nor did he realize that Steve Wagner was waiting in her living room.

———

"Bonni, that's Steve's car. Something must be wrong. Nick's car isn't here."

As Bonni was turning the key to stop the engine of her new Cherokee, Maren was already out of the car and running up the walk to her front door. Bonni was close on her heels, worried for her friend.

When Steve heard the door, he was sitting on the couch in Maren's family room watching TV. Before he could get to the formal living room and entryway, Maren was in the door. She looked alarmed, and Bonni was coming through the door looking concerned.

"What's wrong?" gasped Maren.

"Whoa." He grabbed her arms to stop her. "Everything's fine."

"Where's Nick?"

"He started back about a half hour ago. Everything's okay," he assured her. Relief registered on the faces of both women.

"But how—"

"Nick let me in. He left some winter clothes here and took some things he needed for warmer weather. We had a great time. He's fine, honest." Steve still held Maren's shoulders.

"Oh, thank you," Maren managed, feeling weak. They gave each other a hug, and exchanged a quick kiss, the kind long-time partners display in public, before Maren took off her coat.

She didn't see Bonni's reaction to the homecoming. Bonni had heard so much about Paul and had just enjoyed several hours in his company. Watching the homecoming Bonni felt like she had been punched in the stomach. Her large dark eyes were wide with surprise; her jaw dropped. How, she wondered, could Maren end a romantic weekend with one man and run to the waiting arms of another, literally within minutes?

"I think I'd better be on my way," Bonni said tersely.

"No, stay," Steve insisted. "I have some good news, and you'll appreciate it, too. I've been assigned a class date to train on 747s. I'll be in Denver from May 1st until almost the end of June. The women congratulated him, but Bonni insisted that she needed to get home. "It sounds like you two need some time to chat," she stated dryly, already walking to the door.

Once Bonni had gone they sat facing each other on her old couch. "I've been thinking all weekend Maren… our lives just fit together, like we've been moving toward this relationship all our lives. I'm surprised at how much I missed you, even for a couple of days."

"But, Steve," Maren protested, "we often don't see each other for weeks."

"That's different," he insisted. "That's when I'm out of town. I'm used to knowing you are here. We should take another trip to the cabin. That's where it initially hit me. I was so overwhelmed that day, but I'm afraid I rushed you too much. I want you to know I'm backing off, slowing down, way slow, until you have time to get used to this new dimension of our relationship."

Maren was confused. Maybe Steve was having some reaction because he played father to Nick for the weekend. She hadn't counted on that. She was touched by his revelation and concern for her and relieved at his willingness to slow down, in spite of his preference. His presence in her house did feel reassuring to Maren in several ways. It was more like coming home after a pleasant vacation. Nick had been in capable hands. And Steve was waiting. She was grateful that he respected her privacy and did not inquire about her weekend. Seeing him was like a splash of real life, she decided, jolting her back from the fantasy she had enjoyed in Colorado.

Chapter 18

Maren worked a long day Monday and a half day on Tuesday. During her medical appointment in Edgelawn Tuesday afternoon with Dr. Logan, he told her again that the pain would continue to worsen until she had the hysterectomy. She wanted to wait until July, when the boys would be home and some of their problems resolved. Ziff had told her if they could get Nick through the school year and back in his home environment for the summer months, it could be enough to pull him away from Lois and the cult. Maren couldn't agree to be unavailable to him for four to six weeks, not right now.

Matt needed some help, too, sorting out which road to start down, if indeed he had closed the door permanently on a career in law. She called the boys several times a week now and was beginning to feel that she was walking on eggs in her efforts to make only supportive comments to each.

By midweek she needed time out to do some processing, and the Metra ride home provided an opportunity. She had received a summons to testify in court about little Allison. She mused about that for the first few miles of the trip. What could she testify? Her records contained everything. Why not just send them?

She recalled her recent run-in with the supervisor from the state agency about a number of issues. The woman had come late in the afternoon, without warning, to review Allison's status with the therapists, and Maren had used the opportunity to complain to her about the number of strangers the child was expected to relate to.

A different transporter brought Allison to the hospital each week. Today, a man drove the van. Allison had obviously been crying for a long time before arriving at St. John's. How could they use a male transporter, knowing she had a history of possible sexual abuse? This particular transporter didn't have a very soothing manner with her either. Maybe that made it seem worse than it was. The supervisor basically told Maren to "butt out."

Maren had expressed concern about the apparent lack of interest of the foster parents, too. The foster parents never transported the child themselves and never returned Maren's calls. They didn't attended therapy sessions either. She was told again to butt out. With support from the other therapists on the team, Maren had held her ground. The supervisor had backed down finally and agreed to make sure at least one foster parent would attend at least one therapy session each month. The problem, according to the woman, was that if the foster parents were allowed to visit therapy, the biological mother would demand to visit therapy, too. Maren had been so upset after the meeting that she went out for a walk to calm down.

The last thing she had done before leaving for the day was to place a call to Dr. Schumann and dump the story in his lap. She hadn't been sure it was the right thing to do, but if the court would listen to anyone, maybe it would listen to the prominent pediatrician.

As the wheels ran over the tracks in a comforting rhythm, Maren let loose of the drama of the day and began turning her thoughts westward.

She had been puzzled when Bonni had phoned Monday evening and the two nearly had a fight. Bonni had told her she was more than puzzled. After a few preliminary questions, Bonni had become more pointed.

"What kind of chat did you two have last night?" she had asked in an almost accusing tone. When Maren gave no substantive answer, she had warned, "You're headed for disaster, Maren, one way or another. You're living two lives, connected only by the thread of the railroad tracks. What does that do to you on the inside? What are you doing to Paul and to Steve? How can you ever have a whole life?"

Maren had never known Bonni to be so upset and still didn't understand her concern. "People have different facets to their personalities, and different friends," Maren had responded calmly. "Maybe the Metra is a kind of twilight zone between one part of my life and another; but both are parts of the whole." Bonni had ended the conversation with an ominous prediction. "Maren, you may be fooling yourself, but it's plain to me you are headed for a crash landing."

The slowing speed of the train brought Maren back to the present. It shouldn't be slowing; this was the express. Maybe they were farther west than she thought. She looked out her window. Being in the first car gave her a good view. In the distance she could see pedestrians standing between tracks. Maybe Metra employees were on strike or trying to catch a ride between stops.

The train stopped, and the door of her car opened. The conductor who had taken Maren's ticket walked through the car and exited without comment. He returned a moment later looking pale and very sober. He had his arm around what appeared to be the engineer from another train, possibly the train she could see on the other track, headed toward Chicago. The man looked ill. Several other crewmembers from the other train came into Maren's car, too.

"A breakdown?" she asked one conductor as he sat down across from her.

"An accident, ma'am," he replied dolefully. He put his head in his hands and leaned forward, elbows on his knees. Muffled sobbing sounds came from his throat. "Oh Jesus, Jesus," he moaned softly.

Alarmed, Maren asked if anyone was hurt. "Fatality, fatality, a suicide, ma'am . . . We tried to stop, we tried to stop." He repeated the words over and over. Then the car was quiet except for the man's labored breathing.

Another conductor came on board and announced over the intercom that passengers from the other train would board and be returned to the next station where they would wait for an eastbound train. There were only a few eastbound passengers this time of day.

The train began to creep forward, and Maren could see police as the train neared the point of impact. According to one crewmember, a woman had run onto the track in the face of the eastbound express. It had been at top speed. There was no possibility that the engineer could have stopped before the impact, although he did brake. Once stopped, he had backed the train to the area where Maren now saw it parked.

Just in front of the engine were two forms, one on each side of the tracks. There must have been two victims, Maren thought. But as they passed beside the forms, she realized the grotesque truth. The woman had been literally cut in half. Legs and abdomen were just being covered. The feet, now shoeless, stuck out. A head and upper body was on the other side, not yet covered.

Maren stared, horrified. It was incongruous. Nothing in her experience helped her reconcile the scene. Her mind couldn't assimilate it as reality. A body belonged together, in one piece, even if badly injured.

Finally, a policeman covered the torso. Two little humps of flesh under the blanket proclaimed that this was once a woman. The rest of the ride was eerily quiet. Passengers and extra crewmembers were left at the station. No one complained about being behind schedule. No one spoke.

Maren didn't remember the drive home. She didn't remember taking a shower. She didn't eat. There was no one to share such a gory story with, but she needed to talk. She remembered pushing buttons on her phone and that Paul answered. It took him less than fifty minutes to get to her door.

—

Much of the following weekend was spent with Paul and his family. Maren and Paul finally got their bike ride along the lake. They stopped at the travel agency so Maren could meet Elizabeth. They went out to dinner with Penny and Jim in the evening and had dessert at their home.

Maren's initial fondness for Penny increased, and she liked Jim immediately. Penny was beginning to look pregnant, and they were so obviously happy together. Erin was a beautiful child, but strong willed in a beguiling way. She had waited up to see if fondue chocolate and fruit were as good as Mommy had promised.

Maren spent the night at Paul's, and early Sunday morning he took her to Mass at the church where he had been confirmed. Unlike Maren's confirmation, his had been an important event in his life, a turning point.

They met Bob and Gloria for lunch at their condo. During the course of the meal Paul's parents mentioned that their forty-second anniversary would be in a few weeks. They reminisced about the early days of their marriage. They had been independent young people, each pulling in roughly the same direction but at different times and in different ways. They had fought numerous battles, each admitted.

Bob reached tenderly for Gloria's hand at the table and looked into her eyes. "I'd have been lost without you," he said without embarrassment.

Gloria addressed Maren. "My life would have been so empty without Bob. Not just because of the children, but because he brought out the best in me. And I'd like to think I had something to do with keeping him out of trouble. My parents were sure that because he was so much older than I was, and kind of a free spirit, I would have nothing but heartache. The truth is he kept my heart from breaking through so many difficult times, and we've both been blessed with good times and good health."

Maren was touched, but wondered if Paul had put them up to sharing those particular thoughts today. She glanced at him sideways, but he just smiled an openly affectionate smile and reached for her hand under the table.

Bob changed the subject to Maren's sons. He peppered her with questions and was genuinely interested in receiving in-depth answers. He mentioned that he would like to go with Paul sometime to meet Nick. He hoped Maren didn't mind, which, of course, she did not.

That accomplished, he moved on to Matt. Bob's younger sister, Cloris, was in California, he informed her. He planned to visit her in the next couple of weeks. Did Maren think Matt would meet with him, maybe go sailing with him and some of the family?

Bob had such a warm, genuine smile. There was a calmness about him reflected in his voice. She told him Matt could use a break from the law courses that he was only finishing at her insistence. She knew Matt would enjoy Bob and the sailing immensely.

⁓

The thunder started just outside Springfield. An hour into his drive the rain began. There were heavy thunderstorms the rest of the way. Instead of staying on Route 55 into Chicago, Paul turned north and headed for Edgelawn. He was eager to see Maren and tell her about his visit with Nick. She would be so pleased.

Thunderstorms were becoming a tradition with them. It had rained the first night after their dinner at the Yellow Duck, Paul remembered, and the first night they kissed, too. Maren told him later she thought thunderstorms were romantic. "Very romantic," she had said with emphasis.

As he negotiated the rain-slick highway, he thought about how their relationship had deepened since the trip to Pine Bluff. He imagined her surprised expression when she would open the door.

The rain was just tapering off when he pulled into her driveway. He would have a Coke, fill her in on his visit with Nick, and head back to the city. It had already been a very long day.

The house looked dark from the driveway, although a strange car was parked in front of the garage. Maybe Bonni's. It was so late, who else could it be? They must be in the family room in the back, he guessed. He rang the bell a second time. Paul's expectant smile disintegrated when the door was swung wide by Steve Wagner. Steve's smile also faded.

After cool greetings the two men stood uneasily between the kitchen and the family room, as if not sure exactly where each belonged.

"Maren is changing clothes," Steve explained. "She'll be right out."

Paul, without intending to, scanned the scene for evidence of what had transpired here while he was driving through the storm. Dirty dishes, smeared with tomato sauce, were stacked in the sink. Steve was casually dressed and in stocking feet. His breath betrayed the fact that wine had accompanied or followed the meal.

After pacing back and forth a few times Paul spotted an almost empty bottle of Merlot on the floor next to the couch. Two empty wine glasses were on the glass coffee table in front of the couch. It was only then that he heard quiet music playing through the stereo system.

The silence between the two was becoming intolerable when they heard Maren's bedroom door. She was also in stocking feet and had obviously pulled on a warm-up suit in haste. She was still zipping up the jacket as she came around the corner. She was mid-sentence asking

Steve who was at the door when she saw Paul standing silently by the kitchen island, in the spotlight of a recessed ceiling fixture. The tension in the room was palpable.

"Paul, what are you doing . . . I wasn't expecting you. It's the middle of the week," she finished lamely.

"Obviously," Paul responded tersely. "I saw Nick today after my meeting in Springfield. I thought you might want to know."

"Steve was just leaving." Maren looked pleadingly at her dinner guest.

"Yeah," Steve agreed with a broad smile. "It's really too late for guests. I don't want to wear out my welcome, since I am a frequent visitor."

Paul made no response. His face remained expressionless, and he didn't take his eyes off Maren. He watched her retrieve Steve's shoes from under the couch and hand them to him. Steve walked stocking-footed through the arch to the living room, carrying the shoes.

"See you Saturday," he called cheerfully over his shoulder as he closed the front door behind him. He didn't say good-bye to Paul, and Paul made no effort to be polite at Steve's departure.

"He came for dinner," Maren said, uncomfortable that she was put in the position of explaining her friend's presence.

"It must have been a messy meal if you had to change clothes." Paul's voice cut through her.

"It was," she began. Feeling defensive, she stopped. "I don't have to explain my behavior to you."

"Can you explain it to yourself?" he challenged coldly but without anger.

"You have no right to criticize my social life. You don't share details of your social life with me. You disappear for days at a time without explanation." She stopped, not wanting to reveal how many times she had hoped to see him or talk with him when he was unavailable.

She noticed finally that his jacket and hair were wet and that his eyes were strained and bloodshot. "You look tired. Can I get you some food? There's leftover spaghetti." As she walked toward the refrigerator, she stepped into the pool of light that came from the recessed fixture above his head. His nearness made her ache with regret. She wished she hadn't spoken so harshly.

"Just a Coke. I need to head for home." He spoke now in a quiet monotone, disappointed that his second visit to Maren's home had not met his expectations.

Chapter 19

Judy informed Maren that Dr. Nolan had scheduled the first thyroplasty at St. John's. The strobe would not arrive until fall, but he was eager to start servicing his own patients, rather than referring them to the university hospitals. The agreement between Metro ENT and the hospital called for one of the speech pathologists to observe phonosurgeries and certain laryngeal procedures. Judy felt Maren should observe, since Judy had not yet attended a conference.

Maren was unfamiliar with the patient, so Judy briefed her. Ronald Kelly was a seventy-two-year-old man who weighed two hundred pounds before his left CVA., which occurred while Maren had been at the videostroboscopy conference after the holidays. He now weighed one-sixty-five.

There was dense hemi-paresis on his right side. Judy had done several video swallow studies. His severe dysphagia was being managed with altered diet, thickened liquids, and some compensatory techniques, such as turning his head to the right for swallowing. He also suffered from severe aphasia and was aphonic, no voice at all. It was impossible to assess language because his voice was inaudible, and reading and writing were now nearly nonexistent skills.

Judy had used an amplification device with him once before he was discharged, but there hadn't been enough voice to amplify. When he was rested, he could only whisper, and that with determined effort. He had gone to live with his son and had around-the-clock professional caregivers who couldn't understand him at all. He was totally isolated by his inability to communicate. Depression had set in.

Judy had emphasized the need for an ENT evaluation, and Mr. Kelly had seen Dr. Nolan the day after he returned from the phonosurgery conference. Dr. Nolan had diagnosed unilateral vocal fold paralysis and recommended thyroplasty. Judy had agreed that Ron Kelly was a good candidate. Speech was his best chance at communicating. In the event the laryngeal nerve did recover, the procedure could be revised.

Maren wished Paul had studied with Dr. Hiroshu in Wisconsin, instead of Nolan. She had read articles but only vaguely understood the procedures discussed. She knew of techniques that involved injecting a substance into a paralyzed vocal fold to "bulk it up," but otolaryngologists seemed to prefer thyroplasty. It had proved to be quite successful in reducing or eliminating any swallowing problems, and it gave the patient a voice instantly. Most doctors waited six months or longer to be sure there wouldn't be spontaneous recovery. That was a long time for a geriatric patient to be unable to communicate. With thyroplasty Mr. Kelly would be able to speak in the operating room. It did seem like a good option for him.

Maren had reviewed articles that detailed the procedure and had attempted to explain it to Judy in order to better understand it herself. Mr. Kelly would be sedated and given local anesthetics. An incision would be made in his neck and a rectangular piece cut out of his thyroid cartilage, creating a window to the muscles of the larynx. The surgeon would insert a small, rectangular piece of plastic through the window and position it against the side of the vocal fold. The plastic block would push the paralyzed vocal fold toward the midline, where the healthy vocal fold could meet it. If the nerve recovered at the end of six months and the vocal fold began to move, the chunk of plastic could be removed with another short surgical procedure.

Today was the big day. Maren had been detained in Radiology and was late getting to the OR. She wished she didn't have to have any contact with Dr. Nolan, but short of making an issue of what had happened at the conference, she had no choice.

As she entered operating room 2 Dr. Nolan looked up. "Oh good, you're just in time. I'm cutting the window in the cartilage now." Maren was in scrubs already, but Dr. Nolan directed the circulating nurse to gown and glove her, so she could stand closer to the patient. Maren thought he was either able to totally separate social from professional events, or he had no memory of the incident in her hotel room.

She tried to orient herself to the anatomy. Studying pictures and models of the laryngeal muscles was not the same as looking inside the neck of a living person. Dr. Nolan began instructing her, and she was grateful. She had difficulty hearing him clearly through his mask though. She noticed the way Mr. Kelly was strapped in on the right side of the table, only on one side.

"How you doing, Kelly?" Dr. Nolan asked loudly. "We're almost there."

Amazing to do this with only local anesthetics and a sedative, she thought, but keeping the patient awake was important. The anesthesiologist could vary the drip to evoke the state of consciousness required. For the present, Mr. Kelly had no voice to answer.

"Why is just one arm strapped?" Maren asked the nurse.

"Oh, you know, that's the bad arm from his stroke. It just dangles."

Of course, thought Maren, still trying to assimilate all the details of the case. Mr. Kelly had a left CVA, therefore his right side was paralyzed.

With a sudden realization, she stopped breathing. She was looking at the surgical opening on the left side of Mr. Kelly's neck.

It should be the right vocal fold that's paralyzed! Why would Dr. Nolan be doing the thyroplasty on his left side? Is it possible he is making a mistake? Not possible, her mind responded.

She could think of no reason why he would operate on the strong side. What could she do at this point? Should she say something? She was only present at the invitation of the ENT group, as an observer.

As the disturbing questions raced through Maren's mind, Dr. Nolan was placing the piece of thyroid cartilage on a small tray. It was passed by Maren's frozen stare. It was too late to preserve the integrity of the cartilage.

Dr. Nolan had pre-cut several rectangles from the plastic material so he could quickly choose the size he found was required for this particular patient. He carved a notch on each, designed to catch on the edge of the thyroid cartilage and keep the chunk from going in too far or becoming dislodged. The pieces were about the size of the *enter* key on her computer keyboard, but half as thick.

"Hey, Kelly," yelled Dr. Nolan, as if the man were deaf. "Sing 'Take Me Out To The Ball Game.'"

Mr. Kelly's lips moved, but there was only a faint whisper.

"Umm, guess we'll try the next size," mumbled Dr. Nolan under his mask.

This was repeated twice more while Maren watched in silence. Each chunk was bigger, so that it went deeper into the neck. Each time Mr. Kelly failed to produce voice, her fear that Dr. Nolan was operating on the wrong side increased. She began to feel queasy as she watched the surgeon insert and push the largest boat-shaped piece into position.

Finally, in response to Dr. Nolan's demand to sing, Mr. Kelly demonstrated a hoarse whisper. Maren raised her eyes to meet the surgeon's, questioning what he would do next. They were not Paul's clear, steady eyes. These eyes were watery and bloodshot.

Somewhere in the back of Maren's mind another troubling question began to form. *Is it possible Dr. Nolan was drinking before surgery? Soap opera thoughts*, Maren scolded herself.

"What do you think, Maren?" Dr. Nolan's voice was husky.

Before she could answer, he directed her to walk to the head of the table. There, a flexible scope was already inserted through Mr. Kelly's nose. It was clamped in position and provided her a view of the vocal folds.

"Tell me whether we need to be more anterior or posterior," he commanded.

Maren adjusted the focus and tried to reorient herself to right and left, anterior and posterior. Since she was now sitting behind the top of the patient's head, she no longer had to think her left was his right. That should have made it easier, but she felt a wave of nausea. Did the scope reverse the image? She wasn't sure. *What am I doing here? This isn't my job. How can this be happening?*

"Doctor," she said as calmly as she could, "I'm confused. This man should have a right paralysis, and you're placing the block on the left."

Dr. Nolan snorted. "You need to study your neurology some more." He ran the words "some more" together, producing a word that sounded like the name of the campfire treat, s'more. "Look here." She watched the left vocal fold move as he probed in the patient's neck. "Did you see that move?"

"Yes," she answered immediately, "but . . . "

"And that," he said again, interrupting her. "Was that more anterior or posterior? That's front and back to you," he added scornfully. She didn't answer immediately. "Well, which is it?"

"More in the back," she answered in layman's terms, now that she was completely shaken. A tense silence filled the room.

Instead of carefully cutting another larger shim like the other rectangle pieces, Dr. Nolan strode to the table where supplies were laid out and quickly cut a sliver of the plastic material. He returned to the patient, and Maren cautiously walked around the supply table to return to the operating table.

"You're not sterile," the circulating nurse snapped at her. "She was out of the field, Doctor,"

"Well, just stand there then, and tell me, is the patient's voice louder now?"

Maren watched from several feet away as he pushed the sliver of plastic through the cartilage window and placed the largest shim on top.

"Sing, Kelly," the surgeon commanded.

This time Mr. Kelly sang. It was a hoarse voice, very hoarse. And something else—he produced two tones at once, every time he spoke, like a chord. She knew the term to describe it was *diplophonia*.

"Is he louder?" Dr. Nolan demanded again.

"Yes, Doctor," Maren answered dutifully, without contributing her perceptual judgment.

"Thank you, Miss speech therapist, for your expertise," the doctor sneered. Even in her state of confusion, Maren's trained ear detected that the /sh/ sound was substituted for /ch/ in the word. "Speesh," he pronounced it.

"Then you may go," he commanded in a condescending tone.

The nurses were silent, and astonished looks were exchanged behind surgical masks. Even the anesthesiologist had dropped his magazine to watch the little drama in front of him. Maren was virtually being thrown out of the OR.

She stumbled into the hall, still wearing the gown and gloves over scrubs. She was shaking, her eyes filling with tears. She turned and started blindly down the corridor, but slammed into the chest of a tall person walking in the opposite direction.

"Whoa," said a familiar voice. "Where you going in such a rush?"

Maren looked up into the friendly face of Dr. Charles Ziffarelli. She was afraid she would sob if she started to talk. "Ziff," she choked out, wanting to hug him.

Ziff had caught her shoulders as they collided He immediately saw the distress in her eyes. The sound of her voice let him know she needed help. He took her by the arm and led her to the door to the women's lockers.

"Get dressed," he directed, calmly. "I'll meet you on the other side."

When she appeared, tears were falling noiselessly down her cheeks. "Let's get you some air," he said. He assumed she had heard bad news about Nick.

His office was on first floor, but a long public walk from the OR, so he guided her through the back emergency door to the parking lot. He unlocked his car and held the door for her. Once inside his car she broke down completely. He waited without comment until she became quiet and he could begin to piece together what had happened. While the picture wasn't pretty, at least it wasn't about Nick.

Ziff couldn't break confidentiality to tell her that one of Nolan's partners had already consulted with him about Nolan's drinking. Ziff wasn't familiar with the surgery she described and advised her to talk to Paul about it before taking any other action. He got her permission to talk to Paul himself about the whole thing.

When Maren came to the end of her story, Ziff confessed he had thought something terrible had happened to Nick. "Teenagers involved with cults usually have some"—he hesitated, not wanting to upset her again— "have a hard time breaking free." What he was thinking was that they don't often come through the experience unscathed, and he wanted to warn her.

Maren looked sympathetically at Ziff and realized she had given him quite a scare. "I'm sorry I worried you about Nick. I believe he will escape from the group, almost unscathed."

Odd, he thought, that she should use the very word in his mind. "Well, we always hope that will be the case." He was patronizing her and she knew it.

"Yes, well, I said 'I believe,' and my belief is based on more than some kind of naive hope. It's based on faith and experience."

She told him briefly about Nick's fall from the tree at Lake Mazon and how that vision had appeared in her mind without her call for it or for any comfort. It happened at the very instant that she would have given up hope of Nick's rescue. "That's the Holy Spirit," she assured him.

He looked at her without comment, unconvinced, but impressed.

"You are looking much better," he pronounced. "Do you think you're ready to go back inside?"

She walked with Ziff around the corner of the building to the west side entrance that led down to the lower-level speech office. Fortunately, the outpatients in the afternoon were the children she was co-treating with PT and OT. She could lean on the other therapists for once.

Maren paged Paul and arranged to meet him at his house. She also called Steve Wagner to cancel their dinner at her place. Steve had promised to cook. That meant he would grill steaks or pick up Chinese, but even so Maren always appreciated having him there. How the food was prepared didn't matter. There was some hospital business, she told him; she needed to discuss an incident she had witnessed. She didn't mention where the discussion would take place or with whom.

———

Maren arrived at Paul's house first. She called her answering machine to retrieve messages, in case one of the boys had phoned. The only call was from her gynecologist. He had left his home number in case she needed to contact him after hours.

This can't be good, she thought as she dialed. Dr. Logan answered the phone. Her Pap smear showed some cell changes. He wanted her to stop stalling and schedule her surgery no later than the first of June.

"That's only a month from now," she complained.

"It's six weeks, Maren, and the end of June at the absolute latest," he said sternly.

Paul came in as she was ending the call. Instead of a greeting she said, "I have to schedule surgery." She said the word *surgery* as if her doctor had told her to drink poison.

Paul didn't understand; he saw the hysterectomy as a solution, a way for Maren to permanently eliminate the pain she suffered. Surgery was an option he employed on a daily basis to provide healthier lives for patients.

"Paul, I hate surgery."

Not knowing the events of the day, Paul asked if she was afraid of the anesthetic; many patients were.

"You don't understand. I hate surgery. I hated seeing that first tonsillectomy I watched."

"But you were fine," he answered, vaguely aware of the change of subject.

"I was sick for hours afterwards," she insisted.

Paul was caught off guard. He wasn't sure which part of her statements to address, her concern with her own surgery or her newly stated distaste for all surgery. Before he could decide, she went on.

"I don't know how anyone can get used to the sights and smells, the unbelievable invasion of personhood. It's inhuman. You all think you're God, tinkering inside human beings, violating their privacy while you crack jokes. All in a day's work, and if you make a mistake, 'Oops, sorry about that,' and off to the next table in the next room. Keep on schedule. Time to take out another part, a larynx, a kidney, a uterus . . ."

She was clearly hysterical, something Paul didn't handle well. On a personal level he was stunned and wounded at her dismissal of all surgeons and all surgery. The night of the train accident he had held her hand and listened to her graphic description of the corpse. She had told him there was no one else she could have shared it with. That had made him feel there was nothing he couldn't share with her. He had told her about the young man whose face was split open the day before their trip to Denver and what it did to him inside.

Now he wondered if he had made a mistake, opening that part of himself to her. She was hysterical, and he was confused. Not a good combination, he realized instantly. He tried in a logical way to empathize and to calm her, because that was his way.

"Maren, when I was in med school, I was revolted at some of what I observed, but the fascination and the possibility of making a difference in someone's life is what made me go back."

Over time, he had learned to edit his reports to his family. Eventually, there were only a few specific friends in the field that he could always be open with. He had been shocked and sickened on many occasions, but always he had to go back. He felt he had no choice, as if it was his destiny. Clearly, Maren had a choice.

Quietly and somewhat sadly he tried to explain to her. "You really do get used to it. After standing in an OR for hours, fatigue and hunger set in. They keep you from being overly empathetic. After a while it's a job. You learn to do it well, whether you're hungry or tired or sick, just like any other job."

"And forget that the person on the table has feelings."

"Sometimes, yes," he admitted sadly, "but the really good surgical team is always aware and always uses techniques that will minimize pain and ensure the fastest healing. I never treat an old man without thinking it might be my dad, or a child without knowing it could be Erin."

"And how do you live with that?" she asked, momentarily calmed by the honest emotion in his voice. "Drink?" She was referring to Nolan, but Paul couldn't know that.

"It's not an easy life, Maren. There is a tremendous amount of pressure. And, yes, abuse of alcohol and drugs does occur." He finished quietly, hoping her hysteria would dissolve if he stayed calm.

"Well, I'm not a doctor, not a surgeon"—she raised her voice again—"and I don't want to be."

"Maren, you're a health professional." He was arguing with her now and didn't like it. "At some level you deal with the same issues."

"No. No, you're one of them, but I'm not going to be," she continued with a louder voice. Paul was no longer sure what they were discussing, but he knew it had escalated into some sort of ugly argument.

"One of who?"

"Surgeons! You help each other, all right. You cover for each other. Rick Nolan was drunk and operated on the wrong side, but I know you'll defend him." Her anger over what she had witnessed in the OR finally burst out.

Now Paul realized there was another basis for the argument. He refrained from defending himself and instead inquired about the incident. He understood the thyroplasty procedure better than Maren did, even though he had never performed one. After her description he had more questions than she would ever be able to answer. How much swelling was there by the time the patient achieved voice? What did the flexible scope exam show prior to surgery? Was there a history of intubation that might have injured the left cord? Was it possible the elderly patient's cords were both bowed due to aging?

Paul was always hesitant of accusing another physician. Malpractice lawsuits could so easily be brought. Even the most skilled doctors were vulnerable.

"Maybe there are some other considerations," he suggested.

He tried to present some possibilities, but her fear, frustration, and humiliation from the morning mixed with the anxiety over her own health had turned to sheer generalized anger. Her ability to think clearly was disabled by emotion.

"Maren, I just meant Nolan may have had good reason for doing what he did, even if he had been drinking. You've learned a lot, but there could be other facts that you weren't aware of." He continued with his faulty approach, appealing to her rational side, when she was beyond reason. Penny would have told him it was time to listen, but their conversations had never covered situations like this one.

"I know Mr. Kelly's voice quality would be better if the thyroplasty had been done on the correct side. His time in surgery would have been less, less anesthetic, probably less discomfort and swelling, and for sure no extra chunk of plastic floating around. And you're defending Rick Nolan, just like I said you would," she accused.

"I'm just saying we may not have all the facts."

Paul was right; they did not have all the facts. Only Dr. Charles Ziffarelli would after further conversations with Nolan's partner Ferraro and with Paul.

Chapter 20

After dinner at Penny and Jim's on Friday night, Paul was restless, and sensing his son's distress, Bob said he needed a walk. It was obvious that Paul was glum, as Bob called it. Paul was rarely glum, and when he was, the cause could usually be traced to a relationship or his office colleagues. Bob flipped a mental coin and asked about Maren. Paul was ready to share his hurt and confusion, and he found his father's calm acceptance reassuring.

"A woman's body is a wonderful mystery," Bob counseled. "You may be the doctor, son"—he chuckled softly—"but when you've lived with a woman for twenty or thirty years, you'll develop a different kind of appreciation. A woman may be constant, but her body is constantly changing. They have more input than we do; input from hormones and emotions, as well as intellectual input. If a woman is sensitive, like your mother, she feels things more intensely than we do."

He assured Paul that everything would work out and encouraged him to discuss the incident with Gloria. "Your mother will give you a different perspective than I can," he promised.

The opportunity to talk with his mother would not present itself for two weeks, during which time Maren was never available to him. Meanwhile, Paul had several conversations with Ziff. The first was the morning after the argument with Maren. Ziff had paged Paul to come to his office, where Ziff did most of the talking. He told Paul about his encounter with Maren and asked detailed questions about the nature of the surgery she had observed.

The second conversation was the following week, after a workout on the tennis court, when Paul finally decided to confide in Ziff about the nature of his relationship with Maren. He told his friend almost everything, omitting only the complication of Maren's relationship with Steve Wagner. He ended with his confusion over their recent argument.

If Ziff was surprised that Paul was dating Maren, there was no sign of it. He had said only that he appreciated getting all the pieces of the Nolan puzzle, and he let Paul know he couldn't share some of what he knew. Ziff had a gut feeling that the problems surrounding Rick Nolan were not going to be resolved quickly, so he set aside hospital business for the moment and focused on Paul's personal concerns.

"By the time Maren took the message from her doctor that she needed surgery, you were no longer talking to a professional who had observed surgery. You were talking with an overstressed patient who had personally just observed a surgeon who appeared to be incompetent. She obviously transferred the incident to herself and projected herself as the patient."

Paul understood Ziff's train of thought immediately and smiled at the analysis. "Maybe, but what you should also know is that Nolan was drunk at the conference Maren went to and forced his way into her room. It was pretty ugly," Paul finished, with a facial expression that let Ziff know, without details, what had occurred.

"Is that a fact?" Ziff stared off into space as he assimilated one more piece of evidence.

Paul didn't ask for advice from Ziff; he knew where to get the best. Since Bob had decided to make the California trip alone, Gloria was likely to be available all weekend. He stopped by to see her after Saturday morning's hospital rounds. She made coffee for herself, got Paul a cola, and they sat at the table in her small kitchen. He confessed to her that he was having problems understanding Maren. He told her about the impending surgery and about their argument, but didn't mention his encounter with Steve at Maren's home.

Gloria took off on a track that Paul didn't think was relevant, but he listened politely anyway. "The example you had at home was pretty traditional," Gloria said. "I was at home, your dad worked."

"You always had outside interests and projects," insisted Paul, not sure what his mom was implying.

"Yes, but they were secondary and everyone knew it. I took care of the home by staying in touch with my feelings and making sure the emotional needs of my husband and children were met. Your dad appreciates that now and acknowledges what an intricate, complex job it was, but he really didn't understand what I was doing in those early years."

Paul wondered if she was merely reminiscing, not really attempting to address his concerns. "I know that it's good for the family to have one partner fill that role, but I'm always attracted to a more goal-oriented woman who has a life of her own," he explained.

"You understand each other immediately," affirmed Gloria.

Now Paul knew his mother had something specific in mind. He had always been impressed with her mind. She kept up with issues and had keen insights. He waited without interrupting.

"Women today are more goal oriented, as you say," she continued slowly. "At least, they have new kinds of goals. I think that as women become more focused on technology and data, they lose touch with their feelings, just as men generally have in the past. They become better companions for men on one hand, but in doing so they give up a certain amount of time and energy that used to be available to focus on their inner selves and the inner selves of their partners. I'm not saying that's a bad exchange, but between the two partners a new system needs to be worked out to nurture the relationship to greater depths. If that doesn't happen, the deeper realms of their relationship will never be explored or experienced. That would be a great loss."

Paul noticed how carefully she avoided words like *shallow* and *superficial*. He got the message though. He sat quietly, thinking through some of his past relationships and the one he now had with Maren. Just as he decided their conversation was at an end, Gloria spoke again.

"I personally think that the traditional female skills, which were taken for granted in the past, will be lost, in the sense that they won't be handed down from mother to daughter. Men, who want a rich and satisfying personal relationship in addition to enjoying a woman as a work companion, will have to assume more responsibility for the emotional side of the relationship."

Paul smiled. "And have you some guidelines?"

"No."

"But you have some ideas," he coaxed.

"I think a man will have to nurture the feelings of his partner. Only when she experiences her own feelings more fully will his be nurtured. He could begin by simply asking how she feels, providing quiet time to just be, giving them both permission to change focus from outer to inner, to explore the art in addition to the science of love. When a woman is out of touch with herself, emotions will become more volatile."

Gloria stopped. She had come to the point of Paul's argument with Maren and wanted to be sure she wasn't critical of her son's chosen partner. She felt she had been as specific as she could get. Gloria wanted to support her son in his journey, but also allow space for him to work out problems for himself.

"What if the man is not into nurturing feelings?" prodded Paul.

"You're a sensitive person, Paul, just add a little romance." Realizing he needed more encouragement, she smiled and added, "Give her some time to mull things over. If it's meant to work out, it will."

Maren withdrew to Edgelawn as much as possible following the incident in the OR and her argument with Paul. He called several times the weeks following their quarrel, but she hadn't been ready to see him. She made excuses. She planted flowers, did spring cleaning, shopped, and baked. She talked with old friends and with her sister. She spent more time with Steve, too. He listened to her abbreviated description of the surgery and didn't hesitate to give his opinion.

"The guy should be reported, Maren," he said bluntly. "You're the only one who can prevent other, more serious incidents. Wouldn't you hope someone would protect you from a surgeon like him?"

Steve didn't know about her previous difficulty with Rick Nolan. Just as well, she thought. Steve was so emotional, he'd probably punch him in the nose. He didn't know about her argument with Paul either. Maren wasn't ready to discuss their falling out with anyone; it was still too unsettling. She needed to process it over and over in her mind first. She thought about discussing it with Ziff after he told her he knew that she and Paul were dating, but Ziff hadn't known her when she was married to Jack. Somehow that seemed important.

Saturday morning, while Paul talked with his mother, Maren was on the golf course with Bonni. They enjoyed the first two holes without conversation. As Bonni sipped out of her coffee mug, she tipped it at steeper angles, and as she did so became more talkative. As always, there was a stream of questions.

Maren answered gladly. "Nick is the same, still keeping company with Lois, but at least getting his assignments done. He'll be home for the summer in a few weeks. Matt needs lots of encouragement lately, since he's decided to abandon law school. He's getting a nice break this weekend. He's sailing with Bob McCloud, Bob's sister Cloris, and one of her sons. Matt is a typical firstborn son—he's disciplined. He'll get his class credits and be ready to sort out his life when he gets home."

"Speaking of the McClouds," Bonni interrupted, "how's Paul?"

"Oh, we're not seeing each other much," Maren answered vaguely. "I've been busy here at home."

Wondering if Maren had decided to terminate her friendship with Paul to pursue the one with Steve, she risked pressing for details. Maren was not able to concentrate on golf and dodge Bonni's queries tactfully. She topped the ball. It popped in front of the tee, three feet from where they stood. She threw Bonni a disgusted look.

"Was that look for me, the shot, or Paul?" Bonni asked with raised eyebrows. Before Maren could answer, Bonni advised, "Take another shot. We're not keeping score today, and there's no one behind us waiting."

"The look was for all three," answered Maren, pulling a new ball from her pocket and teeing up again. "We had a disagreement."

"Take your shot, then tell me," suggested Bonni.

As they walked down the fairway, Maren summarized the events of Stormy Wednesday, as she called it.

"So you argued," Bonni repeated, waiting for the rest of the story. "But your disagreement was about what exactly?"

"It doesn't matter, does it? What matters is we are too different, and I am not going to live in a relationship with yelling and screaming again."

"Paul screamed at you?" Bonni was incredulous.

"I screamed at him, and that's all I want to say about it for now."

No amount of coaxing would change Maren's mind. Bonni decided to ask about Steve, and Maren reported breezily how comfortable their relationship had become. "He's really being quite considerate and not intruding too quickly into my emotional space." Bonni wanted to ask about their physical space, but sensed Maren had revealed as much as she wanted for the time being. She pulled a five-iron from her bag, shaking her head at the mix of messages her friend had just given her. "It will be interesting to see how this plays out," she said, as if referring to their golf game.

Matt's call came before she could get dinner together on Monday evening.

"I had a great time sailing with the McClouds, Mom. I wish you and Paul could have been here."

"That just wasn't possible," Maren answered, knowing that no explanation was really necessary. Still, she was uncomfortable skirting the issue of her relationship with Paul. There was no reason Matt couldn't enjoy a one-time outing with Paul's dad, aunt, and cousin, she rationalized to herself. Cloris's son Jason was only a couple of years older than Matt, yet it was Bob he mostly talked about, especially Bob's sailing skill.

"Did you know that Bob races?" he asked, awe in his voice. "He said the way to improve your skills is to race. He's in really good shape. He's a very patient teacher, too." Maren wasn't surprised. Paul also was a good teacher, she admitted, a lump forming in her throat that she couldn't explain. "I thought I would like sailing," Matt continued, "but I didn't think I'd find it so relaxing and at the same time so much of a challenge."

"I wish you were this enthusiastic about law," Maren interjected, hoping to steer the conversation away from a subject that stirred emotions in her she preferred to keep safely in check.

"Mom, I not only don't enjoy my present courses, I hate law school. I should have quit at the semester and stayed home in January. The last few months have been a colossal waste of time."

"Matt, no, nothing you learn is a waste. You have a solid bachelor's degree in business. The year of law will come in handy someday, you'll see." She spoke with more conviction than she felt, urging him to get through finals so he would get credit for his courses.

"Mom, I'll do it, but mainly to please you. I've decided to come home in June and get some kind of job. Maybe I'm supposed to come home to help Nick." His voice quavered, revealing his uncertainty.

Maren's heart ached for him. It was hard to see her firstborn struggle. "It will all work out, Matt. I promise."

"Thanks, Mom. Thanks for always being there. I love you."

"I love you, too, son. Good night."

Tuesday morning when she turned to leave the ICA Maren noticed an acquaintance from her church, Regina D'amico. Regina's dad was having a leg amputated due to diabetes. She squealed with pleasure at seeing Maren. A familiar face in an unfamiliar hospital was comforting to family as well as patients. Maren chatted a few minutes and moved on.

Her next patient was so weak her voice was nearly inaudible. Eighty-year-old Celia Ellingham had suffered a severe left CVA. Maren couldn't elicit a single functional verbal response. The woman sat slouched in her wheelchair, bending nearly in half. Maren was afraid Celia would continue rolling forward and fall to the floor. She asked the nurse if Celia could be put in bed, and if by chance she had just finished physical therapy. The answers were no to the former and yes to the latter. The OT team needed to see her before she could go back to bed.

What can they possibly do that could be considered therapy? Maren wondered. Speech therapy didn't work that way. The patient had to be strong enough to provide the response; she couldn't simply manipulate her patients.

She walked down the hall, hoping for more success with Bill Talaricco, a right CVA patient. She had attempted to see him three times earlier, but he had always been out for a test or having another therapy. This time he was in his room, but he was disoriented. He hardly moved his tongue when she directed him to protrude it or move it side to side. Maren pulled a pack of long cotton swabs from one pocket and a small jelly container from another. With Bill's wife and daughter watching, Maren dabbed the cotton swab in jelly and dotted it on his lip, first on the right side where it would be easiest for him to reach. She placed the dots progressively closer to the left corner, then inside his cheek.

He moved his tongue much farther with the sweet motivation of the jelly. Maren noticed that Bill had an extremely short lingual frenum; he was tongue-tied. He would never have normal range of motion, she decided. Next she asked if Bill wore glasses. Staff members who had taped information sheets on the wall and written comments in his chart complained that he didn't read their instructions. Sure enough Bill couldn't read without his glasses, and the two women kept forgetting to bring them.

One more reminder can't hurt, thought Maren, adding a note on the exercise sheet, "Bring glasses."

Tuesday ended quietly, both at work and at home. She hadn't seen Paul at the hospital, and there were no phone messages on her home answering machine. She wondered if it was broken. Using that as an excuse, she called Nick and asked him to call back to see if the machine would pick up. It did. They had a short conversation with no mention of Lois or the group.

"Classes are going well. I think I'll make all As and Bs. I don't want you to worry about me, Mom. I love you and I'll see you real soon." Maren was definitely encouraged. He hadn't spoken to her with that amount of affection for months.

Wednesday and Thursday were equally quiet days. Paul evidently had no patients at St. John's, and no time or desire to call her. She wouldn't allow herself to call him.

Friday was a beautiful spring day, calling her to her garden. Instead of answering the call to the garden though, she was evaluating Joni Mason, a fifty-nine-year-old African American woman. Maren had tried twice on Thursday to see her and had failed. Judy had seen her in acute care earlier in the week. Joni had suffered a CVA a year ago and now had suffered two more in quick succession. She was NPO but had twice pulled her NG tube out. During the bedside swallow evaluation Judy had done, Joni had swallowed two times with small amounts of applesauce. Then she had stopped. She had held the food in her mouth and clamped her lips closed. She wouldn't swallow again, but she didn't expectorate. Her daughter had spent fully five minutes getting the food out of her mouth while Judy watched, puzzled.

"How many people are in the room?" Maren now asked.

"One, two, three, four." Joni answered by counting her two grown children, Maren, and herself.

"Make a fist." She did. "Where are we? What month is it?"

Joni answered each question appropriately and followed simple directions adequately. Maren was impressed.

"Would you like some food?"

"No."

"Would you like a drink?"

"No."

"Would you like some ice chips?"

"Yes, I would."

Maren knew one of the patient's daughters had given her ice previously. She visualized tiny bits of ice melting on Joni's tongue and slipping down her throat in such small amounts that a swallow would probably not even be triggered. She brought in a cup of ice anyway. Some of the pieces were a bit large, but she got a tiny one on the tip of the spoon. Joni barely opened her lips to let it pass. She crunched the ice chip and swallowed. Maren gave her another and another, larger and larger pieces. Joni crushed and crunched each one, moving them from side to side in her mouth without difficulty. Each time after she chewed, she swallowed.

Somewhere in Maren's training she remembered something about teeth coming into occlusion, signaling the brain that it was time to swallow. It was not a true reflex, more of a habit pattern. She stood concentrating, feeling like a good detective going over a list of clues.

There was nothing wrong with the swallow function Judy observed. Those two swallows were good. I can rule out apraxia, since the few verbal responses elicited were well articulated. There are signs of right hemisphere brain injury—lack of initiation, reduced eye contact, reduced inflection, distractibility, preoccupation with a corner of the bedding, and repetitious hand movements. Probably cognitive impairment similar to Alzheimer's.

She wondered if there might be associated seizures, but didn't mention that concern.

"What does she like to eat that's crunchy?" Maren asked the brother and sister.

In the next few minutes they watched Joni eat a graham cracker Maren produced from her pocket. Maren asked the nurse to obtain an order for a mechanical soft diet with ground meat. She wasn't ready to recommend that a cognitively impaired woman try a hunk of beef or a carrot, but Joni definitely needed to chew before she would swallow.

Maren went one step further by calling the dietitian to emphasize that she didn't want gelatin or custard on Joni's trays, just chewables. Hopefully, Joni would start drinking liquids after getting some solids. In the chart Maren wrote a recommendation for an evaluation of right hemisphere function. Judy would have to do it on Monday, since Maren was due in Radiology next and was taking Monday off.

Eighty-seven-year-old Elvira Gallager was waiting with her daughter in the radiology waiting room. Elvira would have been at least four feet ten inches if she stood up straight, but her back was humped and her head was forward in a geriatric posture. She weighed only ninety-five pounds with her shoes on, her daughter reported. Weight loss and aspiration during an upper GI study were the daughter's concerns. Maren took a careful case history and asked specific questions about the size of meals, number of bites, frequency of meals, and medication. Elvira took no medications. The only clinically significant signs were her weak voice and a mild tremor.

Maren had requested additional food from the kitchen—ground meat, a half sandwich, and fruit. They went through two bites of each, and three different liquid consistencies during the evaluation. Elvira handled everything well. There wasn't even a trace of residue on the pharyngeal walls, which indicated a strong muscle squeeze. In other words, she swallowed like a forty-year-old.

Finally, Maren asked the tech to have her swallow the thin barium liquid with consecutive drinks. *Gulp, gulp, gulp, gulp* . . . Now, trace wisps of liquid entered the laryngeal vestibule, the chamber just above her vocal folds. It drifted silently to the level of the vocal folds without any reaction from Elvira. It would likely float into her trachea and drop to her lungs, since she obviously didn't feel it. Maren asked her to cough and watched the black tracing on the screen pop back up. This time it was swallowed appropriately.

Elvira couldn't explain the weight loss. Maren cautioned her against consecutive drinks, since that was the only kind of swallow that placed her at risk for aspiration.

"I only drink like that during barium studies," Elvira told her seriously.

Maren smiled inwardly. *Patient to avoid barium studies,* she imagined writing in her report.

Elvira walked toward the restroom door, but turned back to Maren. "I just wish they would find out why my stomach hurts after I eat."

Maren talked with Elvira's daughter while they waited. "I wish I could tell you why her stomach hurts after she eats, but I can't."

"If everything checks out with a gastroenterologist," Tonya said, "I'm thinking it might be just lack of social interaction. That can really affect you, you know—lack of social life."

How well I know, thought Maren. She wished Tonya and Elvira good luck and left the radiology area. She walked past the surgery waiting room and stopped to spend a few minutes with her friend Regina and her mother and brother.

"People think we've conquered diabetes," said Regina. "Even with treatment, there's blindness and limb amputation due to poor circulation. It's a serious disease."

Maren's pager beeped, interrupting their visit. Rita wanted to let her know there was a new order for an evaluation. By the time Maren finished the paperwork from that patient it was nearly five o'clock. She kept thinking Paul might look in the speech office, but he didn't. The word *estranged* trickled into her mind and lingered. She kept remembering Bonni's facial expression and incredulous question, "Paul screamed?" Maren had to admit to herself over and over that he had not.

She wasn't tired from the day, but there was nothing to look forward to. It was a three-day weekend, too, since a few weeks ago she had worked a Saturday for Judy and was taking Monday off in compensation. Unfortunately, she had nothing planned for the evening, nothing planned for the weekend, and nothing to do but go home. At least her garden waited.

Buck up, she ordered herself. After all, it had been a good week, a week filled with frustration and sadness, but also accomplishment and hope. The pace had been steady, but Maren didn't feel sapped, as she sometimes did. There was nothing really outstanding today, just routine speech-language services. It was the individuals and their emotions that could leave her exhilarated or exhausted. The patients and their families had been so grateful for the smallest kindness during the past week. What a variety there had been. The staff seemed more cheerful and friendly than usual this week, too. Thankfully, no one had mentioned the surgery incident.

"Maybe spring is having a good effect," she said out loud.

Chapter 21

Maren needn't have worried about plans for the weekend; there was plenty in store for her. She found four calls from Steve on her answering machine, each one inviting her to spend time with him. She agreed to breakfast. Of course he had a flight in mind.

He picked her up early Saturday, and they spent the entire day together. He flew them to Kentucky to see a friend of his who owned a horse farm. If May was wonderful in Illinois, it was positively magic in Kentucky, and the magic stayed with them all day.

He delivered her to her doorstep at sunset, and she invited him in. He declined. A 3:00 A.M. departure, the start of a two-day trip, awaited him. When he kissed her good-bye, she felt again that he was holding her entire being with his lips, that she was suspended by a fragile thread and spinning uncontrollably below him. He kept his hands on the doorframe and made a point of telling her how difficult that was.

Sunday she went to church and out to brunch with a group of teacher friends, and took care of house chores. On Monday she finally got to work in her flowerbeds. It was mid afternoon when Bonni pulled into her driveway.

Bonni hesitated, wishing she didn't have to be the one, but there was no one else. Bonni had asked her old friend Jeff to do everything he could to stay close to the cult and keep track of Nick and Lois. Jeff had gotten a copy of Nick's schedule and had made some contacts with instructors. They had let him know that Nick hadn't been to class since Tuesday. Now, the week before finals, the cult had moved.

When Maren saw Bonni coming, she was cleaning out dead leaves from under the spirea. She stretched her back and began pulling off her gardening gloves. The clouded expression on Bonni's face as she crossed the width of the driveway to the front walk warned her. Bonni took the direct approach and greeted her friend bluntly. "The cult has moved out."

Maren felt a clamp grab her stomach. "What do you mean, moved?" she asked.

"They've all disappeared from their dorms and classes. Jeff told me the authorities feel there is probably an assigned rendezvous somewhere." She stopped short of revealing that no one had seen or talked to Nick since the previous Tuesday.

"But I talked to him last Tuesday. He sounded good. He was anxious to come home. He said his grades were good. He sounded good," she repeated in disbelief, remembering how he had ended their conversation. "Don't worry about me," he had said. "I love you, Mom. I'll see you real soon."

"I'm telling you, none of the group leaders has been seen or heard from since Tuesday," Bonni stated more urgently, trying to convince Maren. "Did you talk to him Saturday or Sunday?" Without answering, Maren threw the cotton gloves on the porch and headed for the phone. It was true that she hadn't been able to reach him over the weekend.

They went inside, and Maren punched his number into the phone and waited. He wasn't in his room, nor was his roommate. She left a short message on his answering machine. Bonni sat with her as she called the university police to file a missing person's report. She told them about her last conversation with Nick on Tuesday and that she hadn't been able to reach him since. The university police were aware of the group but could give her no information as to the students' whereabouts.

Maren called Matt in case Nick had contacted him. It was only then that she started to cry. Matt offered to fly home immediately, but Maren thought it best for him to stay where Nick could contact him, if he tried.

While Maren was washing her tear-streaked face, Bonni turned the Rolodex on Maren's kitchen desk and copied several phone numbers. She left a message on Steve Wagner's answering machine and paged

Paul McCloud. Next she did something she hadn't done in all her flying career; she called in sick.

~

Paul got Bonni's page as he was leaving for his attorney's office. This afternoon was the signing of the lease for his new office. The deal had taken far longer to work out than he would have thought possible. Not only were the tenants moving, ownership of the building was suddenly in question. His lawyer had finally given his official okay to the deal, but another complication had erupted. A relative of the new owner wanted to lease part of the building, and the part he was interested in included Paul's suite. If Paul didn't sign within twenty-four hours, Ken had said, the relative could claim it. That would leave Paul facing another year with Lancaster and Granger.

Paul saw that the number on his pager was Maren's and returned the call immediately. He was surprised to hear Bonni's voice. She quickly filled him in. Paul told her he didn't believe the boy had moved out with the cult. In fact, he was sure he knew where Nick was.

He asked Bonni for Steve's number, but the first call he made was to Ziff. Yes, Ziff would go out to Maren's as soon as he could get free. Without hesitation, Paul dialed Steve. No answer. He left his pager number. At that precise moment, Steve, returning from his two-day trip, was driving into his garage. Paul had just contacted United Airlines and identified himself as Dr. McCloud with an emergency message when Steve returned his call.

Steve agreed that Nick would not rendezvous with the cult, at least not voluntarily. He thought Nick would head for home or go north to the cottage. Paul convinced him otherwise. In one of the conversations Ziff had suggested Paul orchestrate, Paul had encouraged Nick to talk about what he would do if he ever needed to "just escape from the world for a while." That had led to a longer day than Paul had planned.

They had driven across the state line to Indiana. Not far from where Nick's dad had grown up was a small hidden cave. Jack and the boys had explored it years before and had even camped there. Nick had never forgotten the special time with his dad. That they had been spelunking had been their secret from Maren. Nick had made Paul promise he'd never tell anyone they had been there. Now, Paul was in a bind. He hoped Jack might have taken Steve to the cave at some time. If Steve could go to Indiana, Paul would be free to keep his promise to Nick and keep his appointment to sign the lease.

Unfortunately, Steve remembered only that Jack had talked about taking the boys to a cave. He had never personally camped in that area with Jack or the boys. He suggested Jack's mom, Mary Kepple, might know. She still lived in the old house. Holding on to his last hope of signing the lease on time, Paul suggested Steve call Nick's grandmother.

"If she doesn't know the location, I'll start for Indiana immediately."

"I've got a better idea," Steve countered. "Meet me at the airport in an hour. It can't be more than a half hour flight in the Comanche. We'll rent a car at the airport, and you can drive us to the cave. If I reach Mary and he's there, I'll call to cancel."

Paul agreed, knowing the boy's safety was more important than the lease or his promise.

Steve called Maren, told her he might know where Nick was, and asked her to contact Nick's grandmother. "Have her call my cell phone right away," he directed.

He grabbed his keys and drove to the hanger. Mary called just as he was ready to take off. She hadn't seen her grandson and didn't know about the cave, but agreed to meet Steve at the county airport.

Paul was waiting, medical bag in hand, when Steve landed. The two men flew at low altitude without conversation, watching the roads for the old car Steve had helped Nick buy.

As she had promised, Mary was waiting. She recognized the plane and Steve. Paul introduced himself as a doctor and friend of the family. He threw his bag in the back seat and climbed in the front. They drove southwest through Tippecanoe County in Mary Kepple's old red Chevy. Paul had approached the area from the west before; now they were somewhere east of the cave entrance. Mary knew the back roads though and drove them adeptly along the ones that roughly followed the Wabash River.

Maren was surprised to find Ziff standing on her small front porch.

"I was in the neighborhood and thought I would drop in to see how you're doing," Ziff explained, sounding like a pastor. "Paul gave me directions." He answered her question before she could ask.

"The cult has moved out," Maren informed him, not aware of Paul's part in the unfolding drama. She led him through the living room to the family room and kitchen in the back, where Bonni stood craning her neck to see if it was someone with news of Nick.

"This is my good friend Bonni Daley. She's been keeping me company." The tall Bonni found she had to look up slightly to meet Ziff's eyes. She knew immediately his visit was not a coincidence.

Maren slipped automatically into a hostess mode, offering Ziff food and drink. Ziff glanced at Bonni, his eyebrows raised, asking for a clue as to Maren's emotional state and whether it would be good to accept or reject food. Bonni nodded quickly, so Ziff asked what Maren had in mind. Bonni suggested coffee would be good. Maren had homemade poppy seed rolls, as a result of her recent baking binge, and set some slices on a plate along with sliced cheese and fruit. Instead of helping, Bonnie sat at the table with Ziff, allowing her friend the comfort of purposeful activity.

"I guess this is the rough day I thought you were having a few weeks ago," Ziff returned to the cult topic.

"Oh, she's doing really well," Bonni interjected defensively before Maren could answer.

Maren relayed to Ziff that a family friend named Steve thought he knew where Nick might have gone to escape the cult. The possibility seemed to give Maren so much hope that Ziff only glanced again at Bonni to express his doubt with his eyes. To prepare Maren he asked, "Has Nick called to let you know his plan?"

"No," admitted Maren, sensing his drift, "but I told you, I know he'll be okay."

When Maren finally sat down, Bonni reached around her coffee mug to hold her friend's hand; but Maren pulled back, rejecting the role of grieving mother. "I don't know where Nick is, and I'm not an expert on cults, but I am sure Nick will be okay."

Then, for Bonni's benefit, she retold the story of Nick's fall from the tree and the timely image that had come unbidden to mind the day Bonni originally told her about the cult. She stood and moved to the sliding glass door now, distancing herself from them and their assumption that Nick was lost.

"I was standing in this very spot. I'll admit I'm scared, but I know things look the worst before a breakthrough. I'm ready to get through this last step, to get him home and put the cult as far behind us as his fall from the tree."

"We don't have much daylight," warned Steve. "If we don't find him soon . . ." His voice trailed off as he laid the large flashlight he had carried from the plane on the seat next to Paul's bag.

He didn't need to finish his warning. Mary and Paul looked at the flashlight and fervently hoped they wouldn't need it. Mary wondered how old the battery in her little flashlight in the glove box was by now. She never checked it. Paul realized glumly that he had only a penlight in his medical bag.

They drove in silence for twenty minutes. Steve was the first to spot Nick's car. It was parked on a dirt path about twenty-five yards off the road, near a large, old oak tree. Some books and a battery-depleted cell phone were on the back seat. A few minutes later Paul found the cave entrance. Mary waited by Nick's car in case he returned from some other location.

Steve turned on his flashlight and moved ahead of Paul into the cave, calling Nick's name. Paul followed, medical bag in hand. They hadn't gone far when they had to slow their pace. The floor of the cave was extremely wet and slippery. Steve had taken time to change clothes, but his rubber-soled jogging shoes weren't much of an advantage over Paul's leather dress shoes. It was like walking on ice.

Light filtered into the cave from some other entrance, assuaging their fear of darkness. They saw him at the same time, lying unconscious next to his gear.

Paul realized immediately that Nick's arm was broken and applied a makeshift splint. Together, they carried him to the back seat of Mary's Chevy, where Paul treated a cut over the boy's eye, while Steve tried without success to put through calls with his cell phone. "Out of range," he mumbled with disgust.

When Nick awoke in pain, Paul gave him an injection. Mary got the bottled water she always kept in her trunk, and Nick drank freely before falling asleep, again. Paul was relieved that there seemed to be no signs of traumatic brain injury from the fall, and he no longer had to worry about starting an IV.

After discussing options, the men decided to fly back to Chicago to get treatment for Nick at University Circle Hospital. After dropping them off at the airport Mary went home to call Maren.

In Chicago Paul drove them to the hospital, where Steve called Maren for permission to treat Nick while Paul spoke to the emergency room physicians.

Nick's arm was cast, and he was given more pain medication and fluids. This time he managed to rouse long enough to recognize that Paul was there overseeing his care.

Back at the airport Paul helped Steve load Nick into the Comanche and wished them a good flight. At two in the morning, nearly twelve hours after Bonni arrived with the bad news, Steve brought Nick home. Maren had been listening for the car and was in the driveway before Steve could open the passenger door. Bonni and Ziff were close behind.

Maren took in her son's state at a glance. Even in the shadowed light from her porch she could tell that he wasn't badly injured. His left arm was in a cast, his face bruised, and his forehead bandaged, but otherwise he looked fine.

He held his cast aside to receive her hug. Tears flowed freely now and emotion could be contained no longer. She sobbed quietly as Steve helped them both into the house.

"Thank God, thank God," she kept repeating, interspersed with, "Thank you, Steve."

Once inside the house she realized Nick was crying, too. This time it was slipping into the role of mother that restored her calm. Steve helped her take Nick upstairs to his bed, where she realized that Steve was exhausted, too.

Nick was asleep before they left the room. She led Steve downstairs and suggested everyone needed time to rest; talk could come later. She was anxious now to be alone with her son. She hugged and thanked each one, assuring them that she appreciated their concern. She was ready to get some sleep. Steve was glad to excuse himself and finish this incredibly long day. He left without ever being introduced to Ziff.

"We're going, too," Bonni assured Steve, and the two went to find a place for breakfast.

Maren checked on Nick once more and then slipped into her own bed. If Bonni's friend hadn't been called by his contacts, they wouldn't have known to look for Nick. If Steve hadn't gotten the car for him, he may have had no way to escape. If Steve hadn't flown to meet Mary, Nick might still be in the cave. If it hadn't been for Ziff and Bonni, Maren would have had to suffer the anxious wait by herself.

"The prodigal has returned," was her last thought before she fell into an exhausted sleep.

In the morning Maren took breakfast to Nick's room and listened while he ate and talked. He had been sedated and sleeping through most of the journey home, and was pretty fuzzy on details of the rescue. He did explain how he had started to pull away from the cult when talk of the exodus had begun.

The group was to leave in twos and threes starting Wednesday. He was scheduled for Friday or Saturday. That way the group wouldn't arouse suspicion. They were to meet with others from all over the country at some compound in Nebraska.

When one member had tried to go home but was strong-armed into staying, Nick had begun to believe they might take him against his will. His roommate had gone home to study for finals. After assuring Maren in their phone conversation on Tuesday that he loved her and would be home soon, Nick had packed his clothes and books in his old station wagon and left before dawn Thursday morning. He took precautions to be sure he wasn't followed. He had to stop several times to buy food and gear for his camping trip, as he called it.

"After the weekend, once I was sure the group had moved out, I was going to go stay at Grandma's and call you. But on Sunday, I slipped and fell inside the cave."

He wasn't clear on details after that. He thought he remembered being outside the cave, trying to start the car, but was unable to provide a really reliable account of the events after his fall. He had had a rough couple of days before, as he put it, "Grandma and Steve found me."

Maren was relieved to have him home. Although she wanted more answers, she asked few questions.

Summer: West Wind's Time

West Wind brings a time of comfort on the land.
Every living thing now has a chance
to grow, to rest, produce new seed,
and be the best that each can be,
before the cycle can repeat.
Gentle breezes blow.

Chapter 22

Maren sat in the speech office alone, not wanting to stay, but not wanting to go home. Nick's arm was healing, and he had arranged to take finals late; so this morning he had gone back to Champaign. Although Matt's classes had been finished for over a week, it was taking some time to sublet his apartment and pack. He would ship his belongings and fly home after Memorial Day. Steve was training in Denver. Her home was empty, and she felt weighted down with decisions. She had always enjoyed a best friend to help her sort through her thoughts. Now when she had so many different issues on her mind, she wondered why she was left so alone.

At the hospital there was hope that Radiology would improve. Rumor had it that the latest patient satisfaction survey had produced numerous complaints about the department. "Good old public opinion might finally turn the tide," Judy had said with a chuckle. Judy had reported that another group of doctors had already been interviewed.

The more distressing issue of Dr. Nolan's incompetence lingered. Maren had finally told Judy of her experience with Rick Nolan at the stroboscopy seminar, as well as the details of the surgery she had observed. At Judy's insistence, Maren had gone to Lenny with the surgery story.

"He put his tail between his legs and ran," she had recounted to Judy after the interview. "He sucked in his breath, let out a long whistle, and in a politically correct way said that Dr. Nolan was not subject to the authority of the head of rehabilitation." He had also told Maren if she wanted to pursue the incident she could fill out an incident report, but she was on her own.

It was a lot of doubletalk, Maren brooded. *He knew about it before I talked to him. He knew I have no proof.* Maren didn't know if she wanted to pursue it. A malpractice threat was a political time bomb for a hospital. There had been six individuals in the OR that day. Nothing official had ever been reported, yet each of those individuals, except for Rick Nolan, had said something about it to someone. Word spread. Rumors grew. A month after the incident an undercurrent still ran throughout the hospital. The word *malpractice* hung in the air. The ramifications of a lawsuit were tremendous. There would be multiple counter lawsuits, as well as job loss. It would be a PR nightmare, and extremely stressful for Maren. Fortunately, she had not had to confront Rick Nolan again. That wouldn't be the case if there was a lawsuit.

She tried to focus again on the good news that Nick was clearly free of the influence of the cult. He had in fact told Maren he had been wary of the control issue from the start. He credited his parents with having taught him to think for himself.

He always was headstrong, Maren reflected, *and that's not a bad trait to have if it's based on a solid value system.*

The bad news on the home front was that Maren still had not scheduled her surgery, and June was screaming toward her. She usually discussed issues with the boys, she needed to decide this on her own. They would help her, but she didn't want them to be responsible for her. She knew from experience that seeing one's parents in pain is one of life's greatest stresses.

There were also several other issues she had put on a back burner. A tear escaped and slid miserably down the side of her nose, making her feel more wretched. *I'll think about all that after the surgery*, she told herself, gathering her purse to leave. She pulled the office door closed behind her, turned into the dimly lighted hall toward the back steps, and went out to the employees' parking lot. She usually looked to see if Paul was there, but he never was.

As she unlocked her car, she thought she heard someone call her name. When she turned, she saw Paul hurrying from the doctor's parking zone toward her.

"Maren, I was hoping to catch you. I've been wondering when your surgery will be."

"I haven't scheduled it yet." Suddenly she was nervous and a bit defensive. Paul was incredulous, and his expression showed it. He didn't criticize, but he wished silently that she would take care of herself.

"Things have been pretty hectic with Nick and everything."

"Well, lucky it was a clean break and his left arm. He can still write finals. He's young, he'll heal quickly. And so will you, after your surgery."

She looked away at the trees on the perimeter of the parking lot without responding, so he continued. "Maren, let me set up your surgery. I'd like to help you. I could handpick your surgical team. You could stay at my place for a few days until you feel up to being home with the boys. Jamie's been asking about you. She wants to help you, too. She could stay with you for a few days." Maren looked back to Paul as he finished sympathetically, "You need some support." His voice broke on the word *support*. She was startled at the emotion that betrayed and was touched by his concern.

"Thank you, Paul," she answered quietly, it's just that my doctor doesn't come to St. John's, and I wouldn't consider anyone else."

"I'd still like you to be where I could keep an eye on you. Maren, you need some support," he repeated more firmly.

For the first time since *Stormy Wednesday*, Maren spoke to him from her heart. "It's really kind of you to want to help, Paul, but I need to be home, in Edgelawn. There are some things I need to sort out, and I need to do that where I live, not where I work or at your house. Thank you for offering, though. I really do appreciate it."

She replayed their conversation mentally on the drive home. "Left arm," he had said. *How did he know it was Nick's left arm?* She was positive she had not mentioned that in the few brief words they had exchanged at the hospital since the accident. *Maybe Nick is keeping in touch with him. Or Ziff could have told him*, she supposed.

Her answering machine indicated three messages. Thinking they might all be from Steve, she punched the button as she kicked off her shoes. The first was Gloria McCloud. "Please call." The second was

Matt, and the third from her sister Ruth. Matt would arrive on a six fifteen flight tomorrow, instead of next week. Could she pick him up? Ruth was just checking in to see how her little sister was doing.

She tossed a potato in the microwave—her dinner. *No more meals on the run once the boys arrive. I'll have to stock the cabinets, too, maybe cook ahead.*

The boys could cook, but it would take some organizing, and a return to motherhood. Suddenly, she felt overwhelmed at the prospect of recuperating from surgery while continuing to juggle all of her normal activities. She would, she finally admitted to herself, need help. The sermon on Sunday had been about being willing to be a gracious receiver. "Without receivers there can be no givers," the pastor had said, quoting the apostle Paul. "It's good to be a giver, but it's also good to be a receiver." *I suppose it was a message I needed to hear.*

She returned Gloria's call first. Maren had no mother to turn to. Ruth was too far away to give more than moral support. And Bonni's trips kept her out of town most of the time. Gloria was not only available, she was empathetic about the right issue. "I know you must be concerned for the boys," she said. "Bob and I would like to take them under our wings a bit, at least during your hospitalization."

They talked at length, and although Maren had mixed emotions about accepting help from Paul's parents, she allowed herself to process the arrangements with Gloria. Surgery would be Friday, the third week of June, one of the options Dr. Logan had offered. Maren would take six weeks of medical leave. Bob and Gloria would sit with the boys during surgery and take them to their home or to a restaurant for a meal after visiting with Maren. They would try to arrange a time to go sailing. "Of course, they are young men, and we know they will have their own plans," Gloria acknowledged realistically.

Gloria told her that Jamie had offered to go to Edgelawn two or three days a week until Maren could determine what she needed. That would keep the boys from being tied to her. They needed to get jobs, and Matt had told Maren a couple of friends at universities in the Midwest wanted him to visit. Maren hoped he would feel free to go. She hoped the visits would help him sort out his life.

As Maren hung up, she wondered if the boys would go along with her suggestions. She called Matt first, then Nick. Each surprised her in two ways. First, each assumed she would have her surgery at St. John's, "where Paul could watch out for you," Nick said matter-of-factly. She was surprised and a little annoyed that Paul had discussed her health with the boys. Of course, they knew little of her relationship with Paul and nothing of their estrangement. Each of them also reported to her that Paul was planning to be with them during the surgery. She let them know unequivocally that surgery would be in Edgelawn, not at St. John's. They had difficulty understanding her logic, but assured her they would be glad to have a meal with Paul's parents, especially if it meant an opportunity to go sailing on Lake Michigan.

While Matt was sleeping in on Monday morning, Maren began a pediatric case that was to become one of the most memorable of her career. At first Maren only heard her. In fact everyone could hear the swearing and screaming of the small, dark-haired child. "You bastard, don't come near me. I'll spit on you." Her shrieks pierced the halls. It was obviously the voice of a little girl.

Actually, mused Maren, *the articulation is perfect—the sentence structure functional. But there is definitely a paucity of appropriate vocabulary.*

Curious, she stepped away from her desk and peered up the hall to the waiting area near Rita's desk. A young child with long curly black hair and beautiful creamy complexion was crawling awkwardly on her hands and knees. Maren judged the girl to be three or four years old. It was odd to see a child of that size crawling along behind Amber and Libby. The therapists allowed her to crawl because each time they tried to touch her, more shrieks and profanity erupted.

Maren walked quietly to Rita's desk and asked about the child.

"Her name is Cissily, and there goes her mother, Jeanette." Rita pointed out a beautiful blond woman who could have been a model for body-building equipment. She was carrying a dark-skinned infant toward the back steps. "Amber and Libby finally convinced her to leave during the sessions. Cissily's easier to deal with when it's just the three of them."

Maren shivered inwardly. She would not like to be left alone with this small terror. The word *possessed* came to mind. Maren could imagine the child kicking, biting, scratching, spitting, and throwing anything she could pick up. She was wild, more animal than human—trapped and dangerous.

At the end of the day Maren made time to talk with Amber about Cissily. PT and OT had been seeing the girl four times a week for a month. The mother had been physically abused during the pregnancy and had received no medical care until the birth. She hadn't seen Cissily's father since the morning he dropped her off at one of the city hospitals when she went into labor. The mother's cousin and her husband had taken them in six months ago.

"Where did they live before that?"

"In her car and at a homeless shelter," reported Amber flatly.

"For two and a half years?"

"Well, I suppose she may have lived with the new baby's father for a time. That little girl was born drug-addicted. Odd as it may seem, Jeanette started seeing the baby's dad again recently. He's in a drug rehab program, and they're getting counseling."

"Meanwhile, she's safe with the cousin?"

Amber's reply was equivocal. "We've seen the cousin's husband. He's transported them and stayed to observe therapy. Hopefully he has learned some better discipline methods. He is providing food and shelter."

"How did the mother ever manage Cissily, living in a car and then pregnant?"

"She's messed up her life, she knows that, but she's really devoted to Cissily. We've been trying to convince her to apply through public aid for a wheelchair. It's going to be awhile before we get Cissily on her feet. The mom's been carrying the two kids everywhere. She's a strong woman, but in a few more months she won't be able to haul them both by herself."

"Surely she knows that."

"She's afraid if we put Cissily in a wheelchair she'll never learn to walk."

"What's the official diagnosis?"

"Delayed development with severe visual impairment."

"I'd like to review her records. Her speech is clear, but her language is obviously limited. Do you have previous records?"

Amber paused and looked directly at Maren for emphasis. "We're it."

"What do you mean? She's three years old!"

Amber didn't reply. She let the implications sink in.

"You mean they've not had any testing or any therapy or medical care until a month ago?" Maren was astonished that with all the social services available, a patient could still fall through the cracks. Still, it was difficult to identify needs when the patient lived in a car or was in and out of a homeless shelter.

When the mother returned, Amber introduced Maren and explained that they would like to have her join the team. Jeanette was pleased. She knew there would be no problem getting the order from the physician who was currently overseeing Cissily's care.

On Wednesday before the joint therapy session Amber told Maren, "We've mainly used behavior modification techniques and established a routine, so far. It's only the past few sessions that we've been able to start sensory integration therapy. Cissily loves the massaging and brushing." Maren explained to the other therapists she wanted to observe silently, introduce her presence gradually, and try not to set back the progress they had achieved.

Maren went in quietly and was watched as the pudgy child smiled and was peaceful, while they used soft brushes on her arms, legs, and even the soles of her feet. Anything might set off her behavior, though. Initially, Amber and Libby had suffered some bites and bruises from kicks and thrown toys, but now they usually accomplished therapy without injury. They had never completed an entire session without at least one episode of screaming and profanity.

As Maren was contemplating all this, Cissily turned her head jerkily, like a little bird on the lawn, until her left eye apparently got Maren in view. She stared soberly, without a sound.

Amber was barely five feet tall and nearly twenty years Maren's junior, but she, like Maren, had a special sensitivity to her patients, an ability to heal the whole person. She sat on the mat with the girl and waited momentarily to see how Cissily would react.

"That's Maren," Amber said quietly. "She's going to help us."

It was time for Maren to officially join the circle. "Hi, Cissily. How are you?"

"Hi, Cissily. How are you?" came the echo that told Maren she had a lot of work to do.

Mostly they played—rolling a ball, tossing bean bags, and manipulating musical toys. Cissily obviously enjoyed the addition of Maren to her world; and Maren enjoyed Cissily, but wanted goals to be established and attained.

Maren planned to start a list of social phrases and introduce the use of appropriate names and pronouns. Having a child repeat words and phrases could be beneficial, but what Cissily was doing was called echolalia. It was not a good sign. "She needs to display some socially appropriate responses," Maren explained to the other therapists.

As luck would have it, Maren was late getting to the PT room on Thursday. She opened the door quietly. They purposely kept the overhead light off and used quiet voices while working with Cissily. They even played melodic background music on a tape to help calm the girl enough that she could receive the sensory input. Amber had not yet finished the calming massage and sensory integration techniques they used as the initial routine of each session.

The unexpected interruption broke the tranquility. When the blast of light and sound from outside the dim, controlled environment caught Cissily's attention, she was set off. She sat up and began shaking her hands the way a worried mom would shake down a thermometer.

"Don't you come near me!" she shrieked. "You bastard."

"Hands in your lap, Cissily," came Amber's calm command. By now Cissily was trained to respond automatically. As soon as she did, Amber gave her positive verbal reinforcement. "I like the way you keep your hands quiet."

"Hands in lap," Cissily echoed again.

Taking her cue, Maren provided more positive reinforcement. "I like your quiet talking, Cissily. Your voice is pretty."

"Your voice is pretty," the girl repeated dreamily.

"Thank you," responded Maren.

"Thank you," echoed the child.

"Do you want to play ball?" Before Cissily could parrot the question, Maren gave her another phrase. "I want to play ball."

"I want to play ball," came the quiet response. It was a start.

On Friday, Cissily arrived in an agitated state. Jeanette said their routine had been interrupted when the baby got sick. Cissily couldn't tolerate the slightest deviation in routine. She was swearing like a drunken sailor as she crawled across the tile to the PT room. She sobbed in between profane epithets, but there were no tears.

"Who's this?" asked Maren in mock confusion. "I don't know this loud girl. What's your name?"

The sound of Maren's gentle voice distracted the child from her tantrum. "What's your name?" she echoed.

"My name is Maren."

"My name is—" began the echo.

"Cissily," Maren interjected.

"Cissily," the girl repeated. Maren tried again.

"What's your name?"

"Cissily." She spoke her name quite clearly, giving the first real response of her life.

The three therapists restrained themselves from cheering, settling for smiles of satisfaction. Such a small event was a major accomplishment for them all.

Cissily turned her head again, until her good eye could see Maren. Her view of the whole world was evidently through a small, probably foggy peephole.

Such a serious expression for such a small girl, thought Maren. *Fortunately, her auditory sense is excellent.* Cissily moved her head, surveying the group, most likely seen as fuzzy shapes.

The therapists picked up blocks and released them into a dishpan full of sand. Next, Amber put Cissily's hand in the container. Cissily would happily have felt it for hours, squeezing and sifting. Libby hid objects in the sand for the girl to recover.

They transitioned, with some difficulty, to working on the big therapy ball. Cissily sat on it, and they rotated it to force her to balance. When they put her on her stomach and rolled her back and forth, she squealed with delight. Maren capitalized on each activity by introducing appropriate language. She motioned Amber to stop the movement of the ball. Cissily began to make loud noises.

"Roll the ball, please," Maren modeled.

"Roll the ball, please," echoed Cissily.

The reward was quickly provided. After two such demonstrations, Cissily got the idea and responded spontaneously each time Amber and Libby were ready to end the session.

It was a good day. When the hour was nearly up, they always gave Cissily verbal cues to prepare her. "It's almost time to go. We have to put away the toys." Having three adults for entertainment could be a glorious experience for any three-year-old. They were afraid Cissily might not want to leave. The child's body clock seemed to have adjusted to the schedule, though; at the end of the session she started crawling toward the door, before they cued her.

Cissily was making definite progress in all areas, but coming from a school background, Maren had urgent concerns about getting her placed in an appropriate educational setting for fall. She caught Amber's arm and expressed her concerns as Libby walked out beside Cissily. Amber told her Jeanette already had contacted their local school district. They would be placing Cissily in a BD room, a room with children who had behavior disorders. Maren was shocked.

"Behavior disorders? You mean various ages or a preschool group?"

"I don't really know. Why? If you have a better idea, we'll be asked for input before the placement is final."

"Don't you think," asked Maren carefully, "that there's a better diagnosis for Cissily than Developmental Delay with 'behavior disorder'?"

"What do you have in mind?"

"I mean, I think she has autistic characteristics."

Suggesting that a child might be autistic was not to be done lightly, but to call her a behavior problem was short-sighted at best and foolish at worst. Maren watched for Amber's reaction. The physical therapist began to nod her head in agreement.

"Yes," she said, "I think I had the same thought in the back of my mind."

"How will Jeanette take this?"

"I don't know. How do you tell a parent something like that?"

"Very carefully," Maren replied, giving silent thanks for her past counseling courses and clinic mentors. She had been taught how to skillfully lead parents along until they felt they were making the diagnosis, not the professional.

Libby and Amber wanted no part of the parent conference. They would work with Cissily while Maren alone "broke Jeanette's heart." In preparation, Maren searched her files for a checklist of symptoms and characteristics. She had been taught there were specific criteria that had to be met in order to use the diagnostic descriptor *Autistic*. The only reason for a diagnostic label was to improve the treatment or education of a patient, so Maren also researched some school districts to find a more appropriate setting for a child on the low end of the autistic spectrum. Even if Cissily had to be transported, or the family had to move, the quality of life of the child, as well as the rest of the family, might be immeasurably enhanced.

It was Friday, the end of the second week of co-treating Cissily when Maren gave copies of a list she had to each therapist who worked with Cissily. Each checked symptoms and characteristics she felt were applicable. The parent conference with Jeanette took place during the morning session. Maren waited until the girl's mom completed her copy of the checklist.

"I wanted to ask you about your school plans for Cissily," Maren began. "I'm sure you know that once she turned three she was eligible for some kind of placement in the public schools."

"Yes, I've been in touch with our district. She won't be eligible for a regular preschool class because of her behavior problems."

"Behavior problems," Maren repeated, again incredulous that anyone could sum up Cissily's disabilities as if she merely behaved badly. There would be children three to ten with various learning problems, the common denominator being that they were difficult to control.

Maren had a mental image of Cissily retreating, screaming to a corner, and losing the ground they had only recently gained. She forged ahead. "The other therapists and I have gone over this checklist to get a better total picture of Cissily. Let's see which characteristics you believe apply."

There were three categories. Group A, Reciprocal Social Interaction; group B, Impairments of Communication; and group C, Limitation of

Activities and Interests. There were five or six characteristics in each category. Jeanette read the therapists' list and agreed with all but one that they had checked. She marked three additional characteristics the staff had not included.

"Jeanette, this list is part of the process we use to identify children with autism." She read the introductory paragraph, which defined autism as a developmental disability that affects verbal and nonverbal communication and social interaction. It stated that autism adversely affects a child's educational performance; and it went on to describe characteristics often associated with autism, such as repetitive activities and stereotyped movements.

Cissily more than qualified. Maren always expected parents to scream or strike out at her in anger when she gave them such tragic news, but they never did. Jeanette reacted with relief, as if a light had been turned on. "Yes," she said, staring straight ahead, "that is like Cissily."

Now for the hard part, thought Maren. "Your school district apparently doesn't have any classes for children with autism, but there is a special school only a twenty- or thirty-minute drive from here that specializes in the care of children with multiple handicaps. Cissily would qualify, and I'm sure they would know just how to help her. The only thing is it's a boarding school. Cissily would have to live there."

Jeanette seemed not to hear. She was still focused on how it all made sense now. "Is she autistic because her father hit me while I was pregnant?" was the only thing the tall woman wanted to know.

"Of course no one can say for sure, but many children are autistic when there is no history of prenatal trauma."

"It all makes sense," Jeanette kept repeating, her face devoid of expression. "Thank you."

Maren was amazed that there was not the slightest indication of disappointment, grief, or loss—loss of the hope that her beautiful little girl would eventually be normal. Perhaps she didn't yet realize.

As Maren watched the woman walk across the hall to meet her daughter, she wondered about the source of Jeanette's relief. Maybe it was affirmation that she hadn't caused the disability by staying too long in a bad relationship, or that the new diagnosis opened the door for better treatment. Possibly it was related to the fact that she could now get someone to care for Cissily and be free to meet the demands of a rapidly growing infant.

Maren took a deep breath and let out an audible sigh, releasing her own tension. She would probably never know the answers to her questions. There were lots of things she would never know about her patients. Often she wasn't even sure she had helped them.

Maren was sitting at her desk, writing her note in Cissily's chart when Paul appeared in the open doorway. She felt awkward. Even though they had made a sort of peace, it wasn't the way it had been before. She didn't want to ignore him, but really couldn't retreat from him totally. There were reminders everywhere. The boys talked about him, Gloria called, Jamie was coming to help, and now he was standing next to her in the cramped office.

Paul expressed his concern. He thought the rumors over the thyroplasty would have died down by now, but they hadn't. Judy had told him Maren was virtually hiding out in the rehab office, that she covered all the videos in Radiology and saw all the outpatients. That explained why he hadn't seen her; she only went upstairs when Judy couldn't keep up with the patient load. Judy had told him she thought Maren was looking forward to her six-week medical leave as an escape. She had also confided that she was afraid once Maren was away from all the controversy she would never return.

"Stay in town tonight, have dinner," he pleaded. His words reminiscent of an earlier time. "Chad and Connie have been asking for you, and I miss you, too."

The office was so small he had to edge between the side of the desk and the open door in order to close it behind him. When Maren stood, she was practically nose to nose with him in the confined space. The fragrance of his aftershave reached her, triggering the return of memories she had tucked away. She couldn't seem to answer him and lowered her eyes, feeling a kind of panic. For a moment Paul thought she was swaying. He took hold of her shoulders and stooped slightly, tilting his head, to peek under her eyelashes.

"No strings attached Maren, just dinner."

"But Matt and Nick are expecting me."

"You could call them." He was being logical.

She couldn't though. She didn't trust herself with him, at least not alone, and not on his turf.

He tried again. "Why don't we meet the guys somewhere?"

"Okay, I could try to reach them," she replied, thinking they would probably not be available.

The boys were both home though and answered her call on the first ring. They had been concerned about her for various reasons, so they encouraged her to go without them. Maren was adamant about including them, and Nick, remembering his mom mentioning the Yellow Duck, suggested eating there. Matt didn't know about the Yellow Duck, but was anxious to meet his sailing mentor Bob's son, his mom's friend, in person. It was settled. The boys would meet Paul and Maren at the Yellow Duck. His hope rekindled, Paul left without further discussion.

Maren enjoyed the fuss Chad and Connie made over her when she arrived. As she waited alone in the corner booth, she sipped iced tea and reflected on what was about to take place. In a few minutes Nick and Matt would be there next to her, bridging the gap between her worlds. It seemed momentous somehow.

The door opened and there they were, dwarfing Chad and seeing her immediately. Matt surveyed the room more like an older brother than a son, judging, she assumed, whether it was appropriate for Mom.

"Well, do you like it?" she asked lightly.

"This could be very romantic," Matt stated seriously. Neither son noticed the color rise in Maren's face.

She turned the conversation around to distract Matt from his observation. "Speaking of romance, have you heard from Ellie?"

"We broke it off…" Matt replied as the boys sat down, "…before I came home. We had a lot in common, as long as we were in law school, but I finally realized our basic values were very different. It was pretty superficial really."

Before Maren could respond, Paul came in. He greeted each son with a combination hand shake and hug, and greeted Maren with a kiss on her cheek. Maren blushed again. This time Matt didn't miss it, and while observing the two of them, something occurred to him that he had never before considered.

The conversation quickly turned to plans for her surgery, again derailing Matt's train of thought about a possible romance. She protested when they talked of Paul being at the hospital.

"Why wouldn't you want him there?" Nick asked naively. "You'd have your own personal medical advocate."

It was clear Nick still thought Paul would go in the OR with her. She thought she had made that clear earlier. She firmly vetoed the idea, but the three men stood pat on having Paul at the hospital. It was decided; he would wait with his parents and her sons. The arrangement brought him back into her life, including, she realized, her life at the other end of the tracks.

It was Wednesday, the last day she would see Cissily before her surgery. As she entered the room, Amber looked relieved.

"I'm glad you're here. Cissily missed you."

Cissily was in the middle of a rage. No one knew exactly what had set her off. She had begun by shaking her hands and progressed to thrashing her head back and forth, causing the soft blackringlets to flop from one side to the other. Loose strands hung in her face. Something new—the strands of hair were stuck to her wet face. There were real tears.

"Cissily," Maren called sympathetically, "I missed you on Monday." Maren had not been able to co-treat because of the demands of acute care.

Her greeting brought loud sobs and worse language than they had heard since beginning her therapy. It was the worst swearing and condemnation Maren had ever had directed at her. She wondered if Cissily had felt abandoned when she didn't work with them on Monday. She put her hand on Cissily's back and rubbed it gently.

"Don't you come near me, you . . ." Cissily's sentence trailed off as Maren started singing a song she often sang with her geriatric patients.

"You are my sunshine, my only sunshine. You make me happy, when skies are gray. You'll never know, dear, how much I love you. Please don't take my sunshine away."

Cissily began to relax. She sniffed and became quiet.

Libby and Amber joined in the next round as Maren repeated, "You are my sunshine, my only sunshine . . ." At the end a thin, high-pitched, three-year-old voice with a faraway quality joined them, "Please don't take my sunshine away."

A dreamy smile spread across the little girl's face. Tears ran down Amber's cheeks.

"Cissily missed you," Amber repeated softly.

Maren's own eyes brimmed over. They had glimpsed the child within.

Chapter 23

The thunderstorm woke her before five o'clock Sunday morning. Fortunately, everyone could sleep late this morning; but the flashes of light, the sounds of wind, and the sheets of rain hitting the windows prevented Maren from going back to sleep.

She was glad her bedroom was on the main floor. It made the recuperation process easier. She poked her feet into her white scuff slippers and padded into the kitchen to make a cup of tea by the light of the frequent lightning. Now that she was up hunger nipped at her stomach. Toast and tea in hand, she sat propped up on the couch beside the glass coffee table.

Maren was glad to retreat to Edgelawn following her surgery. She needed time to rest and think. As she watched the storm, she was grateful for her safety from this storm and all the storms of her life.

"God is good," she said out loud. There were always good people to help, even if they didn't always get along with each other. She smiled, remembering the events that had taken place a week ago on Saturday afternoon when she came home from the hospital's outpatient surgery center. Her surgery had gone so well she was released after only one night.

She looked at the cards, flowers, and gifts that surrounded her. She was filled with gratitude and wanted to express it. She would write each one a note, but that hardly seemed enough. A party, she thought, to celebrate. She hadn't given a party, a real party, in years. She could ask Jamie to help. Yes, she decided, friends from both ends of the track together on Labor Day weekend—and they'd better get along.

In front of her in the center of the coffee table was the huge Japanese dish garden Steve had sent. He got the idea on his first trip to Japan in the Boeing 747. His note read,

> *Since you won't be gardening for a few weeks, here's a miniature version of what I saw in Japan. When you look at it, just imagine we're walking across that little bridge. That's what I imagined when I saw it. I can't wait until I can bring you here to see the real thing.*

> *Steve*

She knew the dish garden with the tiny bridge was also to remind her to keep him posted on her progress. He had created a terrible scene the day Paul brought her home. He had unexpectedly gotten a two-day break from training and had come to the house expecting to see her. She hadn't informed him of her surgery plans because he was already in Denver for the lengthy training. She knew that when pilots were at the training center they were scheduled in the simulator or in class day and night. When they weren't assigned, they studied, so she hadn't expected to hear from him until he took his check ride at the end of June.

The storm let up and dawn threatened to overcome the dark. Maren needed to talk, but it wasn't yet seven o'clock. On the East Coast it was an hour later, so she picked up the phone and pushed the speed-dial button for her sister Ruth in Maryland. They hadn't really talked since the week Nick came home. Ruth answered on the first ring.

"Good morning."

"I hope I'm not waking you."

"Of course not," Ruth assured her. "You know Calvin is always up early. He's already making rounds, and I'm on my second cup of coffee. Please thank Matt again for calling me after your surgery. How are you doing?"

Before she could stop herself, Maren was retelling the events since her surgery.

"So Paul took you home?" Ruth was trying to get a read on the status of her sister's relationship with the young physician.

"Yes, but Steve got to the house a few minutes before noon. The boys had to tell him the news about my surgery and that Paul would be bringing me home from the hospital at any minute. I had asked the boys to stay home and get lunch ready for the four of us."

"You hadn't told Steve you were having surgery?"

"Not the date. He was in 747 training in Denver. They only let the pilots out if they die on duty," she exaggerated. "I didn't know he would get a two-day break. Anyway, he was furious that he hadn't been told. He contained himself long enough to get a few details from Matt and Nick, just before Paul and I drove up. Paul was walking around the car to help me out when Steve bolted out the front door, fists and teeth clenched, the boys right on his heels."

"Oh, Maren, what did you do?"

"I couldn't do anything. Before I could get a word in, Steve started shouting sarcastically about what a cozy gathering it was. 'I'd just like to know what's going on here,' he yelled. Then he turned on Paul and said, 'I've been looking out for Maren for years, before you were even out of school.' Paul didn't even answer. He pushed past Steve to open my car door before I could get out on my own."

"Keep going. Don't leave anything out."

"Steve was pretty upset with me, too, and I suppose I can't blame him. From his perspective I had cut him off. I can always tell when his feelings are hurt. The hurt comes off as anger. He looked straight at me and said, 'And this is the thanks I get? No one even gives me a call. Maren, I might have wanted to be at your side, you know. This is not like you. You're obviously under some foreign influence.' He glowered at Paul and announced to the whole neighborhood, 'We've seen each other through thick and thin, through marriage, divorce, sickness, and death.' It sounded like the marriage vows."

"Except he left out health and happiness," Ruth observed. "What did Matt and Nick do?"

"They were speechless. I tried to explain things from the car, but by then no one was listening to me. Paul mixed it up, too—not loud, but with that icy-cold tone of his. He told Steve, 'If you cared about anyone other than yourself, you would close your mouth and get the hell out of here until you learn how to behave.'"

"The calm physician lost his cool?"

"Yes, he did. I've never heard him swear before." Maren had heard Paul use what she called his "cold-steel tone" several times before—once at the hospital and once in her kitchen. He never raised his voice; he cut with it, like a scalpel.

"I thought Steve was actually going to punch Paul at that point," she continued, "but Matt got between them. Matt's big, but not as heavy as Steve, so Nick joined the tussle, waving his cast threateningly in the air and yelling for them to knock it off."

Ruth giggled as she visualized the scene. "I'm sorry, Maren. I know it wasn't funny to you at the time." Maren couldn't help laughing along with her sister. Having someone to debrief with was a big relief.

"I guess it was a pretty funny scene. I suppose my neighbors enjoyed it, but I was afraid Nick would either injure someone with his cast or re-break his arm. I'm not sure what might have happened if the boys hadn't come between the two men. I was yelling for them to stop, and somehow between the pushing and shoving and shouting Steve shuffled off to his car, punched it with his fist, and roared away."

"What a welcome home. How does it feel to have two grown men fighting over you?"

"Over me? I never thought of it like that. I think they were each just wanting to be in control. You know, one is a pilot, the other a doctor. They're used to being in charge, that's all."

"Maybe," was Ruth's only response. "Have you heard from them again?"

"Oh sure. Steve stalked off, but he came over the next day, full of concern that he had upset me. I apologized for not letting him know."

"You took the blame?" Ruth was incredulous.

"Not entirely. I pointed out that he had been out of town and under a lot of pressure and couldn't have been here anyway. He apologized for losing his temper, and we chalked it off to the stresses we had both been under."

"Did he apologize to Paul and the boys?"

"Not yet, but he sent me a lovely dish garden and note." Maren ended the story and turned the conversation to Ruth's children Lisa, Lauren, and Doug.

Three weeks after her surgery, Maren was tired of lying around the house. She wasn't sleeping well. *Not enough activity*, she decided, resolving to start taking longer walks.

The garbage truck rumbled through, waking her just before dawn. Since sleep continued to elude her, she got up, dressed and went to the family room where she kept the basket of get-well cards on the fireplace hearth next to the dish garden Steve had sent. She looked at it and tried to imagine walking across the miniature bridge.

Paul's card was tucked behind all the others in the basket. She had already read it a dozen times, but reached for it again. He had placed the sealed envelope on her hospital tray when he left after her surgery. She had been dozing and hadn't opened it until midnight. She remembered asking the nurse to turn up the light so she could read it. There was a night sky on the front, a moon and stars. Inside, Paul had written,

> *In spite of everything, even when nothing seems certain, there are three things you can be sure of… the sun will rise, the stars will shine, and I care.*

> *Love, Paul*

Matt and Nick had brought her a beautiful bouquet from her garden, but Paul hadn't sent flowers. Two days after she arrived home a package was delivered with a note.

> *Dear Maren,*

> *I wanted to send flowers that would have special meaning, but couldn't find a florist who could do an arrangement of Colorado columbine. I did find these. They will never wilt. I hope they will*

always provide you with memories of the peace and relaxation we found in Pine Bluff.

Love always, Paul

She had been astonished to unwrap an original acrylic painting of a scene right out of the hills west of Denver. She looked at it, hanging above her fireplace. There was the cold, blue, early spring sky with a snow-peaked mountain in the background. Blue spruce and pine trees looked as if they were growing right out of the frame. But the focal point was a cluster of lavender and white columbine, like the one that had delighted her on their hike. Behind the columbine was a narrow dirt road that had several curves and led the viewer's eye subtly to the hills, then disappeared.

She had been overwhelmed with emotion, in a way she rarely experienced. Paul's cards and the painting were so romantic. They revealed a facet of his personality she hadn't seen before. The picture did make her feel peaceful, and it did remind her of their time together. She didn't know how to thank him. She only knew her spirit, as well as her body, was healing. As Nick had put it, she was being recycled.

She made coffee and sat down to enjoy her cards again. She thought fondly of Bonni as she re-read hers. Bonni's note promised a lunch outing that was scheduled for tomorrow. Since Maren still wasn't allowed to drive, she was eagerly looking forward to the excursion with her friend.

Maren was always hungry for news from St. John's. It came along, with Judy's card, in an eight-by-ten-inch manila envelope that also held mail from others at the hospital.

Dear Maren,

Hope you're enjoying your rest. I know you need it, but Michelle from Rehab International and I are running our legs off. Like you always say, when the barometer drops, we get a flock of new CVAs.

I wanted you to know that Jason's mother called and scheduled him for therapy twice a week. She didn't grovel or anything, but she did say Jason wasn't making any progress at the other facility. Her husband finally put his foot down. He said Jason not only hadn't improved, he had actually lost ground. He told her straight out to get Jason back to the therapists at St. John's. Since that was primarily you, please hurry and get well. I can't remember those cues you were using with him, and Michelle never heard of them. By the way, they did say to tell you to get well soon, and Jason sent this hand-drawn picture of himself. Pretty good, don't you think? He even put individual fingers on the hands.

Struggling along without you, Judy

Maren smiled. Yes, the big dark eyes and long lashes were Jason, all right; and the hands did have individual fingers. The only problem was, the hands were attached where ears should be. Next time she talked to Judy she'd ask if that meant they needed to do some *ear training*, as listening practice was sometimes called.

A computer-generated card from Amber was enclosed, too. She had taken a picture of Cissily and printed it on the card. The front said, "Get well soon, Maren." When she opened it, there was Cissily, caught in her dreamy smile.

I thought you might like to know Jeanette's cousin helped her and the two kids move to a small house in another school district. Cissily will be in a class for preschoolers with special disabilities. Three others are autistic. She will get PT, OT, and speech in addition to her educational activities. I think, once she adjusts, she'll make fantastic progress. Until school starts they're still coming here, but only twice a week.

Maren could picture Amber's satisfied smile, framed by her long, brown hair. She had added a more personal note at the end.

Maren, I have learned so much working with you! I've never seen co-treatment work so effectively. Evan, Tony, and Jake miss you, too. Get well, and hurry back. Amber

Maren was teary. *I'm the one who learned,* she thought. *I really didn't even know how to co-treat before working with Amber and Libby.*

Rita had stuffed her handmade card in the same manila envelope. She had folded a piece of typing paper into a card and had drawn a vase full of daisies on the front. In bold marker she had printed, "Get Well Soon." On the left side of the opened card, she had penned a note.

> *FYI: Lenny and Carolyn took a two-week vacation at the same time. They sure did look <u>refreshed</u> when they returned. No one I know dared ask where either one went.*

Maren smiled. *If Rita doesn't know where they went, no one knows.*

She put the St. John's mail aside and picked up the pretty card from her church. "We miss you in choir. Get well soon," it proclaimed. *Time flies,* she thought. *I haven't been to choir in almost a year.* There was no time for it with the long commute.

Last was a plain white envelope with Ziff's home address boldly hand-printed in the corner. The note inside was typed on hospital stationery.

Dear Maren,

> *I'm glad to hear your surgery went well. Your timing was perfect. Nick's crisis was past, and Matt was home to keep both of you company. It is just as well you haven't been here. In the past few weeks things have gotten pretty ugly. Alan Weingarten promised he'd fill you in on that. I just want you to know what a pleasure it has been to walk through these last difficult months with you. Your faith has been an inspiration to me. You are truly grounded. Being a psychiatrist, I deal with some pretty mixed-up souls. Let me tell you, your soul is okay. I tried to assure Paul that your friendship has a pretty solid foundation. He just smiled and said, 'I know.'*

> *P.S. If you think Nick needs to talk through his experiences I would be glad to come out. Your home is a special place for me. See you soon,*

Ziff

Maren appreciated the kind words, but thought it was a good thing Ziff didn't know how mixed up she continued to be on several issues. She couldn't figure out why Ziff said her home was a special place. He'd only been there once. *Oh, probably that motherly thing again.*

She sighed, stood, and stretched. The coffee had gotten cold. She poured a fresh cup, made a piece of toast, and curled up on the couch again. She felt tired in spite of the coffee. It had been a damp, rainy month, but she wasn't sure she could blame her restlessness entirely on the weather. When she did sleep, she was visited by crazy dreams. Her hospital nurse had taught her to lie on her side and hold a pillow on her stomach for support, but she sometimes woke on her back with it on top of her. Once, she dreamed a big dog-like animal had knocked her flat and was holding her down. The next night she did without the pillow, but dreamed she and Nick were lost somewhere--in St. Louis, she thought-- at a small airport. They had a plane, but there was no pilot. She had been trying to take off when she awoke.

Another night she dreamed she was in labor, actually having a baby. Was it Paul's baby or Steve's, or was she simply reprising her mother role? Maybe it had some other symbolic meaning. She believed the dreams were certain proof of how mixed up she continued to be. There would be no more babies, ever. She would ask Ziff if bizarre dreams were common after surgery, or if possibly she wasn't as grounded as he thought. She hadn't dreamed about Matt yet. She hoped it would be a happy dream, if it came.

She was almost afraid to sleep; but as she stretched out on the couch, in front of the Japanese dish garden and the Colorado columbine painting the untouched hot coffee beside her, she fell into a dreamless slumber.

Chapter 24

Matt returned to working in a neighbor's sporting goods store. He had spent several summers there before, and it was not what he had expected to do this year—not with five years of college training behind him. He knew it wouldn't be an exciting summer, but he could easily get time off to visit schools. It was looking less and less likely that Nick would get any kind of summer job. "Who would hire a college student with a broken arm?" he asked Maren. She agreed the likelihood was small and was really grateful to have him home. He helped around the house and brought her a new stack of mail every afternoon.

"It must be McCloud day," Nick said seriously. "The return addresses are for Bob and Gloria, the Rev. Frank McCloud, and Cloris and Mike."

She opened Bob and Gloria's first. There was a Monet print on the front of the card, no doubt from the Art Institute. Inside Gloria had penned,

> *You and your boys have become part of our family. We enjoyed entertaining Matt and Nick while you were in the hospital, but we miss your smiling face. Get well soon.*
>
> *Bob and Gloria*

Frank had scrawled a note on hotel letterhead.

Dear Maren, I wanted you to know I offered Mass for you the morning of your surgery. I'm looking forward to hearing reports of rapid healing. I followed your advice and saw a doctor for the acid problem. He prescribed some medication. I've been following the suggestions you gave me, or trying to follow them. It is difficult to sleep in an elevated bed and eat regularly when I seem to be in a different city and bed almost every night. Yes, I recognize that's part of the problem, and I'm working on a solution, with the help of my confessor. The graduation address went well, I think. I was truly amazed at the reception I received there. I thought they would have preferred a Sister Sarah to a Father Frank. I send my love and prayers for you and your family. I'm hoping to see you again soon. Frank

He included a typed copy of the graduation address about the woman at the well. She had heard of Mass being said for dead people, and usually a list of them all at one time. *Wow, a whole Mass to myself while I'm still alive. That's quite an honor.* It reminded her of something her pastor had once told her. "Jesus died just for you. Even if no one else existed, he would have done it for you."

Cloris sent an empathetic message to Maren and greetings to her sailing buddy Matt. She had undergone the same surgery a year earlier and wished she had done it sooner.

Mike and I have four marvelous sons. I didn't need that equipment anymore. You'll see; your worries will melt away. I hope we get to meet you soon.

Mike and Cloris

The notes and cards warmed Maren with the love they conveyed. Mail was the high point of most of her days. Penny, Jim, and Erin had each signed the bottom of a pretty Hallmark card. Penny added a short note.

Busy at the shop. Getting bigger by the minute. Can't wait for you to see. I'm due to deliver a sister for Erin on December 15th. Love ya, Pen

Maren imagined how happy Penny must be. It was so good to have someone so sweet, who had suffered so much, finally realize her dreams. Everything was certainly going Penny's way. Mention of the travel bureau made Maren wonder about Elizabeth. She realized the next piece of mail was an official M & M Travel envelope, and it was from Elizabeth.

I'm anxious for you to get well. I am tired of carrying the electric larynx around with me. I forgot where I put it yesterday and just used sign language all day. I know Paul told me about esophagus speech and the TEP talk before, but now that I know a speech therapist personally, I might have more confidence.

See you soon,

Elizabeth

The only time Maren had met Elizabeth she had been impressed with the woman's courage and level of activity. Maren could picture Paul's aunt clearly. Her pure white hair wasn't in itself amazing, but that it was nearly waist length was. She had most of it braided and wound around her head the day they met, but one strand had hung purposefully across her shoulder. She had the piercing McCloud deep blue eyes, set in a sun-cracked face. She wore no makeup; she didn't need any. It was important for her to talk at the shop, but she never seemed able to place the electrolarynx on the sweet spot twice in a row. In spite of less-than-perfect technique with the electrolarynx, the listener could detect a strong, decisive tone when she did use it. Too bad all the years of smoking had now robbed her of her natural voice.

Maren had learned from Gloria that Elizabeth had survived an abusive marriage and three miscarriages. After the last miscarriage, she had extricated herself from the relationship, gotten a less-than-adequate financial settlement, reclaimed her maiden name, and begun to support herself for the first time in her life. When the cancer diagnosis was confirmed, Elizabeth had wanted to stop with only radiation, but Paul, then a resident, had studied her chart, consulted experts and intervened. According to Gloria, Paul had put his foot down. "Aunt Elizabeth," he had scolded, "you have a lot of living left to do. You haven't begun to teach Penny the travel business. Let's clean this out and give you a fresh start." She was a tough lady and had done well after the surgery.

Elizabeth had questioned Maren closely on the various kinds of alaryngeal speech. Of course Paul had given her all the information previously, but Elizabeth had not been ready to listen. The tracheo-esophageal puncture technique he had recommended, known as TEP, had been unacceptable to her. Elizabeth had wanted no more procedures.

Maren had immediately judged that Elizabeth would do better with a TEP than the electrolarynx, and they were discussing it before the older woman realized it. Paul's eyes had opened wide in disbelief, as he stood by quietly listening. Maren had explained it in the simplest of terms, never using the words *procedure* or *surgery*.

"Paul could use an instrument to reach through your stoma to the wall of your esophagus," Maren had said simply. "He would poke a little hole there and place a prosthesis, a little valve, to keep it open and to keep food from getting into your airway. Then you could cover your stoma with your finger and force the air to go through your esophagus and out your mouth. It would be instant voice. I bet you'd like it." Maren had smiled her most beguiling smile.

After their meeting Maren had commented to Paul, "It would be a blessing if her customers could understand her again."

"It'd be a blessing if her family could understand her," Paul had replied dryly, clearly out of patience with his lovable aunt.

Evidently Elizabeth was now interested, and Maren knew what was coming. The eldest of the McCloud clan would drive a bargain. She would get the TEP if Paul was the surgeon and Maren her personal therapist.

The following morning Nick again deposited the morning's mail on the coffee table next to the couch in the family room. There was a collective card from Maren's three teacher friends. Sandy had written,

> *Get well soon; but if you want to stay healthy, don't come back here. It would be nice to be able to just help children, but bureaucracy and paperwork reign supreme! Sandy*

Maren hadn't mentioned to anyone that she had actually been thinking of going back to the school to work. Her contract at St. John's would expire the last week of August. If she took her vacation week right after the medical leave, she'd only have a few weeks left. The schools could get along for a couple of weeks with substitute therapists. Maren knew there were job openings; there always were openings for SLPs. Sandy's note precipitated a return to those thoughts.

No more commuting. No more hospital politics. No more dying patients. Also, no more routine interaction with Paul . . . Her thinking went on a tangent. *I wonder if our friendship would be as appealing if we didn't have the hospital connection. Matt and his former friend Ellie broke up when he left law school. Maybe Paul and I would find we really have nothing in common either, nothing to sustain a relationship.*

She tried to block out those thoughts as she opened a card Rita had forwarded from Terry Trenton, a college student who was legally deaf. Terry had been one of the outpatients Maren had seen the last few weeks before her leave. Terry wore bilateral hearing aids and read lips. One-on-one she communicated quite well. Her speech was completely intelligible and even had fairly good inflection. Her complaint had been that she couldn't be heard if there was any interfering noise. She always sat at the front of her classrooms, so she could read lips. Lip reading augmented her hearing, but Terry had difficulty giving oral presentations in class, and she had to choose restaurants carefully. Noisy bars or bowling alleys were out, because she could neither hear nor make herself heard.

Terry was very talented, fluent in two kinds of sign language. She would make a great social worker, but she would need to project her voice more effectively to secure employment. Maren had insisted on an ENT exam to rule out the possibility that Terry had bowed vocal folds or some other anomaly that might cause her inability to make her voice louder. That wasn't likely, but SLPs never worked with voice until the patient had been seen by a doctor.

The ENT exam had been normal, and Terry had scheduled two appointments per week. She needed to improve her respiratory support first. She hardly took in any air, and mainly squeezed muscles in her throat in her attempts to be louder. Maren had explained speech respiration to her. "The diaphragm inverts and the rib muscles pull out, opening the lungs. Air naturally rushes in." Patients usually thought they needed to do something with their chest and neck, and invariably got into trouble.

The next challenge had been to stop Terry from hyperventilating—another common mistake patients made when they focused on their breathing.

It had taken Terry only a few sessions to move through a GILCU—gradually increasing length and complexity of utterance—sequence using her new muscle patterns. When her roommate reported she could hear Terry from one end of the house to the other, Maren had asked the young woman to practice using a loud voice in the grocery and at a bowling alley. Then Terry had wanted more. She wanted to improve her articulation. Mainly, it had been just her /s/ blends, clusters of consonants that sometimes gave her listeners difficulty. They had worked on prolonging the sounds just a bit. It had been crucial to have Terry monitor her speech using kinesthetic feedback. She needed to feel her speech muscles, since she couldn't monitor by listening.

Maren had enjoyed working with a young, healthy adult who progressed so rapidly. She was thankful to have been able to help the young woman, since her prior experience with deaf education was limited. Terry wrote that she had been through the interview process with a social service agency in the city and had been hired. She felt Maren had helped make it possible. Maren was grateful for the card.

The phone rang, putting an end to her daydreaming. It was Jamie, returning her call. Jamie would be pleased to help with the party. She would be out on Monday, and they could begin making plans. As she ended the call Maren realized that if she intended to make an announcement to her friends about a job change by Labor Day, she would have to come to a decision soon.

⸻

As the days passed, the cards in the mailbox were fewer in number, and Maren was able to be more active. She did find two greeting-card-sized envelopes in her mailbox on the first day she was allowed to drive. She parked in the garage and carried parcels and mail into the kitchen. The first was from her mother-in-law, Mary Kepple. Mary had phoned a number of times, but was not much on correspondence. There was a picture of a cake on the front. Maren suspected it was supposed to be a birthday card. It said, "Celebrate life! If I could be there, I would bake you a cake!" A short note stated Mary would "be there with bells on for the party."

The second was a newsy letter and some photos from Steve's daughter Megan who was in Paris for the summer on an exchange program. The trip had been arranged the previous summer, and Megan was having a great time. She mentioned feeling disappointed that she no longer had a home to invite a French student to visit, because of her parents' divorce. She ended with,

> *I miss your e-mail notes. Miss our chats, too. Will be home mid-August. See you then.*

> *Megan*

There was a business-sized envelope from St. John's. Inside was a postcard Rita had forwarded from Gwen Tremont. Gwen had been primarily Maren's patient and was on an extended cruise with her husband. The sixty-eight-year-old had suffered a massive left-sided CVA that primarily affected the language area of her brain. The result had been severe expressive aphasia, which included speaking, writing, and caused some apraxia. Her comprehension had been affected to a lesser degree.

The first day Maren had seen her, Gwen couldn't say much more than "Yes, hello." She had said, "Yes, hello," or "Yes, thank you," for nearly everything. She had stopped frequently, as if trying to think of the right words. When she did speak, she had produced only jargon or real words that sounded like sentences but had no meaning. Sometimes, Maren had understood the gist of the message by observing Gwen's gestures and noting the sounds misplaced in the words. "Nor, Nor," Gwen would say, pointing to the door. She always liked a neat room; the bathroom door should be closed. /T/, /d/, and /n/—all sounds formed with the tongue tip behind the upper incisors—were used interchangeably. Gwen's tongue tip was in the appropriate place to form /d/ for *door*, but the /n/ sound came out; so *door* became "nor."

Gwen had learned quickly to limit herself to the few clear phrases she could articulate. Her family had informed Maren that

Gwen had been a high school English teacher and had loved reading. Unfortunately, when printed material was placed in front of her, she would shake her head and assume the look of a lost child. She had been very frustrated.

They had begun therapy by working on automatic sequences and familiar songs, and as the apraxia resolved, they had progressed to phrase completion. Maren would say, "up and . . ." Gwen would say, "down." Maren would say, "salt and . . ." Gwen would say, "pepper." Maren had tried the same phrases with printed cards. At first Maren had to read the cards, "Black and...; boy and . . . ; stop and. . . ." After a day or two, Gwen had begun to read the cards with her.

Writing therapy was always time consuming, so they had put it on hold while focusing on reading. Maren had used choral reading. One day she presented a few printed sentences about Gwen's background— information she had gleaned from conversations with her and with her husband. Gwen had read two out of three sentences on her own.

Alec, Gwen's husband, had taken the initiative to write a three-page history of his wife's life. It had been a turning point in the recovery process. Gwen had needed help on one or two words per sentence, but had become more motivated when she realized she was actually reading. The woman's progress had been amazingly fast. Her family had believed it was God's healing touch, administered through Maren that made the difference. Maren hadn't argued with them, but in her estimation it was also Gwen's family that made the difference.

Gwen's speech and reading had improved dramatically, but she continued to have long pauses while she waited for the right word to come to mind. Writing continued to elude her, even during six weeks of outpatient treatment. Gwen had managed to copy some lines and shapes the last time Maren worked with her. That had been the week of the couple's wedding anniversary. They left the next morning on a cruise to celebrate their marriage and the new life they had been given because of good medical care and speech therapy.

Maren read the postcard Gwen had obviously written by herself.

Italy is the best. You should honeymoon here someday. Gwen

Misty-eyed, Maren forced her thoughts back to the present. There was an envelope from Metro ENT in the stack. It almost certainly was not a get-well greeting. She held it, unopened, thinking about her last conversation with Dr. Weingarten—the day before her surgery, her last day at work. There had been no more outpatients, and Judy had gone to the nursing home. Maren had considered it a good week because no one had commented about Metro ENT or the thyroplasty. She had enjoyed several pleasant exchanges with Paul. There had been less tension everywhere, and she had begun to relax.

She had been within two hours of her medical leave when her pager beeped. It was Alan Weingarten. He indicated that he and Dr. Ferraro were prepared to do whatever it took to get Nolan out of their practice. He had asked her if she would testify in court, if it came to that. She had agreed, but continued to hope it would not go that far. She had dictated a deposition into Dr. Weingarten's tape recorder before she left the hospital that day, and was to sign the typed version when she returned. She ripped open the envelope with her index finger and pulled out a handwritten note.

> *I'm sorry to say Nolan is not going out without a battle. It looks like this is going to be pretty ugly after all. I'll call you with the details. We'll need your signature on your deposition soon. Please call the number below to schedule a time to meet with our attorney as soon as you are able. Maybe once Rick sees all the evidence in black and white he'll be more cooperative.*

As she was reading the note, Steve walked through the open garage, tapped on the back door, and before she could answer let himself in. Instantly, he knew something was wrong. She reminded him about the case and shared the contents of the note she was still holding.

"You don't have to go through with it, you know," he said, concern in his voice. "Quit your job. There are plenty of jobs out here. You and I both know that. You don't have to put yourself on the line."

"You told me I should report Nolan, not allow someone else to suffer because of him."

"That was before your surgery, and now it's the end of your contract. They must have more evidence on this guy than just your say-so."

Steve could be so convincing. He was always so sure of what was the best thing at the time. Surely Weingarten and Ferraro wouldn't consider going to court with only one witness. Still, she wondered if Steve was being objective. Did he understand all the ramifications? Weingarten and Ferraro were counting on her support. The hospital might not renew her contract if this blew open. Steve should like that part; she would have to find work closer to home. Or did he think she would do that anyway when the contract was up? She didn't ask. She was confused and the subject somehow changed. They walked around the yard, and he helped water her flowers.

When he left, he turned and gave her a quick kiss. "I just want you to be happy," he said. "When you're happy, I'm happy." She knew he meant it.

After lunch the following day Paul called. He told her he missed her, but it was hard for him to get out to Edgelawn. Was she up to meeting him part-way for dinner? She was glad for the opportunity after being so restricted. It would make her feel more normal, even if she had to take an early nap to have enough energy. Nick had gone with Matt to visit Matt's friend in grad school at the University of Wisconsin–Madison. They had stayed close to home since her surgery, and Maren had wanted them to feel free to spend the night with friends on the campus. *I don't mind a bit of freedom for myself either,* she admitted.

During the drive she alternately looked forward to seeing Paul and worried that they would have nothing to talk about. She had no trouble finding the Thai restaurant in the strip mall just off the highway.

After they placed their order, she asked how things were going at his office. For an answer he made a face.

"You should move out," she suggested empathetically.

"I tried, but I didn't sign the lease in time, and someone else jumped on it. He's in. I'm out."

Maren was surprised at what he said as well as the way he said it. His curt, humorless answer was the first she had heard of a possible new office. It was obviously a big disappointment, and she couldn't understand why he had missed such an important deadline. He declined to discuss it further and asked her about her get-well cards.

It wasn't like him to be so ill-tempered. Maybe things had changed between them after all.

She babbled self-consciously about all the cards and notes. He listened and waited patiently until she began to relax. Eventually she told him about Alan Weingarten's letter. "I get knots in my stomach just thinking about going back to work and testifying at some sort of hearing." The rest came out quickly. She had to see how it sounded, how he would react. "I'm thinking seriously of going back to working in the schools, getting away from the hospital, procedures, politics . . . malpractice."

She waited for his response, expecting him to mount a defense of her work at St. John's. Instead he reached for her hand and held it quietly in both of his. He kept his eyes on their hands for what seemed like a long time without saying anything. She thought he looked sad, but really couldn't be sure what he was thinking.

Paul couldn't speak. He was afraid of saying the wrong thing, but that was only part of it. He was afraid of losing her. He didn't want to believe she could just walk away, yet the possibility could not be ignored. He sensed that if she decided to turn her back on the hospital, she might turn her back on the complexities of their relationship just as easily. He wouldn't argue with her; she had to make her own path.

His throat finally relaxed enough to speak, but his voice was hoarse. "You have to make your own decisions, Maren," was all he could manage.

⚬

The most memorable event of the summer was a hot night in July a week later. Paul invited his family and Maren's to his house for dinner. It was the first time the boys had seen Paul's home. The dining room table was cleared of books so that all nine of them could sit around the heavy library table with room to spare. Elizabeth missed the evening, since she was on a promotional trip for the shop. Paul prepared everything, even some kind of chocolate mousse.

Penny brought a booster chair for Erin, who spent much of her time trying to figure out how two grown men could be Maren's little boys. Bob and Gloria seemed relaxed being guests in their son's house.

Maren reflected later how the conversation had flowed more easily than she had anticipated.

After that evening, Bob and Gloria called regularly. They came to Edgelawn with Paul once, but more often just phoned. Bob and Matt spent quite a bit of time together, and Maren knew Bob was having some influence on Matt's thinking. She thought Bob was guiding Matt into some kind of advanced degree in business, but Matt would only say he was still considering several options.

He will have to make his own decisions, she decided, realizing instantly those had been Paul's words to her. Unfortunately, it was too late for Matt to apply for the fall semester.

Nick didn't need her help to move to campus this school year. Nick and a friend from high school found an apartment off campus and began moving in. He never mentioned Lois again. He was on his way to becoming an architect.

At the end of her medical leave Maren still didn't feel ready for the long days necessitated by commuting, so her physician prescribed two weeks of part-time work before releasing her for full-time. She used the extra days at home to plan the party and visit friends.

Bonni Daley met Maren after breakfast on the second Saturday in August. They were to grocery shop and have lunch, which naturally included a long chat. While shopping for party supplies, including Japanese torches that would repel insects, they caught up on each other's lives. Bonni summarized her travels quickly; she wanted to hear the next chapter of Maren's life at St. John's and on the home front.

"Your guest list has grown since I talked with you last."

"I even invited Weingarten and Ferraro and their wives. Those two doctors were very supportive when Lenny tried to bully me into forgetting the surgery incident." Bonni insisted on lifting the heavier beverages into the trunk herself, leaving Maren to load paper goods into the back seat.

"I really can't blame the hospital for its position, though. I'm the only hospital employee who is directly connected to the scandal, since no one else has come forward to testify. Without me it's just an issue within Metro ENT."

"The only evidence on this guy is the one surgery incident and your hassle with him in Wisconsin?"

"Alan Weingarten told me that there were two DUI arrests on Nolan's record in the past year alone, and that one of their office nurses had complained of sexual harassment. I didn't say anything about the trouble I had with him in Wisconsin in my deposition, but I will add it if that RN isn't taken seriously. Matt's first-year-law-student opinion is that if it's malpractice they're going for, they had better have the suit brought by an injured party. They need a patient complaint, but the patient is unaware that there was any question about the treatment he received. No one is about to suggest it to him. Matt warned me that the Metro partners better have something powerful up their sleeves, or there will likely be a countersuit, which could make me a defendant."

"Oh, Maren, I would think one of the nurses in the OR or the anesthesiologist would step forward."

"No one is knowledgeable enough about that procedure."

"Or willing to accuse a doctor of being drunk?"

"Lenny has a point though, that if Metro wants Nolan out of their practice, they could handle it without dragging the hospital through the courts. If Nolan leaves Metro, he couldn't practice within some specified distance of St. John's. There's usually a no-compete clause in a contract. I'm sure Lenny was acting on orders from higher up, because he made it clear that Rehab International is supplying St. John's with a part-time SLP to help Judy while I'm on medical leave. He said point-blank they would probably not need to have two full-time therapists in the fall. It was a threat, but one that can easily be carried out."

"He tried to blackmail you into keeping your mouth closed?"

"Well, yes, but Judy has fulfilled her year of obligation to Rehab International now and is free to work full time for St. John's. That means my position is no longer secure. I knew that going in. Now it's a loophole allowing them to let me go. As an ex-employee, I would be distanced from St. John's during any publicity."

"But don't they need more than Judy's full-time position now?"

"Yes, they really do. But if I decide to withdraw my deposition, they'll keep me, even if they reduce my hours. If I don't withdraw it, they'll let Judy struggle for a few weeks then maybe use registry SLPs or hire someone else part-time. Either way the hospital will slide out of the scandal almost untouched."

"What do Paul and Ziff have to say about the whole thing?"

"Paul listens but doesn't ask any questions. He did ask questions on Stormy Wednesday, and I haven't forgotten them. Judy and I are not providing the patient with services, so we have no right to request records. We'll probably never know some of the facts."

"Does Paul give any advice?" Bonni pressed.

"Just to stand fast, not to second-guess myself. He says I acted in good faith. He knows I haven't filed an incident report or talked to the patient. I just gave the facts that were available to me, at Metro ENT's request."

"What about Ziff?"

"What do you mean?"

"I mean, I would think he still has input into this whole thing somehow."

"Whatever Ziff knows is strictly between Ziff and his clients."

"So, he can talk to each one of you but not tell the other what he knows?"

"He can encourage individuals to share information, but he can't divulge anything."

"What are you going to do?"

"Drop the groceries off at home and take us to Lolly's for lunch," Maren answered, putting an end to the conversation.

Chapter 25

Maren had most of the food catered. Mary Kepple came early to do some baking, but a friend from church had been commissioned to bake and decorate a three-tier marbled cake. Incredibly, Bonni and Steve were both in town the day of the party. Steve was scheduled for a five o'clock departure the following morning, so he warned Maren he would have to leave early. He flew the Comanche to northern Michigan to bring Megan from school for the occasion and the weekend. Bonni had bid her schedule for the month around Maren's event to be certain she could be present. She wanted to be there from setup to cleanup. Uncle Frank was in Indonesia, but promised to celebrate there.

Jamie brought her oldest daughter Nola to help serve and clean up, freeing Maren to enjoy the evening. Bob and Gloria came early, with enough champagne for everyone, and Paul was predictably late. Penny, now seven months pregnant, came with Jim but left Erin with a friend. Judy, Rita, Amber, Libby, and most of the permanent rehab staff came with spouses or guests. They provided Frisbees and other lawn games, as promised. Maren's yard was small, but they could spill over onto the public area, along the creek. A few friends from church and the school district where Maren had worked completed the gathering.

It was a lovely evening with the flickering, soft glow of moonlight and torches providing light for the game and conversation areas. Maren began circulating, chatting with each group.

Steve, always the extrovert, was regaling the Weingartens and Ferraros with airline stories. The group stood near one of the torches listening to his story. It was weather related, and he finished by reminding them how bad the ice storm had been the past January. "When I took Megan back to school, it was two days in a motel. Nothing with wings or wheels moved," he emphasized.

Maren was puzzled. That was the trip she had made with Megan. Those were the two days she had spent helping Megan pull herself together, after Pam disappeared. Steve noticed Maren, put his arm on her back, and propelled her to one of the tables with champagne.

"Let me buy you a drink," he joked, "since I can't have one."

"I thought maybe you had been drinking," Maren half teased. "I could have sworn I was the one who was caught in that ice storm."

"Well, that's what I meant. Same thing. I asked you to do it for me."

"So, by extension, you did it?"

"Yeah," he smiled proudly, "that's the way it is when you're that close to someone." He gave her shoulder a squeeze to demonstrate how close.

The rehab staff came and dragged him off to complete a volleyball team before she could answer, so she returned to the Weingartens and Ferraros. The women thanked her warmly for the invitation. Alan held up his glass for a toast.

"To success," he proposed.

"Success?" Maren questioned.

"That's not a wish or a question, Maren. It's a statement. Rick bowed out yesterday when a patient complained about medication he had prescribed. She called me out of the blue and was more than willing to provide a written statement. Added to your incident and Llana's harassment complaint, it turned the tide. The patient said if Rick hadn't been so busy looking down her blouse, he might have checked her chart or asked her for allergy precautions. Fortunately, her pharmacist caught the error before she dispensed it. Rick's on his way to Florida even as we speak. He intends to manage a retirement home and be a beach bum."

"Well," commented Mrs. Ferraro dryly, "he's already accomplished half his plan. He is a bum."

Maren held her glass up, but reworded the toast. "To high standards of practice." The four echoed her sentiment.

"What did I just miss?" inquired Paul as he stepped into the light from the torch. They quickly explained. "I'll drink to that," he happily agreed, tipping an imaginary glass.

Jamie saw the gesture from across the lawn and hurried over with a tray of plastic champagne flutes. "No champagne," Paul said after greeting her, "just some food and a soft drink."

She went to the kitchen and met Mary Kepple at the refrigerator. "Dr. Paul is looking for a soft drink."

"Oh, is he here? I must go tell him hello. I never did get to thank him for helping Nicky." Mary volunteered to deliver the cola to Paul, and met him on the lawn. He and Maren were walking toward the house.

"Paul, it's so good to see you again. I never got a chance to thank you for finding Nick and treating his injuries. It's a rare doctor who'll make house calls these days."

"What do you mean?" Maren asked, "I didn't know you had met Paul." She turned to Paul. "I thought you saw Nick and Steve when they got to the hospital."

Mary answered before Paul could respond. "Why, if Paul hadn't found the cave for us, Nicky might have died in there. Things happened so fast after we found him. They took off, and I didn't get to say anything. I just want to thank you." She handed him the cola and gave him a hug and grandmotherly kiss.

Paul only managed, "Good to see you again," and concentrated on draining his glass of cola.

Steve and Nick had walked up behind Mary while she was talking and overheard everything. While Maren was trying to understand the ramifications of what her mother-in-law had just revealed, Steve turned, without a word, and wandered back to the volleyball game.

Paul hadn't had much opportunity to talk with Nick or Matt during the weeks since the accident and never discussed the cult or Nick's rescue with either one. He hadn't wanted to burden Maren with the fact that he had lost the office lease because of the flight to Indiana, so he never discussed it with her, either.

Nick, who had spent plenty of time during the summer ruminating on the details of his rescue, really only remembered regaining consciousness at the hospital and seeing Steve and Paul there.

Snippets of images had revisited him from time to time, causing him to realize there was more to it than that. Neither Steve nor his mom ever mentioned Paul in connection with the incident. He had wondered why, but there had been no comfortable opportunity to bring it up. Now he realized Steve and his grandmother couldn't possibly have found him so quickly without Paul. The pieces finally fit together.

"Why is everyone looking so serious?" Mary asked. "I thought this was a celebration."

Nick stepped forward and put his arm around her. "It is, Grandma, a celebration for the friends that helped Mom and a celebration for the friends that helped me." He looked over the top of her head, smiling knowingly at Paul. "I want to say thank you, too."

———

Penny, looking wonderfully healthy with the glow of pregnancy, waved Paul over to her group. He excused himself and joined them. She caught his arm and pulled him down on a lawn chair. She and Jim had been getting acquainted with Bonni and Ziff. The effervescent Bonni and the guileless Penny had connected immediately. Jim was quiet, but Ziff, adept at social as well as psychiatric skills, quickly drew him into the conversation.

"We were just talking about the influences in our lives that caused us to be where we are today," Penny explained. "Not at Maren's party, in our careers," she hastily added. "It's Bonni's turn."

Bonni reviewed her close relationship with her dad and their shared love of flying. She wouldn't have applied to the airlines, though, if her marriage hadn't dissolved. "Now it will be really difficult to find a life mate," she finished. "I have the triple threat—I'm tall, used to being in a position of authority, and am not child-bearing material."

Ziff gave her a critical look. "You don't know that, just because you didn't have a child in the short time you were married. And you're not all that tall."

Having no clever comeback, she merely smiled and continued looking down at them from where she was standing. Ziff returned her smile and slowly stood, stretching to his full six-foot-three. Now he looked down at her. "Doesn't bother me," he said with a grin.

Penny asked how Ziff had chosen psychiatry. "Actually," he said quietly, looking affectionately at Paul as he sat down, "it was Paul's friendship that gave me the support I needed to continue." He didn't go into detail; instead he turned the conversation to Paul. "Your turn for tell and tell."

Paul's life plan was a sore point at the moment. Everyone knew the first part of his story. He had developed great hopes for making a difference in the lives of children during Penny's medical odyssey. Now he was a captive in the offices of Lancaster and Granger. He looked sad and hesitant.

"Tell them about your offer," prodded Penny.

He tried to cut her off with a sharp look, but it was too late. He had not even told Ziff about that. They all pressed him, and Penny, exerting her considerable influence, insisted that he really needed to talk about it. Paul reluctantly gave in and shared the news.

"A friend from residency called me right after Maren's surgery. He was looking for a pediatric otolaryngologist for the practice he was joining just outside Denver. They plan to be affiliated with a private university that is becoming known for its children's hospital. The group wanted to start the interview process immediately. I would have had to start the first of this month though."

All eyebrows went up. "Wow," they all said at once.

"Sounds like what you've always wanted," Jim said cautiously, wondering why Paul wasn't as happy as the listeners.

"You should understand why I didn't pursue it, Jim. You wouldn't have considered taking a position out of this area before you and Penny were married. They needed an answer within a couple of weeks. I'm not sure where Maren and I are at this point. Besides, it would take longer than that to wind down here. I can't just take off."

Paul had already argued about it with Penny, but he hadn't even bothered telling his parents about the offer. He admitted to himself that he could wind down the practice in a very short time, if necessary. The timing wasn't right, but the truth was he was bitterly disappointed. He had been trying to put it out of his mind. He wasn't pleased with his sister for bringing the subject up at the party.

"Did you discuss it with Maren?" Ziff asked.

"No, and I don't want anyone else to discuss it with her either!"

Jamie and Nola helped clean up and left shortly after midnight. It was after one when Matt took Megan home. Nick walked with his grandmother to the guest room, told her good night, and went to his own bedroom. Paul and Maren were still standing in the driveway at two o'clock, waving good-bye to the last guests—Ziff and Bonni who left together in Ziff's sports car.

"They were together all evening," Maren said.

Paul smiled. "You've been out of the loop. When's the last time you had a long talk with Bonni?"

"Well, we . . ." Maren stopped, realizing she had done most of the talking at their last get-together. Her eyes opened wide. "You mean . . . ?"

"Ever since the night we brought Nick home."

"That brings us back to some unanswered questions, Paul. Why don't you stay here tonight? It's too late to start back, and I... I . . ." He waited, wondering how she would complete the request. "I just don't want you to go."

"I could get a room at the Hilton," he teased.

"There isn't one in Edgelawn. Besides, I have a guest room." Then she remembered—all the beds were filled. Only the couch in the family room was available. "You can have my room," she offered. "I'll take the couch. I've slept there lots of nights since the surgery, and I don't think I can sleep anyway."

"Why don't we both stay on the couch?" he suggested, putting his arms around her and giving her a squeeze. "We'll pretend we're in Pine Bluff."

Just the mention of Pine Bluff sent a surge of pleasure through her body. She took his hand and led him inside the darkened house to the couch. The moonlight shone through the sliding glass door in the dinette area and spilled into the small family room.

First, he took off his shoes and pushed them purposefully under the couch. Then he reclined against the arm of the couch and pulled her next to him. They sat against each other without speaking, enjoying the quiet and the moonlight. After a time she began to question him about what Mary had said.

"Not tonight," he said gently. "I've already turned off the faucet."

"Promise to download in the morning?"

"Promise."

Their relationship seemed to be back on track, and he was hungry for the taste of her. He found her mouth and parted her lips with his. She returned his deep, soft kiss eagerly. Lost in their embrace, they did not hear the garage door or Matt opening the back door.

Driving Megan home had taken longer than Matt had planned, and he was anxious to turn in. He left his shoes in the garage and turned the door handle carefully. He didn't want to wake anyone, so he refrained from turning on the overhead light. After allowing a moment for his eyes to adjust, he took the few steps through the back entryway. There was plenty of moonlight coming through the windows. He noticed a form on the couch. Thinking a guest may have had too much champagne, he took one extra step into the room to see who it was. Just as he realized it was a couple snuggling there, they heard him and abruptly sat upright.

"Matt," came Maren's surprised voice. "I'm glad you're home."

It was his mother and . . . He hoped it was . . . He strained forward to see. It was.

"Yeah, just me. Night, Mom. Night, Paul." He smiled a pleased smile as he tiptoed around the corner and up the stairs to his room in the dark.

Cautantowwit's Season

Cautantowwit rules the earth
and all that is upon it.
He completes the work or joy
left undone by other gods.
Days of windless warmth with clear blue skies
and long cool nights, lighted by the yellow-orange moon,
are numbered by Creator God alone.

Chapter 26

Paul was unshaven and still wearing the rumpled clothes he had slept in when Mary Kepple came downstairs Sunday morning. She had already showered and dressed. She made the coffee, toast, and juice, while Paul cooked over-easy eggs and microwaved bacon. They made small talk while they worked, but Paul's mind was racing. He wondered if Mary was aware of his relationship with Maren. He wondered what her reaction would be.

This is Jack's mother—Maren's mother-in-law, the boys' grandmother. How will she feel about her son's widow being in a serious relationship with any man, let alone a younger man? I need to be considerate of her, of her son's memory, he cautioned himself. *I think she respects me, but... I have no idea how to go about this.*

They ate breakfast across the round, glass table from one another. Mary studied his face over the top of her coffee mug. She knew what she knew and finally decided to be blunt.

"You and Maren are going to get married, aren't you?"

Paul almost choked on a swallow of juice, but managed to say, "I have been trying to talk her into doing that very thing, yes."

"She hasn't agreed?"

"Not yet, but I haven't given up."

"She doesn't have a father or mother or brother to ask. Be sure you ask the boys."

"I'll do that, I promise. Does that mean you approve?"

"Jack was so much older than she was. She was good for him, but I always kind of worried about how it would be for her in later years. While I worried about it, the good Lord knew it would never be a problem. Things have a way of working out."

"I couldn't agree more."

"Good, then it's settled. Good luck."

Matt and Nick had come down the stairs and were walking into the kitchen.

"Smells like breakfast," Nick greeted them.

"Good luck about what?" Matt asked.

"I'll leave you men to talk about that while I go pack," Mary responded, setting her plate on the counter. She gave each grandson a hug and kiss as they passed by.

"How would you guys like a Paul McCloud omelet?" Paul asked cheerfully.

While he took orders for ingredients and prepared breakfast for them, the three talked about the party and the boys' plans for the future. Paul was impressed that each was technical, but also relational, obviously a combination of Maren and Jack.

"I won't be able to get into grad school this fall," lamented Matt. "I wasted last year in law school, but I'm thinking of some kind of engineering—just can't figure out what the best fit is, maybe mechanical."

"Have you looked into biomedical engineering?"

"No, no one ever suggested that."

"Your year of law and bachelor's in business could be very beneficial in biomed."

"I'm all set to go back and get my degree in architecture," Nick interjected smugly into their discussion. "I'm already counting the days until fall break."

"When is that?" Paul wanted to know.

"End of October."

A plan was forming in Paul's mind as he delivered their omelets. "How would you, both of you, like to visit Colorado for that break?" Paul asked. Their faces brightened at the prospect; but before they could speak, Paul continued. "There's just one small thing I need to know," he asked, raising his eyebrows and pursing his lips. "Would it be okay with the two of you if your mother and I get married while we're there?"

"I told you!" Matt exclaimed to Nick.

"I saw it, too," Nick replied, in his defense.

"We've been talking about this ever since the night we met you and Mom at the Yellow Duck," Matt explained. Nick and I are pretty much on our own, now. It seems like you and Mom... just seem to belong together."

Maren joined them a few minutes after her sons had given their consent. When she came to the table, Paul, looking like an unshaven waiter with a dish towel over his shoulder, greeted her and set a cup of coffee with extra cream in front of her.

In that moment, from that small gesture she knew. *This is the way my life will be.*

It was a startling epiphany. She was finally letting go of the past and was ready to start a new life, or at least a new chapter of her life.

"This is cozy," she commented carefully.

Paul was afraid to let the moment pass. It wasn't what he had envisioned as a romantic moment, but he had been asking her in one way or another for months, so he guessed it didn't really matter.

"It is cozy," he repeated boldly. "It's so cozy we should make it permanent. Mary gave her approval this morning, and Matt and Nick have just given their okay. We could be married in Pine Bluff during Nick's fall break."

Maren wasn't as surprised by the proposal as the short time line.

"Can we do it that soon?"

"We'll pick out a ring one day this week," he said with a grin, noting she had basically said yes.

"We still have differences, things to discuss." She was reluctant again.

"And we always will, Maren, but with love and patience and the grace of God it will all work out."

Much to Maren's surprise and the boys' delight, Paul suddenly dropped to his knees beside Maren's chair. "Marry me, Maren. I promise you'll never regret it."

Maren knew her visit with Steve would be difficult, so she went to his place on Tuesday evening, hoping to make it easier for him. He told her she was making a mistake—that she was only infatuated with Paul because he was a doctor where she worked. "Once you come back to Edgelawn," he insisted, referring to the approaching end of her contract at St. John's, "you'll realize that we belong together."

"No, Steve," she replied calmly. "You and I have known each other a long time. We have a common history. I love you. You've been a good friend. I hope we can continue to be friends. But Paul is my future. I love him in a different way. My life is with him, now."

That stopped him momentarily, but when she told him how soon the wedding would be, he rekindled his objections. If anything, his arguments strengthened her resolve. "I haven't made this decision lightly or quickly," she assured him. "It's time for me, and for you, to move on with our lives."

She invited him to attend one of the premarital counseling sessions Ziff and Uncle Frank were going to provide. It was to include friends and relatives. He agreed only to think about it. All he could see was that she was deserting him, just like Pam. He was angry at Maren and at Pam all over again. He stayed away for weeks, trying to figure out how to deal with it.

On the last Saturday of September they gathered in Maren's living room. Ziff the Jewish psychiatrist and Uncle Frank the Catholic priest provided everyone with some thoughts to consider. Ziff said that when two people marry, many lives and habit patterns are changed. The purpose of this session, he explained, was to facilitate that process. Frank read the Bible story of the brothers, who each in sequence married their brother's widow; but it was Ziff who spoke about it. "In those days a woman alone might go hungry, be abused, or perish without the protection of a man. We don't assign marriage partners in our culture anymore, but God, in his loving mercy, does inspire individuals to provide for the needs of those left and lonely. In our world," Ziff continued, "this doesn't necessarily mean a lifetime commitment. Many friends may help, and the protection is sometimes required only for a season of life."

While Ziff was pausing to let the idea sink in, he noticed that Steve had slipped quietly in the front door and was leaning sullenly against the doorway. He stared at Maren's old friend for a moment; and then, as if changing from one concept to another, he turned to look directly at Maren and Paul.

It was Father Frank who continued the homily. "In the case of Paul and Maren, a wonderful love has been born, a love that is a lifetime commitment that will be celebrated and sanctified a few weeks from now in the sacrament of marriage." He spoke for a few moments about the exclusive nature of marriage, but added that as a married couple Maren and Paul would need the ongoing support of their friends in a new way. Ziff concluded by inviting the guests to share stories about their friendship with Paul or Maren and talk about how life might be different in the future for each of them.

After that evening, Maren noticed a change in Steve. He called several times and seemed more relaxed, more at peace than he had been since Jack's death. He told her how happy he was for her, and that he felt free, like he was getting another chance at life. He even offered to give her away at the wedding. Maren gently declined, encouraging him to save the giving away for Megan's wedding. Steve told her he would not make the trip to Pine Bluff. Instead he offered to provide transportation for family and friends to and from the airport. He would tell them all good-bye at the jetway.

＊

They were married at two in the afternoon, the warmest part of the day, on the last Saturday of October. It was during Nick's fall break, just as Paul had promised. They had talked about having the ceremony on the old bridge, where they had stood watching the streams descend from the mountain, but sentimentality was tempered by common sense.

The guests were seated on cushioned folding chairs set on a wooden platform built in the back yard by Martin, the caretaker of the Pine Bluff home. There were no aisles, no ushers, no *bride's* or *groom's* side. Matt and Nick stood with Maren and Paul, signifying their approval. Maren's sister Ruth and her daughters, Lisa and Lauren, were given the chairs closest to the couple, since they were the only representatives from

Maren's family. Lauren, planning for her own wedding someday, was making mental notes of every aspect of the ceremony. Unfortunately, Calvin was in London on some kind of business, and their son, Doug, was on a strict schedule in medical school. The entire McCloud clan was present. Cloris had been in Pine Bluff all week getting groceries and preparing food for the wedding dinner—her gift to Maren and Paul.

The group was few enough in number they could have crowded into the living room if the weather took a turn; but it didn't. It was a spectacular Indian summer afternoon; only light jackets were needed.

Father Frank had arranged time off to officiate at the ceremony. He began the service by referencing the seventeenth chapter of the book of Acts. "We worship God, who made the universe and everything in it. This God is Lord of heaven and earth and does not dwell in temples made with hands. So here we are"—he gestured with his hands up and around at the sky, mountains, trees, and valley— "in God's house to worship and to celebrate the union of Maren and Paul.

"Some say a marriage is like a partnership such as in a business or game of tennis. Each contributes, each receives, each has the same goals for success which they hope will bring happiness to both partners. But a Christian marriage is different from the partnerships of the world," Frank explained. "A Christian marriage is the joining of two lives the way two vibrant streams spring from a source, develop a form and force of their own, and then meet each other. At first you can see that there are still two distinct entities, side by side. A little farther on, the water droplets become so intermixed that the streams take on a new form, guided and fed by powers outside themselves. As the streams submit to the higher forces, they dance joyfully along the path provided, not seeking to accomplish goals, simply being what they were created to be."

As he spoke, Maren and Paul exchanged quizzical looks, each silently asking if the other had talked to Frank about their view from their wooden bridge. Each gave the other a subtle facial gesture of denial.

Rays of afternoon sunlight filtered through the towering pine trees, giving a heavenly glow to the scene as the bride and groom took their vows and exchanged identical Celtic friendship rings inset with diamonds.

After eating, visiting, and opening a few gifts, the newlyweds left for a nearby resort, allowing family members to stay at the house. Their honeymoon really began when they returned Sunday evening, after everyone had gone. Cloris had left the refrigerator and cabinets stocked. The couple had only to relax and enjoy the week.

When the evening air turned cool, Paul built a fire in the stone fireplace and put on some of their favorite CDs. He stretched out on the plush carpet in the warmth of the fire to wait while Maren changed clothes. Tonight he would make no promises about his expressions of affection. Still, he was nervous. He wondered if she was ready yet to accept him completely. He could wait, even on their honeymoon.

He stared into the fire, traveling back in time in his mind. He was fourteen years old; his father was talking to him bluntly about sexuality.

"Sex is powerful," Bob had emphasized, as they put the boat away. "Like a giant wave, it demands your attention. It can move you in a positive direction or capsize you. Make sure you control it, not vice versa. Make sure, when you choose a partner, it's a good thing for her as well as you. Never, under any circumstances, use your sexuality to hurt or exploit another person. And sometimes it takes a cool head to decide what is helpful and what is harmful." Because they were both busy working with the boat, neither was embarrassed. Bob took other opportunities to educate Paul about issues of pregnancy and disease, but it was the emotional advice that he remembered most clearly.

The fire caught the log Paul had added to the twigs, and burned brighter. His other advisor, oddly enough, had been Uncle Frank. Who would have thought a priest could talk so knowledgeably about sex. Paul sometimes wondered if Frank had always been celibate, but he never dared to ask. It had been a few years after his dad's talk with him that the subject somehow came up while he and Frank were skiing.

"Whenever you make love to someone, you become one with that person," Frank insisted. Be very sure when you join together with someone physically that you want to be one with her—because you will be, whether you think you will or not. There's no such thing as casual sex." They had talked about the ramifications of that and why

Frank believed marriage was the best way to have a healthy, happy sex life.

Paul was certain he and Maren would in time come together, like the two streams on the mountain. The proof he offered himself was that she was increasingly affectionate since their engagement. Still, he was willing to be patient with himself and with them together.

Chapter 27

Weingarten and Ferraro gave Maren and Paul two wedding gifts. One came wrapped, a beautiful set of crystal goblets. The other resulted because they used their considerable influence to make sure Maren's position at the hospital was secure. Maren didn't know exactly what had transpired or with whom, but when she had returned from her medical leave, there was a contract waiting for her. It was a generous offer for a part-time position, between twenty and thirty hours per week, to be determined by mutual agreement. Maren signed the new contract, knowing Paul would have to remain in the cramped and crabby offices of Lancaster and Granger.

The newlyweds kept both houses, spending days off in Edgelawn as often as they could. Nick was doing well in his classes and was working on an independent study that involved designing an addition to Paul's house. It was the oldest son whose future was still a blank page. Matt kept his job at the sporting goods store in Edgelawn and applied to several universities. While he spent some time with them in Chicago, he was not always there on weekends, and Maren was fairly sure he excused himself intentionally. She once overheard part of a phone conversation between her two sons, in which Matt was arranging to meet Nick on campus the following weekend. "Oh, I'm sure they do," she had heard him inform his younger brother.

When Matt was home with them, he frequently had long after-dinner talks with Paul over a game of chess. Maren was delighted to watch their relationship grow and often excused herself to allow them time by themselves. One evening as Maren and Paul were fixing dinner together, Paul asked her why she usually left the room when Matt was present.

"I don't want to hinder your relationship," she responded, realizing instantly it was an old habit pattern. Jack had needed to be alone to bond with the boys; her presence seemed to limit their interaction.

"I have other opportunities to be with Matt one-on-one. I think it's important for him to become comfortable being with us together," Paul responded.

Assured that Paul wouldn't in any way be intimidated by her presence, Maren brought a plate of warm brownies and set it on the drop-leaf table behind the couch. Matt had seemed especially happy during dinner. Now, he shared with them the news he had gotten in the mail that day. He had been accepted at the University of Wisconsin–Madison and would start classes in January, working toward a graduate degree in biomedical engineering. Maren couldn't have been more pleased, and judging by the expression on Paul's face, neither could he.

When they slipped into Paul's queen-sized bed that night, Maren reached for him and directed his hands to her, as she had done the first time, murmuring appreciation for his every touch. Paul had not expected her to provide so much guidance. His worry had been that it would be his sole responsibility to find the way. He had never imagined she would give him a map. Thankfully, their marriage took his mind off the disappointments at his office. He always looked forward to the end of each day when he would learn more about her and about them, together.

Working only part time and eliminating the commute helped reduce Maren's stress. She began to feel more relaxed as her energy and joy were rekindled. She knew she performed better than ever at the hospital, as well as at home. She was more preoccupied by thoughts of her new life with Paul than she had anticipated, but there was no time for her mind to wander when she was at St. John's. The demands of patients commanded her full attention. She now saw most of the outpatients, and the number they served had grown significantly.

She always enjoyed the ongoing relationships that developed with outpatients, while Judy preferred acute care.

Maren also spent more time with her new family members in the city, but she continued to miss life in Edgelawn. She was especially lonely when Paul had to travel for meetings or was called out at night. This was the third night this week Paul either had a meeting or was called to the hospital. She had become used to being alone as a widow, but now that she was married being alone seemed lonelier somehow.

She called Bonni; no answer. She pushed the buttons for her sister's home. Ruth answered.

"Hello."

"Hi. What's happening on the East Coast?"

"Maren, it's good to hear your voice. How's married life?"

"Well, Paul's working again, so I'm single tonight."

"That's hard on newlyweds, I'll bet," Ruth reflected, hearing the sadness in her sister's voice.

"I think it's harder on me, actually. Paul still has the same routine. I'm not in 'my' house. This is still Paul's house."

"What do you do when he's gone so much?"

"Call you. No one stops by here, and the phone rarely rings for me. I didn't mind going out at night by myself in Edgelawn, but I don't like to . . . well, I don't have any place to go. Anyway, it's such a hassle to drive and just as much trouble to take a cab."

"You do sound unhappy."

"I'm not sure if that's it. I miss the wildlife along the creek. I miss hearing the bullfrogs and seeing the heron and finches in my backyard."

"Maren, it's fall, there aren't any heron or finches or bullfrogs."

"There are grasses with seed heads," she answered defensively. "They remind me that spring will come, the hummingbirds will return. I know I'll never see them here. I miss watching the sun go down, and I can only see a sunrise if I drive to the lakefront."

"Maren, I think you're homesick. Maybe you should talk about this with Paul."

"Maybe. I do still feel like a visitor here. I wonder if Paul feels that way in my house. He probably does. He grew up in the city, went to med school in a city, and chose the city for his life's work. I'd like to talk to him about it, but when he's home, he's sleeping. I was married a long time to Jack before . . ." She stopped. "I don't want to make comparisons. This is a different time in life, a different place, and I'm a different person."

Ruth tried to assure her things would work out, but finished their conversation with a wise reminder, "You know better than I that change will come. It will just take some time. I'll be praying for you."

Maren hung up the phone, and prayed that the changes to come would bring them closer, not send them walking on parallel but separate paths. She loved and admired Paul and enjoyed the way their friendship kindled their passion, and their passion deepened their friendship. But it was a fact that they had not resolved all their differences. There were worrisome moments when she still thought about their ages and the implications of that, but those moments were brief and less frequent now.

It also concerned her that they had no worship experience through a church. He was what people called a nonpracticing Catholic, and she had given up her church with the move to the city. They always prayed briefly together in the mornings, and both believed they were meant to be together. *Things will work out,* she assured herself again.

—

She was asleep when Paul came in. He was mentally exhausted and relieved to be alone for a while, although he felt guilty for leaving Maren on her own so much. Now that she was working part time she seemed more dependent on him. He didn't like the feeling that he had to keep her occupied or entertained. He knew it wasn't her nature to be dependent, but there it was. She had few friends in the city, mainly Paul and his family.

It wasn't that way for him in Edgelawn. He enjoyed relaxing at her place. He loved the time alone with her, and Ziff and Bonni were usually available for socializing. He could keep busy or just enjoy being away from his office, where he felt more uncomfortable than ever. He reflected on the latest office unpleasantness, as he showered in the hall bathroom so he wouldn't wake Maren.

He returned to the living room in his warm-up suit and put another log in the fireplace. While he stoked the fire, he told himself this had been just an especially bad week. At a deeper level he knew it would always be like this, as long as he was in private practice. He knew that he had no professional future in the suburbs, at least not specializing in pediatrics; so a move to Edgelawn would just exchange one problem for another.

He stretched out by the fireplace in his wing-backed, plaid lounger and rested his feet on the oversized ottoman. He silently cursed the arrangement he endured with Lancaster and Granger, reminding himself again that he had almost escaped. If only he had been able to sign that contract in time to secure his own office space. Still, it was a small price to pay for the newfound satisfaction he enjoyed at home. He wanted to make Maren as happy as she made him.

It just wasn't the right timing, he told himself once more. *Even if I had gotten the new office, that wouldn't help Maren adjust to living in the city.* On the brighter side, he was gaining a reputation in pediatrics. Once again, he couldn't see any other option but to continue as they were. He would have to be patient. He could wait for it to work out. His patience had paid off waiting for Maren, and she was indeed worth the wait. Since their wedding, he was experiencing a satisfaction he had never known existed. He had expected the adjustment to living with another person, even one he loved, to be lengthy and difficult. It was amazing to him how quickly day-to-day life with Maren seemed perfectly normal.

The warmth of the fire seeped through him, relaxed his muscles, and reminded him of her warmth. He smiled at the thought of living the rest of his days with her. Their lives would fit together; it would just take some time. He drifted into sleep before the log was consumed.

Maren found him there in the morning, wrapped in the afghan they had purchased on their honeymoon. She woke him with a kiss, and they chatted while fixing breakfast.

"The boys will come home for Thanksgiving, won't they?" Paul asked.

"Yes. Do you want to be here or in Edgelawn?"

"How about if we stay here, and you and I cook for the whole family?"

Maren's eyes opened wide. "How many of the whole family do you mean?"

"Just Mom and Dad, Penny, Jim, and Erin, Aunt Elizabeth, and the boys. Then we can show the guys around the city, see a play, or something."

The holiday had been on Maren's mind, too. Last year Paul and his sister's family had been at Bob and Gloria's condo. It would be crowded there with the addition of Maren and the boys, so it made sense for the newlyweds to host the day. Her townhouse had more room than Paul's house, and she would have preferred cooking in the larger kitchen in Edgelawn. They didn't want to ask the very pregnant Penny to travel though, so she eagerly agreed. Cooking a holiday meal with Paul would be a new adventure.

"I'll call and invite everyone tonight," Maren said. "And by the way, I'm staying late to see an outpatient. How about meeting at the Yellow Duck for a late dinner?"

Stephanie Mills was the outpatient Maren would see at five thirty. Stephanie had been coming for therapy biweekly since Maren's first month at St. John's. One of the family physicians, who had been pleased with the services provided by Judy and Maren, had prescribed speech therapy as well as Prozac for the young woman. Of her twenty-six years of life, Stephanie had stuttered severely for twenty-three. The prescription for therapy and the antidepressant came about because of a suicide attempt.

Stephanie had never met another individual who stuttered, never had a date, and had few friends outside her family. Although she had taken classes at the community college, she hadn't been able to interview well enough to secure an office job; so she had settled for employment at a local discount store stocking shelves and ordering merchandise. Maren recalled that the intake interview had been a litany.

"What do you think causes it?"

"I don't know."

"Do you think other people stutter?"

"I don't know."

"What do you think makes your speech more fluent?"

"I don't know."

"What do you expect speech therapy to do for you?"

"I don't know."

She remembered how Stephanie's tears had run silently down her brown cheeks as she told Maren her life story. The young woman had been desperate and therefore willing to do whatever Maren told her. They had worked patiently, week after week, peeling away the layers of nonspeech behaviors.

As Maren was planning the session for Stephanie, Judy paged her. Dr. Weingarten needed Judy to do a stroboscopy. Would Maren see an inpatient? It was one of Paul's patients, so Judy assumed Maren would know all about her. Judy clearly didn't understand about turning off the faucet, or evening meetings, or being on call, or for that matter, being a newlywed.

Maren went to the medical records room and requested the child's past records. Her name was Lorraine, but everyone called her Lolo. Judy had first seen her over a year ago when she was three and already had compiled a long and complicated medical history: pervasive developmental delay, cardiac abnormalities, severe visual impairment, low muscle tone, severe dysphagia, hydrocephalus, and of course severely delayed speech and language. She had undergone heart surgery shortly after birth and additional surgery was planned, if she lived long enough.

Lolo was being nourished through a G tube when Judy had first seen her. Now she was eating baby food. She had a tracheostomy and had been on a ventilator most of her life since she was subject to respiratory infections and was considered medically fragile. Lolo's home health nurse had requested a Passy-Muir speaking valve, thinking the child would simply start speaking if it was installed. Maren had very little experience with speaking valves; in fact she had never evaluated an adult for one, let alone a child. She paged Judy for advice.

Judy's suggestion was to call Paul, and then do a routine speech evaluation. Paul returned her page almost immediately. "The purpose of Lolo's present hospitalization is to reevaluate her medical stability and determine recommendations for the next year of her life. Our goal is to continue to wean her from the ventilator. Don't get too attached to her though," Paul warned quietly. "She has Ivemark syndrome."

Since Maren had never heard of the rare syndrome, Paul explained. "Before thirty days of gestation a bilateral one-sidedness develops.

There's symmetry where she should be asymmetrical. Almost every part of her head and body has some abnormality. Her heart anomalies will likely cause cyanosis and heart failure. That's the major cause of early death in these kids."

Paul gave her an additional insight. "Lolo's parents have two other children together, and they're rarely at Lolo's bedside."

"I'm sure they have many other problems," Maren answered, not wanting to be judgmental. She thanked Paul and went to the child's room.

Lolo was the size of a chubby eighteen-month-old. She looked up at Maren silently from her bed, with eyes that appeared blurred through coke-bottle-thick glasses. She could be upright only with the help of an elaborate standing device from Physical Therapy, but Maren did raise the head of the bed slightly.

With a twist of her fingers Maren secured a small, round plastic object, the Passy-Muir valve, to the end of Lolo's trach tube. Lolo had never heard her own voice and had not developed cooing, babbling, or word approximations. Without the speaking valve the child's breathing was accomplished through the tube in her neck; no air passed through her larynx to vibrate her vocal folds. The valve directed air returning from her lungs to pass by the tube in her neck without leaking out. The air continued, as with normal individuals, up through her vocal folds, and out her mouth or nose. The air vibrated her vocal folds, like blades of grass Maren had held between her thumbs and blown on years ago. Both the grass and vocal folds produced sound when they vibrated.

The next breath the little girl took was audible, and Lolo could tell that something was different. Maren coaxed her to make more sounds. Lolo obviously heard herself; she smiled with each vocalization. Maren was amazed at the instant change. Intuitively, Maren initiated vocal play to encourage inflection and variety. To her delight and surprise, her little patient responded beautifully.

Paul slid in the booth across from Maren. He asked about Lolo, and Maren gave him her report, ending with questions about the speaking valve. Paul suggested she check the Passy-Muir website.

"Who was the late patient?" he asked, helping her download the events of her day; so she could relax with him.

The back, corner booth was more private than the others, and they had adopted it as their own. They could talk more openly there, but Maren leaned closer and spoke in a confidential voice. "... the young woman who's a severe stutterer. I've mentioned her before."

"You've been working with her for quite a while."

"It's been a little over a year."

"What exactly determines if a patient is a severe stutterer?"

"They incorporate nonspeech behaviors into their speech pattern and have complete blocks, times when they can't produce any sound. Stephanie's blocks were so hard her face used to be contorted in pain, physical pain from the muscle tension and emotional pain from being trapped in her own body every time the flow of speech was choked off. Her eyebrows would rise in the center, on a diagonal line, giving her a perplexed expression. Her cheeks would suck in. Her tongue would protrude beyond her lips. Every neck and facial muscle would be rigid. During those blocks I thought she looked suspended, frozen in a ghastly pose, totally helpless. Her blocks used to last for almost ten seconds. It was excruciating for her and almost as difficult for me to watch."

"When did it start?" He had almost no experience with stuttering, except for one boy currently in his practice. He was looking for insight and information.

"It's usually between three and five. Kids are often teased in grade school, shunned in high school, and treated differently by their coworkers," Maren explained compassionately.

Wondering what would happen with his young patient, Paul asked the prognosis.

"We prefer to work with the parents of children with dysfluencies as early as possible. The prognosis is good then, but with adults it's a matter of increasing the control of speech and improving the speaker's fluency. No one uses the word *cure*, but I usually tell patients that only God knows their potential. I've seen some amazing changes.

"Stephanie has taken responsibility for her speech. She's eliminated her blocks and become more confident. The biggest breakthrough came when she met a young man in her workplace who stutters. Since then she has a better attitude. She recently told me she'll call to order pizza delivery now, something she would never have done before therapy. She goes out more, too, usually with relatives, but sometimes alone. She called yesterday and told me she was bringing a friend to therapy. I didn't expect the friend to be male!"

"Is that significant?"

"It is for her. Frequently, speaking to the opposite sex is one of the most difficult communication situations for someone who stutters. She doesn't even know this young man very well."

"What causes it?"

"If I could tell you that, I'd be famous. The truth is no one knows for sure. There's more research about stuttering than any other communication disorder, but only theories about the etiology. We do know there are several kinds of stuttering—developmental, neurogenic, and psychological."

"It's not emotionally based?"

"Stress and emotion certainly play a part in forming the whole pattern, but neither nervousness or emotional instability is the cause."

"Maybe," teased Paul, lightening the mood, "it's just because women like to talk faster than their mouths can move."

"Maybe," Maren shot back with a smile, "but three out of four individuals who stutter are male."

Maren felt as if she had been giving a lecture and wanted to move on to other topics.

Paul didn't want to discuss his day. "Tomorrow is my turn," he said, reminding her of their agreement that she was to download at night, and he was to download in the morning.

In reality there was rarely time in the mornings. He did share more on the weekends, but Maren compared it to when the boys were in school. If she hadn't been there when they came in the door, there were many things she would never have heard. She masked her concern by smiling at Chad as he served their food. She wondered what she wasn't hearing from Paul.

Chapter 28

Fascinated, Maren read and reread the information from Passy-Muir Inc. David Muir, who had muscular dystrophy and a tracheostomy, had become ventilator dependent. He had developed the speaking valve for himself. She remembered reading about it when he died. The valve could be used for patients who had a tracheostomy or those who were ventilator dependent.

She watched the educational video, which explained the "no leak" design. She was impressed with the video recordings of patients using the device. She took the manual to the hospital to share with Judy over lunch in the cafeteria. Paul noticed them and sat at their table while he finished a huge chocolate chip cookie and a carton of milk.

Judy was not as impressed as Maren. "It's great, but realistically we're just not going to see many of those patients at a small general hospital like St. John's."

"Don't you think we could use this with some of the ICU patients?" Maren asked, opening the book while juggling a sandwich.

"Maren, most of them are too sick and weak to care whether they talk or not. And we don't service most of those patients long enough to justify keeping speaking valves on hand."

Paul had answered Maren's technical questions earlier. Now he nodded his agreement with Judy. "Specialized services, especially for children, are usually provided in larger medical centers and university hospitals. It was just a fluke that caused Lolo to be admitted to St. John's rather than to Circle. A community hospital is important," Paul finished his little lecture as he finished his milk, "but it's really for more general care."

Maren closed the book sadly. She couldn't argue with their logic about the ICU patients, but she still thought it would be wonderful to help other children in such a powerful way.

—

It happened Friday, while Gloria was at her canasta club. Penny's water broke. She was five days past her due date, and since it was her second baby things could happen quickly. Jim was out of town on an appointment and couldn't get back until at least six o'clock. Paul was in surgery. Bob picked Penny up, and Maren met them in the hospital lobby. St. John's was considered the McCloud family hospital. Penny wouldn't think of delivering anyplace else.

Fortunately, Jim arrived in plenty of time to take over the coaching and to witness the birth of Colleen Elizabeth. Born December 20th at ten fifteen, she was a healthy eight pounds, three ounces and had a shock of dark wavy hair, like her mommy.

At eleven o'clock Paul and Maren held hands and stared lovingly at their new niece through the nursery window. A proud new dad standing next to them asked which one was theirs. Maren was embarrassed, but not Paul. "That one in front," he told the man with a proud smile. "She's the pretty one with all the hair."

When the new father left, they were alone in the hallway; and Maren was more comfortable. "I offered to keep Erin as much as possible until Jim's mother can get in from Florida," she told Paul. He was aware of the close bond that had formed between his wife and sister, and was grateful Penny had enjoyed Maren's support during the last weeks of her pregnancy. He knew it took a special kind of humility to fit into that situation, without competing with Penny's mom. Maren had a knack for gathering people together or gathering them to herself, he decided. He was pleased, very, very pleased. He squeezed her hand in approval.

Bob and Gloria came up behind them just then to see their new granddaughter through the glass. "Welcome to the McCloud family," Bob called to her a little too loudly. "Your grandmother and grandfather are very happy. We've acquired two grown grandsons, and now we have not one but two beautiful granddaughters." Maren was amused to note that he gave this report to no one in particular.

Gloria rolled her eyes and shook her head. "He's beside himself with joy."

Nick was home for Christmas break, and he and Matt had talked until late, so Maren was surprised that they both got up in time to have a family breakfast. They were eager to go meet their new cousin and congratulate Penny and Jim.

Gloria was already sitting with Penny and commented what gentlemanly grandsons she had. She knew that not many young men would make the effort to visit a newborn cousin. Gloria always made a point of complementing Maren or the boys in front of Paul. "Obviously you've done a fine job raising them."

Paul glowed as if he had received the complement himself.

The day was cold and rainy, so Maren and Paul met Bonni and Ziff at the health club Bonni had joined in Edgelawn. Maren wasn't much for tennis, even doubles, so the women opted for a swim in the pool, while the men wore themselves out on the court.

Maren appreciated the value of having good friendships that continued through different phases of life. She knew it was rare for two couples to get along as well as they did. The men and the women had been friends initially, but what made it special was that Paul and Bonni enjoyed each other's company, as did Maren and Ziff.

The four hadn't been able to spend much time together during the holidays. This weekend was a mini-vacation for them—no children, no parents, no jobs, no responsibilities. After swimming laps, the two women relaxed in the whirlpool. A hot shower was followed by baking in the dry sauna. They were the only ones sitting on the wood benches over the steaming rocks while Bonni confided her growing feelings for Ziff; and they discussed ways the couple complemented one another. They also reviewed their differences, but Bonni wasn't distressed by them.

"Look at you and Paul," she stated brightly. "You had serious reservations about your differences, but you've worked them all out. It's wonderful to see the two of you together—the way he looks at you, the way you've become so relaxed."

Maren smiled, enjoying the shower of comments. It was true; everyone told them, including her sons. Matt had told her only last week that when he found someone who fit with him the way Maren and Paul fit together, he would turn in his bachelor button.

Bonni continued in her bubbly, excited voice. "The way you two compromise and sacrifice for each other is just an inspiration."

Maren stiffened at the word *sacrifice*. "What do you mean by that?"

Bonni now walked ahead of Maren to the locker room and didn't see her expression. "Well, you've kept two homes, so you have the best of both worlds. That wouldn't work for everybody, but clearly it's been a perfect solution for you two. Paul was so wise to turn down that job in Colorado, and you to cut your hours."

Maren was stung that some opportunity had evidently been offered and rejected by Paul without her knowledge, but she didn't let on to Bonni. "I had no choice about cutting my hours," was all Maren could manage to say.

Bonni and Ziff left after dinner at the townhouse, and Matt was still out with friends. Paul picked out CDs while Maren lighted and adjusted the gas log. She felt betrayed, humiliated, that her friend knew things about her husband she had not been told. She wondered who else knew his secrets and why she didn't.

Paul turned and opened his arms to her, expecting an intimate evening. His feet firmly planted, he swayed, rather than danced with her in time to the music.

"How are things at the office these days?" she asked stiffly.

"Let's not go there. This is the most carefree day we've had in weeks. Let's stay upbeat."

Maren had learned to wait, to put things on hold until the time was right for her partner, in spite of her need to resolve issues. The trouble was that with Jack there rarely had been a good time, until an argument erupted. She was afraid the same pattern would develop again. She knew it wasn't that Paul didn't want to communicate; it was just that they had little discretionary time. She often found herself wishing they had taken the three-week honeymoon to Italy that they had briefly considered.

Maren's expression told Paul she was not cheerful, in spite of the relaxing day. Their relationship had taken a backseat since Colleen's birth. They had kept Erin while Penny got on her feet again. He knew they needed to get back in touch, but he had physical touch in mind for tonight.

When Maren didn't answer him it was a sure sign something was on her mind. *Why can't she just forget problems for one day?* he wondered. *Why did she ask about the office as soon as Ziff and Bonni were out the door?*

"Can't it wait?" he pleaded.

"It could, but in all honesty I don't think I can. At least I can't and still be good company."

He nodded soberly, and they sat on the sofa by the fire, holding hands.

"Bonni told me you turned down a job in Colorado. I didn't even know there was a job in Colorado."

He didn't want to relive his disappointment. "That was a long time ago," he answered wearily, turning his head away from her. "...before we were married."

She smiled at his time reference. It seemed to him they had always been together, always shared their days and nights. To her, their marriage was new, so recent. "Why did you turn it down?"

"I didn't want to leave Chicago. It was at the time of your surgery. I didn't even look into it really." He tried to sound nonchalant, hoping to put a quick end to the distasteful discussion. "There was too much happening here to even think about leaving."

"You turned it down because you didn't want to leave your Chicago practice?"

He felt like he was on a witness stand; one wrong word would convict him. He wanted to protect her from the truth, protect them both; but he also wanted to be open with her about his feelings.

"I didn't want to leave you, Maren. I couldn't just pick up and leave town without things being settled between us."

"Why didn't you mention it later or at least explore it at the time?"

"There was a narrow time frame. It was a small window . . ." He stopped.

"Of opportunity?"

"Yes."

"Then you were interested?"

"It was a pediatric practice," he admitted, his voice louder than he intended. "I'd be a fool not to be interested. But it wouldn't have been a good thing if it meant leaving without you."

"Now I feel like I've stood in the way of you reaching your goal, your dream."

"Maren, I love you . . ." He spoke slowly, deliberately. "More than . . ." He turned his palms up and looked at them, trying to frame his thoughts. ". . . more than my own hands. I couldn't be happy if I built my life on your sacrifices, you giving up your home, your work at St. John's, your closeness to your sons. I can't do that, Maren, ask you to give up everything you love so I can have a job I might like."

"That's the position you've put me in. You've given up your lifelong dream so I can be in a certain house, work in a certain place. How do you think that makes me feel, knowing you're unhappy day and night—"

"Not nights," he interrupted with a smile.

"But you've sacrificed yourself on the altar of my happiness."

He hadn't thought of it that way. He knew he didn't want the woman he loved to subjugate her life to his. Now Maren was saying he had subjugated his life to hers. He was confused; she was obviously hurt. He shook his head, bewildered, unable to answer.

Even if the time frame had been too short, it was his way of thinking, dealing with it, that bothered her. She understood that he wanted to delay dealing with it at a sensitive time in their relationship, but she thought they should have discussed it at some point.

"Paul, you have tremendous gifts—healing children, teaching medical students. I never want to be the reason your gifts are stifled."

"And you have tremendous gifts—with patients and students and more recently, I see, with bringing family together—my family, our family. How could I cut you off from using your gifts?"

No one had ever told her that her abilities were "tremendous gifts." She stared at him, unable to think of a response. He stared at her, perplexed.

Penny and Colleen were doing well. Erin was delighted with her new baby sister. Nick was happy at the U of I. Matt had started the winter term in Madison. Paul was away at a meeting, and Maren had some time for herself. She hadn't used any of the education days that were allowed in her contract and decided the time was right. *One thing about living in Chicago,* she thought happily, *educational and cultural opportunities are plentiful.* There was always something exciting going on.

It was late February, time for the annual state convention. A Thursday-Friday seminar on treating tracheostomized and ventilator-dependent patients was being offered, and Maren decided to take it. The first day dealt with the adult population; day two, the pediatric population. Passy-Muir was co-sponsoring it and presenting something each day.

At the noon break on the second day she ran into Dale Showalter, one of her mentors from grad school. Her former professor was incredibly knowledgeable, and his ability was matched by his kindness. He was shaped like an overstuffed teddy bear and his manner with students was just as comforting. He had helped her through some rough times when she started grad school. At that point she had felt like a misfit. She had been a new widow, not young enough to be a student, not experienced enough to be staff. When she wasn't taking one of his classes the Showalter's had invited her to their home a few times.

"What a surprise," she exclaimed. "What a wonderful surprise! What are you doing in the Midwest?"

He was obviously as pleased to see her as she was to see him. Dale and his family had moved the day after Maren's graduation. It had been the chance of a lifetime, he had said, to start a department and training program at a relatively new university near the Rockies. The Showalters were country folk, happy to leave the big city.

"Actually, I'm recruiting students and staff. I've attended four seminars or conventions in the past three weeks, all over the country. I need a break." He sighed. "Can you stay around for dinner?"

They met in the hotel dining room at the conclusion of the Passy Muir presentation. After Maren heard about his twins, who were now fifteen years old, she asked how his work was going.

"St. Francis of the Hills University has been growing rapidly for a decade. It isn't far from Denver and is gaining a reputation as the Children's Hospital of the Rockies."

He answered her questions, one by one, while sipping a glass of dark beer. "When I was hired, they already had an exceptional medical school, as well as programs to train occupational and physical therapists. I've been building the speech pathology and audiology department from scratch."

He had worn many hats since taking the position and worked many long hours. Now the program had reached a new level. He needed to delegate some of his workload.

"The speech clinic has been intentionally developed with a pediatric emphasis, to complement the hospital. I'm looking for someone to direct the clinic, someone who has broad pediatric experience."

Dale thought about Maren's talents while they ate salads. *What an accomplishment it would be if I could sign her on*, he mused. He had noticed she was wearing a wedding ring, although she hadn't mentioned remarriage. He couldn't imagine that she wouldn't remarry, but that could limit her options for relocating.

"It's a private, church-sponsored facility," he went on, between bites. "No major political battles like we lived through here at Circle. What they say they will do, they do. There's no problem getting funds, either. It's a quality organization." He wondered what it would take to entice her.

"That sounds exciting, Dale. Paul and I . . . Oh, I didn't tell you. Paul McCloud and I were married last October. Do you remember him?"

Dale congratulated her. He remembered Paul as an extremely talented, likable resident. Dale would never have put the two of them together, but thinking about it now he could see how they would...

Her chatter interrupted his thoughts. "Paul had an offer to join a pediatric practice in Colorado, but we couldn't meet the deadline."

Maybe she would be interested, he thought. *They might be ready for a change. They,* he said to himself again. Timing wasn't everything, but it was frequently the deciding factor. *Joel will be ecstatic if I come back from Chicago with not only the clinic director but a surgeon as well.*

"It was a private practice that was affiliated with a university," she went on, unaware of his thoughts. "I don't know which one, but his friend in the practice is Gill West."

Bingo, Dale thought, barely able to contain his excitement.

"You know him?" asked Maren, seeing his eyes light up.

He began to tell her the details. "We are closely affiliated with that practice, but the administrators of St. Francis decided they want to hire at least one pediatric otolaryngologist outright, someone who has no outside connections."

"I would think one of the guys in Gill West's practice would jump at that."

"Well, some doctors figure they can make more money in private practice." *And they would be absolutely right,* he admitted to himself. "We work with a number of other groups, too, so our CEO is cautious about developing conflicts of interest. Do you think Paul would be interested in that kind of position?" He tried to sound casual.

They talked on through the main course, and he decided to present her an offer over dessert.

Maren turned him down flat. She wanted to be seeing patients, not sitting behind a desk, but she couldn't answer for Paul.

Dale's disappointment was obvious, but he was not one to give up easily. He redesigned his duties mentally. "What if I absorbed most of the administrative duties of the clinic and we created a position for you as coordinator of pediatrics? You would work closely with our ENT department and the hospital, seeing patients and training students, but only for pediatrics.

"We couldn't do that and maintain a full-time position, though. It would probably be only twenty hours a week. When I get overwhelmed again, you would have the opportunity to be full time, or I'll hire a coordinator of adult patients. There are fewer adult patients in the clinic as well as at the hospital, so the coordinator of adult patients could assume some of the administrative tasks you aren't interested in, to create a full-time position for that person."

Maren couldn't deny the excitement she felt growing inside, but she was afraid to express it. He was willing to be so flexible; maybe it could work out. Helping Dale to build a terrific pediatric practice within the university hospital and working closely with Paul, but still part time, seemed like a great package to her. What if Paul had a distaste for being employed by a university hospital? His whole emphasis had always been on private practice.

Dale said they were eager to move forward as quickly as possible, so she promised him they would discuss it immediately and contact him by the following weekend.

Chapter 29

Maren had to work Saturday morning. It was her turn to see the Medicare patients in the rehab wing. She was to meet Paul after he finished his hospital rounds, and she planned to bring up Dale's offer over lunch.

As she finished writing her last note, she heard the overhead speaker. " . . . McCloud to the emergency room." She wasn't used to listening for her new name. She didn't really hear it the first time, then just the end of it. She assumed ER was admitting a new CVA. Recent new guidelines required that when staff was available, an SLP was to document cognitive, language, and swallowing status on admit for CVA patients. She had never imagined she would be answering calls to the emergency room. She suspected some high-profile patient had been sent home prematurely, and this new protocol evolved as a result. She hoped the new arrangement would not be permanent, while Judy hoped it would; it meant more business for the department.

The ER was hectic. "Accident," someone told her.

Four beds were occupied behind drawn curtains. She could hear moans and tense, professional voices giving orders. She tried to stay out of the way. She didn't like ER. It was too intense.

"Where's the CVA?" she asked a nurse.

"No CVA. All from the same accident."

Maren was about to retreat, thinking the page was a mistake, when Paul rushed out from behind one of the curtains. She had thought he was at Circle this morning. He literally ran into her, grabbing her arms to keep from knocking her down. He was pale and looked shaken, as she had never seen him.

His voice was almost inaudible when he tried to tell her. "It's Penny and Jim… and Erin."

Her heart clutched with fear. She glanced toward the bed nearest them, hidden behind a curtain.

"Don't. Don't look," he said hoarsely, grabbing her wrist to prevent her. He pulled her back and hugged her against his chest, momentarily burying his face in her hair. A groan escaped from his throat. He spoke several words, but she only understood, "God."

"The baby?" asked Maren.

"She wasn't with them. Penny . . ." Maren couldn't hear all that he was saying. "…broken ribs, face, neck . . ." He stopped, momentarily unable to continue. "That's why they paged me. They didn't know it was my sister. I'll start in surgery, but we need someone in plastics."

He was regaining his composure now, years of training and experience taking control. "Call Ian Jones."

"What about Erin?"

"Minor injuries really, and shock. She was strapped in her seat. Jim's a probable concussion."

Maren thought immediately about the possibility of traumatic brain injury. Even minimal brain injury could have long-term effects.

"Call Jones," he repeated more urgently. "Ask him to hurry," he pleaded as he rushed off to scrub. He turned back once more. "Please, call Mom and Dad, and stay with them in the surgery lounge."

Maren wasn't used to being in the ER, but the ER nurse she turned to for help not only pointed out the phone but also gave her the staff directory that would have a list of plastic surgeons, including Dr. Jones's quick-dial home number.

She tried to stay calm as she dialed. Paul had introduced her to Ian Jones once at a party, and she was hoping he would remember her. He answered the phone and he did remember her. He told her he would meet Paul in the OR.

Next, she made the call she was dreading, to Bob and Gloria. She forced her voice to stay low and calm as she told them what little she knew.

When they arrived, they had Colleen with them. Maren sat with them in the surgery waiting area until Paul came out. The three went to him and formed a circle with their arms around each other. Maren noticed he was not wearing scrubs, which he would have worn in the OR. She knew instantly that he had changed clothes to protect his parents from seeing Penny's blood.

"Erin's okay," he told his parents. He almost smiled, then closed his eyes and put his head down. His shoulders shook, and he momentarily lost control. "I think the girls will have parents."

Maren looked intently at him. "They'll have parents no matter what," she assured him. His worried blue eyes locked her eyes in his penetrating gaze, and she knew that he was thinking the same thing. If it came to that, Paul and Maren would take the children.

They didn't leave the hospital for twenty-four hours, and when they did, they knew that Penny and Jim would survive. Penny's injuries were the worst, including a ruptured spleen. She had a long recovery ahead of her.

Maren thought about the sweetest sister anyone could ever have. All the pain she had already suffered in her life, and now this. She prayed that Ian Jones could restore her face and that she would emotionally survive the multiple reconstructive surgeries Paul told her would be required.

Jim had not regained consciousness, and Maren prayed he would wake up soon. She knew that each hour he was unconscious reduced the prognosis for complete recovery. In the back of her mind she was already planning a coma stimulation program.

A week went by—a week filled with images Maren wanted to delete from her memory, but she knew they were etched there permanently. She and Paul had juggled their normal work routine, visits with Penny and Jim, and caring for the girls. Gloria and Bob had taken the girls home with them last night, ordering Paul and Maren to rest. Instead, they stayed late at the hospital. By the time they showered and fell into bed, it was long after midnight.

Maren woke first, reminding herself it was Sunday. She lay quietly next to Paul, thinking about her husband's grief. Several times during the previous week she had seen him in tears. She knew he was exhausted. They both were, and this afternoon they would bring Erin and Colleen back home with them. Again this week Gloria would care for them at their house when Maren had to work. They had all felt it was best for the girls to have the stability of staying in one place.

Maren watched Paul sleep. She wanted to comfort him, but hesitated to disturb him. He certainly needed to rest. His body jumped just then, and he cried out in his sleep. She curled her fingers and stroked his bare chest with the back of them.

He opened his eyes, those deep blue eyes, just inches from hers. They looked darker today as he stared silently at her. Slowly, he reached out a hand to explore her neck and the curl of her hair. His fingers returned to her neck and traced it to her cheek. He caressed her face. "I'm so glad you're here. It would have destroyed me to have suffered through this alone."

She pressed his hand to her lips and held it there. He pulled her closer, comforted by the softness of her body against his. They lay with their arms around each other, she wishing she could help him release his pain and tension, he wishing he could wipe out the awful memories.

"Every time I close my eyes I see her face," he said, his voice a whisper.

He felt Maren's body against his, urging him, but the image of his sister's smashed face intruded. He couldn't take pleasure while Penny was lying in a hospital bed. He fought to push the specter from his mind's eye. With immense effort he closed his eyes and forced himself to replay, as he had many times before, the scene in front of the fireplace in Pine Bluff.

He had been so controlled, moved so slowly. Maren had begun to guide his hands and murmur her appreciation and enjoyment. Her voice had become music, as he lost the sound of the CDs and heard only her breathing, her sighs, her low moans of pleasure. She had repeated his name, and as her excitement increased, she called him more urgently.

He was seeing it clearly now. He was keeping himself in check, enjoying giving her pleasure. Her fears had finally melted. She knew herself so well, knew what she needed, and she hadn't been shy about telling him. "Paul, I need . . ." Her desires had been fulfilled and her needs satisfied ahead of his own, until at some point, after what amount of time he didn't know, he gave up the control he had fought to maintain for so long.

His body suddenly ached all over, reminding him that he was in Chicago, not Pine Bluff. His eyes flew open. "Maren, I need you."

It had been thirty hours before Jim regained consciousness and two weeks before he had been released from the hospital. He continued having mild memory problems, headaches, and difficulty concentrating—typical for patients with minimal traumatic brain injury.

Penny's worst scars appeared to be emotional, not physical. Her plastic surgeries were, so far, highly successful. She was terribly depressed and suffered from severe anxiety in spite of medication. It was heartbreaking to see someone as active, fun loving, and beautiful as Penny thrown into a pit of desolation.

Maren and Paul kept the girls for almost three weeks, until Gloria, Jim's mother, and Jim felt they could handle them. Today they were going home, and Maren would miss them. Having the girls had turned out to be a blessing; there was no other word for it. Maren had enjoyed them thoroughly, and the children had obviously felt secure.

Paul had been absolutely transformed. No matter what kind of day he had, or what kind of setbacks Penny had suffered, when he was with the girls, he had been temporarily released from it all. He had carried Erin on his back and read her stories, and he had been good at calming Colleen. When she was fretful, he had held her on his chest on the couch and covered them both with an afghan until she fell asleep. He even had sung to her on several occasions. Maren had never heard Paul sing a solo before and was surprised at his talent. He told her it was from years of singing at Mass.

One night she watched him hold a penlight in Colleen's mouth. He told Erin, "We're going to make a pumpkin with your baby sister." Erin had squealed with delight. Watching them together had stirred something maternal in Maren, something she thought had been cut out.

After feeding the girls Maren shared scrambled eggs, fresh bagels, and juice with Paul at their kitchen table, while he expressed his latest concerns about Penny.

"I'm going to call Ziff today and have him work with her. She isn't coming out of it on her own, even with the meds."

"I hope I didn't overstep my boundaries, but I talked to him yesterday. He had already visited her as a friend of the family, but there was no referral. I told him you would make sure there was an official order in the chart today."

He squeezed her hand and nodded his approval and appreciation. "Always looking out for the patient… Promise me you'll never go into administration."

The color drained from her face; her expression froze. She closed her eyes as if trying to blot out what she had done, or rather, had forgotten to do. She had totally forgotten her conversation with Dale Showalter.

Chapter 30

Family and close friends gathered at Maren's townhouse in Edgelawn on Labor Day weekend. Maren and Paul had been living there for over a month, since the closing on his house. The boys and Mary Kepple had arrived on Friday. Maren's sister, Ruth, and her husband, Calvin, who was in the country for a change, flew in on Saturday from Baltimore. Bob and Gloria drove out in Paul and Maren's new SUV early Monday morning. Elizabeth rode with Penny, Jim, and the girls.

Matt and Nick were getting reacquainted with an aunt and uncle they had spent very little time with during their growing-up years. After hearing the latest about their cousins, Lisa, Doug, and Lauren, the boys took soft drinks to the deck. Calvin, Bob, and Gloria joined them to enjoy the view and have a glass of wine.

Matt wanted to know more about his uncle's work. "Why did you give up your private practice, Uncle Calvin?"

"I suppose I just got to an age or a stage of life when I had the opportunity to do something different. I wanted to do something global, not just in my own backyard. The Dodd's have always lived on the East Coast. I grew up in Maryland, went to school there, got married, and raised a family there. And after Lauren graduated from college, I felt pulled to do something more challenging."

"He was one of the first in our area to do heart catheterizations," Ruth interjected proudly, as she set the Mexican dip and chips on the table in front of them. "How he could get bored with that, I'll never understand."

"I wasn't bored exactly, just looking for a different kind of challenge. I had never been out of the country until I joined Pediatric Possibilities."

Matt knew Calvin was one of the original members of the organization, and since Matt was one year closer to his degree in biomedical engineering, he wanted to hear more about medical experiences.

"Pediatric Possibilities is a privately funded, international organization whose mission is to provide medical care in regions challenged by natural or man-made disasters," he explained. "The focus is primarily children, although we serve adults when necessary. We work cooperatively with many organizations, including the military, sharing and reinforcing resources."

Maren could overhear bits and pieces of the conversation through the screen door. When Ruth returned to the kitchen to help clean and cut fruit, Maren had a few questions of her own.

"Did you know how much international travel would be involved when Calvin started with this organization?"

"No. Calvin was one of the first doctors from the U.S., so there weren't many guidelines. He was in London to sign on, at the time of your wedding, if you recall."

Maren had been disappointed that her sister's whole family hadn't been at the wedding, but really hadn't absorbed all the details at the time.

"I'm just glad you and the girls made it and that Calvin could come for this weekend. You've spent a lot of years working to support him through medical school and then raising the children. Don't you wish he would just retire and spend some time in the garden with you?"

"That's what I had in mind, but it all started during the two-year Bible study we committed to through our church, when Lauren was only a junior at Salisbury. We had never done anything like that before. He began to get restless, not with the study, but at work. He read more and more about medical challenges in other countries. Then some of his colleagues from England visited us and talked to us about Pediatric Possibilities. He was drawn to it so strongly—it was like he couldn't resist. I had to honor that. Fortunately, he didn't really start traveling until after Lauren graduated, and I have gotten to do quite a bit of sightseeing in the world as a result. Maybe that gardening part will come later."

Maren knew her sister had worked hard to build a good marriage. She had been an administrative assistant to a congressman in DC when she met Calvin. After Lisa was born, Ruth had quit her job and had devoted herself totally to family ever since. The sisters had watched each other's struggles from afar.

"I've been hoping we could be closer, now that the children are grown, and

here you are moving farther away," Ruth lamented. "By the way, how did you get out of your contract at the hospital? And how did you sell a house, buy a house, interview for the new positions, and still have time for a major Labor Day party? You and Paul have had a lot to deal with this past year Maren."

"It was stressful for a while, but everything has worked out. There was always someone who was able to help when we thought we couldn't hold it together any longer. The closing was planned to coincide with Paul's last day at the office, and by mutual agreement, St. John's hired a second full-time SLP, freeing me to make several trips to Colorado with Paul. We interviewed at the same time, and we were pleased with the job descriptions and the offers."

The truth was Maren was more pleased than Paul. He was taking a significant cut in income, while Maren would gross considerably more than she had at St. John's. In exchange for the reduction of income, Paul hoped to have considerably more professional freedom, opportunities to continue to develop his pediatric skills, more regular hours, and no office management.

"I'm sure it will be fine," Maren stated. "We're both excited about working together, not just in the same facility, but actually making joint decisions and recommendations. We'll plan and carry out the treatment of more children in a few years than he would have seen in Chicago in our careers."

Bonni and Ziff arrived at the same time, but in separate cars. They joined Paul and Jim on the back lawn, where they were starting two propane grills to cook burgers, chicken, and brats for the crowd.

"We're keeping Maren's townhouse," Paul explained to them, "at least until Nick graduates and Matt finishes grad school. The cookout today will probably be the last family gathering for a while, but the boys will come out to Colorado for Thanksgiving, and Mom is already planning Christmas in Pine Bluff."

Paul still had some reservations about the move. One of the strongest was that he would be working directly for the hospital, but it was clearly a step in the right direction for their marriage. "The best part is Maren and I will have a home that's ours, not hers or mine. Finally getting away from Lancaster and Granger ranks right up there, though."

Bonni carried her covered salad up the wood steps to the deck, said hello to the group there, and went into the house through the sliding screen door. She joined Maren and Ruth in the kitchen. Bonni remembered meeting Ruth at the wedding but reintroduced herself for Ruth's benefit.

Ruth pointed to Calvin, sitting between Maren's boys on the deck. "He's mine, the talkative one in the sun," she commented loudly enough for Calvin to overhear. He looked up, grinned his good-natured, ear-to-ear smile, waved, and called hello to Bonni.

"I hear the whole clan will gather at Pine Bluff for Christmas," Bonni commented to Maren.

"Including the West Coast contingent and Frank."

"What I want to know is how you finally got together with the people at St. Francis. You told me you forgot to call your friend and thought the positions would be filled."

"That was because of us," Penny called matter-of-factly from the adjoining family room, where she was feeding Colleen in a portable high chair.

"But Jamie saved the day," Maren answered. "She was at the house, babysitting for the girls, and took the call from Dale Showalter. How she found out so much in a few minutes on the phone, we will never know."

"It's just her gift," Penny interjected.

"Jamie explained the circumstances, and Dale told her not to trouble us until things settled down. He told her some unexpected complications had developed and St. Francis of the Hills' administrators wouldn't be moving forward as quickly as they had originally planned. He promised he would call again in a few weeks, but I contacted him first. We told him family came first, and he was okay with that. Fortunately, Penny started doing better about that time."

Penny pulled Colleen from the high chair and set her on the rug near Erin and some toys. "Thanks to you and Paul," she stated, going to the sink to wash the baby's bowl, cup, and spoon.

"How are you doing now, Penny?" Bonni asked.

"By the grace of God, a lot of family support, and professional skill, again provided through my brother, I'm practically healed. Look—only a few pock marks, no worse than if I had marks from teenage acne." She tipped her face up to the light and pulled back her long dark hair with her left hand to reveal the physical reminders of the accident.

Bonni examined Penny's tiny scars. It did look as if she might have had acne at some time in her life—evidence of a difficult past. Penny had never had acne, but the difficult past was a reality.

"Jim and I are closer than ever, and I know that's not always the case when such traumas occur. Some women have accidents, lose their husbands, and have to go on alone. I suppose that could happen yet. You never know what the future holds."

Maren looked anxiously at Penny, wondering if her attitude was healthy and realistic or evidence of continued depression. Before she could decide, Paul came to the deck to get the meat for the grill. As Maren handed the container through the door, she heard Bob going over the travel plans for Calvin's benefit.

"We'll leave the SUV here today for Paul and Maren to drive. They'll leave sometime tomorrow and have a few days vacation on the road. The movers won't deliver furniture until next Monday. Gloria and I will take their Lexus home today and drive it out next week. We'll help unpack, and then fly home."

"I'm keeping Mom's car," Nick put in, "since Matt already has a wagon. I sold my old beater. I won't have time to work on it this year. I need something more reliable."

Jamie and her family arrived just then. Her husband John set up the badminton they had promised to bring. Elizabeth walked around the yard inspecting Maren's plantings, while Jamie and the girls carried containers of food through the front hall to the kitchen.

"Now we can eat," called Paul, seeing them through the screen door. "The shrimp Creole is here." Jamie had in fact brought several of Paul's favorite dishes. "Let's get this meat cooking." He waved his arm, indicating help would be welcome. The men followed him down the wood steps, and Gloria went into the house to greet Jamie, Nola, and Natalie.

"Natalie," repeated Bonni wistfully, "that's such a pretty name."

While the group mingled and visited, Maren slipped out to the deck for a moment to watch Paul supervise the cooking. He kept up a constant chatter as he flipped burgers, turned chicken breasts, and brushed more sauce on bratwursts. His old glibness and energy had returned; she knew he was happy.

Maren laughed at one of Paul's wisecracks, and Elizabeth sassed him back, using her new TEP voice.

Jamie saw Maren on the deck and took advantage of the moment. She closed the screen door behind her and stood quietly next to Maren, watching and listening to the group below. Paul had always been Jamie's favorite. Everyone had doted on Penny, and Jamie loved her, too. Paul had a quality of….of mercy, she decided, that touched everyone he met. How she loved seeing him with someone who could return his love full measure. It was being completed, she believed.

"According to the Weather Channel, the nip of fall is already in the air in the Rockies," Jamie said, peacefully.

"Yes, I heard," Maren answered. "But a beautiful Indian summer is expected."

She knew Jamie was thinking about the legend, and she was inclined to agree with her about Cautantowwit's season. She had the feeling, after having watched Paul with his nieces that out there somewhere a child was waiting for parents.

"You were right, Jamie," she said, smiling. "Our days are numbered by Creator God alone."

Printed in the United States
131723LV00006B/7/P